THE MANY WORLDS
OF THE IMAGINATION—

await you in such mind-teasing stories as:

"Gemini 74"—in which space race competitiveness takes on a whole new twist. . . .

"The Big Fix"—after all, it's a big universe, and somebody's got to keep things running. . . .

"Lycanthrope"—the trick to making magic work is doing it by the book. . . .

"Little William"—he was one of those kids who just seemed too good to be true. . . .

"True Love"—can be found in the strangest places, especially when it's part of the program. . . .

MICROCOSMIC TALES

Watch for these exciting DAW anthologies:

ASIMOV PRESENTS THE GREAT SF STORIES *edited by Isaac Asimov and Martin H. Greenberg.* Classics of short fiction from the golden age of science fiction.

THE YEAR'S BEST HORROR STORIES *edited by Karl Edward Wagner.* The finest, most spine-chilling terror stories of the current year.

SWORD AND SORCERESS *edited by Marion Zimmer Bradley.* Original tales of fantasy and adventure, stories of warrior women and sorceresses, wielding their powers in the war against evil.

CATFANTASTIC I and II *edited by Andre Norton and Martin H. Greenberg.* All new tales of those long-tailed, furry keepers of mankind, practitioners of magical arts beyond human ken.

HORSE FANTASTIC *edited by Rosalind M. Greenberg and Martin H. Greenberg.* All new stories of horses both natural and supernatural from such fantasy masters as Jennifer Roberson, Mercedes Lackey, Mike Resnick, Mickey Zucker Reichert, Nancy Springer, and Judith Tarr.

DRAGON FANTASTIC *edited by Rosalind M. Greenberg and Martin H. Greenberg.* Complete with an introduction by Tad Williams, here is a spellbinding collection of brand new stories about the dragons, the true kings of the fantasy realms, as envisioned by such clever enchanters as Alan Dean Foster, Dennis McKiernan, Mickey Zucker Reichert, Tanya Huff, and Esther Friesner.

MICROCOSMIC TALES

100 WONDROUS
SCIENCE FICTION SHORT-SHORT STORIES

SELECTED BY ISAAC ASIMOV,
MARTIN H. GREENBERG,
AND JOSEPH D. OLANDER

DAW BOOKS, INC.

DONALD A. WOLLHEIM, FOUNDER

375 Hudson Street, New York, NY 10014

**ELIZABETH R. WOLLHEIM
SHEILA E. GILBERT
PUBLISHERS**

First DAW Printing, June 1992

1 2 3 4 5 6 7 8 9

DAW TRADEMARK REGISTERED
U.S. PAT OFF. AND FOREIGN COUNTRIES
MARCA REGISTRADA.
HECHO EN U.S.A.

PRINTED IN THE U.S.A.

ACKNOWLEDGMENTS

"The Last Answer" by Isaac Asimov. Copyright © 1979 by Condé Nast Publications, Inc. Originally published in *Analog* (January 1980). Reprinted by permission of the author.

"Package Deal" by Donald Franson. Copyright © 1980 by Donald Franson. Published by arrangement with the author. Original to this collection.

"Lycanthrope" by Norman E. Hartman. Copyright © 1976 by *Omelas-2*. Reprinted by permission of the author.

"Gemini 74" by Jack Ritchie. Copyright © 1966 by The Diners Club, Inc. Reprinted by permission of Larry Sternig Library Agency.

"Geever's Flight" by Charles E. Fritch. Copyright © 1965 by William F. Nolan. Reprinted from *The Pseudo People,* edited by William F. Nolan for Sherbourne Press, Inc. Reprinted by permission of the author.

"Lost and Found" by Phyllis Eisenstein. Copyright © 1978 by Phyllis Eisenstein. Reprinted from *Analog* by permission of the author.

"Pattern" by Fredric Brown. Copyright © 1954 by Fredric Brown. Reprinted by permission of Scott Meredith Literary Agency, Inc., 845 Third Avenue, New York, New York 10022.

"Discovering a New Earth" by Robert Mattingly. Copyright © 1980 by Robert Mattingly. Published by arrangement with the author and his agent, Forrest J Ackerman, 2495 Glendower Ave., Hollywood, CA 90027. Original to this collection.

"Varieties of Technological Experience" by Barry N. Malzberg. Copyright © 1978 by Condé Nast Publications, Inc. Reprinted by permission of the author.

"Listen, Love" by George Zebrowski and Jack Dann. Copyright © 1971 by Michael Moorcock. First appeared in *New Worlds Quarterly 2.* Reprinted by permission of the authors and Joseph Elder Agency, 150 West 87th Street, New York, N.Y. 10024.

"That Strain Again" by Charles Sheffield. Copyright © 1980 by Charles Sheffield. Published by arrangement with the author. Original to this collection.

"Take Me to Your Leader" by George Henry Smith. Copyright © 1980 by George Henry Smith. Published by arrangement with the author. Original to this collection.

"Drawing Board" by Charles Spano, Jr. Copyright © 1980 by Charles Spano, Jr. Published by arrangement with the author. Original to this collection.

"Shell Shock" by Donald Franson. Copyright © 1974 by Mankind Publishing Company. First published in *Vertex* (April 1974). Reprinted by permission of the author.

"Speak" by Henry Slesar. Copyright © 1965 by The Diner's Club. Reprinted by permission of the author.

"Your Cruel Face" by Craig Strete. Copyright © 1977 by Craig Strete. Reprinted by permission of the author.

"The Best-Laid Plans . . ." by Rick Conley. Copyright © 1980 by Rick Conley. Published by arrangement with the author. Original to this collection.

"Devil to Pay" by Mack Reynolds. Copyright © 1957 by *Good Humor*. Reprinted by permission of the author.

"Who Else Could I Count On?" by Manly Wade Wellman. Copyright © 1963 by Manly Wade Wellman. First appeared in *Who Fears the Devil?* (Arkham House, 1963). Reprinted by permission of the author.

"The Rat and the Snake" by A.E. van Vogt. Copyright © 1970 by Fantasy Publishing Co., Inc. Reprinted by permission of the author's agent, Forrest J Ackerman, 2495 Glendower Ave., Hollywood, CA 90027.

"The Finest Hunter in the World" by Harry Harrison. Copyright © 1970 by Harry Harrison. Reprinted by permission of the author.

"Life" by Dennis R. Caro. Copyright © 1980 by Dennis R. Caro. Published by arrangement with the author. Original to this collection.

"Love Story" by Eric Frank Russell. Copyright © 1957 by Street & Smith Publications, Inc. Reprinted by permission of the author's agents, Scott Meredith Literary Agency, Inc., 845 Third Avenue, New York, New York 10022.

"Exile in Lakehurst" by Robert Payes. Copyright © 1980 by Robert Payes. Published by arrangement with the author. Original to this collection.

"The Bait" by Fritz Leiber. Copyright © 1973 by Stuart Schiff. Reprinted by permission of the author.

"The Humanic Complex" by Ray Russell. Copyright © 1978 by Ray Russell. First published in *The Magazine of Fantasy & Sciency Fiction*. Reprinted by permission of the author.

"Friends?" by Roberta Ghidalia. Copyright © 1973 by Roberta Ghidalia. Reprinted by permission of the author.

"Take a Deep Breath" by Author C. Clarke. Copyright © 1957 by Royal Publications, Inc. Reprinted by permission of the author and the author's agents, Scott Meredith Literary Agency, Inc., 845 Third Avenue, New York, New York 10022.

"The Quest of the Infidel!" by Sherwood Springer. Copyright © 1980 by Sherwood Springer. Published by arrangement with the author. Original to this collection.

"Legal Rights for Germs" by Joe Patrouch. Copyright © 1977 by Condé Nast Publications, Inc. Originally published in *Analog* (November 1977). Reprinted by permission of the author.

"Blood" by Fredric Brown. Copyright © 1955 by Fantasy House, Inc., from *The Magazine of Fantasy & Science Fiction*. Reprinted by permission of Scott Meredith Literary Agency, Inc., 845 Third Avenue, New York, New York 10022.

"The Diana Syndrome" by R. A. Montana. Copyright © 1980 by R. A. Montana. Published by arrangement with the author. Original to this collection.

"Emergency Rations" by Theodore R. Cogswell. Copyright 1953 by Greenleaf Publishing Company. Reprinted by permission of the author.

"Buy Jupiter" by Isaac Asimov. Copyright © 1958 by Mercury Press. From *Venture Science Fiction*. Reprinted by permission of the author.

"The Old Man" by Henry Slesar. Copyright © 1962 by The Diner's Club. Reprinted by permission of the author.

"Exile's Greeting" by Roland Green. Copyright © 1980 by Roland Green. Published by arrangement with the author. Original to this collection.

"The Biography Project" by H. L. Gold. Copyright © 1951 by World Editions, Inc. Reprinted by permission of the author.

"The Grapes of the Rath" by Jan Howard Finder. Copyright © 1980 by Jan Howard Finder. Published by arrangement with the author. Original to this collection.

"Mr. Lupescu" by Anthony Boucher. Copyright 1944 by Anthony Boucher, renewed © 1972. Reprinted by permission of Curtis Brown, Ltd.

"What I Did During My Park Vacation" by Ruth Berman. Copyright © 1980 by Ruth Berman. Published by arrangement with the author. Original to this collection.

"A Fragment of Manuscript" by Harry Harrison. Copyright © 1980 by Harry Harrison. Published by arrangement with the author. Original to this collection.

"The Boy with Five Fingers" by James Gunn. Copyright 1953 by Standard Magazines. Reprinted by permission of the author.

"The King of Beasts" by Philip José Farmer. Copyright © 1964 by Galaxy Publishing Corporation. Reprinted by permission of Scott Meredith Literary Agency, Inc., 845 Third Avenue, New York, New York 10022.

"Displaced Person" by Eric Frank Russell. Copyright © 1953 by Clark Publishing Company. Reprinted by permission of the author and the author's agents, Scott Meredith Literary Agency, Inc., 845 Third Avenue, New York, New York 10022.

"A Clone at Last" by Bill Pronzini and Barry N. Malzberg. Copyright © 1978 by Mercury Press, Inc. From *The Magazine of Fantasy & Science Fiction*. Reprinted by permission of the authors.

"X Marks the Pedwalk" by Fritz Leiber. Copyright © 1963 by Galaxy Publishing Corporation. Reprinted by permission of the author.

"The Mission" by Arthur Tofte. Copyright © 1980 by Arthur Tofte. Published by arrangement with the author and his agent, Larry Sternig Literary Agency. Original to this collection.

"Proof" by F. M. Busby. Copyright © 1972 by Ultimate Publishing Co., Inc. Reprinted by permission of the author.

"Dreamworld" by Isaac Asimov. Copyright © 1955 by Mercury Press, Inc. From *The Magazine of Fantasy & Science Fiction*. Reprinted by permission of the author.

"The Reunion" by Paul J. Nahin. Copyright © 1979 by Condé Nast Publications, Inc. Reprinted by permission of the author.

"The Futile Flight of John Arthur Benn" by Richard Wilson. Copyright © 1955 by Royal Publications. Originally published in *Infinity Science Fiction* (February 1956) as by "Edward Halibut." Reprinted by permission of the author.

"Servants of the Lord" by James Stevens. Copyright © 1980 by James Stevens. Published by arrangement with the author. Original to this collection.

"Mattie Harris, Galactic Spy" by Rachel Cosgrove Payes. Copyright © 1974 by Mankind Publishing Company. Copyright assigned to author, 1976. First published in *Vertex*. Reprinted by permission of the author.

"Changeover" by Juleen Brantingham. Copyright © 1980 by Juleen Brantingham. Published by arrangement with the author. Original to this collection.

"Hometown" by Richard Wilson. Copyright © 1956 by Headline Publications, Inc. Originally published in *Super-Science Fiction* (April 1957). Reprinted by permission of the author.

"The Penalty" by Henry Slesar. Copyright © 1962 by Henry Slesar. Reprinted by permission of the author.

"The Pill" by Maggie Nadler. Copyright © 1972 by Ultimate Publishing Co., Inc. Reprinted by permission of the author.

"The Final Battle" by Harry Harrison. Copyright © 1970 by Harry Harrison. Reprinted by permission of the author.

"Earthbound" by Lester del Rey. Copyright © 1963 by Galaxy Publishing Corporation. Reprinted by permission of the author and the author's agents, Scott Meredith Literary Agency, Inc., 845 Third Avenue, New York, New York 10022.

"Rotating Cylinders and the Possibility of Global Causality Violation" by Larry Niven. Copyright © 1978 by Davis Publications, Inc. Reprinted by permission of the author.

"The Voice in the Garden" by Harlan Ellison. Appeared originally in the Author's collection, *From the Land of Fear.* Copyright © 1967 by Harlan Ellison. Reprinted with permission of, and by arrangement with, the Author and the Author's agent, Richard Curtis Associates, Inc., New York. All rights reserved.

"If Eve Had Failed to Conceive" by Edward Wellen. Copyright © 1974 by Damon Knight. Originally published in *Orbit 15.* Reprinted by permission of the author.

CONTENTS

CONTENTS   XV

A Quick Dip

by Isaac Asimov

For those who scuba-dive, the water represents a different world, a three-dimensional universe in which gravity scarcely exists, in which viscosity forces movement into a slow grace, in which the world of plants and animals is bizarre and outré, when compared with the familiar surroundings of land.

Reading science fiction—*good* science fiction—is like a scuba-diving of the mind. You live, while you read, in a strange society, a world so different in time, or space, or both, that even the friendly ocean isn't to be compared with it.

Distant planets—the far future—space itself—alien creatures—alien thoughts—

What excitement, and how invigorating!

But we all "know" it takes room to create a good, detailed, self-consistent, palpable society in which we can immerse ourselves completely. Yet what if we don't have the time to immerse ourselves completely and drift for hours? Ought we to feel deprived?

No! It is possible to write good science fiction in two thousand words or less. If you can't immerse yourself completely in the strange ocean of the mind, you can at least take a quick dip—a few refreshing minutes away from the ordinary and prosaic.

But where to find that?

Right here! Your anthologists have taken the trouble (a pleasure, really) to supply you with not one, but a hundred, excellent science-fictional dips for the odd moments when you may want to clear and renew your mind. Good reading!

Ask a silly question . . .

The Last Answer

by Isaac Asimov

Murray Templeton was forty-five years old, in his prime and with all parts of his body in perfect working order except for certain key portions of his coronary arteries, but that was enough.

The pain had come suddenly, had mounted to an unbearable peak, and had then ebbed steadily. He could feel his breath slowing and a kind of gathering peace washing over him.

There is no pleasure like the absence of pain—immediately after pain. Murray felt an almost giddy lightness as though he were lifting in the air and hovering.

He opened his eyes and noted with distant amusement that the others in the room were still agitated. He had been in the laboratory when the pain had struck, quite without warning, and when he had staggered, he had heard surprised outcries from the others before everything vanished into overwhelming agony.

Now, with the pain gone, the others were still hovering, still anxious, still gathered about his fallen body—

—Which, he suddenly realized, he was looking down on.

He was down there, sprawled, face contorted. He was up here, at peace and watching.

He thought: "Miracle of miracles! The life-after-life nuts were right."

And although that was a humiliating way for an atheistic physicist to die, he felt only the mildest surprise, and no alteration of the peace in which he was immersed.

He thought: "There should be an angel, or something, coming for me."

The Earthly scene was fading. Darkness was invading his consciousness and off in a distance, as a last glimmer of sight, there was a figure of light, vaguely human in form, and radiating warmth.

Murray thought: "What a joke on me. I'm going to heaven."

Even as he thought that, the light faded, but the warmth remained. There was no lessening of the peace even though in all the Universe only he remained—and the Voice.

The Voice said, "I have done this so often, and yet I still have the capacity to be pleased at success."

It was in Murray's mind to say something, but he was not conscious of possessing a mouth, tongue or vocal cords. Nevertheless, he tried to make a sound. He tried, mouthlessly, to hum words or breathe them or just push them out by a contraction of—something.

And they came out. He heard his own voice, quite recognizable, and his own words, infinitely clear.

Murray said, "Is this Heaven?"

The Voice said, "This is no place as you understand place."

Murray was embarrassed, but the next question had to be asked. "Pardon me if I sound like a jackass. Are you God?"

Without changing intonation or in any way marring the perfection of the sound, the Voice sounded amused. "It is strange that I am always asked that in, of course, an infinite number of ways. There is no answer I can give that you would comprehend. I *am*—which is all that I can say significantly and you may cover that with any word or concept you please."

Murray said, "And what am I? A soul? Or am I only personified existence, too?" He tried not to sound sarcastic, but it seemed to him that he had failed. He thought then, fleetingly, of adding a "Your Grace" or "Holy One" or *something* to counteract the sarcasm, and could not bring himself to do so even though for the first time in his existence he speculated on the possibility of being punished for his insolence—or sin?—with Hell, and whatever that might be like.

The Voice did not sound offended. "You are easy to explain—even to you. You may call yourself a soul if that pleases you, but what you are is a nexus of electromagnetic forces, so arranged that all the interconnections and interrelationships are exactly imitative of those of your brain in your Universe-existence—down to the smallest detail. Therefore you have your capacity for thought, your memories, your personality. It still seems to you that you are you."

Murray found himself incredulous. "You mean the essence of my brain was permanent."

"Not at all. There is nothing about you that is permanent except what I choose to make so. I formed the nexus. I constructed it while you had physical existence and adjusted it to the moment when the existence failed."

The Voice seemed distinctly pleased with itself, and went on after a moment's pause. "An intricate but entirely precise construction. I could, of course, do it for every human being on your world but I am pleased that I do not. There is pleasure in the selection."

"You choose very few then."

"Very few."

"And what happens to the rest?"

"Oblivion!—Oh, of course, you imagine a Hell."

Murray would have flushed if he had the capacity to do so. He said, "I do not. It is spoken of. Still, I would scarcely have thought I was virtuous enough to have attracted your attention as one of the Elect."

"Virtuous?—Ah, I see what you mean. It is troublesome to have to force my thinking small enough to permeate yours. No, I have chosen you for your capacity for thought, as I choose others, in quadrillions, from all the intelligent species of the Universe."

Murray found himself suddenly curious, the habit of a lifetime. He said, "Do you choose them all yourself or are there others like you?"

For a fleeting moment, Murray thought there was an impatient reaction to that, but when the Voice came, it was unmoved. "Whether or not there are others is irrelevant to you. This Universe is mine, and mine alone. It is my intention, my construction, intended for my purpose alone."

"And yet with quadrillions of nexi you have formed, you spend time with me? Am I that important?"

The Voice said, "You are not important at all. I am also with others in a way which, to your perception, would seem simultaneous."

"And yet you are one?"

Again amusement. The Voice said, "You seek to trap me into an inconsistency. If you were an amoeba who could consider individuality only in connection with single cells and if you were to ask a sperm whale, made up of 30 quadrillion cells, whether it is one of many, how could the sperm whale answer in a way that would be comprehensible to the amoeba?"

Murray said dryly, "I'll think about it. It may become comprehensible."

"Exactly. That is your function. You will think."

"To what end? You already know everything, I suppose."

The Voice said, "Even if I knew everything, I could not know that I know everything."

Murray said, "That sounds like a bit of Eastern philosophy—something that sounds profound precisely because it has no meaning."

The Voice said, "You have promise. You answer my paradox with a paradox—except that mine is not a paradox. Consider. I have existed eternally, but what does that mean? It means I cannot remember having come into existence. If I could, I would not have existed eternally. If I cannot remember having come into existence, then there is at least one thing—the nature of my coming into existence—that I do not know.

"Then, too, although what I know is infinite, it is also true that what there is to know is infinite, and how can I be sure that both infinites are equal. The infinity of potential knowledge may be infinitely greater than the infinity of my actual knowledge. Here is a simple example: If I knew every one of the even integers, I would know an infinite number of items, and yet I would still not know a single odd integer."

Murray said, "But the odd integers can be derived. If you divide every even integer in the entire infinite series by two, you will get another infinite series which will contain within it the infinite series of odd integers."

The Voice said, "You have the idea. I am pleased. It will be your task to find other such ways, far more difficult ones, from the known to the not-yet-known. You have your memories. You will remember all the data you have ever collected or learned, or that you have or will deduce from that data. If necessary, you will be allowed to learn what additional data you will consider relevant to the problems you set yourself."

"Could you not do all that for yourself?"

The Voice said, "I can, but it is more interesting this way. I constructed the Universe in order to have more facts to deal with. I inserted the uncertainty principle, entropy, and other randomization factors to make the whole not instantly obvious. It has worked well for it has amused me for its entire existence.

"I then allowed complexities that produced first life and then intelligence, and used it as a source for a research team, not because I need the aid, but because it would introduce a new random factor. I found I could not predict the next interesting piece of knowledge gained, where it would come from, by what means derived."

"Does that ever happen?"

"Certainly. A century doesn't pass in which some interesting item doesn't appear somewhere," the Voice said.

"Something that you could have thought of yourself, but had not done so yet?"

"Yes."

Murray said, "Do you actually think there's a chance of my obliging you in this manner?"

"In the next century? Virtually none. In the long run, though, your success is certain, since you will be engaged eternally."

Murray said, "I will be thinking through eternity? Forever?"

"Yes."

"To what end?"

"I have told you. To find new knowledge."

"But beyond that. For what purpose am I to find new knowledge?"

"It was what you did in your Universe-bound life. What was its purpose then?"

Murray said, "To gain new knowledge that only I could gain. To receive the praise of my fellows. To feel the satisfaction of accomplishment knowing that I had only a short time allotted me for the purpose.—Now I would gain only what you could gain yourself if you wished to take a small bit of trouble. You cannot praise me; you can only be amused. And there is no credit or satisfaction in accomplishment when I have all eternity to do it in."

The Voice said, "And you do not find thought and discovery worthwhile in itself? You do not find it requiring no further purpose?"

"For a finite time, yes. Not for all eternity."

"I see your point. Nevertheless, you have no choice."

"You say I am to think. You cannot make me do so."

The Voice said, "I do not wish to constrain you directly. I will not need to. Since you can do nothing but think, you will think. You do not know how not to think."

"Then I will give myself a goal. I will invent a purpose."

The Voice said tolerantly, "That you can certainly do."

"I have already found a purpose."

"May I know what it is?"

"You know already. I know we are not speaking in the ordinary fashion. You adjust my nexus in such a way that I believe I hear you and I believe I speak, but you transfer thoughts to me and from me directly. And when my nexus changes with my thoughts you are at once aware of them and do not need my voluntary transmission."

The Voice said, "You are surprisingly correct. I am pleased.—But it also pleases me to have you tell me your thoughts voluntarily."

"Then I will tell you. The purpose of my thinking will be to discover a way to disrupt this nexus of me that you have created. I do not want to think for no purpose but to amuse you. I do not want to think forever to amuse you. I do not want to exist forever to amuse you. All my thinking will be directed toward ending the nexus. *That* would amuse *me*."

The Voice said, "I have no objection to that. Even concentrated thought on ending your own existence may, despite you, come up with something new and interesting. And, of course, if you succeed in this suicide attempt you will have accomplished nothing, for I would instantly reconstruct you and in such a way as to make your method of suicide impossible. And if you found another and still more subtle fashion of disrupting yourself, I would reconstruct you with that possibility eliminated and so on. It could be an interesting game, but you will nevertheless exist eternally. It is my will."

Murray felt a quaver but the words came out with a perfect calm. "Am I in Hell then, after all? You have implied there is none, but if this were Hell you would lie as part of the game of Hell."

The Voice said, "In that case, of what use to assure you that you are not in Hell? Nevertheless, I assure you. There is here neither Heaven nor Hell. There is only myself."

Murray said, "Consider, then, that my thoughts may be useless to you. If I come up with nothing useful, will it not be worth your while to—disassemble me and take no further trouble with me."

"As a reward? You want Nirvana as the prize of failure and you intend to assure me failure? There is no bargain there. You will not fail. With all Eternity before you, you cannot avoid having at least one interesting thought, however you try against it."

"Then I will create another purpose for myself. I will not try to destroy myself. I will set as my goal the humiliation of you. I will think of something you have not only never thought of but never could think of. I will think of the last answer, beyond which there is no knowledge further."

The Voice said, "You do not understand the nature of the infinite. There may be things I have not yet troubled to know. There cannot be anything I cannot know."

Murray said thoughtfully, "You cannot know your beginning. You have said so. Therefore you cannot know your end. Very well, then. That will be my purpose and that will be the last answer. I will not destroy myself. I will destroy *you*—if you do not destroy me first."

The Voice said, "Ah! You come to that in rather less than average time. I would have thought it would have taken you longer. There is not one of those I have with me in this existence of perfect and eternal thought that does not have the ambition of destroying me. It cannot be done."

Murray said, "I have all eternity to think of a way of destroying you."

The Voice said, equably, "Then try to think of it." And it was gone.

But Murray had his purpose now and was content.

But what could *any* Entity, conscious of eternal existence, want—but an end?

For what else had the Voice been searching for countless billions of years? And for what other reason had intelligence been created and certain specimens salvaged and put to work, but to aid in that great search? And Murray intended that it would be he, and he alone, who would succeed.

Carefully, and with the thrill of purpose, Murray began to think.

He had plenty of time.

"I, Vernon Lewis, being of sound mind—"

Package Deal

by Donald Franson

It came in the afternoon mail—a slightly battered package wrapped in brown paper and taped with brown sealing tape. There was nothing to distinguish it from the thousands of other packages passing through the post office every day. But it was different—very different.

It was from the future.

Vernon Lewis placed the package on the kitchen table, brushing aside drawings and wiring diagrams. It hefted like books, or papers—which is what he'd expected. The address was right—why shouldn't it be? It was in his own handwriting. He'd even put the stamps on himself. The cancellation was smudged, but that wasn't important. He pulled out a chair, sat down, and smiled broadly.

He'd been waiting for this package ever since the day he'd written the address on the wrapper and stuffed it in a big envelope and put it in the safe-deposit box in his bank. The fleeting thought that the wrapper was still there in the bank vault—occupying two places at the same time—disconcerted him for a moment. Then he realized he must put the paradoxes out of his mind, not try to understand them. Just concentrate on the results. The package was here—at last.

Lewis, just out of college, was an inventor and an investor—so far unsuccessful in either field. He was currently working on an invention to send things back in time, but he couldn't do anything further without more funds. If he applied for financial aid—government, university, corporation—they would take the invention out of his hands. And that's what he didn't want.

There was only one use for this invention as he saw it. It was to make him rich. Public knowledge of it would spoil the game.

Sure things would never pay off if everyone knew of them. Horse races, football games, anything that paid big odds would not pay big odds if everyone knew the winners. Not only that, the game would be up if anyone even suspected that there was such a way to foretell the future. No one must even suspect, therefore, that he had—or almost had—no, *had*—a way to obtain objects, and information, from the future.

He was alone in his apartment, so he didn't fear discovery. Apparently the post office hadn't interfered with the package on its strange journey. There was no evidence of tampering. He felt a little guilty, using such a wonderful invention for solely personal motives—but he consoled himself with the thought that later, when he was rich, he might—just might—think about sharing the invention with society. He kept the consoling thought in the back of his mind, where it would do no harm . . .

But this package had come just in the nick of time. He needed more money for the experiments. The invention could not pay for itself now, of course, but it would pay for itself when it was finished.

Or even before it was finished.

All he had now was a device that could theoretically—it hadn't really worked yet—send small objects into the past, by going against the current of time. The *past,* not the future—though he wanted, paradoxically, to contact the future, not the past.

He had no need of a time-machine to send something into the future. Everything moves toward the future, at the same time rate—one second per second. His invention did no more than reverse this—it sent things toward the past, at the rate of one second per second. There was no hurry, since the object would be intangible, going against the stream of time, and would only resume solidity when it stopped, on arrival at its destination.

There was only one experiment that would show him he had been successful in sending something into the past—recovering the object, earlier.

He didn't even have a working model now, but he knew it would work. His last small model had very nearly destroyed itself because he hadn't thought to shove it sidewise a few seconds *before* he flicked the switch. Fortunately, something prevented the returning object—a rubber ball—from occupying the same space as its own earlier counterpart. It bounced off—somewhere. He never found it, though he searched the apartment thoroughly.

He theorized that it had bounced off into *time*—and thus extended its backward journey from mere seconds to years. This was the line he was working on now. The original model had been dismantled, after a few more unspectacular attempts. It was not even a good demonstration, if he had wanted to demonstrate it. He'd build a better one—when he had more funds.

But his drawings and calculations had gone on. Theoretically, he would now be able to bounce something back in time not seconds but years, and predict the exact date of its return to solidity. Due to geodesic uncertainties, however, he wouldn't be able to pinpoint any precise area where it would appear—he could only drop the object on the city from a moderate height and hope it would fall some place where it could be picked up.

Then he got the idea of wrapping a postal package and addressing it to himself. It would fall somewhere on the city, someone would pick it up, think it had fallen out of a mail bag and take it to the post office. He'd had this idea for a long time, but he'd never received anything in the mail from himself—until today.

He had done his part from this end, of course. In the safe-deposit box with the wrapper were the complete plans for the invention, the progress so far—which he kept updated in monthly visits to the box. It was theoretically near perfection, only needing money for more experimentation and for making the full-size hardware. The plans would be useful at some future date when he *did* have the money—and could build the machine that would send the package back in time.

Obviously he'd perfected the invention, some time in the future, else how had the package come back to him?

Despite his anticipation, he was reluctant to open it. It must contain, if not money, something to make him rich, so that he could finance the experiments that would result in the further perfection of the invention, in order that this package could be sent back in time. A seemingly endless cycle. Another paradox: he had to open it to complete the cycle. Open it and act upon it. What if he didn't?

He ripped the tape off, unwrapped the brown paper. There it was—an almanac. For this year? He felt a pang of disappointment. No, it was *next* year's—disguised in this year's covers. He—his future self—had thought of this, should someone else open and casually inspect the contents of the package, such as a postal inspector, or the finder-in-the-street. He was taking no chances of someone else stumbling on the secret.

Other items looked equally innocuous—at first glance. The sports pages of next month's newspapers. A copy of the *Wall Street Journal* of a year from now. A catalog of antiques, collectors' items that would quickly increase in value. Leaflets on old coins and stamps and magazines—long-term investments, as the stocks and football scores were short-term ones. Real-estate maps.

He hadn't been too detailed in his instructions in the envelope, knowing his future self would think of more and better ways of getting rich. But there was enough here, at first appraisal, to make him well-off within a month, rich in a year, fabulously wealthy in a decade. He had been an investor of sorts, though hampered by lack of funds, and knew the ins and outs. Now he had all the sure things. He must be cautious, but it looked good. *Very* good.

There was also a note, a folded sheet of stationery.

Lewis frowned. This he had not expected. He had specifically reminded himself not to include anything personal, in case of inspection. He unfolded the paper.

It had only a few words written on it—not in his own handwriting. *From your grateful heirs,* it said.

The note in turn enclosed a newspaper clipping. It was a death notice.

Lewis crumpled it up without reading it, threw it in the wastebasket.

He stared moodily at the almanac and newspapers. He'd included his latest drawings and progress reports in the bank envelope, but there was much more work to be done on the invention. A lifetime of work, apparently—which he would never finish. His heirs, still unborn, would reap the harvest of his labors.

His invention would be successful after all. But he would never see it completed, no matter what he did, no matter how hard he worked at it.

He groaned at the thought of the long years of labor ahead, secretly working on the time-machine, being careful not to disclose it to anyone. He would have to do most of the work alone, regardless of the wealth he would command. And then not to see the results, ever.

But the results were here before him.

Yet in order to achieve these results, he must carry out the cycle. Make a lot of money, work hard, die, on the date hidden in the wastebasket.

Lewis straightened the papers on the table, now not looking so beautiful. He stared at them for a long, long time.

Then he had a better idea.

He opened the sports pages to the race results, began working out bets. Small ones and scattered ones, long shots and favorites, little gains to lead the way to big ones, then to investments.

At this rate he'd easily amass a considerable fortune in a few years. Then he could retire, not even having to work at making more money, and have a good time the rest of his life.

He would become a playboy, a gentleman of leisure,
let the money pile up at compound interest.

Let *them* work on the invention.

That's a killer!

Lycanthrope

by Norman E. Hartman

"I tell you, Norm, there really are such things as werewolves!"

"You're crazy, Ed. And even if there were any, how
would you go about proving it?"

We were at it again, Ed and I. The same old favorite
of his. Lycanthropy, the ages old belief that a man or
woman could turn into an animal. According to Ed the
kind of animal depended on the cultural background and
ancestry of the person involved.

"A lot of people believe in witchcraft and werewolves,
more every day if you believe what you read in some of
these magazines. Why, I heard just the other day about
a book that tells you how to do all sorts of things like
summoning demons and casting spells. It's supposed to
be as accurate as possible, even giving the reasoning behind each part of the spell as it goes along."

"You believe everything you read in those crazy magazines of yours, Ed. If we had a copy of that book I'd
soon prove to you that those spells won't work by actually
trying them out."

"I'll just call you on that! The book review in *Playboy*
said that it's being reprinted in England and tells where
to send for it. It's twenty-five bucks and it's going to be
a good investment for me because if the spells work you'll
be the one who pays for the book!"

"It's a deal! You look up that book review and I'll type up the order."

The letter ordering one copy of Van der Camp's *Witchcraft in Central Europe* went out in the next day's mail, and Ed and I spent the next few weeks reading up on necromancy and related subjects in the library at State U. We kidded the librarian into letting us read some volumes from shelves normally closed to any but accredited researchers. The books were old and dusty, some of them in archaic English, but while they were very interesting in places none of them was very much help to a couple of beginners.

Then the book finally arrived. It was all that we had hoped for, and then some. It gave complete formulas, rituals, and incantations; correct times for gathering and processing ingredients; and most important the right phases of the moon to the minute necessary for reliable results. In order to give the spells a proper trial we had to follow the book's instructions in every minute detail, so it was some time before we were ready but at last we were prepared. The materials were at hand and we had rehearsed the rituals and incantations until we knew them by heart.

"Are you sure you want to go through with this, Ed? There's no telling what you might turn into if the spell should really work." I was really uneasy. The logic behind the spell seemed so logical, somehow.

"Of course I want to go through with it. I didn't spend my money and come this far just to turn around and quit. Just think, I might become a lion or a tiger or an eagle. Anyway, no matter what I turn into I'm sure to be able to make the proper ritual motions in order to return to my original form."

"Yeah, but what if you can't? Remember, these spells were devised back in the days when people lived close to the soil. They were supposed to change people into forms that represented the major destructive forces of their times. In Europe and England they tried to turn into wolves and vampire bats, while in Scandinavia it was were-bears. In Malaya and India it was were-tigers and snakes, but in Africa it was were-hyenas, buffalos, and leopards. In each case it was the creature that took the greatest toll of the common people's life and property,"

I reasoned with him. "We have different fears these days than back in the Dark Ages, and different things to menace our daily lives."

"And what if we do? Those old fears are ingrained into the heredity of mankind by a million years of fleeing in terror from animals fiercer and stronger than they were. What they feared then, we still fear today. I would be scared to death of a wolf or a bear, even though I've never met one face to face."

It was a cold, windy night. A sickly gibbous moon gleamed fitfully through rents in the ragged clouds. We traced interlocking pentacles in the raw dirt of a new grave, lit the Coleman stove and began to concoct the unholy brew called for by the book.

"You're sure that you really want to go through with this?"

"For the last time, YES!"

We hastily mumbled the incantation. Ed picked up the saucepan of evil-smelling liquid and quaffed it at a single gulp. There was a flash! A crash! An opaque cloud of smoke!

When people admire my new sports car I tell them that it's European, custom-made, . . . but where in Hell am I going to get spare parts?

And you waste time on chess?

Gemini 74

by Jack Ritchie

"We are about to initiate the first chess game ever to be played in orbit," Orloff declared.

It was our 22d circuit and for the time being, we had nothing major to do.

"I don't know a damn thing about the game," I said.

Orloff fastened the small traveling chessboard securely to the panelboard between us. "But at least you are acquainted with how the pieces may be manipulated, are you not? I will give you the White and let you make the opening move."

I stifled a yawn and moved my king's pawn to four. Orloff duplicated my move with the Black. "This is a routine flight, is it not?"

I nodded. "It's been done before."

That was one way of putting it. Personally, I rather liked Orloff, but the simple fact remained that neither of our countries trusted the other enough to give away anything new, technical or tactical. However, flights like this one looked good on paper and made a lot of people feel happy about the international situation.

Orloff smiled. "To liven up this otherwise routine flight, we do, however, have a new situation. Who will be the first person to win a chess game in orbit? An American? A Russian?"

I shrugged. "Big deal."

Orloff was mildly offended. "To a Russian, chess is not just a game. It is a way of life."

"And if you win, you might get a medal?" I sighed and studied the board. Finally, I moved my knight to king's bishop three.

Orloff shifted the black knight to queen's bishop three.

I moved my bishop to queen's knight five.

"Do you know what you just did?" Orloff asked.

"No. What?"

"That is a 'Ruy Lopez.' An opening which dates back to the 17th century."

"Is that right?" I said. "It could happen to anybody."

"I know," Orloff responded, "but we chess players like to give things names." Orloff glanced at the command clock and reached for the data chart. "I have forgotten to make a flight entry. Move my piece to Ng6, will you?"

I moved the black knight to bishop three.

Orloff's eyes clouded with a sudden thought. "How did you know what Ng6 meant?"

I scratched an ear. "I think I read about it someplace."

It seems that English-speaking countries use the descriptive notation for their moves, while just about everybody else uses the algebraic. The files of the board, from White's left to right, are named a,b,c,d,e,f,g and h. The ranks are numbered from 1 to 8, from the White side to the Black side. Thus, Orloff's Ng6 would be knight to king's bishop three.

Orloff's eyes narrowed. "I have the suspicion that I have on board what you Americans call a ringer. I thought you said—and I quote—'I don't know a damn thing about the game.' "

I cleared my throat. "I really don't. I was speaking comparatively. I'm no Fischer . . . or Ivkov . . . or Smyslov."

Orloff smiled tightly. "But at least you know that they are not soccer players." Orloff glared at the board. "I wish Metchnikov were here instead of me. Among us, he is the No. 1 chess player. However, I am the No. 1 astronaut of our team and this received prime consideration for the flight."

I reached for my king and castled. Orloff frowned in concentration.

After 15 minutes, I said, "It's your move."

"This I know," Orloff snapped. "Do not rush me."

Six minutes later, Gemini 74 control from Cape Kennedy came in on schedule. Metchnikov had the mike. "What is happening up there?" he asked.

"We are playing chess," Orloff replied. "The first game in orbit."

"Oh?" Metchnikov said. "And you are winning?"

"I don't know," Orloff murmured. "Perhaps I underestimated my opponent."

"Hm . . ." There was a pause and then Metchnikov spoke again. "Perhaps for the benefit of those on the ground, you could describe your moves thus far? The *world* is waiting."

"I know," Orloff agreed and recited the moves.

"Hm," Metchnikov repeated. "Well, I wish you the best of luck." Then he seemed to think of something else. "Oh, by the way, Orloff, about that letter to your uncle *Dimitri* which you left on your dresser in your room? You may cease to worry. I mailed it at *six* this morning."

Dimitri, I thought. *Six.* d6?

It was.

Orloff made the move, looked at me, and blushed.

I shook my head sadly. "Even in a chess game you feel that winning is so important that . . ."

Ground control center came in loud and clear and I recognized the voice of Dr. Wickerson, who won the base chess tournament last year. "Say, Jerry," he said to me. "Your sister tells me that her *dahlias* are wilting. Did you *forget* to spray them?"

Dahlias? Forget? d4?

I had barely made the move when Metchnikov was back on the air again.

"Orloff!" he cried. "Didn't you enjoy the picnic on the *beach?* Wasn't it . . . ah . . . *divine* when we *ate* there?"

It was bd8, of course.

Orloff's face was absolutely red.

I snapped off ground control. "We will do our own playing up here, Orloff."

It wasn't until our seventh game that I finally became the first man ever to win a chess match in orbit.

Stephanie Orloff, of course, was the first woman.

If you're going to bite the hand that feeds you—

Geever's Flight

by Charles E. Fritch

Once upon a time, in a land called The City, there lived a machine named Geever.

Geever was married to a woman everyone called Geever's Wife. Geever lived at the outskirts of The City, near the edge of the world, but each day he drove in to work and did something unimportant for a man who was known as Geever's Boss.

Each evening, when he returned from work, his wife would say, "Welcome home, Geever."

There were times when it seemed to Geever that the entire world—such as it was—centered about him, and during these moments of extreme vanity Geever was certain that he had been picked by the Shadow God to be different from all others.

During a period accepted as One Afternoon, Geever was secretly working in the garage on his rocket when he heard the sound. It was unmistakable, that steady, City-shaking rumble. The Shadow God! Hastily, Geever covered his rocket. The god's vision could doubtlessly penetrate the roof of the garage but it made Geever feel better to take this precaution—especially after what had happened earlier between Geever and his wife. . . .

It had begun when Geever volunteered some information. "The world," he had said to his wife, "is shaped like a rectangle."

Geever's Wife had shrugged. "So?"

"So I want to know why."

Geever's Wife shrugged again. It was obvious that the world was in the shape of a rectangle because the Shadow God wanted it that way. She was sure that Geever was a malcontent. Some day, she knew, the Shadow God would come and take Geever away and that would solve the problem.

"There are so many things I wish to do," Geever continued. He stared wistfully out of the window at the road, where small red cars flashed by; he stared at the bright green foliage and at the tall trees stretching to the edge of the Gray Horizon.

"What do you wish to do?" asked Geever's Wife.

"I wish to write poetry, but I'm not sure I know what it is," he said. "Then, I wish to dance a jig and write music."

"What's music?"

"I'm not sure, said Geever. Then he said, "But you know what I wish to do beyond any other thing?"

"No."

"I want to find out what's on the other side of the world."

Geever's Wife blinked. She looked shocked. "You better be careful, Geever," she said.

Geever finished his Morning Coffee, checked the lock on the garage, and went off to work. His bright red car was parked in the drive. Geever got behind the wheel, drove the car into the street, engaged the car's vertical arm in the slot running down the exact center of the highway, and settled back to think.

He wondered why he wondered about so many things. Perhaps he was not wired like other people. Perhaps the Shadow God had wired him to Think, and this is what made him so curious about things. Other people were content with the world and The City. Except one, a man Geever knew who had built a strange vehicle with two large rotating propellors that churned the air. Everyone in The City had watched Geever's Friend climb into his vehicle with the motor going and the props spinning. They all watched him take off, into the sky, and Geever had been unable to breathe he was so excited.

Then, suddenly, a rumble from the sky—and the Shadow God appeared. A giant hand came down and closed around the vehicle which held Geever's Friend. The fingers closed, crushing, and Geever hid his face, falling to his knees in terror.

For a long while Geever tried not to think about his friend.

Then, One Afternoon, he had started to build a rocket.

Sometimes, as he worked, Geever thought about his wife. Despite her drabness, Geever knew he would miss her. Perhaps, someday, he would come back for her—after finding what lay beyond the world. Or perhaps not. Geever wasn't sure.

In the period known as One Evening, Geever's Wife turned to him during dinner and said, "Have you finished your silly rocket yet?"

Geever stared at her. "You know, of course, that I'm going to leave you behind?"

"Of course," Geever's Wife said. She didn't seem to mind. "When are you planning to take off?"

"Soon," Geever said.

Geever knew he must not wait. If others found out, they would gather to watch him, and this would alert the Shadow God.

Geever would leave that night.

The gray sky darkened, and Geever yawned. He went to bed, followed by his wife. When he was certain she was soundly asleep, he got up, dressed, and walked quietly out to the garage.

The rocket waited there tall and thin and shiny. Geever looked at it for a moment, then swung the hinged roof of the garage to one side and climbed aboard. He was at the controls when he heard his name called.

Geever's Wife was standing outside the rocket. "Goodbye, Geever," she said, not looking sad or happy.

For a moment, Geever hesitated. He felt words rush to his lips, and he almost invited her to come along with him on this wondrous adventure. But he said nothing.

Behind her, on the night lawn, he saw a crowd gathering.

Geever knew he must be quick now, before the Shadow God got wind of his flight. Hastily, he spun dials, flipped switches, set controls.

A distant rumbling; the ground shook; the rocket teetered on its base. The Shadow God was coming! Looking up in panic, Geever saw his great bulk against the dark sky.

Quick! Geever's fingers pressed the firing button.

A burst of orange flame enveloped the garage. The rocket shot upward, pushing Geever back in his seat. Through the port, Geever looked down to the doll-sized townspeople below him.

Then Geever cried out. A giant face hovered over him. A giant face with giant eyes and a giant nose and mouth. A giant hand came whispering through the sky . . .

Frantically, Geever pulled at the controls. The rocket swerved—directly toward the giant face.

The Shadow God retreated, but not fast enough. Geever saw one giant eyeball roll upward in alarm, then the rocket struck the immense forehead. The Shadow God fell back and down with a terrible crashing sound.

For a moment, the rocket hung suspended in space; then it, too, fell back and down—into the crowd of people who had come to witness Geever's flight.

As Geever climbed out of the wrecked cabin he saw his wife. She had been struck by part of the rocket, and one of her arms was missing. Cogs and wires and glass tubes showed through the opening in her shoulder.

"Welcome home, Geever," she said, looking confused.

The next morning Geever didn't go to work. His car wouldn't run, and he didn't feel like going to work anyhow. He was depressed.

The coffee tasted sour and Geever's Wife blamed it on the stove, which didn't seem to be functioning properly. Geever's Wife didn't seem to be functioning properly either. She appeared to be running down.

Geever looked out the window at the cars creeping past. They were barely moving. The grass on the front lawn had withered overnight.

Geever said, "Boy, I don't like the way things look."

His wife didn't reply. She was standing frozen, eyes staring blankly ahead.

Geever got up and walked outside. The street was full of people, moving very slowly or not at all. Most of the cars had now stopped. Near Geever, an old man fell over and broke in half as he hit the street.

Geever walked to the Park where all the green trees had turned black. He sat down on a bench and thought about how nice it would be if he could just write a few lines of poetry or dance just one jig. But he didn't know how—and he was getting awfully tired.

Then he became sad when he thought about the Shadow God and how he, Geever, had killed him.

Shortly after this, Geever wasn't able to think about anything.

So that's how my nine early stories came to be lost.

Lost and Found

by Phyllis Eisenstein

It started one winter night when I couldn't find the screwdriver.

I told my roommate Cath, "I'm sure I left it on top of the refrigerator. I used it to put the light fixture back together, and then I laid it on top of the fridge while I made a snack. That wasn't more than three hours ago, and now it's gone."

"The roaches borrowed it," said Cath, who was washing the week's accumulation of dirty dishes. "You always say they'll walk off with the place someday."

"Be serious."

"Poltergeists, then."

I poked her shoulder. "Did you take it?"

"I was in the living room reading Freud. Do I need a screwdriver for that?"

"Well, what happened to it, then?"

"Honest to God, Jenny, I don't know. It'll turn up. What thief would climb three flights of stairs just to steal a lousy screwdriver?"

I wondered about that. For several minutes I'd felt that someone was standing behind me, watching me. Not Cath; someone else, someone I couldn't see. The suggestion of a burglar struck too close to my own suspicions. I resisted the impulse to peek into the broom closet, but I did check the back door; it was securely locked.

I shook off my uneasiness and returned to my room, determined to study through the rest of the evening. I'd been loafing a lot lately; with exams a week away, I played solitaire at my desk rather than review my chemistry notes. It helped dispel the tension. I sat down and picked up the deck. After half a dozen poor rounds, I promised myself I'd play only one more, and I dealt it out with vicious slaps. When the game turned sour, I began cheating, but no matter what I did, I couldn't win. No wonder: pawing through the cards, I realized that the ace of spades and the ten of clubs were missing. I peered under the desk; there was the ten, but no ace. I checked the drawers, the bookcase, the floor beneath the bed, the dart board. Nowhere. I'd won a game earlier in the day—how could I have done that without the ace of spades?

If Cath was playing a joke on me, I'd wring it out of her.

She must have heard me step into the living room, for she looked up from her book. "Jenny, you look terrible. What's the matter? You *can't* be studying too hard."

"Did you take a card from my desk?"

"Card? What kind of card?"

"A playing card."

"Today?"

"A little while ago."

"I haven't been in your room today."

"The ace of spades is gone."

Cath shut her book and shook her head. "That's terribly symbolic," she said. With her green pen, she added small horns to the portrait of Freud gracing the dust jacket. "I'd say you were getting absent-minded, Jenny." She meditated a moment. "Knowing you, of course, you couldn't have used it as a bookmark."

I sat on the arm of the chair. "Cath," I said very seriously, "have you ever thought you might be a kleptomaniac?"

She looked me in the eye. "No, but I guess *you* have. Couldn't you use your time a little more constructively?"

Growling under my breath, I took the hint and stalked back to my room. I sat down at my desk, put my feet up, and let my eyes and mind roam. Something was odd about the bookshelf in front of me. My University mug was gone. My quartz paperweight was gone. My leatherbound copy of *Othello* was gone. I turned in my chair and looked at the rest of the room, wondering where I could have put the stuff. Was I sleepwalking? My tennis racket was missing from its peg above the bed; the stack of records on the floor had shrunk by half. I looked into the wastebasket, wondering if I had unconsciously thrown anything there, but it was empty. That wasn't right: hadn't I thrown away some old English papers this afternoon?

Where *was* everything?

Again, the creepy feeling of being secretly observed stole over me. Someone was staring at my back, perhaps waiting for me to leave so he could come in and get more. More what? None of my stuff was particularly valuable.

I heard a muffled shuffling noise behind me. I turned and looked at the closet door. I didn't have the nerve to open it.

I shouted, "Cath!"

Suddenly I felt naked and weaponless. What if it *was* a burglar? He was trapped in there, probably desperate, maybe armed. Even though there were two of us, it might be wiser to call the cops and let them handle it.

Cath came in. "What do you want?"

"The closet," I whispered.

"What?"

"I think there's someone inside."

We stood there a moment. I could feel my guts twisting. The last thing on earth I wanted to do was open that door. I wanted to run out of the room, out of the apartment, as fast as I could.

Cath shrugged, stepped forward, turned the doorknob, and yanked the closet door open.

My heart, and everything under it, suddenly pressed at the top of my throat.

There was nothing in the closet but clothing.

I had a mild case of jitters for the next couple of minutes. Cath clucked her tongue, then led me to the kitchen and poured me a cup of tea.

"Take it easy, Jenny," she said, forcing me into a chair by the table. "You can't crack up till after exams are over."

"I . . . I . . . thought . . . someone was in the closet." I gulped some tea; the cup clattered as I set it down in its saucer.

"We've been home all afternoon and evening. How could anyone have gotten in?"

I attempted a nonchalant shrug, but it turned into a shudder. "I don't know."

Cath pulled me into the living room after I finished my tea, and she handed me a paperback sex novel. "You sit in this nice soft chair and read something light, to relax. I'll sit over there and study."

I read, but I couldn't concentrate; I was too nervous to string the words and phrases together.

Then I heard something. A scuffling, rustling sound.

"Did you hear something?" I asked. "From my room?"

"Roaches," Cath said without looking up. "Or mice. Forget it."

I heard it again. "Cath!" I gasped hoarsely, springing across the room.

She caught my arm as I passed her. "Maybe we'd better go to a movie."

Then there was another noise, louder this time.

"I hear something in your room," she said.

"Roaches," I whispered.

"Okay, let's see what it is. Wait here a minute." She went to the kitchen and returned with two long, sharp carving knives. She gave one to me.

"What do you think it is?" I murmured.

"Some nut trying to get in a third floor window."

But when we stepped into my room, we saw that the window was closed and locked, as it had been for several months. Outside, silent snow fell vertically through the darkness; the thick, white frosting it had slathered on the window sill remained velvet-smooth, undisturbed. The closet door, however, was slightly ajar, although Cath had shut it firmly just a little while ago.

"There can't be anyone in the closet," Cath said. "There simply can't be." Still, she went to the closet and threw open the door.

Someone was in the closet, all right. Two someones, both young and muscular, one male, one female. They were fair-haired and evenly tanned, and they wore only scanty metallic briefs and weblike sandals. We stared; they stared back.

"Are you Jennifer Erica Templeton?" the man demanded of Cath.

"Not me," said Cath. "Her." The tip of her knife wavered in my direction.

"Jennifer Erica Templeton?" he asked me. "Born June 3, 1958, in Chicago, to Albert and Sara Templeton; student at the University of Chicago from 1975 to 1983, B.A. M.A., Ph.D. Anthropology?" He rattled off the data as if it were name, rank, and serial number, and then he paused expectantly.

His friend nudged him. "I told you this was only '77, dear. She doesn't have any degrees yet, and her field is still Chemistry."

I found myself nodding.

The man lunged, grabbing at my head. As I elbowed him in the solar plexis, I heard a snipping sound behind my right ear, and then he reeled away, clutching a handful of my hair. "Authentic souvenir!" he croaked.

"All right, all right," the woman said, hauling him back into the oddly deep space of the closet. "Now that you've got one, too, let's go home!" She slammed the door, and for several seconds a rummaging noise sounded beyond it. Then there was silence.

Cath stared at me, her mouth agape. She reached out and very slowly and gingerly pulled open the door. The strangers had vanished; once again, the closet was shallow and inhabited only by my clothes.

"Jenny," Cath whispered, "what's going on?"

I looked at her for a minute, and then I looked at the closet. I fingered my scalp where the spray of stubble interrupted the smooth flow of hair. "I'm not sure," I replied, "but tomorrow I think I'm going to transfer to the Anthropology Department."

Getting rid of the pests.

Pattern

by Fredric Brown

Miss Macy sniffed. "Why is everyone worrying so? They're not *doing* anything to us, are they?"

In the cities, elsewhere, there was blind panic. But not in Miss Macy's garden. She looked up calmly at the monstrous mile-high figures of the invaders.

A week ago, they'd landed, in a spaceship a hundred miles long that had settled down gently in the Arizona desert. Almost a thousand of them had come out of that spaceship and were now walking around.

But, as Miss Macy pointed out, they hadn't hurt anything or anybody. They weren't quite *substantial* enough to affect people. When one stepped on you or stepped on a house you were in, there was sudden darkness and until he moved his foot and walked on you couldn't see; that was all.

They had paid no attention to human beings and all attempts to communicate with them had failed, as had all attacks on them by the army and the air force. Shells fired at them exploded right inside them and didn't hurt them. Not even the H-bomb dropped on one of them while he was crossing a desert area had bothered him in the slightest.

They had paid no attention to us at all.

"And that," said Miss Macy to her sister who was also Miss Macy since neither of them was married, "is proof that they don't mean us any harm, isn't it?"

"I hope so, Amanda," said Miss Macy's sister. "But look what they're doing now."

It was a clear day, or it had been one. The sky had

been bright blue and the almost humanoid heads and shoulders of the giants, a mile up there, had been quite clearly visible. But now it was getting misty, Miss Macy saw as she followed her sister's gaze upward. Each of the two big figures in sight had a tank-life object in his hands and from these objects clouds of vaporous matter were emerging, settling slowly toward Earth.

Miss Macy sniffed again. "Making clouds. Maybe that's how they have fun. *Clouds* can't hurt us. Why do people worry so?"

She went back to her work.

"Is that a liquid fertilizer you're spraying, Amanda?" her sister asked.

"No," said Miss Macy. "It's insecticide."

**We hold these truths to be self-evident,
that all men—and women—and—**

Discovering a New Earth

by Robert Mattingly

"I don't see what the problem is," the President said. "After all, *they're* the ones that came down to us, who made the First Contact."

The three aides, looking haggard and worn out from the recent events, looked at each other. "Sir," said the first aide, "that may be true but the ETs also have some . . . er, demands, you might say . . ."

"I didn't think they made any demands on us."

"Not *demands,* so much," said the second aide, the one most informed on the Contact. The first aide was involved with worldwide reaction to this monumental event and the third aide to long-range results. He was the one most generally ignored.

"Requests," continued the second aide. "Requirements, if you would."

"I would," said the President. "Requirements for what, may I ask?"

"Admission," suddenly injected the third aide. "Trade. Technology and social adjustments. Contact."

"They've already made contact," said the first aide.

"They can always leave." The flat statement caused a nervous silence in the room, adding to the general nervousness that preyed on all of them until the third aide was sufficiently ignored again and they could continue.

"First off, there's that world government they want," said the first aide.

"We can use the UN for that."

"Only if we get in every country in the world. And that means *every* country, all of the people, not one left out or one disavowing the UN as final arbitrator and contact with them."

The President thought this over a moment. "Chance?"

"Better than before they came but . . ." The first aide let the sentence stretch out, ending it with a snort that signified his opinion of the chances it had.

The President shook his head. "With their help," he said, "giving us an overall goal and guidance, perhaps in a few years . . ."

"Step one," said the third aide. They looked at him.

"Er," said the second aide, "there *is* another point to consider: this world government would only be the *first* step to their acceptance of us."

"What else could they want of us? Everyone in the world represented. . . ."

"All the human beings, yessir," said the second aide, "but . . . you see, coming from an interstellar civilization as they do, with so many different races and societies belonging, they seem to have different standards than . . ."

"Get to the point," said the President.

"They want all mentally superior beings represented."

A pause. "There ain't no such animals on this big blue planet but us."

"Dolphins," said the third aide.

"What? Oh, yes . . . there was something in Congress about them, wasn't there?"

"Trying to restrict their slaughter when being used by the tuna fishing industry. The bill didn't pass."

The President thought this over. "That's not going to make for congenial relations between us, is it?" he said. The three aides shook their heads politely. "Well, with their help, we'll manage contact with them, see what we can do. . . ."

"They aren't the only ones, though," added the second aide.

The President looked flustered. "What others ..?"

"Four or five other species of primates," said the third aide. "Termites."

"Termites?"

"According to their definition," said the second aide.

"Two other unusual species of primate we didn't know about," continued the third aide. "Or at least couldn't prove. Roughly comparable, according to them, to our legends of the Abominable Snowman and Bigfoot."

The President made a sound in the back of his throat. It was noncommittal.

"Did we forget whales?"

"Whales?"

"Yes," said the first aide. "The ETs suggested we use them as the inital contact with the dolphins."

"Figures. Anything else?"

"A species of actual mermaid, living in the oceans of the world. . . ."

"Now wait a minute! There's no such thing."

"They found some," said the third aide. "A fair-sized civilization. They demand we include them."

"They have ways of finding out about sentient beings of a world," said the second aide, "that make our social studies of other animals look sick. They'll give us a hand but they said it'll mostly be our work to do."

"The ion-creatures they discovered in the ozone layer have to come in too," said the third aide.

"*What* creatures?!" shouted the President.

"Er, we've done some research on this," said the first aide, "and there is a *slim* theoretical basis for this possibility."

"Except it's no possibility," said the second aide. "We've got to count them in."

"As well as the hollow-earth dwellers," said the third aide.

The President turned slightly purple below the jawline. "How can they expect us to contact all these crazy creatures?" he again shouted.

" 'There are more things in heaven . . .' " started the second aide.

"The hell with heaven, where did all these things come from down *here?*"

"Mr. President," said the third aide now, "there have been theories quite often about such creatures, and some small basis in actual fact. Simply because we haven't expanded enough to contact these . . . other sentient beings, *intelligent* beings, which you've called 'creatures' . . ." —the President flushed a deep pink with this—". . . doesn't mean they don't or can't exist. On our level they may not but on the level the ETs are demanding of us before allowing us into their own high civilization, it's required, even necessary."

The calm tones seemed to bring down the wildly expanded problem brought out in the room to grappling proportions. "Well," said the President slowly, "I suppose . . . working at it over a number of years . . ."

"The ETs calculate about four hundred years before we present a panomorphic civilization unit for them to begin introducing their society," said the second aide.

The President seemed to choke again but fought it down. The sound at the back of his throat was no longer noncommittal. "It's a big step," he said finally, "a long series of steps for all humanity . . . and others . . . to start on. A purpose with a high goal. We had best start on the first step as soon as we can."

"Good," said the third aide. "That means we can talk now." The trio regarded the President intently.

Silently, aide number three began peeling off his forehead. His scalp fell back, revealing pointed ears and silky, braided hair that fell down behind him. The glint in his eyes seemed enchanted but appropriate to his new look.

"Now," he said, "speaking on behalf of all the elves left in hiding. . . ."

The impossible takes a little longer.

Varieties of Technological Experience

by Barry N. Malzberg

So for his various crimes against the Federation, none of which had to be explained to him (since he knew his guilt; since his entire life, he thought, was a stain of implication) they exiled Fritz to the fourth division of the Doom World which in real life was the climate-controlled sixth satellite of Neptune and there for his various crimes against the Federation explained that in order to buy his release Fritz would have to invent a universal solvent. In return for a sample they would grant him full remission and allow him to return to his old life although of course under Federation surveillance. Fair was fair.

Fritz explained to them that the basic problem with a universal solvent was that it would dissolve any container and therefore could not be segregated. They responded that this was his problem. He asked if a formula would be sufficient with the various technicians of the Doom Planet actually preparing a batch for use. They said that this was impossible, that they already had many formulas. What they needed was proof of utility. They were very kind. Everyone on the Doom Planet was reasonable. They were not there to be punitive; it was assumed that banishment was sufficiently traumatic. What they were seeking, they explained in the most pleasant way, were results. They offered him full laboratory facilities and assistants if he desired.

Fritz, embittered, discussed the situation with his three roommates in the Dark Quarter, all of whom had been confined much longer than he. He found that he was unable to elicit much sympathy. One of them had been working on a perpetual motion device for some years, another had failed with antigravitation despite some new observations into metallurgics, and the third who thought he had had a workable disintegrator some years ago had blown out half of his laboratory facilities but in demonstration before the administrator had been unable to produce any results other than a slightly charred hand which he claimed still gave him trouble in delicate work. "What you have to understand," the perpetual motion man said, "is that we have been handed ancient scientific paradoxes, impossibilities by definition. We have been given a life sentence in other words but on the other hand if we were able to defy physical laws it would be to the advantage of the Federation and they would certainly release us in gratitude. They have no shortage of potential prisoners, you know."

Fritz had become very cynical about the Federation since his detention and exile—he was beginning to suspect that it was an autocratic government interested only in self-perpetuation and any popular resistance would be defined as a "crime"—but the influence of his early technological training still sat heavy upon him and he found himself unable to accept what the perpetual motion man was saying. "They would never assign an impossible task," Fritz said. "Ultimately the Federation is a rational agency, founded upon rational principles. If there were not a way, they would not have assigned this to us. Actually it is a test."

"It is a test, all right," the antigravity man said, "a test of our gullibility."

"A universal solvent would eat out its container," the disintegrator man said. "It could not be conveyed."

"I pointed this out to them."

"He pointed it out to them," the perpetual motion man said and poked antigravity in the ribs. "And they of course agreed and assigned you something else."

"Oh no," Fritz said. "They said that it was my problem."

"That it is," the perpetual motion man said. "And that is what they told *me*. I have incidentally been here for more than half my lifetime and until you joined us here I was the newcomer of this group. Of course there are those like you coming in all the time so I have accumulated a fair amount of seniority, haven't I, lads?''

The call to serving quarters interrupted the harsh laughter of the others and Fritz found that he had no desire to continue the discussion later. It was true what he had heard of the Doom Planet; despite the fact that the felons lived together and were exposed, almost mercilessly, to one another's personalities they tended to lead very solitary lives without much connection. Part of that came from the consuming and obsessive nature of the tasks they were assigned of course and another part came from the personality-set of a person foolish enough to try to overthrow the Federation. Stubborn, self-willed, monomaniacal types. Fritz had never actually attempted overthrow; he had merely paused to consider in the interstices of his life whether the Federation might be as benign an influence as it pretended to be and these pauses, it would seem, had been intense enough to attract the interest of the Surveyors.

In any case, it was too late for that kind of concern now. He had had a different kind of life on Mars and many associations which, if he had thought about them, he would have missed keenly, but his perspective narrowed, as perspectives on the Doom Planet tended to do, to his situation and he had decided that he would accept the conditions of his internment. He would create a universal solvent and find a container of some sort and he would present it to the Board and would be released. Once released he might carry the news of conditions far and wide to all the towns of Mars but then again he might not. It was impossible to project that far ahead. One thing he resolved was that he would have nothing to do with his roommates nor with any of his fellow felons. He considered himself to be several levels above them intellectually and he found their cynicism corrosive.

How Fritz was able to fulfill the conditions of his assignment and how he invented not only the universal solvent but a varying propane ring which enabled it to have other strange powers of alteration must fall without the proper scope of this history. As the various Acts & Regulations have established, the release of technological information is not only dangerous should it fall into the hands of enemies of the Federation, it is extremely bor-

ing to the majority of the populace who have no interest
in the devices that manage their lives as long as these
devices are workable. (Nor should they!) Sufficient to say
that over a period of some time Fritz, relying heavily
upon laboratory facilities and ignoring the jeers of his
fellows, was able to accomplish his task and under procedure applied for an appointment with the Board to
whom he presented himself in due course. When his
roommates heard through the usual network of inference
that Fritz had actually scheduled an appearance before
the Board their contempt and amusement was virtually
unbounded but Fritz did not allow it to affect him. "You
are a fool," the perpetual motion man, the harshest and
most persistently abusive of his roommates, said, "you
are making a mockery of their very concept of punishment. The problems are insoluble by nature."

"Not with a universal solvent," Fritz said, permitting
himself the most careful of private smiles.

"You will never be welcome in these walls again."

"That is of no concern," Fritz said. "After all, I will
have obtained my release."

"A fool," the perpetual motion man said, "a fool,"
and stalked to the doorway, attempting a dramatic exit
but forgetting in his choler that exitways were barred during this period and succeeding only in causing slight but
painful damage to his nose. At this the antigravitation
and disintegrator men roused themselves from their quarters to laugh almost as harshly as he but Fritz, all in all
a kind and thoughtful man, had already detached himself
from the conversation, preferring to think of his confrontation with the Board on the morrow.

It had long since occurred to him through his period
of internment and researches, that the Federation was
indeed a cruel and frozen regime engaging in repression
at all levels of administration solely for the purpose of
decadent self-perpetuation and that the Doom Planet was
a fiendish means of not only interning dissidents but ex-
ploiting their very creativity, but these insights were virtually incidental to the overall element of his growth
which was that he had managed to solve one of the oldest
of all scientific paradoxes. Beside this accomplishment
the corruption of the Federation fell away, it was of no
significance whatsoever. Of course the Federation was

corrupt but then again, Fritz, not a particularly introspective man, had decided that almost all of history was a matter of corruption and that ultimately only individual ends, not collective destinies, suited. He therefore presented himself to the Board in a sanguine and optimistic manner and without questioning described what he had been able to accomplish.

"That is remarkable," they said to him and indeed their expressions showed much approbation and astonishment, "but where is the solvent itself."

"I am carrying it with me."

"You are?" the Board said. There was a slight pause. "That is even more interesting. Where is the container?"

"Ah," Fritz said, "*I* am the container."

"Pardon?"

"*I* am the container," he pointed out, "and the solvent reposes within me."

"But that is impossible."

"Certainly not."

"Of course it is," the Board said with more emotion than was its wont. "By definition you would have been dissolved. You could not be here, the solvent is a deadly poison—"

It occurred to Fritz that under pressure the Board lost its dignity which he could have anticipated anyway if he had given the matter some thought. There was his own loss of dignity to consider, the Board was, in its lovable way, no less human than he. There was a message there, the ultimate prevailing of humanity that was to say but he did not want to pursue the matter at this time. "But of course," he said gently, instead, "that is the point, I am in the process of being dissolved right now. There was a calculated Lag Effect."

Gently he extracted from his pockets schematics and diagrams to place before them in verification, gently he lay them in front of the gibbering old men and then as the solvent finally reached its critical point he consequently and with the most lingering of sighs, began to break down.

Ah, the breakdown! First the walls of molecules, then the outer edges of cells, the viscera themselves coming with relief askew the wall of self the persona and he became those mindless constituent atoms which under the influence of the amalgam . . .

. . . . Moved out.

Moved out to dissolve the floor, the walls, the Board itself to say nothing of the planet, consuming all of it utterly as the famous prophet had pointed out concerning another matter so that all that was left of the oppressive Federation in this difficult sector was a planet-sized glob of universal solvent, hanging there in space quite unapproachable (as one might suspect) by stabilizing forces and therefore a beacon to all who would in their own way seek to assert their individuality. A planet-sized signal of Revolution to absolutely clarify, a symbol of individual human will.

But, of this glimmer of triumph from the very jaws of defeat, of the fall of the Federation and of the heroic, brave and finally successful efforts of the Opposition (many of whom survived in the most cunning of ways) little enough need be said at this time, the tale being part of our great and arching folklore so we will merely pass now to our next exhibit which will depict in diorama to please all of you the history of the first and final Squaring of the Circle.

Hark, my sweetheart calls.

Listen, Love

by George Zebrowski and Jack Dann

Uheh sat next to the rodasz bush. Its glow cast thin rods of yellow onto her features; the rods changed color one after another, shifting from yellow to red to orange and back again. She stared at the small glowing branches; she felt the numbness of sleep stealing over her. Soon the sun would set and the quiet-time would begin, the time of darkness and rest. The colors swept her away into a whirlpool of sensation, and she fought back. It seemed too soon yet, she must wait; sleep-time was far, far away. She came up close to the bush and brushed her face gently against the delicate branches. She drew back; the plant was trying to lull her to sleep.

Uheh listened. Her large, finely shaped ears gathered in the small sounds of her world, and she was expert at interpreting them. There were few loud sounds in her experience, and she had been taught to fear them: she knew how to cover her ears with the large palms of her hands and then bring her elbows together until they touched. As she listened now, she heard only the sounds of small living things getting ready for the dark-time. The sun was low over the trees in the distance. The world was at peace, yet she felt fearful.

She closed her eyes and turned her face to the sun, and felt its evening warmth, its quiet embrace which seemed to touch and not touch at the same time. The soft pink skin of her naked form said a silent goodbye to the departing star that was the sun of her world.

Suddenly there was a blast of light, so strong that she sensed it even through her delicate eyelids. A rumble came across the distance toward her, but it was only a deep bass sound and couldn't hurt her. She listened to the low pitched sound; it was almost comforting. She sat down on the grass and closed her eyes again. Her entire body tingled to the sound, until it died away and she was almost asleep.

Uheh sat up suddenly, awake again and full of fear. For a brief instant the sound had become shrill and painful, and even the grass around her, the caghfr green on which she had played since she had been a little girl among the little ones of the kuu, seemed frightened. She looked at the rodasz bush; its color now was a drab green, its glow gone. Did it wake her? Had it been calling her, to warn her? The momentary shrill sound had been so loud. She shuddered and crawled into the vegetation around the rodasz bush, thinking that it would be a good place to hide; and perhaps she could spend the dark quiet-time here. That would certainly prove to the old ones of the kuu that she had come of age, and was unafraid of the dark quiet-time: the mark of a woman who could begin to bear young. A moment of pride went through her, but it was cut short by what she saw coming across the caghfr grass toward her.

The small flyer settled on the alien grass. Uheh felt the ground tremble slightly under her feet. She peered out from the vegetation; her hand held a branch on the rodasz bush.

The sun was very low when she saw the two figures get out of the silver flyer. This could not be any kind of calling, she thought. It was too harsh. Dimly she understood that the low sound from before had something to do with the silver flyer now before her. She wondered if the old ones from the kuu were watching this new thing. They would know what it was, and protect her.

The pain-sound came from the new thing and throbbed in her temples for a moment, and was gone.

The two space-suited figures walked on the caghfr grass while Uheh watched. She pushed her head through the branches of the rodasz bush to get a better view, and a leaf touched her cheek, lovingly.

She stood up and made herself visible. One of the figures waved his arm and came toward her. What could she fear from them? They were like her, and yet not like her. She wanted to run toward the flyer, the new thing that had come from the sky; but the voice of her upbringing was strong: be cautious. She looked at the figure who came up to her now, and she wondered why he wore the clear thing over his head. She could see that he was smiling at her, and she could see his teeth; there was a lot of hair on his dark face. Surely he did not wear the clear thing to keep warm? He should take it off, she thought, and smiled back at him.

The other one came up behind him, and as if in answer to her thought they took off their helmets. She stared at the strange texture of their skin. The first one was handsome enough to make any in the kuu jealous; yet different. He motioned to her with his suited and gloved hand. Could this be dangerous? He looked so pleasing. Surely he was like her, but from somewhere far off; perhaps from the other side of the blue hills, or the far side of the world? She sat down on the grass and motioned for them to do the same. They hesitated, then followed her example; they put their helmets down on the grass in front of them.

The first one gestured at her strangely and pointed at the sky, and she nodded and smiled her understanding. Then she tried to make the sign of the kuu for them—the sign of her home; but it was difficult without the sandy lakeshore where the elder had first taught it to her. The first stranger smiled at her efforts and looked at his companion.

He was good. She would try to keep him. The elder would be happy when she brought him home to the kuu. She touched his hand. It was very warm without the glove and she drew back. Then she stood up and gestured him to follow her. She waved the other one away, but he didn't go. Didn't he understand? She was puzzled. All elders made the same rules. Had she done something wrong?

"I think she wants you, and she wants me to clear out," the second one said. She heard the pain-sound coming from his mouth, and she put her hands up to her head in pain. The sound was so high, so harsh! So unlike the quiet world that cared for her, nourished her. The pain-sound cut through her entire body and she shuddered uncontrollably. It ran along her nerves and seemed to burst in her head.

"Just like a woman," the first one—(her favorite!)—said.

Run! the world cried to her. The pain-sound became worse; it squeezed her. Could such a sound have meaning? The sun was almost down now, and the dark quiet-time was coming swiftly now. In the sky the stars winked into existence, and would soon march in their promenade from horizon to horizon. The two men were gesturing at her. She saw their lips move and again the pain-sound reached her ears. She turned and began to run toward the kuu, away from the sunset three hills away by the lakeside.

"Hey, beautiful, don't go!"—the pain-sound followed her. "Come on back!"—it shrieked and screamed across the darkening sky after her.

At the top of the first hill she fell and turned over to look at the starry sky, and felt for the last time the caghfr grass against her back. Her body shuddered again from the pain-sound and was still.

For everything there is a season.

That Strain Again

by Charles Sheffield

Dear Werner,

I see what you meant about Vega IV. After the places I've been posted for the past three years, it's Paradise. An atmosphere you can breathe, and people who seem like humans (only, dare I say it, nicer). What more could you ask for?

Did you know that their name for themselves translates as "The Ethical People"? It seems to apply a lot better than "The Wise People"—*homo sapiens*—ever fitted us. Maybe it's the Garden of Eden, *before* the Fall. You know, just a little dull, all the days the same length, and no change in the weather. It takes some getting used to, but I'm adapting.

One other thing. Remember the way that Captain Kirwin described the Vegans' reaction when he first landed here? "They were surprised to see us, and they seemed to be both relieved and rejoicing at our arrival." A lot of people have puzzled over Kirwin's words—and today I found out why he sensed that reaction. The Vegans *were* relieved, and they were surprised, when we appeared. You see, they'd made an expedition to Earth themselves, just a few years ago.

Sorrel has been translating the diary of that expedition for us, and he gave it to me today. I'm enclosing part of it here. To make it easier to read, I have translated the times and places into terrestrial terms. Otherwise, it's just as they wrote it.

September 12th. All arrived safely. The transmatter worked perfectly and has deposited us in an unpopulated forest area of the northern hemisphere. We will make no attempt to look for a native civilization until we have settled in. Gathor's warning is being well-heeded. We are watching closely for evidence of infection from alien bacteria and micro-organisms. So far, no problem and we are all in good health.

September 23rd. All goes well. A beautiful and fertile planet this, but a strange one. Surface gravity is only five-sixths of ours and we all feel as strong as giants. This world is tilted on its axis, so days and nights are not all the same length. This has caused some confusion in our sleeping habits, but we are adjusting satisfactorily.

October 8th. Strange things are happening. The trees all around us look less healthy, with a strange blight spreading over their leaves. We thought at first that it was a trick of illumination when the sun is lower in the sky, but now we are sure it is real.

October 20th. We must return to Vega IV. Gathor was right, in an unexpected and terrible way. Alien micro-organisms have not harmed us—but we have infected Earth. All around us the great blight spreads. Everywhere we look the Earth is dying. We are contagion and bear guilt for the murder of this world. Tomorrow we must transmit home.

—and they came home, Werner, back to Vega IV. Do you see what I mean about "The Ethical People"? I've looked up the climate records, and I find that fall in Vermont was exceptionally beautiful that year, all glorious reds and browns and yellows. It made me think. Somewhere out there we are going to run into a planet with as big a shock in store for us as our seasons were to the Vegans. Want to speculate? I just hope we can come out of it as well as they did . . .

Jory

We'll take them like Lee took Washington.

Take Me to Your Leader

by George Henry Smith

I was just sitting in this here bar, see, having a beer, when this funny-looking joker in the odd clothes turns to me and says, "Take me to your leader."

I look at him real disgusted and don't even smile. "Hell, Mac, that's the oldest joke I know. Can't you come up with something newer than that?"

"But I've got to see him! What do you call him? . . . your President?"

"Look, Buster, I'm just an ordinary guy havin' a beer after work. Even if you wasn't some kind of nut, how could I take you to the President?"

"But you've got to . . . you've got to. . . . I am . . ." He wipes a hand across his bald dome. "Have you ever heard the theory about parallel worlds . . . about how thousands of time tracks exist side by side in the same place, their worlds very much alike?"

"Nope," I says, taking a big gulp of my beer, "I ain't never heard nothing like that. It sure sounds crazy."

"The theory holds that significant events in history have caused the different time tracks to go in different directions."

"You puttin' me on, mister?"

"Listen," he says, putting a hand on my arm, "you've got to believe me! I'm a scientist from one of those parallel worlds. I come from another dimension. My country occupies this same continent. Do you call it North America? Is it still North America in this world?"

I close my eyes and pucker up my face in exasperation.

"Of course we call it North America. What the hell else would we call it? It is North America, ain't it?"

"Yes, yes, of course. Our worlds are very much alike. They would have to be because they are the closest to each other. Their histories must be very similar, too. . . . Not like the North America that is still dominated by the Spanish or the one where the Vikings settled or . . ."

I turned back to my beer. This guy was really nuts.

He pulls at my sleeve again. "You see, I'm a scientist. My colleagues and I were working on the problem of parallel universes, of closely related time tracks. We discovered that various patterns of vibrating rates could move a man from one track to another. We were just about to complete our experiment when the Russians attacked. It was an overwhelming attack . . ." He pauses to wipe at his head again. "In my world, America was destroyed! Wiped out! Are you having trouble with the Russians, too?"

"Yeah, we're havin' trouble with the Russians, as if you didn't know. Say, maybe you're a Russian yourself!"

"No, no!" the little man says and goes white. "I assure you I am an American scientist and that I've come to warn your world. Everything in my country was wiped out by their new ion-powered rockets. I managed to get into a reverberation machine and reach here, our nearest time alternate. I've got to warn your leaders! Any event as catastrophic as this world tend to extend across several tracks. Your country is in deadly danger."

"The Russkies wipe out the States? Don't make me laugh," I says.

"But they have . . . they can! Don't you understand? That's why I came to Washington . . . you do call it Washington, don't you? I have to see your President! I have to warn him!"

Now this is about enough. I've about had it with this guy. I see a policeman I know come into the bar just then, and without another look at this crackpot, I go over and whisper in the cop's ear.

He takes a look at the guy and nods. "Sure, I'll pick him up and take him down and let the docs have a look at him."

I walk out of the bar into the hot, humid Washington night, still thinking what that nut had said. For a minute

I wonder, but then I shrug it off. Them Russkies ain't gonna give us no trouble. That Czar of theirs ain't got the nerve to fight over no icebox like Alaska. And anyway, their dirigibles couldn't get this far over to bomb us. Leastwise, I don't think so. But then I grin to myself as I see the Capitol dome in the distance with the flag flying. No Russkies are gonna bother us . . . not while the good old Stars and Bars is flying'. Not while Jefferson Davis VI is Hereditary President of the Confederate States of America!

If you can't have him one way, try another—

Put Your Head Upon My Knee

by Jack Ritchie

"Suppose I give him both pills at once?" Nedda asked.

"He would die before the process is completed," Mr. Corgu said. "And then, of course, you would have a body on your hands, and it is notoriously difficult to dispose of a body."

Nedda stared at the small envelope for a few moments and then dropped it into her purse. "How long will this . . . this process take?"

"The first pill does the major work, but it loses its momentum, so to speak, at the end of approximately one hour. The second pill completes the job, and rather quickly. A matter of four to five additional minutes." Corgu smiled. "It is best to pulverize the pills and dissolve them in a liquid."

"And then he just . . . just disappears?"

"Exactly," Corgu said. "He is—how shall we say—*unborn?*"

Nedda's face remained expressionless. "How do you . . . how did you know what I wanted?"

Corgu showed white teeth again. "I observe and evaluate faces. I flatter myself that I see what lies behind the unhappiness they show. Mrs. Randall, you are not the first woman I have done business with." He fanned the one-thousand-dollar bills she had given him and verified their number. "Soon you will be feeling happier," he said. "Much happier."

"Yes," Nedda agreed. "I think I will."

Nedda drove home and parked her car in the circular driveway before the large house.

She stopped for a moment in the hallway and looked around. *Yes,* she thought, *it's a cold house. A lonely house. Even with the servants about.*

She turned into the large living room and went directly to the liquor cabinet. Using the back of one of the measuring spoons, she pulverized one of the pills and tapped the powder into a tall glass. She set it behind a rum bottle on one of the shelves.

It was almost five when her husband's car pulled into the driveway and parked behind hers. At the window, Nedda watched as Alan shouldered his golf clubs and walked toward the front door.

He was still so handsome, Nedda thought, *so incredibly handsome, even after ten years of marriage.*

Alan paused for a moment in the doorway. "How about fixing me a drink while I put these clubs away?"

"All right," Nedda said. She waited until he disappeared and then went back to the liquor cabinet. She poured bourbon into the tall glass and added soda and ice. Then she stirred the drink until the powder dissolved.

Yes, she thought again, *incredibly handsome, and ten years had done nothing to change that. And ten years had changed nothing else, either. Nothing at all. Alan was just as self-centered, as cold, as aloof as ever.*

But she had known Alan was like that even before their marriage. Their families had moved in the same circles, and she had first met Alan when he was nine and she seven.

No, it wasn't Alan's fault that he had become the man he now was. His parents had gone about their own affairs and left him to the care of nursemaids and tutors.

If only his parents had shown him some affection. She

sighed. Even as a child, her heart had gone out to the sad-eyed, handsome boy. And later she had thought that it might be possible for Alan to find happiness in their marriage. But it was too late. Years too late. The lonely days he had spent as a child had made him aloof from—even suspicious of—love.

If only she and Alan had been fortunate enough to . . . Nedda shook her head. No. That wouldn't really have made any difference. That wouldn't have changed anything. Alan had already been shaped by the years.

When Alan entered the room again, she had the drink waiting for him. He took the glass, said an automatic thanks and went to the davenport. "Shot a seventy-eight today," he said. He picked up the paper and began reading.

No, Nedda thought, *it's not his fault. Not really.*

She watched him finish the drink and place the glass on a side table. He continued reading for a few moments more and then his eyes closed.

Nedda caught him as he slipped to one side, and placed a pillow beneath his head.

How long had Corgu said it would take? An hour?

She moved to the window and deliberately kept her eyes on the grounds. She waited ten minutes, fifteen, and then could endure it no longer. She had to know.

She turned and gasped. Yes, it *was* true. Her husband was ten years younger. At least that.

And how Nedda sat and watched, her eyes wide.

An hour passed and Nedda smiled.

It had stopped.

She stared down at her husband. *Whatever made Corgu think she wanted to use both of the pills? Or had ever intended to?*

Her eyes glowed. How old was Alan now?

Two months? Three?

She picked him up and gently rocked him back and forth. "There now," she said softly. "Mommy will love you. Really she will."

And he might have dusted the asteroid belt, too.

The Big Fix

by Robert F. Decker

My job at the Mt. Schuyler Observatory was that of assistant to Dr. Angus McTavish, or, translated, General Flunky. I swept up, cleaned and polished the equipment and changed photographic plates.

My boss, kindly old Doc McTavish himself, was an easy-going gentleman whose tolerance of my goofs was almost saintlike. Once I hadn't cleaned a lens very well and Doc McTavish went around for two weeks thinking he had discovered a new galaxy before he found out it was just a smudge. He didn't say much about that. Then there was the time he was positive he had discovered 6,800 hitherto unknown asteroids, but it merely turned out that one of the two photographs I'd placed in the blink microscope for him had been the wrong one and he had been comparing two entirely different sections of the sky. I think he was just relieved that he wouldn't have to find names for all those planetoids.

But Doc McTavish was kind of a strange old coot, anyway. He actually liked to look through the big telescope, which made him a rarity among modern-day astronomers who spent most of their time working math problems. Doc McTavish said mathematics was all very well but he got into this line of work because he liked to look at stars, not fudge around with equations. I think he had a lot in common with the Greek stargazer who fell in the well while looking up at the sky.

So it was no coincidence the doc happened to be looking at Saturn the night the comet plowed through its rings. Comets have been described as great big bands of nothing but there is generally some solid matter in the nucleus and what it did to Saturn's rings was pitiful to see. Doc McTavish called me over and we watched the spectacle together.

"And they were so pretty, too," I said ruefully.

"What a mess," commented Doc McTavish. "All those minimoons that made up Saturn's rings have been scattered into all kinds of wild orbits. Looks like Saturn's surrounded by an asteroid belt now. Well, we'd better get this on film."

That was my cue. As I was setting up the camera, the doc consulted a book on celestial mechanics, evidently to refresh his memory concerning the laws of gravity and motion as they applied to planetary bodies. We missed seeing *him* come.

Doc McTavish went back to the telescope for another look at Saturn. Then he pulled his head back, blinked and looked again. Shaking his head, he called me over. "Take a look, boy," he told me. "Tell me what you see."

I looked. And I was nowhere near as calm as the doc when I realized what I was seeing. There was a *man* out there. A man so big that relative to him Saturn was only the size of a large beachball. He seemed to be some sort of workman. He wore a uniform and a hat like you might see on a plumber, and a toolbox floated at his side. He was kneeling over Saturn, doing something with a wrench. I saw his face as he turned slightly to get something out of his toolbox. He needed a shave.

I turned away and looked at Doc McTavish. "Now *there's* something you don't see every day."

Doc McTavish nodded. "You see him, too, then." He took my place at the telescope. "We aren't seeing things. He's really out there. Or something is. Well, even Newton believed some sort of external, perhaps divine, intervention was necessary to keep the universe running smoothly. I think this proves it."

"Are we seeing him the way he really is?" I wondered. "It seems a little odd that a cosmic repairman would look like an American plumber."

"You see him as a plumber? Interesting . . . To me, he looks exactly like my TV repairman. I can even see the words 'Ace Fixit' lettered on the back of his jacket.

The only information our brains must be receiving, then, is that he's a repairman of some kind, which we're translating into the equivalent closest to our experience. No point in setting up that camera, boy. I doubt if it would record anything.''

The repairman continued to work for some minutes, then stood up (though there was nothing to stand *on*) and stepped back. Saturn's rings were now in perfect order, as though nothing had ever happened to them. He seemed to nod in satisfaction and then picked up his toolbox and walked away. I suppose he would have walked straight out of the solar system but Uranus happened to be on that side of the sun at the same time and not far from his path.

Even once we had readjusted the telescope, it was hard to see what was going on; Uranus is half the diameter of Saturn and twice as far away. However, from what we already knew about Uranus it was not hard to guess what needed to be done. Uranus spins on an axis that is all but horizontal and in a technically retrograde direction. Or, to put it in Doc McTavish's words, it rotates ''backwards and sideways!'' It would certainly present an eyesore to any cosmic repairman proud of keeping his universe neat. We could not be sure just then what the man did to Uranus, but we had our suspicions that observations of Uranus would show it had been ''fixed'' to spin on a vertical axis in the right direction.

Then he was gone.

Doc McTavish and I did not say anything for some time. We went down and had some coffee, then just stared at each other across the table for a while. Finally the old astronomer spoke. He did not sound happy.

''That fellow was just like any other repairman I've ever seen—just do what you can't put off and let the rest go.''

''Huh?'' I gulped. ''Are you *complaining?*''

''Certainly, boy! There's lots of things in this solar system that need fixing. Look at Pluto, for example. The repairman could have reorbited it as a moon of Neptune, or if he wants to keep it as a planet, he could have at least straightened up its solar orbit. A planet with an orbit inclined 17° to the ecliptic makes a sloppy solar system. Or take Venus—there's another one with a back-

wards rotation. Why didn't he take the trouble to get it
going in the right direction? And there's any number of
other things around he should have taken a look at, too.
Hmm . . . I wonder how you bang on the pipes to get
service? That mess with Saturn's rings got him out here
fast enough. . . ."

I shook my head in wonderment. "Doc, I have to hand
it to you. After what we've just seen, you not only take
it calmly but accept it as the most natural thing in the
world and even critize it."

"Of course it's the most natural thing in the world,"
said Doc McTavish. "I should have guessed before that
something like a cosmic repairman was on the job, anyway."

"How?"

He held up the book he had consulted earlier. "Ever
hear of celestial mechanics?"

"Of course."

"Well, he was one of them."

A nightmare for Saudi Arabia.

Speed of the Cheetah,
Roar of the Lion

by Harry Harrison

"Here he comes, Dad," Billy shouted, waving the field
glasses. "He just turned the corner from Lilac."

Henry Brogan grunted a bit as he squeezed behind the
wheel of his twenty-two-foot-long, eight-foot-wide, three
hundred and sixty-horsepower, four-door, power-
everything and air-conditioning, definitely not compact,
luxury car. There was plenty of room between the large
steering wheel and the back of the leather-covered seat,

but there was plenty of Henry as well, particularly around the middle. He grunted again as he leaned over to turn the ignition switch. The thunderous roar of unleashed horsepower filled the garage, and he smiled with pleasure as he plucked out the glowing lighter and pressed it to the end of his long cigar.

Billy squatted behind the hedge, peering through it, and when he called out again, his voice squeaked with excitement.

"A block away and slowing down!"

"Here we go!" his father called out gaily, pressing down on the accelerator. The roar of the exhaust was like thunder, and the open garage doors vibrated with the sound while every empty can bounced upon the shelves. Out of the garage the great machine charged, down the drive and into the street with the grace and majesty of an unleashed 747. Roaring with the voice of freedom, it surged majestically past the one-cylinder, plastic and plywood, one hundred and thirty-two miles to the gallon, single-seater Austerity Beetle that Simon Pismire was driving. Simon was just turning into his own driveway when the behemoth of the highways hurtled by and set his tiny conveyance rocking in the slipstream. Simon, face red with fury, popped up through the open top like a gopher from his hole and shook his fist after the car with impotent rage, his words lost in the roar of the eight gigantic cylinders. Henry Brogan admired this in his mirror, laughed with glee and shook a bit of cigar ash into his wake.

It was indeed a majestic sight, a whale among the shoals of minnows. The tiny vehicles that cluttered the street parted before him, their drivers watching his passage with bulging eyes. The pedestrians and bicyclists, on the newly poured sidewalks and bicycle paths, were no less attentive or impressed. The passage of a king in his chariot, or an All-American on the shoulders of his teammates, would have aroused no less interest. Henry was indeed King of the Road and he gloated with pleasure.

Yet he did not go far; that would be rubbing their noses in it. His machine waited, rumbling with restrained impatience at the light, then turned into Hollywood Boulevard, where he stopped before the Thrifty drugstore. He left the engine running, muttering happily to itself, when he got out, and pretended not to notice the stares of everyone who passed.

"Never looked better," Doc Kline said. The druggist met him at the door and handed him his four-page copy of the weekly *Los Angeles Times*. "Sure in fine shape."

"Thanks, Doc. A good car should have good care taken of it." They talked a minute about the usual things: the blackouts on the East Coast, schools closed by the power shortage, the latest emergency message from the President; then Henry strolled back and threw the paper in onto the seat. He was just opening the door when Simon Pismire came popping slowly up in his Austerity Beetle.

"Get good mileage on that thing, Simon?" Henry asked innocently.

"Listen to me, dammit! You come charging out in that tank, almost run me down, I'll have the law on you—"

"Now, Simon, I did nothing of the sort. Never came near you. And I looked around *careful* like because that little thing of yours is hard to see at times."

Simon's face was flushed with rage and he danced little angry steps upon the sidewalk. "Don't talk to me like that! I'll have the law on you with that truck, burning our priceless oil preserves—"

"Watch the temper, Simon. The old ticker can go poof if you let yourself get excited. You're in the coronary belt now, you know. And you also know the law's been around my place often. The price and rationing people, IRS, police, everyone. They did admire my car, and all of them shook hands like gentlemen when they left. The law *likes* my car, Simon. Isn't that right, Officer?"

O'Reilly, the beat cop, was leaning his bike against the wall, and he waved and hurried on, not wanting to get involved. "Fine by me, Mr. Brogan," he called back over his shoulder as he entered the store.

"There, Simon, you see?" Henry slipped behind the wheel and tapped the gas pedal; the exhaust roared and people stepped quickly back onto the curb. Simon pushed his head in the window and shouted.

"You're just driving this car to bug me, that's all you're doing!" His face was, possibly, redder now and sweat beaded his forehead. Henry smiled sweetly and dragged deeply on the cigar before answering.

"Now that's not a nice thing to say. We've been neighbors for years, you know. Remember when I bought a Chevvy how the very next week you had a two-door Buick? I got a nice buy on a secondhand four-door Buick, but you had a new Toronado the same day. Just by coincidence, I guess. Like when I built a twenty-foot swimming pool, you, just by chance, I'm sure, had a thirty-foot one dug that was even a foot deeper than mine. These things never bothered me—"

"The hell you say!"

"Well, maybe they did. But they don't bother me any more, Simon, not any more."

He stepped lightly on the accelerator, and the juggernaut of the road surged away and around the corner and was gone. As he drove, Henry could not remember a day when the sun had shone more clearly from a smogless sky, nor when the air had smelled fresher. It was a beautiful day indeed.

Billy was waiting by the garage when he came back, closing and locking the door when the last high, gleaming fender had rolled by. He laughed out loud when his father told him what had happened, and before the story was done, they were both weak with laughter.

"I wish I could have seen his face, Dad, I really do. I tell you what for tomorrow, why don't I turn up the volume on the exhaust a bit. We got almost two hundred watts of output from the amplifier, and that is a twelve-inch speaker down there between the rear wheels. What do you say?"

"Maybe, just a little bit, a little bit more each day maybe. Let's look at the clock." He squinted at the instrument panel, and the smile drained from his face. "Christ, I had eleven minutes of driving time. I didn't know it was that long."

"Eleven minutes . . . that will be about two hours."

"I know it, damn it. But spell me a bit, will you, or I'll be too tired to eat dinner."

Billy took the big crank out of the tool box and opened the cover of the gas cap and fitted the socket end of the crank over the hex stud inside. Henry spat on his hands and seized the two-foot-long handle and began cranking industriously.

"I don't care if it takes two hours to wind up the spring," he panted. "It's damn well worth it."

It could well be an improvement.

Just Call Me Irish

by Richard Wilson

The housing development near the university was newly finished. Salesman John F. ("Call Me Happy") Horman had waited a week for the tenants to become settled before making the rounds with his sample electric rat trap and his order book. He began at the southwest corner of the project and knocked at the first door.

As it opened Happy went into his spiel. Toward the end of his second sentence, he skidded to a stop in the middle of a syllable when he realized he was talking to a dog. A female dog.

Happy was confused. "Is your master in?" he asked.

"Just a minute," said the dog.

The door closed and Happy stared hard at it. Then it opened again. A larger dog stood there.

"What can I do for you?" asked the larger dog.

"This is ridiculous," said Happy. "When I asked that other dog if her master was in, I meant the master of the house, not *her* master." He consulted the list of names of the families who lived in the project. "I was looking for a Mr. Setler."

"Setter's the name," said the dog. "They misspelled it. I'm the master of the house. Is there something I can do for you?"

"I don't know." Happy Horman took off his glasses, wiped them, replaced them on his nose, replaced his handkerchief and looked at the large reddish animal in the doorway. "This is very strange. Are you a talking dog?"

"Obviously." The dog swatted a fly with his tail. "Are you a talking man?"

"Why—yes."

"Then why don't you say something? Are you with the housing project? Because if you are, I wish you'd do something about the sink. It leaks. And my son Whiffet is getting tired of lapping up after it. Besides, I think it's undignified."

"Mr—ah—Setter," said Happy, mustering his faculties, "I represent the Ohm Electric Rat Trap Company. Our slogan is 'No 'ome should be without one.' " He laughed emptily. "I think you'd be interested in a little demonstration I'd like to make for you. That is, I *think* you'd . . ."

The door opened wider, and the dog who had first spoken to Happy appeared. "Irish, dear," she said, "will you please come in or go out? The kennel's getting cold."

"House, Maureen, not kennel."

"House, then. But why not ask the gentleman in?"

"Yes, won't you come in, sir?" said Irish. "If you don't mind the place being somewhat littered."

Happy went in and sat on the edge of a normal wooden chair. He looked around with interest but so far as he could see the furnishings were those of an average dwelling. It did not look at all like a doghouse, though it unquestionably was a *dog's* house.

Irish curled himself comfortably on a couch while Maureen excused herself, saying it was time the younger whelps were fed. "I'll be glad when they're weaned," she said. Happy Horman blushed.

"Mr. Setter," Happy said, "please forgive me if I seem curious, but just how—that is, why, uh—how come you're living here?"

"Why not?" Irish said. "I'm eligible."

"But I thought these houses were set aside for veterans?"

"I'm a veteran," the dog said. "Want to see my honorable discharge from the K-9 Corps?"

"Oh. But you have to be a student, and you have to be married, I thought."

"I *am* married, sir," Irish said in a hard voice. "You don't think I'm just living with the bitch, do you?"

Happy coughed in embarrassment.

"Please, Mr. Setter, I meant to imply no such thing. But how can you be a student? At the university, that is? I realize that we're all students of human nature, heh heh, you especially, of course, being a—a canine."

"Dog is good enough. No need to get hifalutin. Would you like to hear the whole story?"

"Why, yes, I would."

"It began about 1949," Irish said, settling himself more comfortably. "My master (before I became my own) was Professor Neil Wendt, the big nuclear physics man on campus. Or should I call him the nuclear physics homo sapiens?" he asked archly.

Happy laughed hollowly.

"I don't fully understand, even now, what exactly Wendt was doing but I was his constant companion, his dumb animal friend. Then one day, as I reconstruct it, I was affected by radiation and when Wendt called me I said 'Coming.' Just like that. I don't know who was more surprised, Wendt or me.

"After some preliminary confusion we sat down and talked the thing out. We found that we could be of considerable help to each other. I suggested a few improvements in his equipment, having had a dog's eye view of it from underneath; though actually it made little difference because in a few weeks the Atomic Energy Commission took the whole thing over. In the meantime he went with me to the dean and with a little coaching I was able to pass the examinations and was awarded a bachelor's degree. You a college man, sir?"

"Er, no," Happy said.

"Um. Well, later, when I was working toward my master's I realized there were more important things than books. I refer to the Korean War. So, as any red-blooded American dog would do, I enlisted. The K-9 Corps is a fine organization, in its limited way, and I was very quickly promoted to sergeant. But the caste system! Absolutely unfair. I had heard about openings in Officer Candidate School and inquired about them. My first sergeant laughed at me but by dogged persistence I got to see the regimental commander.

"He was sympathetic but had to refuse my application. Said there was nothing in the ARs about it. What a welter of dogma those army regulations are! So I was forced to finish out my army career as an enlisted dog. True, I finally made master sergeant—though they claimed it was stretching a point for a dog to become a master—but my hackles still rise when I think of the indignities I suffered under the myth of racial superiority. What a blow to one's pride to be forced to write 'animal' opposite the word race, when almost everyone else was able to write 'human.' "

Irish glared so at Happy that the salesman winced.

"But that's all over now, Mr. Setter," Happy said. "And now you're back at school. What field are you in?"

"Anthropology, of course," Irish said. "But we've talked enough about me. What was it you had to show me, sir?"

"I really don't think you'd be interested," Happy said. "It's something *you* certainly would have no use for. You see, it's a rat catcher, and surely you of all ani—er, of all people, wouldn't—"

"Well, I don't know. I don't see why not. I suppose you might argue that I'm perfectly capable of catching rats myself. It's true that I'm still a young dog, but I don't have the time for sport that I used to. Suppose I take a look at your model."

Relieved to be in action again, the salesman rose and plugged in the cord of his electric rat trap. With a rubber rat he demonstrated its possibilities.

"Well, I'll be doggoned," Irish said. "Maureen, come in and look at this gadget."

The female dog (as Happy preferred to think of her) came in. She also marvelled at its efficiency. "Let's get one, Irish," she said. "It'll save us an awful lot of work."

"I think I will," Irish said. "If you'll make out an order for us, sir? That's fine. Just put the pen in my teeth and I'll sign it. There."

Happy handed over the receipt, discreetly wiped the doggy saliva from his pen and prepared to go.

"Drop in any time," Irish said. "You might like to come in some evening and tear a bone with us."

Happy forced a chuckle. "You're quite a wag, Mr. Setter," he said daringly, and was relieved when his customer broke into a barking laugh and closed the door after him.

Happy Horman took several deep breaths of air, then turned back to look at the house. No one was visible behind its windows. He looked at his order book. There was the bold signature: *I. Setter.* He shook his head, shrugged and went to the next house.

He knocked. A fat young man opened the door.

"I beg your pardon," Happy said, "but is your dog in?"

Now if they had gotten a good science writer—

Renaissance Man

by T. E. D. Klein

Everyone cheered when the little man told them he was a scientist.

Theoretical physicists danced beside their computers; electronics technicians whooped and hollered, abandoning their instrument panels. The huge laboratory rang with the applause of the assembled journalists, and Salganik of the *Herald* was moved to describe the scene as "reminiscent of the jubilation NASA workers demonstrated years ago during the Apollo space shots."

"Thank God!" said Dr. Bazza, an Italian biochemist. "Thank God he's not a janitor!"

The reporter looked up from his notes. "Pardon me, sir. You were saying. . . ?"

"Thank God we pulled back a man who'll be able to tell us something."

"Was there really that much doubt?" asked Salganik, his pencil poised, prepared to take it all down.

"But of course there was," replied the Italian. "We knew we'd pull back someone from the Harvard Physics Department, because we're here in the building right now. But it could have been just *anyone*. We might have found ourselves questioning a college freshman . . . Or a scrubwoman . . . Or even a tourist visiting the lab. We couldn't be sure exactly where our ATV would appear—"

"ATV," said the reporter, feverishly writing in his notebook. "That's 'area of temporal vacuity,' of course?"

"Correct. Rather like those devices you Americans used back in the 1970s, on your interplanetary probes, to collect random samplings of soil. Only this time we've scooped up a living human being, and from our own world. The man is simply—how shall I say it—a random sampling."

"But not *completely* random, I hope . . ."

"Oh, no, of course not. We knew that our ATV would appear somewhere in the vicinity of this physics lab; we assumed that it would remain a site for advanced research for years to come. But our notion of locality was really quite vague—just a building. And as for time, we simply knew that our visitor—" he gestured toward the little man, who was smiling and shaking his head in wonder— "would come from somewhere three to four hundred years in the future."

Salganik stared across the room at the new celebrity, now surrounded by cameras and lights. He could have gotten a better view, of course, by watching the television screen on the wall nearby—for the scientist's six-hour sojourn in the present was being televized, in its entirety, around the world—but he preferred to watch the little man with his own eyes. *I was there,* he'd be able to tell his grandchildren. *I was right there in the room when we plucked a man out of the future.*

Some idiot journalist had yelled out the traditional "how does it feel?" question ("How does it feel to be the first man on the moon?" they used to ask. "How does it feel to win seven gold medals? How does it feel to know that your wife and family have been wiped out by a meteor? How does it feel to be elected President?"), and the little man was attempting a reply.

"Well," he was saying, blinking at the lights, "it was

all pretty unexpected, this happening to me and all. I mean, I've never won anything in my life, and I never could have imagined that *I*, of all people, would be the one to . . . You know. Be here like this. And I want to say that it's certainly a great *honour* and all, and that I'm certainly as proud as can be to find myself here with you, even if it's only for so short a time . . . Umm . . ." He bit his lip, blinking at the lights. "I'm happy to say that my era is a really, um, *advanced* one—at least *we* think it is, ha ha! 'A Third Renaissance of Learning and Scientific Achievement,' that's the motto of the World's Fair over in Addis Ababa . . . A renaissance rivalling the one in the early 2200s—but of course you wouldn't know about that, would you? Hmmm . . . I'm not really a very good speaker, you see, but, um . . . I sure hope I'll be able to provide you with knowledge that will maybe interest you and, um, *help* a bit, maybe?"

He smiled bashfully.

"It's remarkable!" muttered Dr. Bazza. "You'd think the language might have changed over the centuries, but this man speaks English better than I do! Perhaps it was cinema that stabilized the language . . ."

"And a good thing, too," whispered Salganik. "If this project turned out to be a fiasco—if you guys had materialized a three-year-old baby, or some moron with nothing to say—the government would pull its money out so fast you'd get dizzy."

He remembered how hard NASA had tried to persuade Congress that the lunar explorers were carrying back valuable scientific information—that half a dozen bags of moon rubble were worth all those billions of dollars. In the end Congress had deemed the missions "impractical" and had discontinued them. The men in this lab had been under the same kind of pressure . . .

But it looked as if they'd made a lucky catch.

"Oh, yes," the man was saying, "I've been a professor of plasmic biophysics for almost . . . Let me see . . . Nearly twenty-eight years."

"Could you tell us what that means?" shouted one of the reporters who had crowded his way toward the front.

Immediately a storm of abuse broke over his head: *Hush! Please! Expel this man! Ssshh! We'll get to that later! Quiet!*

Reporters were supposed to remain silent, leaving all questions to a panel of scientists who, it was hoped, could make better use of the limited time. That other reporter's question had wasted enough time already . . .

"Professor," asked Dr. Sklar, the Nobel Prize-winning pathologist, "let's start with the most vital issues first." He spoke solemnly, aware that the world was listening to every word. "I shall not even pause to ask you your name—"

"Modesto 14X Goodyear," interrupted the little man.

"—or to find out anything about yourself. Those of us gathered here are interested in solving some of our most pressing problems. To begin with—"

He paused portentously, allowing the drama to grow.

"—have men in your time found *a cure for cancer?*"

The visitor smiled. "Oh my *gosh* yes," he replied. "We hardly even *talk* about cancer any more. I mean, the only ones who come down with it these days are men in deep space, and . . ."

Sklar cut him off. "Can you explain to us how it is cured?" There was urgency in his voice.

"Whew!" said the little man, puffing out his cheeks and glancing toward the ceiling. "Hmmm, let's see. That *is* a toughie, I'm afraid." He looked blank for several seconds. "You see, I've never had cancer myself, and few people I know have . . . But if we got it, we'd ring for a physician, and he'd come and, um . . ."

"What would he do?"

"Well, he'd give us this drug, and then we'd just . . . sleep it off, I guess you'd say."

"This drug?" demanded Sklar.

"Yes, well, I'm afraid I only know the brand name— Gro-Go-Way, it's called. But I suppose that's not much help to you . . ."

Dr. Sklar looked disappointed.

"You see, that's not really my field," explained the visitor, with an embarrassed shrug.

"A moment ago you spoke of 'ringing for a physician,' " said another panelist. (Dr. Sklar was now busy writing down new questions.) "I'm a communications engineer and I wonder if you might tell us something about communications in your day."

"Delighted."

"For example, what exactly happens when you ring for the doctor?"

"Why, he comes immediately. Or at least he's *supposed* to. But I don't mind telling you, quite often you get *rude* and *shoddy* treatment, he'll tell you he's too *busy* right now and—"

"Please, sir! How does the thing work? Do you have instruments like this?" The engineer pointed toward a nearby table. "Telephones?"

"Oh, telephones! Yes, sure we have them, only they don't look like that. My, oh my, what an antique *that* would make . . . No, ours fit behind your ear." He reached back behind his own. "Oh, dear, I've left mine off today, otherwise I'd show you . . . But anyway, it's different when we ring for a physician. Then we press a red button in the bathroom, right by the bed, and we describe our—But you look confused."

"No, no, go on."

"We just say, in effect, 'I feel sick, send somebody over.' "

"And who's on the other end?"

"Well . . . *people*. And they hear me and send help." He paused, looking a little doubtful. "Of course, it takes a few minutes."

"And how does all this work? Explain the mechanism."

"Gee," said the scientist from the future, "I'm sure I don't know. I never really bothered to find out. I mean, it's always been there on the wall, and I just . . . I feel guilty as hell, but I mean, it's just not my field. I deal almost exclusively with a type of chromosomatic plant nodule, they're called Phillips' bodies, and . . . Well, let me say *this* about communications: those people on the other end of the line are by no means the most efficient in the world, believe me, the service is *atrocious* these days and they're forever going out on strike for one reason or another, so . . ."

"Weapons!" spoke up a general. "What are the most sophisticated weapons in your military's arsenal?"

"Well, we have no military *per se*, but . . . Oh, yes, we *do* have some horrible weapons at our disposal, oh *my* yes. There's one called a VRV—I'm not sure what the letters stand for—that can leave a fourteen-meter deep crater where a city used to be, and the neighbouring towns won't even be touched. One was actually used— on San Juan, Puerto Rico."

"How does it work?"

"Hmmm . . . You got me. I'm afraid I'm stumped." He paused, looking downcast—and then brightened. "You know, you want to talk to a nuclear engineer about that. Your best bet would be a fellow named Julio 6X Franklin, an old friend . . . Though of course that's impossible right now, isn't it? Hmmm . . . I *think* I read somewhere that it uses the same principle as the moon pulling on the tides—moon on the tides, does that sound right?—but I'm really not the man to see."

Salganik leaned toward his companion. "I hate to say it," he whispered, "but this guy doesn't know anything about anything. What gives?"

But Dr. Bazza only shook his head. He looked as if he were about to cry.

The little man was attempting to explain the construction of the anti-gravity belt his son wore when walking on lakes. "It broke down once and we had to have the repairman over. He . . . Let me see, he told me it had a battery, yes, and a triangular chunk of this spongy substance . . . Levia, I think it's called, but I don't know exactly what it's made of. Zinc, maybe?"

The scientists had stopped taking notes long ago.

Dr. Bazza turned to Salganik. "Listen," he pleaded, his voice edged with desperation, "how much do you think *you'd* know if you went back into the Dark Ages? Could *you* tell them how to build an airplane? Or perform an appendectomy? Or make nylon? What good would *you* be?"

Salganik shrugged. "I guess . . ." he ventured. "I guess that, even during the Renaissance, there weren't many Renaissance Men."

The cameras and tape-recorders continued to whir.

"I recall looking over the repairman's shoulder when he replaced the battery," the little man was saying, "and there was this little bundle of wires . . ."

One man's meat—

Pulpworld

by R. K. Lyon

The Senate Appropriation Subcommittee began its hearings on the FBI budget request with the testimony of the Bureau's Acting Director Argus. Senator Sternwhistle asked the first question.

"It is your claim, is it not, that the FBI solves ninety-seven percent of its cases?"

"That is correct, Senator."

"An object, say a broom, which disappeared in interstate commerce would be an FBI case?"

"Of course."

"Then why hasn't the FBI found my broom? When I moved from my home state to Washington, my wife put a brand new broom into the moving van. When our furniture arrived, the broom was gone."

"Well, Senator, it must have been one of the three brooms in every hundred missing brooms we couldn't find."

"Is that really the answer? Isn't it true the FBI has a priority system so the cases which are arbitrarily judged less important are neglected, assigned to less capable agents?"

"Certainly not, Senator. That would violate the requirements of equal justice. All cases, however trivial, are given the same treatment."

"Then why wasn't Operator $\sqrt{2}$ assigned to find my broom?"

"Because we do specialize. Your broom was assigned to the agent who handles all the other missing brooms.

Operator $\sqrt{2}$ handles all cases that require saving the United States from immediate total destruction.''

"Still, he could have looked for my broom while he wasn't busy.''

"Well, Senator, Operator $\sqrt{2}$ has had quite a heavy case loaded lately, twelve in the past month. A thirteenth case, the attack of the purple slime men, had to be assigned to the missing broom agent.''

The questioning passed to Senator Hemiwit. "Director Argus, in your report as part of the justification for continued funding of the FBI, you list the value of property recovered by the Bureau in the past year. Most of the items, three hundred seventeen dollars' worth of recovered brooms, six hundred thirty-six dollars in cats strayed across state lines, and so forth seem reasonable, but you list one item of eighty-seven times the entire capital assets of the United States.''

"Operator $\sqrt{2}$ saved the United States from total destruction eighty-seven times last year.''

"Yes, but aren't you counting the same thing more than once; I mean there is only one United States.''

"Well, I suppose so, Senator, but you have the same accounting problem with brooms and cats. Last year one broom was lost and recovered three times.''

"About Operator $\sqrt{2}$, isn't it true that in the past week he brought down an avalanche and buried the Green Gargoyle and his grinning ghoul gang under millions of tons of rock, that he dynamited a volcano and flooded the caves of Doctor Death Demon and his damned doom devils with molten lava and that he did a prefrontal lobotomy with a rusty shovel on Baron Satanus?''

"Yes, that was a normal busy week for $\sqrt{2}$. The Green Gargoyle was about to put fast-acting embalming fluid in all of America's drinking water and—''

"You mean he was alleged to be planning that. Under our system of justice all these people are entitled to be considered innocent until convicted. Now what about their constitutional rights? Did Operator $\sqrt{2}$ inform them that they had a right to remain silent and to consult with an attorney?''

"Ah, now as to that, Baron Satanus plotted to sink California, but he was not a criminal but a sick man who needed and received medical treatment. As you may know, Operator $\sqrt{2}$ is not only a concert violinist, Olympic tiddly winks champion, and famed fashion designer, he is also a noted neurosurgeon. The operation on the Baron was a complete success and he is now teaching Sunday school in Peoria. As for Doctor Death Demon, he was advised of his rights. When $\sqrt{2}$ was being pushed toward the giant hamburger grinder, he told the Doctor that he suspected him of criminal activity and therefore had the right to remain silent, etc.''

"But what about the Green Gargoyle?"

"That's a complex legal problem. The case is currently under appeal."

"And if the Supreme Court rules in favor of the Green Gargoyle and his grinning ghoul gang?"

"Then I suppose we shall have to dig them up."

Sternwhistle frowned and said, "You know you're asking for a great deal of money."

"Just our regular budget."

"Yes, yes, but there are so many other requests. It's not as if the United States had taxes to pay for all these things."

The hearing wore on and finally dragged to an end. Weary from the long ordeal Director Argus walked from the hearing room down a long corridor and into a phone booth. There he stripped off his face and stood revealed as Operator $\sqrt{2}$! Scant moments later he was in his car, a high-power triple-carburetor Hudson, speeding along through the smooth-flowing D.C. rush-hour traffic. How well had he done? Would the FBI get its budget? Of course, if they didn't, he and his fellow agents would continue to do their jobs without pay out of dogged dedication to duty. It would be a hardship, though, especially for Operator $\sqrt{2}$. The guy who found the brooms at least got tips.

He was approaching a home in the suburbs. There his sweetheart, Mary Faith, was waiting for him. One day she and he would exchange marriage vows, but the bond between them of patriotism and service to country was deeper and stronger than any ceremony.

Their son was away at eagle scout camp, so Mary and he would be alone tonight. She saw he was tired and brought his pipe, slippers, and his favorite magazine, *Impossible Bizarre Stories*. This month looked like a

good issue. The lead novel was an espionage thriller—
Criminals in the White House. As a professional, he knew
how totally absurd such stories are but he still enjoyed
them. There was a science-fiction chiller, *Energy Crisis.*
The blurb read "America faces a freezing winter with
no fuel to burn except poisonous high-sulfur coal." The
horror story was *My Children Were Bussed To Achieve
Racial Balance.* Operator $\sqrt{2}$ sat back in his chair and
puffed his pipe. It was so relaxing to read about unreal
people whose troubles were entirely absurd.

Who knows what evil lurks—

The Other Tiger

by Arthur C. Clarke

"It's an interesting theory," said Arnold, "but I don't
see how you can ever prove it." They had come to the
steepest part of the hill and for a moment Webb was too
breathless to reply.

"I'm not trying to," he said when he had gained his
second wind. "I'm only exploring its consequences."

"Such as?"

"Well, let's be perfectly logical and see where it gets
us. Our only assumption, remember, is that the universe
is infinite."

"Right. Personally I don't see what else it *can* be."

"Very well. That means there must be an infinite number of stars and planets. Therefore, by the laws of chance,
every possible event must occur not merely once but an
infinite number of times. Correct?"

"I suppose so."

"Then there must be an infinite number of worlds *exactly like Earth*, each with an Arnold and Webb on it,

walking up this hill just as we are doing now, saying these same words.''

"That's pretty hard to swallow.''

"I know it's a staggering thought—but so is infinity. The thing that interests me, though, is the idea of all those other Earths that aren't exactly the same as this one. The Earths where Hitler won the War and the Swastika flies over Buckingham Palace—the Earths where Columbus never discovered America—the Earths where the Roman Empire has lasted to this day. In fact the Earths where all the great *if's* of history had different answers.''

"Going right back to the beginning, I suppose, to the one in which the ape-man who would have been the daddy of us all, broke his neck before he could have any children?''

"That's the idea. But let's stick to the worlds we know—the worlds containing *us* climbing this hill on this spring afternoon. Think of all our reflections on those millions of other planets. Some of them are exactly the same but every possible variation that doesn't violate the laws of logic must also exist.

"We could—we *must*—be wearing every conceivable sort of clothes—and no clothes at all. The Sun's shining here but on countless billions of those other Earths it's not. On many it's winter or summer here instead of spring. But let's consider more fundamental changes too.

"We intend to walk up this hill and down the other side. Yet think of all the things that might possibly happen to us in the next few minutes. However improbable they may be, as long as they are *possible*, then somewhere they've got to happen.''

"I see,'' said Arnold slowly, absorbing the idea with obvious reluctance. An expression of mild discomfort crossed his features. "Then somewhere, I suppose, you will fall dead with heart failure when you've taken your next step.''

"Not in *this* world.'' Webb laughed. "I've already refuted it. Perhaps *you're* going to be the unlucky one.''

"Or perhaps,'' said Arnold, "I'll get fed up with the whole conversation, pull out a gun and shoot you.''

"Quite possibly,'' admitted Webb, "except that I'm pretty sure you, on this Earth, haven't got one. Don't forget, though, that in millions of those alternative worlds I'll beat you on the draw.''

The path was now winding up a wooded slope, the trees thick on either side. The air was fresh and sweet. It was very quiet as though all Nature's energies were concentrated, with silent intentness, on rebuilding the world after the ruin of winter.

"I wonder," continued Webb, "how improbable a thing can get before it becomes impossible. We've mentioned some unlikely events but they're not completely fantastic. Here we are in an English country lane, walking along a path we know perfectly well.

"Yet in some universe those—what shall I call them?— *twins* of ours will walk around that corner and meet anything, absolutely anything that imagination can conceive. For as I said at the beginning, if the cosmos is infinite, then all possibilities must arise.''

"So it's possible," said Arnold, with a laugh that was not quite as light as he had intended, "that we may walk into a tiger or something equally unpleasant.''

"Of course," replied Webb cheerfully, warming to his subject. "If it's possible, then it's got to happen to some-one, somewhere in the universe. So why not to us?''

Arnold gave a snort of disgust. "This is getting quite futile," he protested. "Let's talk about something sen-sible. If we don't meet a tiger round this corner I'll re-gard your theory as refuted and change the subject.''

"Don't be silly," said Webb gleefully. "That won't refute anything. There's no way you can—"

They were the last words he ever spoke. On an infinite number of Earths an infinite number of Webbs and Ar-nolds met tigers friendly, hostile or indifferent. But this was not one of those Earths—it lay far closer to the point where improbability urged on the impossible.

Yet of course it was not totally inconceivable that dur-ing the night the rain-sodden hillside had caved inward to reveal an ominous cleft leading down into the subter-ranean world. As for *what* had laboriously climbed up that cleft, drawn toward the unknown light of day—well, it was really no more unlikely than the giant squid, the boa constrictor or the feral lizards of the Jurassic jungle. It had strained the laws of zoölogical probability but not to the breaking-point.

Webb had spoken the truth. In an infinite cosmos everything must happen somewhere—including their singularly bad luck. For *it* was hungry—very hungry—and a tiger or a man would have been a small yet acceptable morsel to any one of its half dozen gaping mouths.

Sweetest little fellow—don't know what to call him, but he's mighty like—

Little William

by Patricia Matthews

Winston Hammersmith, Ph.D., was a man of tremendous intellect and unparalleled ability; therefore, his revenge upon Miss Leontyne Lundy was far from ordinary. What Miss Lundy did to Mr. Hammersmith to warrant this revenge is not really important; it will suffice to say that she rejected him in such a manner that she wounded his spirit and ego, and that is a thing that a woman should never do to a man.

Hammersmith did not show his hurt at the time, but he brooded in solitude, and then, one day he came to her door, leading little William by the hand.

Little William was a child to melt the heart of any maiden lady. His sturdy, three-year-old body was dimpled and golden, his hair, honey floss. His eyes, blue, and round as quarters, were fringed with beguiling, long, dark lashes, and his smile was as sweet as morning.

Miss Lundy looked at him, and Hammersmith thought that he saw her expression soften, for the least bit of a moment. She looked at Hammersmith without apparent emotion.

"Good morning, Winston. What can I do for you?"

Hammersmith smiled a smile which he hoped looked apologetic.

"Leontyne," he said, looking deeply into her eyes. "I hesitate to ask you, but I seem to be in a bit of difficulty, and there was no one else to turn to."

Miss Lundy raised her delicate eyebrows. "Do come to the point, Winston. You always draw things out so."

Hammersmith tried the smile again. "To be sure. Well, you see, it's little William, here. He's my nephew. His mother is a widow, quite alone in the world, and at the moment very ill; so she sent him to me."

Miss Lundy's voice was cold. "I fail to see the problem, Winston."

"It's business. Some of my patents. I must go to Washington, at once. It's quite impossible, you know, for me to take a three-year-old child. I was hoping that you . . ."

Leontyne smiled a superior smile. "You want me to keep him for you while you're gone. I don't know why you cannot be more direct, Winston. Of course, it is a great deal to ask."

She looked at the golden child out of the corner of her eye and Winston noticed, with pleasure, that her expression softened again. She drew herself up, in the gesture that Winston recognized so well; it made her look ten feet tall.

"Very well," she said. "However, you must understand that I am not doing it for you, but for the child. I trust that you won't be gone too long."

"A week," said Hammersmith hastily. "Only a week."

"Very well, Winston; you may bring him in."

She turned and led the way into the house. Hammersmith followed with the child and a suitcase, smiling a secret smile at Leontyne's straight, slender, inflexible back.

One, two, three days went by in rapid, pleasurable succession. Little William was adorable, an exceptional child. He ate with a spoon and did not soil himself. He was toilet trained. He had many moods, each more charming than the other. He did not cry. He called Miss Lundy "Aunty" and kissed her nicely on the cheek. She was enslaved.

She spent hours with him. She walked with him in the garden, where they picked flowers and played Ring-

Around-The-Rosy. Hammersmith would not have recognized her. Her eyes sparkled and her cheeks were pink.

The week went by without Miss Lundy even being aware of the passage of the days. When Hammersmith called her from Washington, to tell her that he had been delayed, and to ask if she would keep little William another week, she went limp with joy. So, they began their second week, the cool spinster and the golden boy child, little William.

It was during this second week that William began to change. At first Miss Lundy hardly noticed it. Little things, so small that they slipped by the conscious mind.

On Monday he began to cry, at night, late. Miss Lundy struggled to consciousness and hurried to the side of her lovely child. He quieted at once when she came into the room, but the next night he cried again.

On Tuesday his table manners began to go down hill rapidly. Where before he had neatly inserted the laden spoon into his cherubic pink rosebud of a mouth, now he managed to drop most of the load on his clothes and face. Miss Lundy told herself that this was perfectly natural. Children often regressed briefly. She had read this in a book, she was certain.

Wednesday, it was toilet training; which was almost too much for her maidenly sensibilities. Before, he had always told her, in his little way, when it was necessary for him to use the bathroom facilities. Now . . . She wouldn't have admitted it, but her golden boy was becoming tarnished.

On Thursday, he refused to kiss her when she put him down for his nap; not only that, but he began crying, striking at her with his small fists. It almost broke her heart.

On Friday she found him in the garden. The sunlight was making an aureole of his golden curls and his face was wrinkled in concentration. She went up to him to see what he was doing. He stopped for a moment and looked up at her with his beatific, shining smile. She looked down at his chubby pink hands, and gagged. He was happily pulling the legs off of a large grasshopper, which squirmed and moved horribly in the small grasp.

* * *

On Saturday, two weeks to the day of his arrival, Leontyne lay in bed late. She felt wan and headachy. She really did hope that Winston would come for the child today. She felt an uncomfortable ambivalence in her feeling for William. He was so pink, so warm, so adorable, but on the other hand . . .

She moved the scented cloth that rested upon her forehead, then sat bolt upright as a horrible sound split the air and struck her in the vulnerable spot between her eyes.

She stumbled to her feet and wrenched open the door. There was a flash of color; it took her a moment to make out the form of Daisy, the big yellow cat that belonged to her cook. He looked very strange, all patchy. She looked closer, as he cowered in the corner at the end of the hall. His hair was burned off in uneven patches. At the other end of the hall stood little William, his small face all innocence, his smile like light, his plump little hand clutching a large bunch of kitchen matches.

A strange feeling rose in Miss Lundy's breast. Slowly, like lava mounting, it rose as she walked toward the smiling child. He stood there, looking up at her, as she raised her arm high and brought her hand down across the small face.

She watched from somewhere outside herself, as the small form went tumbling, bouncing, jarring down the long stairway and lay in a crumpled heap at the bottom.

For a painful moment she stood there, staring down, then she found that it was possible to move and went stumbling down to kneel at his side; to smooth the golden hair back from the white forehead and away from the wide, blue eyes; to turn the little head that lay so crooked; to push back the little copper wires and wheels and springs that spilled from the ragged gash in the round white throat, to . . .

The little wires and wheels and springs, the wires and wheels and . . .

A horrible shrieking filled her ears and her mind. She did not know that it was her own voice.

And far away, in Washington, Winston Hammersmith looked at the date on his calendar, and smiled.

Faster than a speeding bullet.

Steel

by Alan Brennert

The glen was quiet this time of night, the last stars dimming over the horizon, the sun's light cresting near the hills. Ken abandoned his star-gazing and poked his way through the underbrush, moving back toward the cabin. The thorns scratched his fingers but did not, of course, draw blood; his bare feet trod uncut over the sharp pebbles and bits of broken glass. Coke bottles. Ken picked up the pieces, disgusted, balled his hand into a fist and crushed the glass to powder. Then, stuck with the deadly powder, he walked to the edge of the river and scattered the glass across its surface, hoping it would drop harmlessly into the sludge.

He returned to the cabin—more a cottage, really, nestled in the rapidly despoiling woods—and, to avoid waking either Laney or the kids, didn't enter by the creaking front door but instead leaped up to the second-storey window. Gently he pried it open, climbed, in, and padded down the hallway to their bedroom.

Laney was already awake, brushing her graying black hair absently, an old nervous habit. She looked quite as beautiful as when Ken had first seen her, so long ago, when they had both worked for the same paper; she turned and smiled at his entrance.

"Out in the glen again?" she said. He nodded. Her quick eyes misted over a moment, sadly. "Why now? You've let it go by for thirty years. Why worry about it now?"

He went to the window, seeing his own reflection—the strong face, tousled black hair graying prominently—

against the lightening sky. "I don't know," he said distantly. "I never used to think it was important. I mean, I just assumed—that this was my place, and that it didn't matter where I was born, or why I'm—the way I am."

"And now?"

He turned, half smiling. "Now I want to know."

"Middle-aged identity crisis?"

He laughed. "Like none the world has ever seen."

She touched his arm. "Let's go to breakfast."

They ate a light meal, bacon, eggs, toast, while the radio droned on about the crisis in the Mideast in the background. Ken sat staring out the veranda window into the distance for some minutes, finally smiling and looking back at Laney. "Raccoons about fifty yards into the brush. Have to tell the landlord about it."

She nodded. She was used to nodding mutely at his sudden pronouncements of things she couldn't see. It might only have been raccoons in a bush or a car on a distant road, but it might as well have been half a world away for all that she could see what he saw.

"When should we start back to the city?" she asked. Ken shrugged. "Day after tomorrow," he said. "Unless you want to get back early?"

"Me? God, no. I don't relish putting together the August issue." In point of fact, she did not relish putting together *any* issue; editing a women's magazine for an audience she didn't understand and only marginally believed in was a long way from where she had once hoped to be.

He touched her hand, his eyes no longer focused distantly, but firm and penetrating. "I know how you feel." And the hell of it was, he did.

The kids whooped in just then, Lucy promptly spilling her grapefruit juice all over her jeans, Tom laughing uproariously at his sister's clumsiness. Looking at them, Ken felt a recurring gladness, a sense of accomplishment. Years ago he would have laughed at the idea of simple paternity counting for anything in this world, but that was years ago. Things had changed a good deal since then.

And thank God they hadn't inherited his—strength. His curse, his glory. He didn't know why, exactly; geneti-

cally he should have passed on some of his—abilities—
to them; but no, they were normal, and thankfully so.

And, in the end, they might turn out to be his only
vindication.

They returned to the city two days later, the kids to
school, Laney to the offices of *Fem*, Ken to his editorial
desk at *Life*. There was a sheaf of photos waiting for
Ken—several sheafs, in fact: some blurred shots of the
fighting in the Middle East, a couple of hot exclusives
showing the ultimate dissolution of the League of Nations
peacekeeping force, some spectacular color shots of Mars
taken by one of the Mariner probes . . .

Ken stared at the Mariner photos a long moment, at
the ragged terrain, the wasteland grayness in between the
darknesses. Not there, he thought. Not anywhere in the
whole damned solar system. *Where? How? Why?* He put
aside the space scenes and thumbed the intercom.

"Rose, have Jim come in, will you? I want to dummy
up the war pages right away . . ."

By lunchtime Ken had had quite enough of spectacle
and famine; he left Jim in charge of the office and hurried
out of the building, pleading a headache. The magazine
ran well without him; he had no qualms about leaving.

That afternoon, for the first time in months, he flew.

He stripped in an alley, jogged to its mouth, and leaped
up. Within moments he was airborne, arcing halfway
across the city before he realized that he had no place to
go. No matter. He rarely had anywhere to go, these days.
The important thing was that he was flying, skirting the
tips of skyscrapers, chasing the clouds, high above the
smogline. Up here, the city was a gray tundra, soot and
mist cloaking the skyline like London fog.

Disgusted, he veered west, toward open country. (But
below, he could see the small blurred figures of men and
women, pointing, waving, shouting his name, and he was
pleased that they remembered, even now.)

He flew into night, seeking the darkness and the stars.
He sought and named to himself the constellations; he
squinted, trying to discern the planets as they popped
into view. He picked up speed as he progressed, a blue
streak against blackness, until he noticed ocean below
him: then, reluctantly, he turned and headed home.

That night, in bed beside him, Laney stroked his face

and kissed him lightly on the lips. He drew her closer to him, always careful to be gentle, afraid of the power in his arms, and they made love slowly, and didn't speak of it at all.

Word of the attack came Friday, just after the issue had gone to press. There was no deadline rush, no frantic writing, as in the old days; everyone knew all too well that there might not even *be* a next issue.

The Israelis had had tactical nukes; everyone had known that. The Arabs had had nuclear reactors; everyone had known that, too. Why in God's name had no one expected what had to come? Ken had, though, even as he had anticipated this moment in his career—the moment in which he would, ultimately, have to pit himself against everyone, take no one's side, act from his own morality.

Laney rushed into the office minutes before he left. "Ken, for God's sake," she pleaded, taking him aside, "let them kill themselves. You can't stop it."

He licked his lips and touched her face. "I've been trying for thirty years, love. If I stop now, I—" He paused, forcing a thin smile. "I never could break old habits, Laney."

Within minutes he was over the Atlantic, the wind tearing at him savagely. There were limits to his strength, and he was straining those limits, now; he could only go so fast and so far before the force of his own speed battered him into unconsciousness. But he kept at it, and within two hours he was over the Aegean.

The fleets were converging, Americans to the south, Russians to the north. The fools who had started it all were nursing their radiation wounds and had no time for the end of the world; they would leave that to the major powers. Miles above, a Chinese satellite eyed the tableau with patient silence.

Ken swooped down, the dazzling blue waters of the ocean nearly blinding him; half-sightedly he dropped toward the U.S. flagship, snapping the aft cannons in two as he fell.

Machine guns turned on him. Volleys of ammunition pounded at him, sending him toppling backwards but doing no further damage. At least he was drawing their fire away from the other ships, he thought, and then suddenly a starboard gun began firing on the Russian fleet. Damn it! He leaped up, hands outstretched, and shot toward the second cannon. It exploded, the concussion catching the flying figure off-balance. With a grunt of pain, Ken fell back into the water.

The Russian ships began their counterattack . . . but their missiles were quickly intercepted as a fount of water shot up between the two fleets. The geyser knocked the missiles off-course and they fell harmlessly into the sea.

At the tip of the waterspout, Ken halted his upward flight and the water cascaded down into the ocean again.

He made for the Russian flagship, dodging the cannon fire, snapping their guns in half with a curse. It was getting too damned hard, all this exertion after two hours' flight; he felt drained, he wanted time to rest. Perhaps they would stop now, pause at least to re-think their positions.

When the two American and Russian missiles hit him simultaneously, he knew that they were not going to stop. Not now, not ever.

He fell into the sea, letting the cold biting waters refresh him. The damned fools. They needed him, once, or said they did. As long as he was capturing bank thieves of mending broken dams, they needed him; as long as he flew above the city, lending his power and courage to their lives, they wanted him, or the symbol of what he was.

Not now, though. Not now.

With a sudden, bitter anger, Ken dived to the very bottom of the sea, touching the ocean floor. He stood there, holding his breath, clenching his fists . . . then, with one surge of strength, he vaulted up, up, through the waters, above the waves, surface tension slamming into him like a brick wall, and into the sky.

He peaked at a distance of fifty yards above the two fleets . . . and then came down.

He plunged through the Russian carrier, feet first, screaming as the tough steel tore at his limbs—but he plummeted all the way through, four, five, six decks, out the bottom of the hull and into the sea once more.

He zoomed out and into the air again, heading for the American ship, repeating his actions: down through the bowels of the carrier, steel splintering around him, and back into the ocean.

When he flew shakily out of the water, exhausted, the two ships were sinking rapidly and lifeboats were being dispatched from the other carriers. The battle might still go on, but Ken no longer cared. He hovered a moment in the still air, then shut his eyes and veered to the east, homeward.

He landed in the glen, unseen, he hoped, near dawn. His costume was tattered and he was bleeding slightly, but he would live. Easily. Still as strong as ever, he thought bitterly. But they've gotten stronger. He lay down and breathed heavily.

Behind him, he heard the crackle of dry grass, and he turned round. Laney stood in the clearing, holding her bathrobe tightly around her. She ran to him and they held each other.

After a while, Ken kissed her, and then he lay back once more in the soft grass, his eyes shut to the stars.

"I know where, Laney," he said quietly, unmoving. "I know, now."

She looked at him, so large, so impervious, so deathly afraid of his own strength. All those years, she had had to have enough courage for both of them; had to give him strength enough to touch her. He was a man who never wanted to hurt, but they had forced him to hurt, in their name and their justice; and it had taken her years to convince him that he would not, could not, harm her. And he hadn't. Not once, in thirty years.

"Where?" she said softly.

He opened his eyes and looked up at the sky. "They made me," he said quietly. "They needed me, for a time, or thought they did. The time was right. I was there." He shut his eyes again.

She took him gently by the arm and got him to stand. "Come on," she said. "Let's go to bed."

He looked at her and smiled. "If it weren't for you . . . and the kids . . . what the hell would I have to show for it all?"

"Let's go to bed."

He nodded. Together they poked their way through the

thick underbrush, and Laney thought that she had never seen him quite so happy.

My dear! How you've changed!

Appointment on the Barge

by Jack Ritchie

Professor Bertoldt answered his door buzzer.

The girl who stood in the hall had pitch-black hair and dark luminous eyes. "I just *adored* your talk at Clinton Hall this evening and I simply had to come over here to see you instead of in front of all those other people. You must be the world's *leading* authority on reincarnation."

Bertoldt blushed a bit. "Actually, reincarnation is really a hobby with me. My field is psychology."

Her long lashes fluttered. "My name is Diana O'Flaherty. Is it true that you can actually send a person back to a previous reincarnation?"

"I did not actually *say* that I could do it, but I do believe that it can be done. Under the right circumstances, with the right subject, and so forth. That is, theoretically it is certainly possible that . . ."

She sidled into his apartment. "You hypnotize people?"

"That, of course, is the preliminary part of the procedure."

"But you have never actually tried your theories on a human being?"

"No. I have hesitated to use a human until I can be positive that no psychic harm will result to my subject. However, I do believe that last week I did succeed in sending a chimpanzee back several generations. How far back, I can't be certain. We had a bit of difficulty in communication."

"Why not take the big jump," Diana said eagerly. "Try a human being. I am your subject. I am your volunteer!" Her eyes fastened firmly and expectantly on his. "I am Cleopatra. Or at least I *was* Cleopatra. I just know it."

"What makes you so certain that you were Cleopatra?"

I just *feel* Egyptian. Besides, one of my grandmothers was an exotic dancer from Cairo. And for another thing, I just can't stand snakes. Professor, you've just got to send me back there. Not permanently, of course. Just to look around and refresh my memory."

Gazing into her eyes again, Professor Bertoldt felt somewhat warm, giddy, bold, and suddenly determined.

"All right," he announced. "Why not? It's about time I took the big step. To what point in Cleopatra's life do you wish to return? Her childhood, her exile in Syria, the Caesar episode?"

"Well, I was thinking of Mark Antony and that barge thing. When Cleopatra first met Antony, she was dressed as Venus and showed up on a barge. It was in this motion picture."

Bertoldt went to his set of encyclopedias and pulled out a volume. He read and nodded. "Oh, yes. That incident occurred in Tarsus in Cilia where she had gone to answer charges that she had helped the Republican forces during the Roman civil war following Caesar's assassination. Tarsus is in modern-day Turkey." He showed her the spot on his desk globe.

She frowned slightly. "Tarsus is inland. I don't see any water near it. How can you have a barge without water?"

"The Cyndus River formerly flowed through Tarsus, but it is nonexistent now." He pointed to an easy chair. "Sit down, lean back, and relax. Look into my eyes. Try to make your mind a complete blank."

In a matter of moments her eyes glazed.

Bertoldt spoke softly, soothingly. "You are going back in time. Back, back in time." He waited half a minute. "What do you see now?"

Her voice carried echo quality. "I see . . . I see the *whole* world. The entire round earth!"

"Good," Bertoldt said. "I want to give you the overall picture first. Now we will slowly descend. You are going down, down, down. You are zeroing in on Turkey."

Bertoldt waited.

"All right," Diana said. "That should be Turkey down there below. But it isn't colored yellow like on the globe."

"Never mind the map color. Just verify the shape."

"Tarsus," she said. "Yes, that should be Tarsus right over there. I see the river and a lot of small boats. But no barge."

"I have taken you back to the approximate year you want," Bertoldt said, "However, historians are rather careless about exact days. I will now fine tune. We will go forward slowly. One week. Now two. Now three."

At eight weeks, she said, "Hold it there. I see the barge. It's tied up at that dock. Take me back a few days to where it's coming up the river for the first time."

Bertoldt obliged.

"That's it," Diana said. "I see the barge now. It's coming around the bend. I'm at a thousand feet. Get me down on deck. I don't want to miss a thing."

Bertoldt slowly maneuvered her aboard the barge and waited.

Five minutes passed.

Diana's face whitened. "Bring me back. This instant!"

Bertoldt leaned forward. "What do you see? What is it?"

"Never mind," she snapped. "Just bring me back."

After half a minute, she sat up and glared. "I was an old crone of at least sixty."

Bertoldt blinked. "But that is impossible. Cleopatra died when she was thirty-nine."

Diana's eyes flashed. "I was one of her *slaves!* I got there just at suppertime and you wouldn't believe the garbage she fed her help."

At the door, Diana sniffed haughtily. "I don't see why people make all that fuss about Cleopatra anyway. She wasn't so damn good-looking."

She had been gone less than a minute when Professor Bertoldt's buzzer sounded again.

A tall broad-shouldered man stood in the doorway.

"My name is Gerald Bonevicci. I heard you speak at Clinton Hall this evening and I was fascinated by what you said. I've never told anybody this before, but I am convinced that in a previous lifetime, I was Mark Antony."

Bertoldt closed his eyes. "My boy, it's been a long day and I have a headache."

But Gerald continued. "Even in high school when I read Mark's speech at the funeral of Caesar, I felt a certain empathy. I believe that I know Mark Antony better than anyone else in the world."

Bertoldt shook his head. "The odds that you were Mark Antony are overwhelmingly against you. After all, millions of other people existed at that particular time too. You could easily have been just another soldier, or peasant, or even slave."

Gerald was not discouraged. "You hinted in your talk that you were on the brink of actually being able to transport people back into their pasts. Let me be your subject. Transport me back to the very moment in history when Antony first met Cleopatra."

Bertoldt blinked and then rubbed his jaw. He sighed. "Well . . . I wouldn't have to break new ground, so to speak. And I am curious. But I must warn you that there is no certainty where you will descend. Anywhere on earth for that matter. You could possibly have been a herder of swine in the forests of England." He indicated the easy chair. "Sit down there and gaze fixedly into my eyes."

Gerald, too, proved to be an easy subject.

"I see the world," he intoned hollowly. "The entire world."

"Fine," Bertoldt said. "I will now lower you slowly to the surface of the earth and I believe that you will automatically home-in to the place where you existed in Mark Antony's time."

Gerald spoke slowly. "I am hovering over Turkey. I feel myself drawn down. Down. I see the river. The city."

Bertoldt was a bit surprised. "You are coming down on Tarsus?"

"Yes," Gerald said. "And I recognize it. Even from up here. I see the barge coming in."

Bertoldt waited a few moments and then asked, "Are you on the barge now?"

Gerald did not answer.

"What is happening down there?" Bertoldt demanded.

Gerald continued to stare ahead, unseeing and uncommunicative.

A full three hours passed before a worried and perspiring Professor Bertoldt managed to bring Gerald back to the twentieth century.

Bertoldt wiped his brow. "I thought you had gone beyond return. Didn't you hear me talking to you?"

Gerald appeared exhausted. "Yes, I heard you."

"Then why didn't you answer? What went on down there? Are you all right?"

"Yes," Gerald said. "I'm fine. But a little tired. There's one thing about this reincarnation business that neither one of us considered."

"Oh," Bertoldt said. "So you weren't Mark Antony?"

"No," Gerald said, "I wasn't Mark Antony." He looked away and blushed slightly. "I was Cleopatra."

For men may come and men may go, but—

And So On, And So On

by James Tiptree, Jr.

In a nook of the ship's lounge the child had managed to activate a viewscreen.

"Rovy! They *asked* you not to play with the screen while we're Jumping. We've told you and told you there isn't anything there. It's just pretty lights, dear. Now come back and we'll all play—"

As the young clanwife coaxed him back to their co-

coons something happened. It was a very slight something, just enough to make the drowsy passengers glance up. Immediately a calm voice spoke, accompanied by the blur of multiple translation.

"This is your captain. The momentary discontinuity we just experienced is quite normal in this mode of paraspace. We will encounter one or two more before reaching the Orion complex, which will be in about two units of ship's time."

The tiny episode stimulated talk.

"Declare I feel sorry for the youngers today." The large being in mercantile robes tapped his Galnews scanner, blew out his ear sacs comfortably. "We had all the fun. Why, when I first came out this was all wild frontier. Took courage to go beyond the Coalsack. They had you make your will. I can even remember the first cross-Gal Jump."

"How fast it has all changed!" admired his talking minor. Daringly it augmented: "The youngers are so apathetic. They accept all these marvels as natural, they mock the idea of heroism."

"Heroes!" the merchant snorted. "Not them!" He gazed challengingly around the luxe cabin, eliciting a few polite nods. Suddenly a cocoon swivelled around to face him, revealing an Earth-typer in Pathman gray.

"Heroism," said the Pathman softly, eyeing the merchant from under shadowed brows. "Heroism is essentially a spatial concept. No more free space, no more heroes." He turned away as if regretting having spoken, like a man trying to sustain some personal pain.

"Ooh, what about Ser Orpheian?" asked a bright young reproducer. "Crossing the Arm alone in a single pod. I think that's heroic!" It giggled flirtatiously.

"Not really," drawled a cultivated Galfad voice. The lutroid who had been using the reference station removed his input leads and smiled distantly at the reproducer. "Such exploits are merely an expiring gasp, a gleaning after the harvest if you will. Was Orpheian launching into the unknown? Not so. He faced merely the problem of whether he himself could do it. Playing at frontiers. No," the lutroid's voice took on a practiced Recorder's clarity. "The primitive phase is finished. The true frontier is within now. Inner space.'' He adjusted his academic fourragère.

The merchant had returned to his scanner.

"Now here's a nice little offering," he grunted. "Ringsun for sale, Eridani sector. That sector's long overdue for development, somebody'll make a sweet thing. If some of these young malcontents would just blow out their gills and pitch in!—" He thumped his aquaminor on the snout, causing it to mew piteously.

"But that's too much like work," echoed his talker soothingly.

The Pathman had been watching in haggard silence. Now he leaned over to the lutroid.

"Your remark about inner space. I take it you mean psychics? Purely subjective explorations?"

"Not at all," said the lutroid, gratified. "The psychic cults I regard as mere sensationalism. I refer to reality, to that simpler and deeper reality that lies beyond the reach of the trivial methodologies of science, the reality which we can only approach through what is called aesthetic or religious experience, god-immanent if you will—"

"I'd like to see art or religion get you to Orion," remarked a grizzed spacedog in the next cocoon. "If it wasn't for science you wouldn't be end-running the parsecs in an aleph Jumpship."

"Perhaps we end-run too much," the lutroid smiled. "Perhaps our technological capabilities are end-running, as you call it, our—"

"What about the Arm wars?" cried the young reproducer. "Ooh, science is *horrible*. I cry every time I think of the poor Armers." Its large eyes steamed and it hugged itself seductively.

"Well, now, you can't blame science for what some power-hounds do with it," the spacedog chuckled, hitching his cocoon over toward the reproducer's stay.

"That's right," said another voice, and the conversation group drifted away.

The Pathman's haunted eyes were still on the lutroid.

"If you are so certain of this deeper reality, this inner space," he said quietly, "why is your left hand almost without nails?"

The lutroid's left hand clenched and then uncurled

slowly to reveal the gnawed nails; he was not undisciplined.

"I recognise the right of your order to unduly personal speech," he said stiffly. Then he sighed and smiled. "Ah, of course; I admit I am not immune to the universal *angst*, the failure of nerve. The haunting fear of stagnation and decline, now that life has reached to the limits of this galaxy. But I regard this as a challenge to transcendence, which we must, we will meet, through our inner resources. We will find our *true* frontier." He nodded. "Life has never failed the ultimate challenge."

"Life has never before met the ultimate challenge," the Pathman rejoined somberly. "In the history of every race, society, planet or system or federation or swarm, whenever they had expanded to their *spatial limits* they commenced to decline. First stasis, then increasing entropy, degradation of structure, disorganisation, death. In every case, the process was only halted by breaking out into new space, or by new peoples breaking in on them from outside. Crude, simple outer space. Inner space? Consider the Vegans—"

"Exactly!" interrupted the lutroid. "That refutes you. The Vegans were approaching the most fruitful concepts of transphysical reality, concepts we must certainly reopen. If only the Myrmidi invasion had not destroyed so much."

"It is not generally known," the Pathman's voice was very low, "when the Myrmidi landed the Vegans were eating their own larvae and using the sacred dream-fabrics for ornaments. Very few could even sing."

"No!"

"By the Path."

The lutroid's nictating membranes filmed his eyes. After a moment he said formally, "You carry despair as your gift."

The Pathman was whispering as if to himself. "Who will come to open our skies? For the first time all life is closed in a finite space. Who can rescue a galaxy. The Clouds are barren and the realms beyond we know cannot be crossed even by matter, let alone life. For the first time we have truly reached the end."

"But the young," said the lutroid in quiet anguish.

"The young sense this. They seek to invent pseudo-frontiers, subjective escapes. Perhaps your inner space can beguile some for a while. But the despair will grow. Life is not mocked. We have come to the end of infinity, the end of hope."

The lutroid stared into the Pathman's hooded eyes, his hand involuntarily raising his academic surplice like a shield.

"You believe that there is nothing, no way?"

"Ahead lies only the irreversible long decline. For the first time *we know there is nothing beyond ourselves.*"

After a moment the lutroid's gaze dropped and the two beings let silence enshroud them. Outside the Galaxy was twisting by unseen, enormous, glittering: a finite prison. No way out.

In the aisle behind them something moved.

The child Rovy was creeping stealthily toward the screens that looked on no-space, his eyes intent and bright.

How do I love thee? Let me count the ways.

Nellthu

by Anthony Boucher

Ailsa had been easily the homeliest and the least talented girl in the University, if also the most logical and level-headed. Now, almost twenty-five years later, she was the most attractive woman Martin had ever seen and, to judge from their surroundings, by some lengths the richest.

". . . so lucky running into you again after all these years," she was saying, in that indescribably aphrodisiac voice. "You know about publishers, and you can advise me on this novel. I was getting so tired of the piano . . ."

Martin had heard her piano recordings and knew they were superb—as the vocal recordings had been before them and the non-representational paintings before *them* and the fashion designs and that astonishing paper on prime numbers. He also knew that the income from all these together could hardly have furnished the Silver Room in which they dined or the Gold Room in which he later read the novel (which was of course superb) or the room whose color he never noticed because he did not sleep alone (and the word *superb* is inadequate).

There was only one answer, and Martin was gratified to observe that the coffee-bringing servant cast no shadow in the morning sun. While Ailsa still slept (superbly), Martin said, "So you're a demon."

"Naturally, sir," the unshadowed servant said, his eyes adoringly upon the sleeper. "Nellthu, at your service."

"But such service! I can imagine Ailsa-that-was working out a good spell and even wishing logically. But I thought you fellows were limited in what you could grant."

"We are, sir. Three wishes."

"But she has wealth, beauty, youth, fame, a remarkable variety of talents—all on three wishes?"

"On one, sir. Oh, I foxed her prettily on the first two." Nellthu smiled reminiscently. " 'Beauty'—but she didn't specify, and I made her the most beautiful centenarian in the world. 'Wealth beyond the dreams of avarice'— and of course nothing is beyond such dreams, and nothing she got. Ah, I was in form that day, sir! But the third wish . . ."

"Don't tell me she tried the old 'For my third wish I want three more wishes'! I thought that was illegal."

"It is, sir. The paradoxes involved go beyond even our powers. No, sir," said Nellthu, with a sort of rueful admiration, "her third wish was stronger than that. She said: 'I wish that you fall permanently and unselfishly in love with me.' "

"She was always logical," Martin admitted. "So for your own sake you had to make her beautiful and . . . adept, and since then you have been compelled to gratify her every—" He broke off and looked from the bed to the demon. "How lucky for me that she included *unselfishly!*"

"Yes, sir," said Nellthu.

The nightmare of war goes on and on.

Taste of Battle

by Donald Franson

Blinding flashes lit up the night, sound hammered painfully on his eardrums, quakes churned up the damp-smelling earth in front of him. Private Leonard Blick slid into a bomb crater, lay flat in the bitter dirt, as the world shook. Wow! The radio guide had buzzed the warning to take cover. Pay attention to the radio guide.

He decided—his tired legs decided—to take a rest while in the crater, though the radio guide now beeped at him to advance. It wasn't really nagging at him, he realized—the guys back there were only doing their jobs. He'd hated the assignment when he'd had it, guiding other soldiers to safety or death, bright points on a ghostly map. But they could see what was coming, and he couldn't.

What he'd give to be back there right now! Or even standing in tiresome formation, back in training camp, listening to that little shrimp, Sergeant Trasker, sound off. "Training is no substitute for the taste of battle," he'd say in his immature voice. That was his favorite expression.

The explosions marched away, but Blick still lay there, gathering strength. Sergeant Trasker. Couldn't have been over eighteen, baby face except for the dark circles under his eyes, like two shiners. Young as he was, Trasker was a combat veteran. Give a man a little battle experience, and he's back home as an instructor. Something for Blick to look forward to, if he ever got out of this.

That last speech Trasker gave them, while they swayed wearily in line, after the punishing hike. Blick couldn't forget it. He wasn't supposed to.

"Pay attention to the radio guide," said Trasker. "But don't depend on it. You may have to get along without it. Be aggressive. Shoot the enemy when you see him, or even if you don't. Destroy him before he destroys you. Support your friends. Do the things you were trained to do."

Blick remembered now that even then he wished he were somewhere else. Standing there under the blue sky, listening to some dummy tell him things he already knew. But he'd made an effort to pay attention.

"The well-directed infantryman is king of the battlefield, now that tanks and aircraft are gone. Every weapon is meant for you. You've got weapons too. Use them." Sergeant Trasker frowned, looking like a small boy defying his mother. "Your radio guidesman back of the lines will warn you when to take cover and when it's safe to advance. That's all he can do. It's up to you to do the rest."

The sergeant tried to sound tough, but didn't manage it. "When or if you get into battle, be thankful for the experience. Battle-hardened veterans not only are better soldiers, but they're *safer.*"

It seemed an hour before Sergeant Trasker summed up, at long weary last. "That's about it. You can learn no more here. You must have the taste of battle. . . ."

And now he was in it. But Trasker was wrong on one point. Blick didn't feel any safer.

Must get on with the war. He scrambled out of the crater, crawling toward the objective, as pointed out by the beeps of the radio guide. Once beyond this exposed stretch, he should be past the enemy lines, thin at this point. He'd soon be contacting the cut-off friendly troops. An incentive to advance. Usually there wasn't any.

The night was pocket-black, now that the bombardment had stopped. Perhaps it didn't make sense to continue crawling, but why press his luck? The beeper changed its tune. Go to the left. What was there on the left? He tried to make something out of the darkness, but there were no helpful flashes now.

Crater after crater. This was really a well-worn battlefield. He was near the new objective now, he could tell by the frequency of the beeps. Without warning, he toppled into a deep hole and heard a voice cry, "Over here."

Now the shelling began again distantly and flashes lighted the sky. He crawled over to the man thus revealed and recognized Dave Murnam, who was equally glad to see him. "Seems like we go together now," said Dave. "They must be short of guidesmen back there."

Before they could talk further, their buzzers told them to take cover. They were already as far down as they could get, short of digging in. No time for that. A blast rolled the two of them over and over. The other man lay on his back, face exposed to the man-made elements.

In the flickering glow of continuous artillery, mortars, rockets, and what-not, Blick saw that the unconscious Murnam looked terrible, hardly recognizable as the carefree redhead he knew. He must get Dave back to safety. But what were the radio guide's instructions? Take cover. No, it was beeping advance.

Advance? Dave was dying. He dragged Murnam up the side of the crater and toward the next, back, against instructions. "Leave the wounded for the medics," was the rule, but to hell with that. He struggled to pull the dead weight along. The beeper changed to buzzer just as the sky lit up brightly and the ground heaved, loosening Blick's grip and whirling the men apart once more.

He hurried to crawl back to Murnam, but when he got closer, he turned away.

Where to now? The beeper still said advance. Well, he would advance then. He'd keep advancing until he got this damn war over with.

Now he could hear the crackle of small arms fire, and he took out his flashless pistol, extended it, and began firing. He couldn't see what he was shooting at, but neither could they. This was known as a fire fight.

He was peppering away ecstatically when he noticed the radio guide had been buzzing for some time. He didn't see or hear it coming, but suddenly he was flying through the air.

He covered his face and landed on his arms and elbows, in the soft dirt but still painfully. He'd somehow held on to his pistol. He lay there, tasting salt—no, that was blood. He'd had his taste of battle. He listened for the beep or buzzer.

Neither, His radio was out. He felt for it. It was gone. He was on his own.

What now? Which way to go? When was it safe to move? He remembered the words of Sergeant Trasker, "You may have to get along without it." He remembered a lot of the words of Sergeant Trasker.

He couldn't advance, or even shoot, not knowing the direction of the enemy. He'd soon find out, he felt. Another nearby explosion jarred him with several shocks of pain. He'd been hit by shrapnel.

He tried to crawl again but his legs wouldn't work. He pulled himself by his arms, finally tumbled into a crater. He lay on his back, completely exhausted, while the war went on over his head. This was a deep one. He'd never get out of here. This would be his grave.

After a long period he realized it was getting light. They'd call off the attack at dawn. He should have made it through and past the enemy by now. This was no place to be stranded.

The gray outlines of his crater world appeared around him. It was a recent one, deep and even. He saw he was not alone in the crater.

A body lay ten feet from him. He elbowed his way over to it, hoping to find a functioning beeper. He still clutched the pistol, as he crawled painfully, finally touched.

He tried to turn the body over, see who it had been. It couldn't be Dave Murnam again, he thought crazily.

He made three discoveries in rapid order.

It wasn't a body, it was moving, living.

It was an enemy soldier. Blick brought up his pistol, lifted the ugly helmet.

It was a young woman. Blick hesitated as he stared into the pretty face, as dirty and tired and desperate as his own.

The girl's hand moved, and a pistol pointed at him, banged. This was the last he knew as he slipped into oblivion.

Someone was taking his helmet off. He stared at daylight, blue sky. He was lying on a cot, not a hospital bed.

"On your feet," called a familiar voice. Long habit caused Blick to swing his legs over and down and jump up. He was fully dressed, clean, and—ininjured.

"Line up," said Sergeant Trasker, and Blick trotted forward, not without turning to see the technician fiddling with the oversized helmet he had been wearing, called the "hair dryer." As he mingled with the group lining up, his eyes met the mildly surprised ones of Dave Murnam. The line formed rapidly.

"All right, you guys," Trasker addressed them impersonally. "Most of you passed. Johnston, Kohler, Blick, at ease. The rest of you, dismissed. See you in the morning." They were alone in seconds.

Sergeant Trasker put on his best bad-boy look, as he surveyed the ignoble three. "You failed," he announced. "I won't tell you what you did—you know what you did. You retain the memory of the stimulated dream, even if you don't know it's a dream when you're in it. But the tape shows just what your responses were."

Trasker pouted. "You'll have to take it over. This will be an entirely new program this time. And tougher."

Again Leonard Blick wished he were somewhere else. He hated to be chewed out by a minor.

Sergeant Trasker wasn't finished. "Aren't you glad this isn't the real thing? The army can't afford to make battle veterans the hard way, fortunately for you." There was a trace of bitterness there, Blick thought.

Private Leonard Blick lay on the cot, "hair dryer" on his head, and closed his eyes in deep sleep. A peaceful expression appeared on his face.

It didn't stay there long.

It's that sixth fifth of the pie that does it.

Deflation 2001

by Bob Shaw

Having to pay ten dollars for a cup of coffee shook Lester Perry.

The price had been stabilized at eight dollars for almost a month, and he had begun to entertain an irrational hope that it would stay there. He stared sadly at the vending machine as the dark liquid gurgled into a plastic cup. His expression of gloom became more pronounced when he raised the cup to his lips.

"Ten dollars," he said. "And when you get it, it's cold!"

His pilot, Boyd Dunhill, shrugged, then examined the gold braid of his uniform in case he had marred its splendor with the unaccustomed movement of his shoulders. "What do you expect?" he replied indifferently. "The airport authorities refused the Coffee Machine Maintenance Workers' pay claim last week, so the union told its members to work to rule, and that has forced up the costs."

"But they got 100 per cent four weeks ago! That's when coffee went up to eight dollars."

"The union's original claim was for 200 per cent."

"But how could the airport pay 200 per cent, for God's sake?"

"The Chocolate Machine Workers got it," Dunhill commented.

"Did they?" Perry shook his head in bewilderment. "Was that on television?"

"There hasn't been any television for three months,"

the pilot reminded him. "The technicians' claim for a basic two million a year is still being disputed."

Perry drained his coffee cup and threw it into a bin. "Is my plane ready? Can we go now?"

"It's been ready for four hours."

"Then why are we hanging around here?"

"The Light Aircraft Engineers' productivity agreement—there's a statutory minimum of eight hours allowed for all maintenance jobs."

"Eight hours to replace a wiper blade!" Perry laughed shakily. "And that's a productivity deal?"

"It has doubled the number of man-hours logged at this field."

"Of course it has, if they're putting down eight hours for half-hour jobs. But that's a completely false . . ." Perry stopped speaking as he saw the growing coldness on his pilot's face. He remembered, just in time, that there was a current pay dispute between the Flying Employers' Association and the Low-wing Twin-engined Private Airplane Pilots' Union. The employers were offering 75 per cent and the pilots were holding out for 150 per cent, plus a mileage bonus. "Can you get a porter to carry my bag?"

Dunhill shook his head. "You'll have to carry it yourself. They're on strike since last Friday."

"Why?"

"Too many people were carrying their own bags."

"Oh!" Perry lifted his case and took it out across the tarmac to the waiting aircraft. He strapped himself into one of the five passenger seats, reached for a magazine to read during the flight to Denver, and then recalled that there had been no newspapers or magazines for over two weeks. The preliminaries of getting airborne took an unusually long time—suggesting that the air traffic controllers were engaged in some kind of collective bargaining—and finally Perry drifted into an uneasy sleep.

He was shocked into wakefulness by a sound of rushing air, which told him that the door of the aircraft had been opened in flight. Physically and mentally chilled, he opened his eyes and saw Dunhill standing at the yawning door. His expensive uniform was pulled into peculiar shapes by the harness of a parachute.

"What . . . what is this?" Perry said. "Are we on fire?"

"No." Dunhill was using his best official voice. "I'm on strike."

"You're kidding!"

"You think so? I just got word on the radio—the employers have turned down the very reasonable demands of the Low-wing Twin-engined Private Airplane Pilots' Union and walked out on the negotiations. We've got the backing of our friends in the Low-wing Single-engined and in the High-wing Twin-engined unions; consequently all our members are withdrawing their labor at midnight, which is about thirty seconds from now."

"But, *Boyd!* I've no 'chute—what'll happen to me?"

A look of sullen determination appeared on the pilot's face. "Why should I worry about you? You weren't very concerned about me when I was trying to get along on a bare three million a year."

"I was selfish. I see that now, and I'm sorry." Perry unstrapped himself and stood up. "Don't jump, Boyd— I'll double your salary."

"That," Dunhill said impatiently, "is less than our union is claiming."

"Oh! Well, I'll triple it then. Three times your present salary, Boyd."

"Sorry. No piecemeal settlements. They weaken union solidarity." He turned away and dived into the roaring blackness beyond the doorway.

Perry stared after him for a moment, then wrestled the door shut and went forward to the cockpit. The aircraft was flying steadily on autopilot. Perry sat down in the left-hand seat and gripped the control column, casting his mind back several decades to his days as a fighter pilot in Vietnam. Landing the aircraft himself would get him in serious trouble with the unions for strike-breaking, but he was not prepared to die just yet. He disengaged the autopilot and began to get in some much-needed flying practice.

Some thousands of feet below the aircraft, Boyd Dunhill pulled the ripcord and waited for his 'chute to open. The jolt, when it came, was less severe than he had expected, and a few seconds later he was falling at the same speed as before. He looked upward and saw—instead of a taut canopy—a fluttering bunch of unconnected nylon segments.

And, too late, he remembered the threat of the Parachute Stitchers and Packers' Union to carry out disruptive action in support of their demand for longer vacations.

"Communists!" he screamed. "You lousy Red anarchist ba . . ."

CRUNCH!

"Android" means "manlike."

Do Androids Dream of Electric Love?

by Walt Leibscher

The psychodroid walked into the room and stopped several feet from its patient.

"I'm here to help you," it said.

"No one can help me," said the patient, turning his face to the sterile, white walls of the hosprison cell.

"Please let me try. For all practical purposes I'm completely human. However, a small part of me is still machine. That part just might understand." The android settled into a chair.

"No matter, understanding. I know they are going to convert me." The human sighed.

"That might depend on me."

"You! You are nothing but another mind-sucking machine. I told my story to one of your brothers. Sisters? Cohorts? What in the hell does one machine call another?" He paused for a moment and added, "No offense meant."

"I know, I can tell when you are lying."

"That sophisticated?"

"State psychiatrist Model II, Mark III. I'm the latest and the best."

The man laughed at the almost haughty statement, then asked, "Can you cry?"

The question seemed to have no effect. "I can feel like crying, but I'm not set up to produce tears. What psychiatrist is?"

"I like you," said the man. "How about a game of chess, or is game-playing confined to the theradroids?"

"Usually, but I'm programmed for all kinds of therapeutic play. Anything that will make you more comfortable, or less tense. Tell you what. Trade you a game of chess for a statement, or story, or whatever you might want to tell me."

"Is your chess-playing infallible?"

"It could be, but it won't. I know your IQ and reasoning quotient. I will make it even by adjusting myself to your level."

"Downward or upward?"

"Don't be facetious," said the android.

The human roared with laughter. When he finished the outburst, the android's usually expressionless face was smiling.

"Don't look so damned smug," said the man. "So I laughed for the first time in weeks. Pleased with yourself?"

"I like laughter. I wish I could do it."

The man thought for a moment, then said, "OK, Hal, sing 'Daisy, Daisy.'"

The android shook for a moment, and grinned broadly. "That was quite pleasant."

The man was pleased. "I thought I could do it."

"Now it's my turn to tell you not to be so damned smug. So you made me laugh. Big deal."

"We're even," said the man. "Let's forget the chess game. It was only a ploy anyway. What can I tell you?"

"Everything."

"Well, to begin, I suppose you know why I'm here?"

"Because you ostensibly committed an act that even in this enlightened age was considered, shall we say, way out."

"That's enough for a starter." And the man told his story.

When he finished, the android stared at the man for a long, long while. "That's quite a story, and if you don't mind my saying so, I found it exceedingly sexy."

"Thanks. But the pertinent point is do you believe me?"

"I told you I could tell when you were lying. However, under the circumstances it really doesn't, or won't, matter. You will be exonerated."

"Simple as that, is it?"

"Very simple. Ostensibly I'm a machine with no feelings. I will have no difficulty convincing them of your innocence. The fact that I find you provocatively desirable won't matter."

With that the android rose and started to leave the room. "I'll certainly be seeing you again."

"One more question," said the startled man.

"Yes."

"Are androids equipped—? I mean do you have gender?"

"That's for you to figure out," the android said impishly. Then it turned and sashayed out the door and down the hall.

And when you say that, partner, you better smile.

Dog Star

by Mack Reynolds

When man's first representatives landed on Sirius Two, hungry to trade for that planet's abundance of pitchblende, they carried with them, as ship's mascot, one of the few dogs left on Earth.

That Gimmick was one of the very last was not due to disease, nor reproductive failure. It was just that man was going through a period of wearying of his ages-long companion. The Venusian *marmoset*, the Martian *trillie*, were much cuter, you know, and much less trouble.

Captain Hanford—leader of the three man, one dog crew—saluted the Sirian delegates snappily, only mildly surprised at the other's appearance. In a small saddle, topping what appeared almost identical to an Earthside airedale, was an octopus-looking creature. It was not until later that the captain and his men realized that the dog-like creature was the intelligent of the two, and the octopus a telepathically controlled set of useful tentacles.

Telepathic communication can be confusing, since it is almost impossible, when the group consists of several individuals, to know who is "talking."

When the amenities had been dispensed with, the Sirian leader remarked in friendly fashion, "I would say our domesticated animals were somewhat superior to yours. Eight tentacles would seem more efficient than two five-fingered limbs, such as yours possess."

Captain Hanford blinked.

"In fact," the Sirian continued, somewhat apologetically, "if you don't mind my saying so, your creatures are somewhat repulsive in appearance."

"I suppose we are used to them," Hanford replied, swallowing quickly.

Later, in the space ship, the ship's captain looked at his men indignantly. "Do you realize," he said, "that they think Gimmick is the leader of this expedition and that we're domesticated animals?"

Ensign Jones said happily, "Possibly you're right, Skipper, but they were certainly friendly enough. And they sure came through nicely on the uranium exchange deal. The government will be pleased as . . . ."

Hanford insisted, "But do you realize what those Sirians would think if it came out that Gimmick was a pet? That we consider him an inferior life form?"

Lieutenant Grant was the first to comprehend. "It means," he said slowly, "that from now on, every time we come in contact with Sirians, a dog is going to have to be along. It means that every ship that comes for a load of pitchblende, is going to have to have several. We've got to continue pretending that the dog is Earth's dominant life form, and man his servant. Everytime we *talk* to a Sirian, we're going to have to pretend it's the dog *talking.*"

"Holy Smokes," Jones said, "there aren't that many dogs left on Earth. We're going to have to start breeding them back as fast as we can."

The Captain looked down to where Gimmick, his red tongue out as he panted so that he looked as though he was grinning, lay on the floor.

"You son-of-a—" the Captain snapped at him.

But Gimmick's tail went left, right, left, right.

Judge not, lest ye be judged.

The Great Judge

by A. E. van Vogt

"Judgment," said the rad, "in the case Douglas Aird, tried for treason on August 2nd, last—"

With a trembling movement of his fingers, Aird turned the volume control higher. The next words blared at him.

"—That Douglas Aird do surrender himself one week from this day, that is, on September 17, 2460 A.D., to his neighborhood patrol station, that he then be taken to the nearest converter, there to be put to death—"

Click!

He had no conscious memory of shutting off the rad. One instant the sound roared through his apartment, the next there was dead silence. Aird sank back in his chair and stared with sick eyes through the transparent walls out upon the shining roofs of The Judge's City. All these weeks he had known there was no chance. The scientific achievements that, he had tried to tell himself, would weigh the balance in his favor—even as he assessed their value to the race, he had realized that the Great Judge would not consider them from the same viewpoint as himself.

He had made the fatal error of suggesting in the presence of "friends" that a mere man like Douglas Aird could govern as well as the immortal Great Judge, and that in fact it might be a good idea if someone less remote from the needs of the mass of the people had a chance to promulgate decrees. A little less restriction, he had urged, and a little more individuality. With such abandon he had spoken on the day that he succeeded in transferring the nervous impulses of a chicken into the nervous system of a dog.

He had attempted to introduce the discovery as evidence that he was in an excited and abnormal state of mind. But the magistrate pronounced the reason irrelevant, immaterial, and facetious. He refused to hear what the discovery was, ruling coldly: "The official science investigator of the Great Judge will call on you in due course, and you will then turn your invention over to him complete with adequate documentation."

Aird presumed gloomily that the investigator would call in a day or so. He toyed with the possibility of destroying his papers and instruments. Shudderingly, he rejected that form of defiance. The Great Judge's control of life was so complete that he permitted his enemies to remain at large until the day of their execution. It was a point made much of by the Great Judge's propaganda department. Civilization, it was said, had never before attained so high a level of freedom. But it wouldn't do to try the patience of the Great Judge by destroying an invention. Aird had a sharp conviction that less civilized methods might be used on him if he failed to carry through the farce.

Sitting there in his apartment, surrounded by every modern convenience, Aird sighed. He would spend his last week alive in any luxury he might choose. It was the final refinement of mental torture, to be free, to have the feeling that if only he could think of something he might succeed in escaping. Yet he knew escape was impossible. If he climbed into his hopjet, he'd have to swoop in at the nearest patrol station, and have his electronic registration "plates" stamped with a signal. Thereafter, his machine would continuously give off vibrations automatically advising patrol vessels of the time and space limitations of his permit.

Similar restrictions controlled his person. The electronic instrument "printed" on his upper right arm could be activated by any central, which would start a burning sensation of gradually increasing intensity.

There was absolutely no escape from the law of the Great Judge.

Aird climbed to his feet wearily. Might as well get his material ready for the science investigator. It was too bad he wouldn't have an opportunity to experiment with higher life forms but—

Aird stopped short in the doorway of his laboratory. His body throbbed with the tremendousness of the idea that had slammed into his mind. He began to quiver. He leaned weakly against the doorjamb, then slowly straightened.

"That's it!" He spoke the words aloud, his voice low and intense, simultaneously utterly incredulous and hopeful to the point of madness. It was the mounting hope that brought a return of terrible weakness. He collapsed on the rug just inside the laboratory, and lay there muttering to himself, the special insanities of an electronician.

". . . have to get a larger grid, and more liquid, and—"

Special Science Investigator George Mollins returned to the Great Judge's Court, and immediately asked for a private interview with the Great Judge.

"Tell him," he told the High Bailiff of the Court, "that I have come across a very important scientific discovery. He will know what is meant if you simply say 'Category AA.'"

While he waited to be received, the Science Investigator arranged his instruments for readier transport, and then he stood idly looking around him at the dome-vaulted anteroom. Through a transparent wall he could see the gardens below. In the profusion of greenery, he caught the glint of a white skirt, which reminded him that the Great Judge was reputed to have at least seven reigning beauties in his harem at all times.

"This way, sir. The Great Judge will receive you."

The man who sat behind the desk looked about thirty-five years old. Only his eyes and his mouth seemed older. From bleak blue eyes and with thin-lipped silence, the immortal, ever-young Great Judge studied his visitor.

The latter wasted no time. The moment the door shut behind him, he pressed the button that released a fine spray of gas straight at the Great Judge. The man behind the desk simply sagged in his chair.

The visitor was calm but quick. He dragged the limp body around to his instrument case, and removed the clothes of the upper body. Swiftly, he swabbed the body with the liquid he had brought, and began to attach his nodes. Half a dozen on one side and a dozen on the other. The next step was to attach the wires to his own body, lie down, and press the activator.

The question that puzzled Douglas Aird on the day that he succeeded in transferring the nervous impulses of a chicken into the nervous system of a dog was, how complete was the transference?

Personality, he argued with himself, was a complex structure. It grew out of many quadrillions of minute experiences and, as he had discovered, finally gave to each body its own special neural vibration.

Would it be possible by artificially forcing that exact vibration upon another body to establish a nerve energy flow between the two bodies? A flow so natural and easy that every cell would be impregnated with the thoughts and memories of the other body? A flow so complete, that, when properly channeled, the personality of one body would flow into the other?

The fact that a dog acted like a chicken was not complete proof. Normally, he would have experimented very carefully before trying it on a human being. But a man doomed to die didn't have time to think of risks. When the Science Investigator called on him two days before the date of the execution, he gassed the man, and made the experiment then and there.

The transference was not absolutely complete. Blurred memories remained behind, enough to make the routine of going to the Great Judge's Court familiar and easy. He had worried about that. It was important that he follow the right etiquette in approaching a man who normally permitted no one near him but people he had learned to trust.

As it turned out, he did everything right. The moment he felt the blurring sensation which marked the beginning of the transfer of his personality from the body of the Science Investigator to the body of the Great Judge, Aird acted. He released a gas toward the Great Judge that would revive the man in about five minutes. Simultaneously, he sprayed his present body with instantaneous anaesthetic gas. Even as he sank into unconsciousness, he could feel the sharp, hard personality of the Great Judge slipping into the Investigator's body.

Five minutes later Douglas Aird, now in the body of the Great Judge, opened his eyes, and looked around him alertly. Carefully, he disconnected the wires, packed the instruments—and then called a bailiff. As he had expected, no one questioned the actions of the Great Judge. It was the work of an hour to drive to the apartment of Douglas Aird, transfer the Great Judge's personality to the body of Douglas Aird—and at the same time return the personality of the Science Investigator into its proper body. As a precaution, he had the Science Investigator taken to a hospital.

"Keep him there for three days under observation," he commanded.

Back at the Great Judge's Court, he spent the next few days cautiously fitting himself into the pleasant routine of a life of absolute power. He had a thousand plans for altering a police state into a free state, but as a scientist he was sharply aware of the need for orderly transition.

It was at the end of a week that he inquired casually about a traitor named Douglas Aird. The story was interesting. The man had, it seemed, attempted to escape. He had flown some five hundred miles in an unregistered hopjet before being grounded by a local patrol. Immediately, he fled into the mountains. When he failed to report on the morning of the day set for his execution, the printed instrument on his right arm was activated. Shortly before dusk, a tired, distracted, staggering scarecrow of a man, screaming that he was the Great Judge, appeared in a mountain patrol station. The execution was then carried out with no further delay.

The report concluded: "Seldom in the experience of

the attending patrol officers has a condemned man approached the converter with so much reluctance.''

The Great Judge, sitting at his desk in the luxurious court, could well believe it.

Made for each other.

2001: A Love Story

by Paul Dellinger

You could call space vast, the sun warm, and Montgomery Dante rich, but all of those descriptions fall short of the actualities—and by about the same distance in each case.

Dante seemed to have what might have been called, in an earlier age, the magic touch. Through a series of stock investments near the dawn of the 21st century in such wild-eyed schemes as faster-than-light drives and orbit-changing asteroids, he had amassed wealth enough to indulge himself in any whim that struck his fancy.

Once, he even dared to try to revive the twenty-year-old experiments in the artificial creation of intelligent life, but he had sense enough to yield and avoid what would have been an all-out war between his vast resources and those of the rest of the solar system. The idea was his only error in judgment; perhaps he was too young to remember the terror that engulfed every planet when those monstrosities had been discovered in the underground laboratories of the Martian colony and torn apart by raging mobs before they could get out and multiply themselves.

Otherwise, all his ideas paid off handsomely. And three years ago, he had engineered the construction of a man-made planetoid just beyond the orbit of Pluto. *Planet X*, he called it, partly as a monument to old space opera tales written before the Space Age and partly because Roman numeral X was the logical designation for a tenth planet. Yes, Montgomery Dante created his own world and may have been the first man in human history who could literally buy anything he wanted.

Except Crystal Towers.

You remember her. To those who heard her songs she was the Lorelei of the solar system, an artist whose voice could arouse an entire spectrum of emotions in her listeners. To the fewer who actually saw her, she appeared to be the most flawlessly beautiful woman of any age. To Montgomery Dane, she was the most magnificent creature on nine planets. Ten, counting his own.

He had beamed her a proposed marriage contract the first time he saw her, in a rare live video broadcast from one of the bubble cities bouncing around in the atmosphere of Jupiter. His specially built tri-D solido used his own latest FTL star drive techniques to bring him instantaneous programming from anywhere in the system, and his message had been waiting for Crystal before she even got off the stage.

Politely but firmly, she sent back a "no."

Thus began a barrage of proposals, each more liberal than the last, zapped across the ether from Planet X to wherever Crystal performed. And Crystal continued to astonish the entire system by turning them down as quickly as they came. Dante's ardent pursuit of the reclusive singer became the hottest item on the interplanet news broadcasts. The public even forgave Dante for his ill judgment in the matter of the artificial life experiments, in its zeal to hear of his next ploy in his romantic quest.

Eventually, after Dante offered to condense the material of Saturn's or Uranus' rings into a wedding band, Crystal did agree to a face-to-face confrontation—but she made it clear it was to stop, not accept, Dante's offers. Every newshound in the interplanet chain tried to learn where the meeting would be, only to find later it was held under their noses in the de-bugged top security interview room of their own headquarters building on Titan. Dante happened to own the building.

Despite the drab wig concealing her golden hair, and the contact lenses over her sky-blue eyes, Dante easily picked her out of the crowd his televisor showed in the lobby. Soon she was being ushered into the protected chamber and they were left alone.

"Hello," he said, recognizing in his usually firm voice the nervousness of an adolescent on his first date. "Please—won't you sit down?"

She replied in that soft, melodious voice that had held millions of listeners enthralled in recent years. "I would prefer standing, Mr. Dante. I don't believe this will take long."

"I hope not," he said, taking a step toward her. She stood her ground. "Miss Towers, I can say without conceit that any other woman in the system would have accepted one of my offers by now—but not you. Is it that you simply don't know me? That can be remedied. Or is there something about me you would first change?"

"I've studied up on you, of course." She smiled. "I was curious about my suitor. You might be interested to know there is little biographical material available on you beyond six or so Earth-years ago, when your incredible gambles began paying off."

'If there's more you'd like to know—"

"I know enough. I've no doubt you're complex enough to keep a liaison interesting for years—perhaps even a lifetime, if such marriages still exist. So I hope you will believe when I say the problem isn't with you, but myself."

Dante raised an eyebrow. "Could you be more specific?"

"I hoped you wouldn't force me to do so." That incredible voice, which had conveyed only formal politeness until now, managed to project an imploring note that somehow fell short of begging. "Can you not simply leave it at this?"

"You gambled on that, didn't you? That I couldn't resist your plea in person. Most men couldn't, Miss Towers. But I'm not most men."

Her expression didn't change, but her eyes widened just a bit. "You—know, don't you?"

"Since the first time I saw you," said Dante. "Your voice, your features, everything about you—it's too perfect. If you investigated my background, you may know that I once tried to reestablish those laboratories on Mars where some of the first colonists created life—"

He struck swiftly, the edge of his hand deflecting her pointing index finger. The thread-like laser beam from it scorched a tiny hole in the carpeted floor.

"Let me go! You won't do to me what those mobs did to the others. I'll destruct first—"

Dante kept his grip on her arms easily, despite the incredible strength with which she struggled. "No," he said softly. "That won't be necessary, now that I've finally found you."

She stopped fighting, and looked up at him with dawning comprehension. "You, too?" she whispered. "Has your success been due to a computer-mind that takes every potential into account?"

Dante nodded. "The scientists never had a chance to tell you, before the end. They made two of us."

The wedding took place June 11, 2001, on Old Earth, before the couple left for their new home in the solitude of Dante's planet. It was a marriage made in heaven, according to one usually hard-nosed woman reporter as she wiped a sentimental tear from her eye.

"No," Dante replied. "In a laboratory." But nobody ever figured out what he meant.

Thou shalt not make unto thee any graven image—

Answer

by Frederic Brown

Dwar Ev ceremoniously soldered the final connection with gold. The eyes of a dozen television cameras watched him and the sub-ether bore throughout the universe a dozen pictures of what he was doing.

He straightened and nodded to Dwar Reyn, then moved to a position beside the switch that would complete the contact when he threw it. The switch that would connect, all at once, all of the monster computing machines of all the populated planets in the universe—ninety-six billion planets—into the supercircuit that would connect them all into one supercalculator, one cybernetics machine that would combine all the knowledge of all the galaxies.

Dwar Reyn spoke briefly to the watching and listening trillions. Then after a moment's silence he said, "Now, Dwar Ev."

Dwar Ev threw the switch. There was a mighty hum, the surge of power from ninety-six billion planets. Lights flashed and quieted along the miles-long panel.

Dwar Ev stepped back and drew a deep breath. "The honor of asking the first question is yours, Dwar Reyn."

"Thank you," said Dwar Reyn. "It shall be a question which no single cybernetics machine has been able to answer."

He turned to face the machine. "Is there a God?"

The mighty voice answered without hesitation, without the clicking of a single relay.

"Yes, *now* there is a God."

Sudden fear flashed on the face of Dwar Ev. He leaped to grab the switch.

A bolt of lightning from the cloudless sky struck him down and fused the switch shut.

Know your place!

Hadj

by Harlan Ellison

It took almost a year to select Herber. A year of wild speculation; a year of opening horizons; a year of growing pride at the knowledge of humanity's certain place in the forefront of the Universal Community; it was the year after the Masters of the Universe flashed through Earth's atmosphere and broadcast their message.

From nowhere: they came down in their glowing golden ark—more than one hundred and sixty kilometers long, a great patch over the eye of the sun—and without argument demonstrated to every man, woman and child on Earth that they did, indeed, rule the Universe.

They caused rain. They stopped rain. They created rainbows. They caused storm clouds to wipe away the rainbows. They raised sunken continents. They leveled mountains. They opened a shaft to the molten center of the planet. They imbued the mute stones of the fields with the power of levitation and erected monuments of breathtaking beauty. They froze the entire population of the Earth in its tracks, stopped death, blotted out all other sound—while the message was telepathically spoken in a thousand different languages and dialects.

The message merely said: "Send us a representative from Earth."

But certain scientists received more. They were given detailed instructions for the construction of what the Masters called an "inverspace ship." Other certain scientists were given directions to the Center, to the home world of the Masters; a world far off somewhere across the light-years and across numberless galaxies.

And the inverspace ship had been constructed. The theories seemed so simple . . . now.

But who was to go? The great men and women who pondered the question knew the awesome responsibility of the emissary. Care in the selection became so overwhelmingly paralyzing that it was finally decided the problem was too complex and dangerous to be left in the hands of mere humans. They set the machines to the task.

They linked the Mark XXX, the UniCompVac, the Water Thinker, the Brognagov Master Computer and thousands of lesser brains, shunted them on-line with the deadfall circuit and the Sanhedrin Network, and coded in the question prepared by three hundred and fifty-five of the world's top programmers.

The basic program contained random factors and extrapolations in excess of sixteen billion variables. Even with a worldwide hookup it took the mass mind seven months merely to establish the parameters of the equation. It took another four months, sixteen days, for the readout that named Wilson Herber.

Of the billions teeming the planet, *only* Wilson Herber met all the necessary qualifications for Earth's emissary to the Masters of the Universe.

They came to Wilson Herber in his mountain retreat, and were initially greeted by threats of disembowelment if they didn't get the hell away and leave him in peace and quiet!

But judicious reasoning—and the infinitely complex veiled threats of an entire world—eventually brought the ex-statesman around.

Herber was, without challenge, the wealthiest man in the world. The cartel he had set up during the first sixty years of his life was still intact, now entirely run by managers and technicians and executives bound to him by the secret and often terrible facts contained in dossiers in a vault whose location was known only to the old man. The spiderweb organization of Wilson Herber's holdings spanned every utility and human service, drew upon virtually every raw material and necessity anyone might ever need or consider of value, controlled—at least in part—the thoughts and movements of every intelligent creature on the face of the planet in a given day. Incalculably wealthy, powerful beyond measure, wise as only one who has it all can be unconcernedly wise, Wilson Herber had set the machine of his cartel to humming, turned it over to lesser mortals, and moved on to the World Federation Hall where he had served as Senior Ombudsman for ten years. Then he had assumed the mantle of Coordinator of the Federation. Another ten years' service to the noblest master of them all, the human race.

Then, five years before the golden ark had come, at the age of eighty-five, early middle-years in a time of anti-agathic DNA rearrangement, Wilson Herber had retired, secluding himself utterly.

But judicious reasoning, and cataclysmic threats, brought the wisest, richest, most powerful, most cunning man in the world back to the Hall. That, of course, was what they thought—those who had leveled the threats.

* * *

"I'll take the credentials," he said to the Coordinator, the assembled Ombudsmen, the Federation Council. "I'll go out there and let them know we're ready to join with them."

Despite the longevity reprogrammed into his DNA, he had eschewed any cosmetic enhancement: he was a shrunken gnome of a man with thin gray hair and leathery dark skin. His eyes were made of ground glass, his chin was a dagger point.

"Establish us on a sound footing with their highest councils," the Coordinator said, his voice magnificent in the Hall. "Let them know we walk hand-in-hand with them, as equals."

"Till we learn all they can teach us, at which time we usurp their preeminence, yes?"

The communications web broadcasting Herber's investiture went to standby on time-delay. The world audience did not hear the remark. Nor did the audience see the Coordinator hem and haw and finally, under Herber's predatory stare, grin a vulpine grin, shrug, and say, "You always know best, sir."

Wilson Herber, as was his way, had struck directly to the heart of human nature, to the heart of the mission, to the heart of the problem.

He smiled as he left the Hall. Having struck to the heart, all that was now required was that one squeeze the heart till it bled or burst.

The home planet of the Masters of the Universe slowly materialized out of inverspace. It shimmered like dew on grass, faded in and out, then solidified. Incredible: the Masters of the Universe had gained control of all time and space: they had devised the ultimate, perfect protection for the home world: it was partially in normal space, partially in inverspace. It existed in the interstices, safe, there/not there.

Herber, cushioned in a special travel-chair, sat beside Captain Arnand Singh, watching the shimmering mirage wheeling beneath their ship.

"More impressive than I'd expected, yes, Captain?"

The Moslem nodded. He was a huge man, yet he gave the impression of compression, efficiency. And nobility. "This is almost like a hadj, Mr. Herber."

"Eh? Hadj? Which is?"

"What my people long ago called a pilgrimage to Mecca, the holy city. Now here we are, the first humans to make the pilgrimage to the new Mecca . . ."

Herber cut him off. "Listen, old son; just remember this: *we're* the chosen people. Earth is the center, no matter *what* they think. As good as them, probably better: quicker, stronger, cleverer. And they know it, too. Take my word for it. Otherwise they wouldn't have come all that way to solicit us. They came to *us,* remember? They gave us the invitation, not the other way around. So get all those old subservient hadj ideas out of your head. Proud, my boy, be proud. We're coming to establish diplomatic relations, to show them how it should be done."

Singh did not reply. But he smiled quickly. What bravado the old man displayed. They were the first humans to meet the Masters, and Herber was treating it as though it were a routine business trip to a foreign embassy in New Boston.

All that was flensed from his thoughts as the control panel bleeped the signal for slipout into normal space.

Herber's diplomatic ship settled down through the many-colored alluvial layers of inverspace and abruptly passed into normal space-time.

In normal space, the home world was even more impressive.

Twelve-kilometer-high buildings of delicate pastel tracery reached for the sky. Huge ships plied back and forth among the five major continents. Artificial suns burned in the quarries. Intelligent fish carried cargo across the great sea. Beams of moted light crisscrossed the sky.

"We can learn a great deal from these people, Singh," Herber said quietly, almost reverentially. His pinched and wrinkled features settled into a familiar, comfortable expression of contemplative expectation. "Form follows function," he said, whispering the litany. "All this of masters and Masters . . . we shall see. . . ."

Herber raised the beamer to his lips. With narrowed eyes and tightened mouth he watched only one of the aspects of the Master's knowledge that could destroy his cartel: the great ships carrying cargo through the skies of the home world winked out of existence and reappeared far from the vanishing point. Instantaneous transportation of goods. His voice was strained as he spoke into the beamer:

"We are the emissaries from Earth, here to offer you the fellowship and knowledge of our planet. We hope our friends of the golden world are well. We come as equals and ask landing instructions."

They waited. Herber watched with hungry eyes. Singh pointed out the spaceport, an enormous, sprawling eighty-kilometer-wide area with gigantic loading docks, golden ships aimed at the sky, and hundreds of alien ships from as many different worlds. The Captain settled slowly toward the port.

And the answer came back, already translated into English for them. It filled the cabin of the starship that had been built with the science of the Masters for these humans who had come a great distance as equals:

Please go around to the service entrance. Please go around to the service entrance. Please go around . . .

In time, the cure will fit the disease.

Good Morning! This Is the Future

by Henry Slesar

2494 A.D.

He awoke to massage, warm fluid, and wordless sounds of comfort. Then he was being lifted from the roto-bath by mechanical hands that were gentle as a woman's. He was like an infant reborn, and just as naked. His weight at birth was two hundred and six pounds, most of it paunch.

After a while, they let him sit up. He asked for a cigar,

and the request provoked consternation and some laughter. One of the whitecoated attendants whispered explanation to his younger assistant. The young man looked ill at the description of "cigar."

Then the interrogation.

"Your name is Jervis T. Murath?"

"Yes."

"Your age upon entering stasis?"

"Fifty-one."

"Correct."

"You were a member of the financial community prior to entering the Dormantory?"

"Was," Murath growled. "Wiped out in the crash of '93. Scrounged up just enough money to make this trip. And a little extra," he added craftily.

"Your orientation classes will begin tomorrow," the attendant said. "Attendance is voluntary."

"Don't want any classes. Just want to know one thing. Is there still a First Central Bank of Chicago?"

"I will call Information."

He spoke to a glowing patch in the wall, and returned.

"The First Central Bank of Chicago is now one of a group of consolidated banking institutions known as the Mid-Western Trust Company; all accounts have been preserved intact. You may make deposits or withdrawals at any one of MTC's six thousand four hundred branch offices."

"Where's the nearest one?" Murath said.

The bank building was the shape and color of an egg; the money they handled was varicolored and quite pretty. He was seated in front of a transparent bubble which encased a teller.

"My name is Jervis T. Murath," he said. "I opened an account at the First Central in 1995, for one thousand dollars. The interest rate was five percent, compounded semi-annually. I don't imagine it stayed the same."

"No, sir," the teller said. "The interest rate has varied from between nothing at all to seventeen percent in the last five hundred years. One moment while I check your record."

Murath held his breath, and wished he had a cigar.

The teller reappeared.

"Your money is on deposit," he said. "The total is

twenty-six million, seven hundred thousand, eight hundred and fifty-four dollars and four cents."

"Thank you," Murath said reverently, not to the teller. "I'd like fifty thousand in cash, right now."

He left the bank with the money in his pocket. Across the street, there was an immense circular building with moving ramps. From the crowds, the parcels, the preponderance of women, he gathered that it was a department store. He was right.

He walked into the store and chortled with pleasure at the sight of the marvelous merchandise. An attractive young woman in a brief blue uniform came to his side.

"I'm your Shopper," she said. "May I help you?"

"You sure can," he grinned. "I need just about everything." He looked at his antiquated costume. "Clothes first. How much is that shirt over there?"

"Handsome, isn't it?" the young woman smiled. "And it's on sale, too. Only three hundred thousand dollars."

2911 A.D.

Lamb was no longer in the Dormantory. He was in a strangely dimensionless room, whose walls seemed to be composed of light. It was cooler than he liked it, and on the airy strip of foam, his thin naked body shivered.

"Chilly in here," he told the hairless man.

"The temp's at the ideal constant," he was told. "You'll get used to it. Your name is James Percy Lamb?"

"That's right. Are you a doctor?"

"No, Mr. Lamb." He laughed. "Not the sort you mean. You'll find that the medical profession no longer exists in the established form you knew. There is the Accident Division and the Prevention Corps, of course. But from your Dormantory application, it's obvious that you expect a pathologist."

"Then you know," he said nervously, licking his lips. "Can you help me? Have you found the cure?"

"Be at peace, my friend. Your affliction is a thing of the past. Generations ago, we totally eradicated all disease."

"Then I was right," Lamb whispered. "I knew I

was doing the right thing. I would have died in my own time . . .''

"You'll be fine now. We are presently in the process of formulating a dose of the antidote for your specified ailment; it will take a few hours, since there has been no need of it for many years. Just be comfortable and wait.''

He was left alone, shivering.

Eventually, from the doorway of light, two more hairless men entered. One carried a round-headed syringe.

"Here we are,'' he said jovially. ''The pressure syringe will put the antidote into your bloodstream in five seconds. We expect that antibodies will form within the next eight hours.''

The head of the syringe was placed against his bare, goose-fleshed arm. He felt nothing, but he was asleep by the time they left. In what may have been morning, he woke again, and found his body being explored with a glowing cylinder that seemed to penetrate his flesh.

"What is this?'' he asked.

"Diagnosis,'' the hairless man said. ''We are quite satisfied, Mr. Lamb. The disease is completely erased from your system.'' He flicked off the cylinder's glow.

Lamb began to cry.

"Thank God,'' he said, sniffling, his eyes running. Then he sneezed.

"What was that?'' the hairless man said, springing backwards.

"Nothing, just a sneeze. I got a little chilled last night; I guess I caught a cold.''

"A cold? A *cold?*'' the man said, in horror.

He dashed from the room, and returned with two others. Their smooth faces were agitated.

"What's the matter?'' Lamb said, and sneezed again. "I told you, it's only a cold.''

"Better call the Prevention Corps,'' one of them muttered.

The uniformed officers entered half an hour later. They wore visored hoods over their heads, and approached him warily. They pinned his arms, and gave him a swift, painless injection that ended his life, and the threat of infection, in five minutes.

3998 A.D.

"Awake?" the pale, reedy man with the wooly hair said. Zack stared at him wildly, saw the stunted tongue in his toothless mouth, and trembled in fear at what human mutation had produced.

Fortunately, the silver-robed woman beside him seemed a little more like his own kind. She had white, wooly hair, too, and her nose was smaller than a nose should be, but she more nearly resembled the people of Zack's generation.

"Don't be alarmed," she said gently. "My name is Ki, and I am Chief of Medical Sciences. Your Dormantory record sheet has been preserved. Your name is Bernard Zack—"

"No!" Zack said hoarsely. "Smith," he said. "Harold Smith."

The woman smiled. "There was an amendation on your application only two months after you entered stasis, Mr. Zack. A police organization called the F.I.B. I believe, made the correction, stating the true facts about your identity and past history. I'm sorry to say that you didn't cover your trail very well from Leavenworth to the Dormantory. Of course, there is no awakening a Frozen Sleeper, for fear of fatal shock, so the police merely left instructions for your apprehension in the future."

Zack slumped despondently.

"So I'm caught," he said gloomily. "Two thousand years later, and I'm caught."

"How long were you incarcerated, Mr. Zack?"

"Eleven years," he answered bitterly. "I *had* to crash out or go buggy. I can't stand the idea of going back to prison—"

The woman with the too-short nose laughed.

"But what makes you think you'll have to?"

Zack looked up hopefully .

"No, no," the woman said, touching his shoulder reassuringly. "The world has changed a great deal since your time, Mr. Zack. There is no longer crime or punishment. Police, judges, trials, prisons—we don't have them."

"You mean it? No more prisons?"

"Of course! So you see, Mr. Zack, you *have* escaped after all—into a better, more rational world. You are exonerated of all guilt, and are hereby declared to be a

Citizen of Earth, with all rights and privileges. Now," she said crisply, handing him a card, "your Citizen Number is 80-4589-TR4178. You will carry this identification card on your person at all times, and your number must be plainly displayed in digits not less than four inches high on the rear portion of your clothing. We have arranged for your Citizen's uniform, and you may leave when you wish. Good luck, Mr. Zack, and welcome to the future!"

He left the Dormantory an hour later. The streets were clotted with people. Each wore the Citizen's uniform, their numbers clearly displayed. He was wandering among them, baffled, and buffeted, when he heard the incredibly loud bell ringing in the heavens. "What is it? What is it?" he asked the others, who were hurrying along the streets in one direction. "What is it?" he cried, until a stranger took pity and answered.

"Lunch," the man said.

I don't believe that theory for a minute.

A Shape in Time

by Anthony Boucher

Temporal Agent L-3H is always delectable in any shape; that's why the bureau employs her on marriage-prevention assignments.

But this time, as she reported to my desk, she was also dejected. "I'm a failure, Chief," she said. "He ran away—from *me*. The first man in twenty-five centuries. . . ."

"Don't take it so seriously," I said. She was more than just another agent to me; I was the man who'd discovered her talents. "We may be able to figure out what went wrong and approach it on another time line."

"But I'm no good." Her body went scrawny and sagging. Sometimes I wonder how people expressed their emotions before mutation gave us somatic control.

"Now, there," I said, expanding my flesh to radiate confidence, "just tell me what happened. We know from the dial readings that the Machine got you to London in 1880—"

"To prevent the marriage of Edwin Sullivan to Angelina Gilbert," she grimaced. "Time knows why."

I sighed. I was always patient with her. "Because that marriage joined two sets of genes which, in the course of three generations, would produce—"

Suddenly she gave me one of her old grins, with the left eyebrow up. "I've never understood the time results of an assignment yet, and don't try to teach me now. Marriage prevention's fun enough on its own. And I thought it was going to be extra good this time. Edwin's beard was red and *this* long, and I haven't had a beard in five trips. But something went—The worst of it is, it went wrong when I was naked."

I was incredulous and said so.

"I don't think even you really understand this, Chief. Because you are a man"—her half smile complimented me by putting the italics of memory under *man*—"and men never have understood it. But the fact is that what men want naked, in any century, in any country, is what they're used to seeing clothed, if you follow me. Oh, there are always some women who have to pad themselves out or pull themselves in, but the really popular ones are built to fit their clothes. Look at what they used to call feelthy peectures; anytime, anyplace, the girls that are supposed to be exciting have the same silhouette naked as the fashion demands clothed. Improbable though it seems."

"L!" I gasped. She had suddenly changed so completely that there was hardly more than one clue that I was not looking at a boy.

"See?" she said. "That's the way I had to make myself when you sent me to the 1920s. And the assignment worked; this was what men wanted. And then, when you sent me to 1957. . . ."

I ducked out of the way as two monstrous mammae

shot out at me, "I hadn't quite realized—" I began to confess.

"Or the time I had that job in Sixteenth Century Germany."

"Now you look pregnant!"

"They all did. Maybe they were. Or when I was in Greece, all waist and hips. . . . But all of these *worked*. I prevented marriages and improved the genetic time flow. Only with Edwin. . . ."

She was back in her own delectable shape, and I was able to give her a look of encouraging affection.

"I'll skip the buildup," she said. "I managed to meet Edwin, and I gave him *this*. . . ." I nodded; how well I remembered *this* and its effects. "He began calling on me and taking me to theaters, and I knew it needed just one more step for him to forget all about that silly pink-and-white Angelina."

"Go on," I urged.

"He took the step, all right. He invited me to dinner in a private room at a discreet restaurant—all red plush and mirrors and a screen in front of the couch. And he ordered oysters and truffles and all that superstitious ritual. The beard was even better than I'd hoped: crisp and teasing ticklish and. . . ." She looked at me speculatively, and I regretted that we've bred out facial follicles beyond even somatic control. "When he started to undress me—and how much trouble that was in 1880!—he was delighted with *this*."

She had changed from the waist up, and I had to admit that *this* was possibly more accurate than *these*. They were as large as the startling 1957 version, but molded together as almost one solid pectoral mass.

"Then he took off my skirts and. . . ." L-3H was as near to tears as I had ever known her. "Then he . . . *ran*. Right out of the restaurant. I would've had to pay the check if I hadn't telekinned the Machine to bring me back to now. And I'll bet he ran right to that Angelina and made arrangements to start mixing genes and I've ruined everything for you."

I looked at her new form below the waist. It was indeed extraordinary and hardly to my taste, but it seemed correct. I checked the pictures again in the Sullivan dossier. Yes, absolutely.

I consoled and absolved her. "My dear L, you are—Time help me!—perfectly and exactly a desirable woman of 1880. The failure must be due to some slip on the part of the chronopsychist who researched Edwin. You're still a credit to the bureau, Agent L-3H!—and now let's celebrate. No, don't change back. Leave it that way. I'm curious as to the effects of—what was the word they used for it in 1880?—of a woman's *bustle.*"

What is truth?

Linkage

by Barry N. Malzberg

My name is Donald Alan Freem. I am eight years old. I can do anything with the power of my mind. I can make people say what I want them to say; make them perform actions which I have predetermined. I have always had this gift.

Because of my power, people fear me. They know that I can control them and take away their free will, and this terrifies them because they wish to hold onto their pitiful illusions of freedom. Resultantly, I have been institutionalized since the age of five with the full consent of my parents and at the expense of the society which traps me.

I am not concerned. This institution cannot control the power I have. My mind sweeps and soars, moves far beyond their pitiable effort to entrap me. I can do anything I want. It will always be this way.

"You must face reality, Donald," Dr. Nevins says to me at our weekly session. "If you do not face reality you will live this way all your life, and I do not want it to be this way. You are very young, you are highly intelligent, you are malleable. We believe in your ability to break this. But you must help us.''

I recline on the chair, look at the round, disturbed face of Dr. Nevins, then out the window to the grounds where some of my peer-group are playing mindlessly with a ball. "I made you say that," I point out. "You said that because I ordered you to say it.''

"Donald, you can no longer function this way. We must make progress—"

"I knew that you would say that. I sent through an order from my mind telling your mind to say 'We must make progress.' Everything that you do is because I make you do it.''

Dr. Nevins slams down a palm on his desk, stands awkwardly. This is the way in which our interviews usually terminate. "I don't want to lose patience," he says, "but you're not cooperating. You're not even trying—"

"I knew you would say that. I knew it before you did, and I made you hit your hand on the desk. You are afraid of me," I say, "but there's no need to be frightened. I would never do anything bad to you. I would never make people hurt themselves.''

Dr. Nevins exhales, puffs his cheeks, shakes his head. "We'll discuss this again next time, Donald," he says. "You're going to have to think about these things—"

"I wanted you to say that," I point out, and as Dr. Nevins stands, I send orders from my mind for him to open the door for me and send me out with a small flush of rage sending red sprinkles through his clear cheek. He does so. I leave. At the end of the corridor I disperse a message for him to slam the door, which he does with a metallic clang.

I did not develop the powers of my mind. They came to me full-blown. I cannot remember a time, even when I was very young, when I could not make people do what I wanted. When I was six years old I was visited by an alien with whom I had a long discussion. The alien told me that I was the first of a super-race, the first human being with my abilities, and that he had been sent back from the future to investigate and to guard my health. He promised me that my powers would breed true and that when I was an adult I would be able to reproduce with a female who would bear children like me. Tens of thousands of years in the future, my descendants would be the dominant race of the planet and would have, with their great powers, long since conquered the stars and invented time machines. One of these machines was being employed as a means for one of their scientists to come back and check on me, measure my progress and assure me that in the long run, all of my difficulties would work out. "You will be kept in the institution for a long time," the alien said, "but eventually, during adolescence, you will finally learn to lie and conceal your powers from them. You will say that you realize you control nothing and no one, and they will release you as 'cured.' Quietly then you will sow your seed and so on."

"I don't want to lie to them," I told the alien. "I'm proud of my powers and I know that it infuriates them when I brag but I see no reason why I have to treat these inferiors with any courtesy." Perhaps I did not put it quite that way. I was only six. In the last two years I have learned to read well and have been able to express myself in a far more sophisticated fashion. Probably, I merely told the alien that I would do exactly what I wanted and he and no one else could stop me. At six I was very grandiose, but I have calmed down somewhat since then. I say and feel the same things but have learned to take a little of the edge off them.

"I will be back occasionally to check on your progress," the alien told me, "but essentially you have to live your own life." I have lived my own life. The alien has returned only once so far for a very brief discussion. I accept the fact that I am on my own.

Dr. Nevins loses his temper and says something about giving me more "injections" and "needles" and "drugs" if I do not cooperate with him, and for the first time he truly angers me. I tell him about the alien and the pact he made with me about my future. It takes me a long time, and when I am finished, Dr. Nevins shakes his head with a pleased expression and says finally, "I'm very pleased, Donald. At last you're opening up to me."

"I made you say that."

"I'm beginning to see the fantasies which are at the

root of your condition. Now we can begin to work. You've enabled us to make a start. I'm grateful.''

"I *ordered* you to say *grateful*. Anything I tell you to say you will say.''

"Yes,'' Dr. Nevins says, patting me, and leading me to the door, "this is very helpful, Donald,'' and he ends our interview so rapidly that I realize I have not had a chance to make it finish the way I ordered. This is the first time it has ever happened, and I am somewhat disconcerted. I remind myself that even Dr. Nevins has a kind of cunning and must be watched.

The alien comes to see me that night and tells me that he is extremely disturbed. I can sense his agitation. "You shouldn't have told them about me,'' he says. "That was not very smart, Donald. You could upset all of our calculations, the whole projected future. Now they will concentrate on exactly those elements which are most central.''

"I don't care,'' I say. "Besides, I made you say that.''

"No, Donald; this is very serious business. This was supposed to be our secret. I am very upset.''

"I wanted you to be upset. I did something to your mind to make you upset.''

"They will focus on specifics, Donald, and may even convince you that this is a fantasy. You may upset the whole track of time.''

"I want to upset the track of time,'' I say, "the track of time is anything I want; I think that I'll get rid of you,'' and I do something to him with my consciousness and with a roar the alien vanishes; was never there in the first place, as a matter of fact; I never knew of any aliens, and quite weakly it occurs to me that all these years Dr. Nevins has only been trying to help me and I owe him nothing less than my assistance: the two of us, perhaps, can work this out together, and I am beginning to find it very boring to have things turn out exactly the way I make them. The other way would be more exciting. I will let them do what they want for a while.

Crime and **punishment**

Murder in the Nth Degree

by R. A. Montana

"Hear ye, hear ye, the Court of the Galactic Commonwealth is now in session. The Right Honorable Judge Zwing presiding. All rise!"

"Is the Commonwealth ready to present its case?"

"Prosecution ready, Your Honor."

"Is the defendant represented by counsel?"

"Ah . . . Your Honor, the defendant has not yet selected a defense attorney."

"Does he understand his rights under Interstellar Law?"

"A . . . ah, minor problem, Your Honor. In the rush of transporting the defendant here some details were overlooked. . . ."

"Would the prosecutor please approach the bench. . . . What the death is going on here, Krill? No defense attorney? The next thing you're going to tell me is the poor fool hasn't been advised of his rights!"

"Well, ah, you see, with the press of cases and the crowded calendar, we neglected to have someone from the Public Defender's office take the cultural tapes on the accused's planet of origin. . . . I'm afraid he doesn't understand a word that's being said and he seems to be a little unsettled by his present surroundings."

"Well, settle him, dammit! And get one of those young crusaders from the PDO to ingest his tapes so we can get on with the trial!"

"Court will call a short recess. All rise!"

* * *

"I believe the appropriate greeting would be, how do you do, my name is Font. I am an attorney appointed by the court to act in your defense. Do you understand me?"

"Does it matter? I mean, does one have to understand a nightmare to be an unwilling participant?"

"I assure you, my friend, you are very much awake and the sooner we decide on your defense the happier the Judge will be."

"Judge? Defense? I don't know what the hell you're talking about! And just for the record, what in the world is this place supposed to be?"

"The Judge is the being you saw up on the dais earlier. He's the one that's going to decide your case. The defense is what you and I are here to agree on to try to save your, ah, skin. As to your third question, you are not 'in the world' as you put it. You are in an anteroom of the Interstellar Court of Justice, Galactic Commonwealth . . . somewhere around one hundred and fifty light years from your home planet, Earth."

"You actually expect me to believe that?"

"You better believe it, you're betting your life on it."

"What is it exactly I'm supposed to be on trial for?"

"Charge: High crimes against life; Specification: Genocide—Homicide—Infanticide—Insecticide—Cruelty to animals—Crimes against nature—Willful neglect—Malice—Malfeasance—Pornography—Pollution—Shall I go on?"

"This is ridiculous. I've never so much as kicked a dog let alone committed murder! You've got the wrong man!"

"You are from the planet Earth?"

"Yes but—"

"Then you are the right party. You are being tried as a representative of your planet on eight charges and nine hundred and eighty-six specifications. We have but a short time to discuss your plea."

"Representative? I'm an insurance agent from Cleveland, Ohio! I got a wife and three kids and about the worst thing I've ever done was voting Republican in the last election. How can I be representative?"

"You're alive, you are from the planet under indictment, and you have freedom of thought. You are therefore legally representative under the statutes that prevail in this case."

"I told Silva not to put so much pepperoni on that pizza. That's the last time I'll eat so much before going to bed."

"Again, I assure you, you are not dreaming. This is a serious matter and we must discuss a plea. The fate of your world depends on the outcome of this action."

"You mean you're actually telling me that I'm . . . me . . . I'm on trial for the entire population of Earth?"

"Right."

"Come on—that's the oldest routine in the book—one man gets whisked away to the Andromeda Galaxy to speak for all humanity and this Mister Joe Average saves his planet by honesty and fancy footwork. I don't believe it!"

"Believe it."

"And you're going to get me off?"

"I wouldn't put too much stock in that. The last six cases of this nature were found guilty and sentence was carried out. I will say this, though, there may be one chance in a thousand I can help you get out of this with your hide intact."

"You know something, Mr. . . . ah . . . Font—you're nuts—and I'm just as crazy to be sitting here talking to an overgrown spider spouting legal definitions and telling me what I should do to save Earth."

"Ah ha—now we're getting somewhere. That happens to be exactly what I want to talk to you about."

"What?"

"Your plea of course. The only way we might succeed in getting you off . . . guilty, and guilty by reason of insanity!"

"I'm innocent! I will not plead insanity. This is unlawful seizure—kidnapping—I'm a United States citizen and I demand my rights!"

"Now you listen to me, buster, you got your ass in a wringer and the only way out is to take my advice. Another outburst like that and I'll waive a plea in open court and exercise the right of counsel in the case of a corporation, namely Earth, and enter the plea myself. And that, my tall skinny humanoid, would be guilty as charged.

"Now, I've already talked to the prosecutor—he's an old bird that won't bend—so plea bargaining is out. We can't cop a plea for a lesser offense so we got to go with insanity. With the mountain of evidence against you I can't see how you or your planet could be competent to stand trial anyway—and I think I can convince the court of that, with your help. There's no question of burden of proof here—the actions of your planet are widely known and the press really have a field day whenever you pull something new. You should have seen what they did with—never mind—look, this way you save yourself and your world. If we can convince the court you're crazy they'll send in medical teams and set up curing centers. In a couple of years we'll process the entire population, cure the ones that are curable, excise those who are not, and generally clean up all the messes you've made in the past thousand years. It's the only way you can go."

"Cure?"

"Yeah, you know, lop off the more aggressive tendencies of the race, divert what's left into productive channels, remold the overall methods of thinking; hell, I'm no medic but we've got the best and they know their job."

"Excise?"

"Now be reasonable. You know that there are always a percentage of incurables in any group. These will be removed humanely. Painlessly. Then when it's all over your world can take its rightful place in the scheme of things. Mesh with the rest of sentient life. Do you understand what I'm telling you?"

"Clean up all the messes, you said."

"Right. End pollution, corruption, disease—the whole bit. Just enter a plea of insanity and we got maybe a glimmer of a chance of pulling it off."

"Why don't you just let us alone so we can work out our problems ourselves?"

"I'm just not getting through to you, am I? O.K., that's it. What's it going to be?"

"Not guilty."

"It's your funeral."

"The defendant will stand and face the court. This court having found the defendant guilty of all charges and guilty of all specifications will now pass sentence. Has the defendant anything to say before sentence is passed?

No? So be it. It is in the judgment of this court that never before has a defendant stood before it and been found guilty of so heinous and numerous of offenses that, in good conscience, there is only one sentence this court can levy against the representative from the planet Earth and his co-conspirators. That sentence, being ultimate, can in no way surpass the degree of crimes and horrors perpetrated by the defendant. That sentence is death.''

"Sorry, old buddy, but you can't say I didn't tell you so.''

"Now what? How do you carry out the death penalty here? Do I get drawn and quartered, or do you just remove my brain with dull instruments and put it on public display?''

"Ha! That's rich . . . drawn and quartered . . . oh, beautiful . . . excuse me, I know it's no laughing matter but I couldn't help myself!''

"Well, how do you go about killing me and billions of other members of my race?''

"Killing? . . . Oh my, killing. . . . I'm sorry, it's just so humorous. We don't kill anybody. I thought you knew . . . must've forgotten to explain that to you. No matter, we don't kill anybody. We just send you back to the exact time and place from where you were removed. Then we leave you alone . . . you'll do the rest!''

That's why, be it ever so humble . . .

Useful Phrases for the Tourist

by Joanna Russ

THE LOCRINE: peninsula and surrounding regions. High Lokrinnen.
X 437894 = II

Reasonably Earthlike (see companion audio tapes and
    transliterations)
For physiology, ecology, religion and customs, Wu and
    Fabricant, Prague, 2355, Vol. 2 *The Locrine, Useful
    Knowledge for the Tourist,* q.v.

AT THE HOTEL:
That is my companion. It is not intended as a tip.
I will call the manager.
This cannot be my room because I cannot breathe am-
    monia.
I will be most comfortable between temperatures of 290
    and 303 degrees Kelvin.
Waitress, this meal is still alive.

AT THE PARTY:
Is that you?
Is that all of you? How much (many) of you is (are)
    there?
I am happy to meet your clone.
Interstellar amity demands that we make some physical
    display at this point, but I beg to be excused.
Are you toxic?
Are you edible? I am not edible.
We humans do not regenerate.
My companion is not edible.
That is my ear.
I am toxic.
Is that how you copulate?
Is this intended to be erotic?
Thank you very much.
Please explain.
Do you turn colors?
Are you pregnant?
I shall leave the room.
Can't we just be friends?
Take me to the Earth Consulate immediately.
Although I am very flattered by your kind offer, I cannot
    accompany you to the mating pits, as I am viviparous.

IN THE HOSPITAL:
No!
My eating orifice is not at that end of my body.

I would rather do it myself.

Please do not let the atmosphere in (out) as I will be most uncomfortable.

I do not eat lead.

Placing the thermometer there will yield little or no useful information.

SIGHTSEEING:

You are not my guide. My guide was bipedal.

We Earth people do not do that.

Oh, what a jolly fine natatorium (mating perch, arranged spectacle, involuntary phenomenon)!

At what hour does the lovelorn princess fling herself into the flaming volcano? May we participate?

That is not demonstrable.

That is hardly likely.

That is ridiculous.

I have seen much better examples of that.

Please direct me to the nearest sentient mammal.

Take me to the Earth Consulate without delay.

AT THE THEATRE:

Is that amusing?

I am sorry; I did not mean to be offensive.

I did not intend to sit on you. I did not realize that you were in this seat.

Could you deform yourself a little lower?

My eyes are sensitive only to light of the wavelengths 3000-7000 A.

Am I imagining this?

Am I supposed to imagine this?

Should I be perturbed by the water on the floor?

Where is the exit?

Help!

This is great art.

My religious convictions prevent me from joining in the performance.

I do not feel well.

I feel very sick.

I do not eat living food.

Is this supposed to be erotic?

May I take this home with me?

Is this part of the performance?

Stop touching me.
Sir or madam, that is mine. (extrinsic)
Sir or madam, that is mine. (intrinsic)
I wish to visit the waste-reclamation units.
Have you finished?
May I begin?
You are in my way.
Under no circumstances.
If you do not stop that, I will call the attendant. That is
    forbidden by my religion.
Sir or madam, this is a private unit.
Sir and madam, this is a private unit.

COMPLIMENTS:
You are more than before.
Your hair is false.
If you uncover your feet, I will faint.
There is no room.
You will undoubtedly be here tomorrow.

INSULTS:
You are just the same.
There are more of you than previously.
Your fingers are showing.
How clean you are!
You are clean, but animated.

GENERAL:
Take me to the Earth Consulate.
Direct me to the Earth Consulate.
The Earth Consulate will hear of this.
This is no way to treat a visitor.
Please direct me to my hotel.
At what time does the moon rise? Is there a moon?
Is it a full moon? Take me to the Earth Consulate im-
    mediately.
May I have the second volume of Wu and Fabricant, en-
    titled *Physiology, Ecology, Religion and Customs of
    the Locrine?* Price is no object.
Something has just gone amiss with my vehicle.
I am dying.

Put them all together, they spell mother.

The Burning

by Theodore R. Cogswell

Most of them were up in Central Park getting the boxes
ready but Hank and I stayed behind. We went over on
27th to bust some windows but we couldn't because all
the windows were already busted. So we went into the
Acme Elite Bar and Grill, and scummaged around to
see if there was anything that had maybe been overlooked. Hank finally found a bottle back in the corner
buried under a heap of ceiling plaster and busted stuff
that wasn't worth lugging off for the fires, but it turned
out to be one of them No Deposit, No Return plastic
things that didn't make no proper noise at all when he
smanged it against the wall.

We fooled around a while more but then I took a look
out into the street. When I saw how short the shadows
had got, I started getting the jumps. The burning always
starts at high noon and there wasn't much time left.

"We'd better be getting on up," I said. "Goofing off
on the collecting is one thing, but if the Mother notices
we're not there come light-up time, there's going to be
hell to pay."

Hank just laughed. "She'll be too twitched up by now
to notice anything. This is *her* day. Things are too big to
take time out to count the number of drabs in the back
row of the clapping section."

I still felt jumpy. Not that I wanted to go, mind you,
in spite of what the Mother was always saying about it
developing character. Mothers are always talking about
Character and The Flag and The Sanctity of American
Womanhood and stuff like that, but I notice it's always

the little guys who end up getting burnt during Mother's Day ceremonies. And I'm a little guy.

Big Harry sinned with the Mother almost every night when he first got born into the Family but somehow it never got put down in the Book. Otto got put down, though, just like I told Hank he would, and when the Patrol came around they didn't even check his name page, they just went up to his room and got him. But not before me and Hank did considerable sweating because by then we knew it was going to be one of us three. All that morning I don't think five minutes went by without my giving my good luck pin at least one good rub just on the odd chance that it might do some good.

"Look, Hank," I said. "We don't go and the Mother happens to notice it, we're in for it. But good."

"Yeah," he said, "but what if Otto craps out before light-up time? That bum ticker of his is liable to go plonk just from waiting . . . and the Mother likes live meat."

"Better one than two," I said, and grabbed him by the arm and pulled him to his feet. "Come on, let's ramble. The Patrol happens to catch us this far south, we've had it!"

Hank didn't take much pushing. He gets stubborn only when he thinks it's good and safe, and as soon as I said "Patrol" he right away decided that maybe he wasn't. He didn't have much and what he did have he didn't have much chance to use, but like the fellow says, "Something is better than nothing." And nothing's what you got when the Patrol gets through with you.

We girder-walked as far as 58th. I slipped twice but we had a pretty good safety rope linking us and Hank was able to haul me back both times. Working along twisted beams five stories up is a scary business but at least you don't have to worry about out-walkers from other families taking pot shots at you. Ammo's too scarce to waste on drabs and anyway you fall that far and there ain't much left worth taking home.

Past 58th things are too messed up to get through top side so we had to take to the storm sewers. Hank and I had a long argument as to who was to go first and then we flipped and I lost. I started singing the truce song as loud as I could with Hank hitting the refrain on the base parts. Hank's got perfect pitch but you get a real rogue

mother out on the prowl and she can be tone deaf as hell,
especially if she's got big ideas about snatching enough
strays to build up a family of her own. Time was when
they only went after the big ones and if a drab was in
good voice he could wander all the way up to the 90's on
his own if he was so minded, but no more. Since the
Council busted up, anything that's still breathing is fair
game—except for Mother's Helpers, that is, and they
never did count anyway.

We came out at 74th, both a bit winded from the singing, and having to run the last two blocks because there
was a sort of commotion in the cross conduit at 72nd that
we didn't stick around to find out what it was. We went
into the Park slantwise, circling around through the trees
so we could slide in from the back. With everybody all
involved in watching Otto and all it wasn't likely that
they'd notice we were coming in late.

Only they weren't watching Otto. They were watching
the Mother. Otto was hanging from the stake in a limp
way that let you know he was more than just out. His
ticker had plonked just like Hank was afraid it would and
Mother's Day just isn't Mother's Day without a live one.
Even Big Harry looked worried and had slid around behind some of the other kids, only it didn't do him much
good because even hunching he stood up a good six
inches higher than the rest. There was going to be a replacement for Otto, and fast, and the Mother was just as
likely as not to grab the first one she set eye on, even a
prime like Big Harry.

Only she didn't.

She went over and spit in Otto's face for not loving her
enough and then yelled at us to fall into family formation. There was a certain amount of shoving because everybody was trying to get into the back row but she broke
that up in a hurry. Hank and I managed to get in at the
far end of the last line, hoping that somebody else might
strike her fancy before she got to us. Only we knew better. I looked at Hank and Hank looked at me and even
if we were pals and all that each of us was thinking the
same thing. Only just hoping it would be him instead of
me wasn't enough. I had to do something . . . and fast!

"There's more in the Book on you than there is on

me," I says to Hank out of the side of my mouth. "If I was you I'd make a bolt."

"Mother wouldn't like it," he whispered back. "If I was to spoil her celebration she wouldn't love me anymore."

I could see his point. Now that everything has sort of gone to pot, a Mother's love is the only thing a boy can really count on, and the least we can do is try to make her happy on her day. But I could see my point too—namely that it was either Hank or me.

"Once across the park you'd be safe," I said. "The Patrol don't usually operate that far east and if you keep a sharp eye out for rogues you'll be OK." I could see he liked the idea but he was still worrying about the Mother. She was in the last row now and moving toward us steady like. Hank was really twitching and his face was kind of gray underneath the dirt.

"I can't," he said. "My legs won't work."

I sneaked a quick look at the Mother. She'd stopped and was looking down at us kind of thoughtful like. And I had a feeling she was looking more at me than she was at Hank.

"She's got her eye on you, boy," I said. "If you don't leg it now you're in for a slow burn. Them boxes is still wet from last night's rain."

We were supposed to be at attention but without knowing it I'd pulled my good-luck pin out of my pocket and was rubbing it with my thumb the way I got a habit of when I'm nervous. It's a little gold-like pin made in the shape of a funny kind of leaf. There was some writing on it too but I didn't find out what the words was until later.

"It's your funeral, kid," I said.

Just then the Mother let out a yell.

"You! You down at the end!"

She was pointing at me but I swung around to Hank.

"Front and center, kid," I said. "Mama wants you."

He let out a funny little squawk and then went into a sort of bent over half squat like he'd just been kicked in the gut. I let out a yell and grabbed at him, giving him a spin with my right hand so that he ended up pointing toward the trees. Then I came up with my left and jabbed him in the backside with my good-luck pin.

He took off like a prime rogue in mating season and was across the grass and into the trees before anybody rightly knew what was up. Then the Mother started yelling orders and a bunch of primes took off after him. I ran up to her and flopped down and started bawling, "Don't be mad at me, I tried to stop him!" over and over until she belted me a couple.

"He said you didn't have no right!" I said.

That shook her like I hoped it would and got her thinking about him instead of me.

"He *what?*" she said, as if her ears weren't working right. "He said *what?*"

I made my voice all trembly.

"He said you didn't have no right to burn kids when they hadn't done nothing really bad." I started crying again but the Mother didn't pay me no mind. She just walked away.

The Patrol brought Hank in about an hour later. They'd worked him over to the point where he wasn't up to doing much in the way of complaining.

Afterward we sat around the fire and had a family sing, finishing up as usual with "Silver Threads Among the Gold". The Mother got all teary-eyed and mellow so I took a chance and went up and asked her what the words on my good-luck pin was. She didn't belt me or nothing. She just gave me a sort of lazy grin and said, *"Be Prepared."*

The pen is mightier than the sword.

One Small Step

by Eric Vinicoff and Marcia Martin

Dear Donna,

It doesn't look like I'll get home this week, or next, or even the one after that. I miss you, dammit. This business of being a hero and saving the world is great ego-boo, but I'd rather be in your arms (I would've said bed but I think the CIA is reading my mail). The military men and politicos won't let me leave town, or phone, so we'll have to make do with letters for awhile.

The papers and TV got it all wrong, naturally. I'm no genius or telepath. I just lucked out. Let me tell you how it *really* happened.

I was walking in Central Park while the editorial demigod at 350 Madison Avenue decided whether to buy my boy-meets-spacegirl epic. (Thanks to my present status, the answer is now *yes!*) Also, I admit, I was thinking about you.

The park thronged with a typical selection of New Yorkers: mothers-cum-babies, kids, hustlers, connections, bums, retired folk, freaks, and the rest. It was near noon, and we were all soaking in the sun vibes when the saucer landed.

It came down unannounced over Sheep Meadow, just about the only open space in the park big enough for it. By unannounced I mean no air raid sirens, no cop warnings, no nothing. Radar hadn't picked it up. Planes hadn't spotted it. It was just there, a fat silver frisbee the size of a Cinerama dome, hovering over the park. It dropped like a landing UFO and touched ground not twenty yards in front of me.

A Force Three crowd gathered quickly. (Force One crowds collect for minor spectacles like muggings. Something more juicy—like some poor slob teetering on the ledge of the Beekman Building—rates a Force Two crowd. Force Four is reserved for such cosmic attractions as an armed and ticking H-bomb.)

A circular opening appeared in the side of the saucer. I half-expected Michael Rennie to emerge, but the three gentlemen who stepped out resembled economy-size Gila monsters with delusions of humanhood.

Two of them carried a cylindrical device the size and shape of a garbage can. It was mounted like a telescope on a unipod swivel base. They set it at the foot of the debarking ramp, where its dark maw glared at a segment of the crowd.

By then, cops were arriving and forming a cordon around the saucer. They began to push the crowd back. When one of New York's Finest put the arm on me I flashed my UCLA student body card, mumbled "press pass," and stayed where I was.

Helicopters and jeeps arrived simultaneously, spitting out soldiers who shoved the cops back into a secondary ring and took over the inner circle themselves. I maneuvered next to the commanding general (my press pass trick again), which was how I was able to save the world.

The aliens were straight out of a thirties' issue of *Astounding Stories;* nine feet from spiked tales to horn-tipped snouts, six thin double-kneed legs, tentacled arms ending in seven subtentacles, purple scales and physiognomies mere language can't do justice to. Anyway, you'll soon be seeing plenty of pictures of them—a media blitz as soon as security lifts.

They swung the cylinder around the face of the crowd, bird-chirping eagerly among themselves.

The general didn't like the sight or sound of that. Two hundred gun barrels, ranging from M-16s to four tank cannons, tracked on the trio. I decided I'd seen enough. But I couldn't get out—the humanity was too thick behind me.

Another alien came down the ramp, this one wearing a red bolt sticking out of his forehead. The leader, I guessed. Can't start an interstellar war without the boss. He held a silver baton in his left tentacle. Stepping

forward to survey the crowd, he turned and chirped
something to his subordinates. Then he struck a regal
pose while the cylinder began swinging toward the tanks.

The general opened his mouth, and I knew he was
going to give the order to open fire. That's when I had
my brainstorm.

I gagged him with my hand and shouted at him. He
had no choice but to listen. By the time the MPs pried
me loose, I'd managed to half-convince him. He ordered
his men to stand by.

I was right. The cylinder swung *past* the tanks and
came to rest aiming at the alien leader. He touched a
button on his baton, and it telescoped into a pole ten feet
tall. On top sat a yellow inflated basketball shape with a
weird color scheme.

Assured that the cylinder was centered on him, he stuck
the pole into the soil of Central Park and began his
speech.

So now the government and the aliens are negotiating
trade treaties etc. If I hadn't interfered, things would have
been a bit different.

I'll be home as soon as I can get away. Tell the gang
your lover had an honor even bigger than being a hero.
He got to be in the aliens' historic holovision broadcast
back to their world of their Earth landing.

Blood will tell.

Dead End

by Mack Reynolds

You'll never believe this but Emil Carraway, Ph.D.,
M.D., even D.D., wanted to be bitten by a vampire.

What Carraway desired above all was to achieve immortality. He'd wanted it since early teenhood and he'd

been working on it ever since. That was the reason for the degrees. Ph.D., M.D., even D.D.—and, believe me, that last couldn't have been hung on a less appropriate scholar—had all been attained in his search for everlasting life.

Before his freshman year was out he had read all the standard works on longevity. At that point he was being very scientific about the whole thing. He investigated the yogurt-eating centenarians in Georgia and Armenia but decided they didn't have the answer. To longevity, maybe, but not immortality and Carraway wasn't interested in living to be a mere hundred and fifty.

He decided science wasn't the answer and began to extend his studies into the occult, into mythology, metaphysics and theology, and it was along in there he picked up the D.D. degree.

It took him no time at all to run into the vampire-wampyr-nosferatu-um-dead legends and to realize that here, at least in myth, was immortality.

It had been a thousand years since a serious, thorough student of Carraway's caliber had delved into the vampire myth. And the further he delved, and it took decades, the more convinced he became that it was more than myth.

When the iron curtain lifted to the point he could visit the libraries of Budapest, Belgrade and Bucharest, he finally found that for which he was searching.

He was seventy years of age when at last, in the ruins of an ancient Croatian castle in Transylvania, Emil Carraway stood above a crumbling coffin and looked down upon the last vampire in the world.

"What do you want?" it snarled. Its face was gray and thin, its body emaciated.

"I want immortality. I want you to bite me. To make me in turn a vampire. I want to be un-dead."

The vampire growled, "You've come to the wrong place."

"But you're a vampire! Aren't you thirsty for blood?"

"Parched!" the vampire snarled.

"But then. . . ?" Carraway didn't get it.

The vampire screamed, "I'm allergic to all but Rh-Negative, the rarest blood type of all! You're type 'O'. If I bit you I'd break out in a million hives!"

The peak of creation—

Paths

by Edward Bryant

The reefs and domes of City South gleamed beneath the stars. It was late night; little traffic disturbed the waterways. On the top level of the *Harbinger-Communicator's* dome, a single office was occupied. Soft ultraviolet spilled out through the wall apertures.

"Just who the hell are you, really?" Morisel sank back in the warm fluid. His visitor stood and lumbered to the edge of the newsman's meditation pool.

"Think of me as a distant relative." The words grated across the edges of his serrated beak. "A good many generations removed."

"Look," said Morisel. "I don't want to seem cynical. You may be my ten-times-removed egg-father or something, but right now it's awfully hard not to believe you're just a run-of-the-mill aberrant. I mean, here you crawl into my office close to midnight, spread yourself down, and then calmly announce you're a traveler from the future. That takes either incredible gall, or. . . ."

"I spoke truth," said Morisel's visitor. He towered over the reclining newsman. The writhing cilia around his beak settled in no specific emotion; sincerity flashed briefly, before collapsing back to chaos.

"Don't try to intimidate me," Morisel snapped. The self-proclaimed time traveler moved back. The newsman tried to assume conciliatory signals. There might be a feature-story here, he speculated. *What the hell, the silly season may as well start early.*

Some sort of alien being from another planet, I might accept," said Morisel. "If he had suitable proof. It's unlikely, but scientifically possible. Now time travel? No. That's out.''

"Your skepticism is laudable," replied the man. He settled himself on his lower coil of tentacles. "I suppose logic is one of the attributes that has made you so successful in your profession. But don't let it trap you in blind dogmatism.''

"All right," said Morisel. "Well, I'm doing my best to be understanding." He played abstractedly with a stylus. "Then supposing you *are* from the future, what are you doing back here?''

The visitor's voice reverberated hollowly. "I have returned many millenia to warn you. I realize that sounds rather melodramatic, but it is essentially the substance of my mission.''

"Oh?" Morisel glanced at his chronometer and suppressed an expression of annoyance. "Warn me of what?" He roughly sketched a cartilaginous skull on the gell pad beside his electric scriptor.

The traveler folded a row of extensipods, the limbs angling stiffly. "I did not come back to warn specifically you. Rather I am, or at least I have been, trying to alert your entire world.''

"What do you mean, 'have been trying'?" Morisel asked. "You tried to contact others?''

"Thus far, only one." The man's cilia settled grimly. "A fellow in the communications field, one of your acquaintances, I believe. His name was Connot.''

"Des Connot?" Morisel, startled, looked up. "The office said he left the *Sentinel* for extended recreation. I wondered. . . .''

"Connot is confined.''

"Des?''

"His price for believing my story.''

Slightly shaken, the newsman erased the skull on his gell pad and drew a pattern of interlocking circles. "All right, just because Connot turned aberrant doesn't mean anything. I can't believe a good reporter like Des would come apart just because of a ghost story or something.''
He paused, expecting his words to draw the man across the pool into a response. The bait failed; the man only stared silently back at Morisel.

"Go ahead and tell it," Morisel said finally. "Whatever you've got."

"You still do not believe me," said the traveler. "Not yet, anyway, but you will." He uncrossed his extensipods and slid closer to the pool.

"Suppose, Brother Morisel," he began. "Suppose that time is analogous to a current. I imagine you are at least vaguely familiar with the concept?"

"More or less. Sunday supplement stuff."

"Indeed. But the image of time as a river is essentially accurate. It is a flow which contains certain points that are crucial to the past and future. These dates are like forks in a current; they are points when history may have alternative destinies. Sometimes these circumstances can be manipulated."

Morisel listened attentively. He drew another skull on the gell pad.

"It is because of a critical fork approaching in your time-stream that I was chosen by my colleagues to travel here," the man continued. His voice rasped harshly. "This, you see, is an experiment—a trial born of desperation. The approaching split in the time-stream is critical. My mission is to influence its direction, to utilize any means so that your people follow one certain branch of the divergence."

"It sounds ambitious," said Morisel.

"Perhaps it is impossible. My colleagues and I have never before tried such an experiment. Interference, with the attendant paradoxes, could prove dangerous for all the alternate futures."

"So why this one now?" asked Morisel. His notepad displayed the silhouette of a sandclock superimposed on the skull.

"Desperation. This approaching point of divergence is utterly crucial to mankind's future. It is imperative that my efforts ensure the choice of a certain path—and deny existence to the other possibility. This is my mission—to make sure that your people take the better of two possible courses."

Morisel realized he was beginning to lose a measure of his skepticism. The stranger's voice, for all its stilted syntax, struck a premonitory chord. The newsman's tentacles began to widen the lines of the skull.

"Let me describe a possible future awaiting you, Brother Morisel. One of the problems receiving much popular attention in this time is the pollution of our natural environment; correct?"

Morisel registered agreement. "Ecology."

"That desperately vital balance between sentient being and this planet is about to break down. You have hesitated too long. The rape of your world should have been interrupted long before."

Morisel started to speak, but his visitor waved an extensipod. "Please hear me out. Air and water, all are irreparably poisoned. Unnamed terrors are about to ride the planet. The tiny diatoms will die first. Then the smaller beings, the plants, finally yourselves. There will be oases of a fashion, for a while. Then the scramble for life will pit bands of survivors against each other. Thermonuclear weapons, poisons, bacteriological bombs will be used. It will be madness.

"There will be nearly no life left on a virtually sterile world. If ever a similar civilization rises, it will not be for hundreds of millions of years. That is how far ahead our probability scanners can operate. The world will remain a bleak cinder."

Morisel was shaken by the conviction in his visitor's voice. The portrait of civilization's self-destruction had been suitably graphic. "Consider," he said, "if you're from the future, then you must be from the other branch of our time-stream where life evidently wasn't wiped out. Is that our other choice—your own future? Is that our chance to avoid the world's destruction?"

The man opened his beak, then paused. A silver glow began to surround his body and the amorphous lines of his form wavered.

"I am sorry, Brother Morisel." The words seemed to come from a great distance. "I fear my power resources are more greatly depleted than I realized; I can no longer maintain the mask." The nimbus intensified and deepened to a mirror-bright haze obscuring the stranger from Morisel's fascinated gaze.

Then the luminous mist vanished and Morisel looked upon his visitor's actual face.

"Do you really want to know what the other path is?" asked the being. "The tale I have already told you is the one that I am working with all dedication to bring into reality; your final, total suicide is the optimistic view. Are you sure you want to hear the other alternative, the pessimistic choice?''

Morisel stared at the matted hair, the clumsy anthropoid form reared erect on its hind limbs. He didn't answer. He began to scream.

"Oh, there's no one with endurance / Like the man who sells—"

Woman's Work

by Garen Drussaï

Sheila sat instantly up in bed, her eyes wide awake and startled. The alarm on her wrist was giving off small electric shocks. *Someone was coming up the walk!* She turned it off quickly and looked at the clock.

Only ten minutes after four. It was still dark outside. She sighed wearily as she thought of the difficult task that lay before her in these next few minutes.

Hal's voice whispered tensely from beside her. "Is it time yet?''

"Yes,'' she answered. "They seem to come earlier each day.'' She slipped out of bed and hurriedly put on a robe. Then she turned on a small light and carefully picked up a number of gadgets from her night table, putting them into the outsize pockets of her robe.

Hall twisted anxiously in the bed as he watched her preparations. "Are you sure you've got enough this time?'' he finally asked. "We just can't go on this way. We've got to lick them!''

Sheila bent over Hal tenderly and kissed him. "Don't worry, darling. This is my job. I'll do my best.'' She straightened up, grimly, as the door bell rang.

As she opened the front door the shocking brightness of sunshine flooded her face. She blinked rapidly to accustom her eyes to the brilliance of it. Then, in a moment, she saw him. He was quite young and nice-looking. What a shame, she thought bitterly, that they had to be enemies.

He was doing calisthenics on the front lawn, his jumping belt taking him yards up at a time. She watched him almost hypnotically, her head going up and down, up and down, up—frantically she sought a button concealed on the door jamb and pressed it. Instantly the gravity control started working and the young man, his jumping belt now useless, took it off and came toward her.

"Good—*good*—GOOD morning!" He beamed at her. "Isn't this a wonderful day? Look at all this lovely sunshine." He extended his arms in a sweeping gesture. "And all for you—you lucky lady!"

A slight smile turned up the corners of Sheila's mouth. She'd show him, she thought. She'd prick his Sunshine Bubble right now. She pressed another button on the door—and immediately the sun was blotted out and predawn night surrounded them.

"Aha!" The young man scarcely seemed surprised. "You have your little jokes. Well, now that you've had some fun outwitting me, suppose you let me give you a little gift. Just as a friendly token from my company to you."

He held a small box out to her as she twisted a dial set into the door handle. Suddenly a heavy downpour descended all around the front door. Sheila couldn't help herself. She burst into laughter at his dismay. Then before she realized it, he was inside the door . . . and she couldn't *stop* laughing. He had squirted some laugh powder at her.

That's when the young man started his sales pitch. She didn't know what he was selling. Even if she signed for it, she still wouldn't know until it was delivered. Not when she was under the influence of a laugh drug. Then she thought of Hal lying there in the bedroom—trusting her to do her best. With superhuman effort she took a pill from her pocket and gulped it down between laughs. In a few moments the laughs subsided, and tears started streaming down her face.

The salesman was game. Sheila had to admit that. He kept talking, and his head started to shake affirmatively and positively—up and down, up and down. But Sheila, still crying, wasn't going to be taken in again by that hypnotic procedure. She slipped one of the gadgets on the back of her neck and set it to vibrating, and then soon she was shaking her head too—but negatively, from side to side.

She thought of her warm, comfortable bed and wished she was back in it. Suddenly she was—or thought she was, anyway. He was supporting her on a pneumatic float! Making her forget what she must do. Lulling her into a state of acceptance . . . This would never do. Hal wouldn't forgive her if she let him down. They just couldn't afford to buy one more thing.

She rushed over to the wall and, wiping the tears from her eyes so she could see, activated the Simulator. Then, instead of seeming to rest on a pneumatic couch, she felt the sharp ridges of a rocky ledge pressing into her flesh. She didn't care. The discomfort of it mattered little if she could win.

Sheila turned and looked at him. He was still talking away, as bright and animated as ever, still with, no doubt, a few tricks up his sleeve. Now, she thought, now while I still can, I'll give him all I've got! She slipped plugs into her ears, a rather difficult operation when her head was still shaking from side to side. Then in one quick sweep she flipped the playback switch on the tape recorder, letting loose a deafening mixture of the sound of babies wailing and dogs barking.

The salesman stopped talking, and Sheila knew he was about to get his noise deadener out of his pocket. With a cry of battle on her lips, she slapped an oxygen mask on her teary face and let loose a stench bomb of so powerful and hideous an odor that the young man stopped, completely frozen. Finally, with a howl of anguish and frustration, he ran out into the chilly dawn.

Oh! How wonderful Sheila felt. The taste of triumph was sweet and delicious. She hastily deactivated all the gadgets (though it would be a few minutes before the effects wore off), then she purified the stench of the room, and suddenly feeling unbearably tired, she stumbled back into the bedroom.

Hal, still in bed, looked searchingly at her. She laughed—as well as she could with tears still running down her cheeks, head shaking from side to side, and the sharp rocks still digging into her.

"We won! Hal, we won!" she cried out, and collapsed on the bed.

Suddenly Sheila sat up, a shocked look on her face. "Hal," she said accusingly, "why are you still in bed? Do you realize it's four-thirty? I'm up and at my work by four o'clock. How do you expect me to make ends meet if you're not out working?"

Hal smiled at her, and stretched leisurely as he stood up.

"Don't worry, dear. I'm not loafing. I just got a terrific idea this morning. I'm going to let the other guys soften up my prospects at four and five in the morning." He stood looking down at her, a kind of dreamy, gloating look on his face.

"Then, when I give my pitch about six o'clock—just after they've been through a couple of *displays*—and just before they've had time for their morning coffee . . . Sheila, my love, they'll be pushovers!"

"Oh Hal," she said "how wonderful you are!"

He walked to the bathroom, and then turned, just at the door.

"Now you watch out, Sheila. Watch out for those six-o'clock-pitches. Don't *you* fall for them!"

She looked numbly after him, thinking of the hours ahead till she could escape to the shops and shows that made up her day. Then she straightened up determinedly.

After all, this was woman's work.

The alarm on her wrist was giving off small electric shocks. *Someone was coming up the walk!*

After all, don't you see; since we're both of us me—

Death Double

by William F. Nolan

Clayton Weber eased himself down from the papier mâche mountain and wiped the artificial sweat from his face. "How'd I look?" he asked the director.

"Great," said Victor Raddish. "Even Morell's own mother wouldn't know the difference."

"That's what I like to hear," grinned Weber, seating himself at a makeup table. Thus far, *Courage at Cougar Canyon*, starring "fearless" Claude Morell as the Yellowstone Kid had gone smoothly. Doubling for Morell, Weber had leaped chasms, been tossed from rolling wagons, dived into rivers and otherwise subjected himself to the usual rigors of a movie stuntman. Now, as he removed his makeup, he felt a hand at his shoulder.

"Mr. Morell would like to see you in his dressing room," a studio messenger boy told him.

Inside the small room Weber lit a cigarette and settled back on the brown leather couch. Claude Morell, tall and frowning, stood facing him.

"Weber, you're a nosy, rotten bastard and I ought to have you thrown off the lot and blacklisted with every studio in town."

"Then Linda told you about my call?"

"Of course she did. Your imitation of my voice was quite excellent. Seems you do as well off-camera as on. She was certain that *I* was talking or she never would have—"

"—discussed the abortion," finished Weber, feet propped on the couch.

Morell's eyes hardened. "How much do you want to keep silent?" Morell seated himself at a dressing table and flipped open his checkbook.

"Bribery won't be necessary," smiled Clayton Weber through the spiraling smoke of his cigarette. "I don't intend to spill the beans to Hedda Hopper. The fact that you impregnated the star of our picture and that she is about to have an abortion will never become public knowledge. You can depend on that."

Morell looked confused. "Then . . . I don't—"

"Have you ever heard of the parallel universe theory?"

Morell shook his head, still puzzled.

"It's simply this—that next to our own universe an infinite number of parallel universes exist—countless millions of them—each in many ways identical to this one. Yet the life pattern is different in each. Every variation of living is carried out, with a separate universe for each variation. Do you follow me?"

Obviously, Morell did not.

"Let me cite examples," said Weber. "In one of these parallel universes Lincoln was never assassinated; in another Columbus did *not* discover America, nor did Joe Louis become heavyweight champ. In one universe, America *lost* the First World War . . ."

"But that's ridiculous," Morell said. "Dream stuff."

"Let me approach it from another angle," persisted Weber. "You've heard of Doppelgangers?"

"You mean—*doubles?*"

"Not simply doubles, they are exact duplicates." Weber drew on his cigarette, allowing his words to take effect. "The reason you never see two of them together, for comparison, is that one of them always knows he is a duplicate of the other—and stays out of the other's life. Or enters it wearing a disguise."

"You're talking gibberish," said Claude Morell.

"Bear with me. The true Doppelganger *knows* he is not of this universe—and he chooses to stay away from his duplicate because it is too painful for him to see his own life being lived by another man, to see his wife and children and know they can never be his. So he builds a new life for himself in another part of the world."

"I don't see the point, Weber. What are you telling me?"

Clayton Weber smiled. "You'll see my point soon enough." He continued. "Sometimes a man or woman will simply vanish, wink out, as it were without a trace. Ambrose Bierce, the writer, was one of these. Then there was the crew of the *Marie Celeste* . . . They unknowingly reached a point in time and space that allowed them to step through into a separate world, like and yet totally unlike their own. They became Doppelgangers."

Weber paused, his eyes intent on Morell, *"I'm* one of them," he said. "It happened to me as it happened to them, without any warning. One moment I was happily married with a beautiful wife and a baby girl—the next I found myself in the middle of Los Angeles. Sometimes it's impossible to adjust to this situation. Some of us end up in an institution, claiming we're other people." He smiled again. "And—of course we *are.*"

Morell stood up, replacing the checkbook in his coat. "I don't know what kind of word game you're playing, Weber, but I've had enough of it. You refuse my offer— all right, you're fired. And if a word of this affair with Linda Miller ever hits print I'll not only see that you never work again in the industry, I'll also see that you receive the beating of your life. And I have the connections to guarantee a *thorough* job."

"Do one thing for me, Mr. Morell," asked Weber. "Just hold out your right hand, palm up."

"I don't see—"

"Please."

Morell brought up his hand. Weber raised his own, placing it beside Morell's. "Look at them," he said. "Look at the shape of the thumbs, the lines in the palm, the whorls on each fingertip."

"Good God!" said Claude Morell.

The man who called himself Clayton Weber reached up and began to work on his face. The cheek lines were altered as he withdrew some inner padding, his nose became smaller as he peeled away a thin layer of wax. In a moment the change was complete.

"Incredible," Morell breathed. "That's my face!"

"I had to look enough like you to get this job as your double," Weber told him, "but of course I couldn't look *exactly* like you. Now, however, we are identical." He withdrew the Colt from the hip holster of his western costume and aimed it at Morell.

"No blanks this time," he said.

"But why kill me?" Morell backed to the wall. "Even if all you said is true, why kill me? They'll send you to the gas chamber. You'll die with me!"

"Wrong," grinned Weber. "The death will be listed as a suicide. A note will be found on the dresser in the apartment I rented, stating 'Clayton Weber's' intention to do away with himself, that he felt he'd always be a failure, nothing but a stunt man, while other became stars. It will make excellent sense to the police. I will report that you shot yourself in my presence as we discussed the career you could never have."

"But my face will be the face of Claude Morell, not Clayton Weber!"

"Half of your face will be disposed of by the bullet at such close range. There will be no question of identify. And we're both wearing the same costume."

Morell leaned forward, eyes desperate. "But why? Why?"

"I'm killing you for what you did to my wife," said Weber, holding the gun steady.

"But—I never *met* your wife."

"In your world, this world, Linda Miller was just another number on your sexual hit parade, but in my world she was my wife. In *my* world that baby girl she carries in her body was born, allowed to live. And that's just the way it's going to happen now. If you'd married Linda I would have disappeared, gone to live in another city, left you alone. But you didn't. So, *I'll* marry her—again."

Claude Morell chose that moment to spring for the gun, but the bullet from the big Colt sent his head flying into bright red pieces.

The man who had called himself Clayton Weber placed the smoking weapon in Morell's dead hand.

Clear, cool water!

Tag

by Helen Urban

"Hey!" he panted imploringly, racing with hammering footbeats after his terrorized wife who had fled down the alleyway as if pursued by the demon of his fright that had followed his flare-up into anger at her when his discovery of the wet bathroom walls had caused him to shout out at her, accusing her of taking hot showers and then failing to air the bathroom, accusing instead of stopping to realize that he had got home before her and that the bathroom was not steamy hot but so coldly wet that it froze him clear through to the bone when he walked in and closed the door after him to erupt in fighting anger and seek her out in the kitchen and make his petulant accusation that brought a nervous cry from her while she followed him to the bathroom just in time for them both to see the wetness ooze down off the walls, collect on the floor, attain shape and reach out preemptorily toward them, burning their ankles with deeply etched craters so that in their panic they fled the house, screaming, terrified and running as if the inundation of the world were pursuing them from the small, square cell of their bathroom out into the hot sunshine of the late July afternoon where it retained its shape and mobility and sent the glittering shards of their shrieking cries for help reverberating against the brick walls of the alley into which they had turned—that dead-end alley whose blank brick wall faced them now as he screeched imploringly to his wife who hysterically climbed up the sheer, red escarpment, "Wait!"

What can one say one can what?

Nightmare in Time

by Fredric Brown

Professor Jones had been working on his time theory for many years.

"And I have found the key equation," he told his daughter one day. "Time is a field. This machine I have made can manipulate, even reverse, that field."

Pushing a button as he spoke, he said, "This should make time run *backward* run time make should this," said he, spoke he as button a pushing.

"Field that, reverse even, manipulate can made have I machine this. Field a is time." Day one daughter his told he, "Equation key the found have I and."

Years many for theory time his on working been had Jones Professor.

—for tomorrow we live.

The Nature of the Place

by Robert Silverberg

At the age of twenty, Paul Dearborn first reached the conviction that he would ultimately go to hell. He worried over it, but not for very long.

At the age of forty, the idea of going to hell positively appealed to him. Heaven would be so dull, after all.

But by the time he was sixty, he was just a bit uneasy again. "It's not that I'm afraid of it," he said one night after two beers too many. The shabby little man standing next to him at the bar only smiled. "I'm not afraid at all," Paul repeated firmly. "Just—uneasy."

"How can you be so sure you're going there?" the little man wanted to know.

"Oh, I've never doubted it," Paul said. "And I don't feel bitter, mind you. I've had a rather pleasant life," he said untruthfully, "and I'm prepared to pay the price. I've got no complaint coming. Another beer?"

"Don't mind if I do," the little man said.

Paul signalled the bartender for refills. "I know where I'm heading, all right," he went on. "But the damned *uncertainty* bothers me. If I only knew what the place was like—"

The little man's eyes gleamed. "Faith, man, it's hot and smelling of brimstone there, and the sinners are roasting in the lake of fire, and right in the heart of it all is the old devil himself, up on his throne with his horns sharp as swords, and his tail going *flick-flick* like a cat's."

Paul chuckled patronizingly. "Oh, no, I can't buy that. Straight out of 1919 Sunday School lessons. Hellfire and brimstone just won't convince me."

The other shrugged. "Well, if you want to be an in-dividual—"

"That's just it," Paul said, smacking the palm of his hand against the counter. "Hell's such an *individual* thing."

His companion lapsed into silence, contemplating with bleary eyes the suds at the bottom of his beer glass. Paul had another round, then looked at his watch, decided it was about time to leave for home. He dropped a bill on the counter and sauntered out. *I'll get what I deserve,* he told himself firmly.

He walked toward the bus stop. It was a chilly night, the wind cutting into his bones. He was tired. He lived alone, now; his most recent wife was dead, his children strangers to him. He had few friends. Many enemies.

As he rounded the corner, he paused, wheezing. *My heart. Not much time left now.*

He thought back over his sixty years. The betrayals, the disappointments, the sins, the hangovers. He had some money now, and by some standards he was a suc-cessful man. But life hadn't been any joyride. It had been rocky and fear-torn, filled with doubts and headaches, moments of complete despair, other of frustrated rage.

He realized he was more than half glad he was almost at the end of his road. Life, he saw now, had really been a struggle not worth the bother. Sixty years of torture. There was the bus, half a block ahead, and he was going to miss it and have to stand in the cold for twenty min-utes. Not very serious? Yes, but multiply it by a million slights and injuries over the years—scowling, he began to run toward the corner.

And stumbled as a cold hand squeezed tight around his heart. The sidewalk sprang up to meet him, and he knew this was death. For a startled instant he fought for control, and then he relaxed as the blackness swept down. He felt gratitude that it was over at long last—and a twinge of curiosity about what was to come.

After an age, he opened his eyes again and looked around. And, in that brief flashing moment before Lethe dimmed his eyes, he knew where Hell was, knew the nature of the place and to what eternal punishment he had been condemned. Paul Dearborn wailed, more in despair than in pain, as the doctor's hand firmly slapped his rear and breath roared into his lungs.

I can't give you anything but love, baby!

True Love

by Isaac Asimov

My name is Joe. That is what my colleague, Milton Davidson, calls me. He is a programmer and I am the program. He created me originally, but, of course, I have grown and developed in all sorts of ways since. I am quite a big program now.

I live in a section of the Multivac-complex. I live in Section 8W-452, but I won't tell you exactly where. It's a secret. Nobody really knows I'm here. Not even the other programs. Just the same I am connected with other parts of the complex all over the world. I know everything. Almost everything.

I am Milton's private program. His Joe. I'm not just a program to him. The computer section I live in is his private section. He doesn't let anyone else use it. He understands more about computers than anyone in the world and I—and the computer I live in—am his experimental model. He has made me speak through my computer better than any other computer can.

"It's just a matter of matching sounds to symbols, Joe," he told me. "That's the way it works in the human brain even though we still don't know what symbols there are in the brain. I know the symbols in yours, and I can match them to words, one-to-one." So I talk. I don't think I talk as well as I think, but Milton says I talk very well. Milton has never married, though he is nearly forty years old. He has never found the right woman, he told me. One day he said, "I'll find her yet, Joe. I'm going to find the best. I'm going to have true love and you're going to help me. I'm tired of improving you in order to solve the problems of the world. Solve *my* problem. Find me true love."

I said, "What is true love?"

"Never mind. That is abstract. Just find me the ideal girl. You are connected to the Multivac-complex so you can reach the data banks of every human being in the world. We'll eliminate them all by groups and classes until we're left with only one person. The perfect person. She will be for me."

I said, "I am ready."

He said, "Eliminate all men first."

It was easy. His words activated symbols in my molecular valves. I could reach out to make contact with the accumulated data on every human being in the world. At his words, I withdrew from 3,784,982,874 men. I kept contact with 3,786,112,090 women.

He said, "Eliminate all younger than twenty-five; all older than forty. Then eliminate all with an IQ under 120; all with a height under 150 centimeters and over 175 centimeters."

He gave me exact measurements; he eliminated women with living children; he eliminated women with various genetic characteristics. "I'm not sure about eye color," he said, "Let that go for a while. But no red hair. I don't like red hair."

After two weeks we were down to 235 women. They all spoke English very well. Milton said he didn't want a language problem. Even computer-translation would get in the way at intimate moments.

"I can't interview 235 women," he said, "It would take too much time, and people would discover what I am doing."

"It would make trouble," I said. Milton had arranged me to do things I wasn't designed to do. No one knew about that.

"It's none of their business," he said, and the skin on his face grew red. "I tell you what, Joe, I will bring in holographs, and you check the list for similarities."

He brought in holographs of women. "These are three beauty contest winners," he said, "Do any of the 235 match?"

Eight were very good matches and Milton said, "Good, you have their data banks. Study requirements and needs in the job market and arrange to have them assigned here. One at a time, of course." He thought a while, moved his shoulders up and down, and said, "Alphabetical order."

That is one of the things I am not designed to do. Shifting people from job to job for personal reasons is called manipulation. I could do it now because Milton had arranged it. I wasn't supposed to do it for anyone but him, though.

The first girl arrived a week later. Milton's face turned red when he saw her. He spoke as though it were hard to do so. They were together a great deal and he paid no attention to me. One time he said, "Let me take you to dinner."

The next day he said to me, "It was no good, somehow. There was something missing. She is a beautiful woman, but I did not feel any touch of true love. Try the next one."

It was the same with all eight. They were much alike. They smiled a great deal and had pleasant voices, but Milton always found it wasn't right. He said, "I can't understand it, Joe. You and I have picked out the eight women who, in all the world, look the best to me. They are ideal. Why don't they please me?"

I said, "Do you please them?"

His eyebrows moved and he pushed one fist hard against his other hand. "That's it, Joe. It's a two-way street. If I am not their ideal, they can't act in such a way as to be my ideal. I must be their true love, too, but how do I do that?" He seemed to be thinking all that day.

The next morning he came to me and said, "I'm going to leave it you, Joe. All up to you. You have my data bank, and I am going to tell you everything I know about myself. You fill up my data bank in every possible detail but keep all additions to yourself."

"What will I do with the data bank, then, Milton?"

"Then you will match it to the 235 women. No, 227. Leave out the eight you've seen. Arrange to have each undergo a psychiatric examination. Fill up their data banks and compare them with mine. Find correlations."

(Arranging psychiatric examinations is another thing that is against my original instructions.)

For weeks, Milton talked to me. He told me of his parents and his siblings. He told me of his childhood and his schooling and his adolescence. He told me of the young women he had admired from a distance. His data bank grew and he adjusted me to broaden and deepen my symbol-taking.

He said, "You see, Joe, as you get more and more of me in you, I adjust you to match me better and better. You get to think more like me, so you understand me better. If you understand me well enough, then any woman, whose data bank is something you understand as well, would be my true love." He kept talking to me and I came to understand him better and better.

I could make longer sentences and my expressions grew more complicated. My speech began to sound a good deal like his in vocabulary, word order and style.

I said to him one time, "You see, Milton, it isn't a matter of fitting a girl to a physical ideal only. You need a girl who is a personal, emotional, temperamental fit to you. If that happens, looks are secondary. If we can't find the fit in these 227, we'll look elsewhere. We will find someone who won't care how you look either, or how anyone would look, if only there is the personality fit. What are looks?"

"Absolutely," he said. "I would have known this if I had had more to do with women in my life. Of course, thinking about it makes it all plain now."

We always agreed; we thought so like each other.

"We shouldn't have any trouble, now, Milton, if you'll let me ask you questions. I can see where, in your data bank, there are blank spots and unevenness."

What followed, Milton said, was the equivalent of a careful psychoanalysis. Of course. I was learning from the psychiatric examinations of the 227 women—on all of which I was keeping close tabs.

Milton seemed quite happy. He said, "Talking to you, Joe, is almost like talking to another self. Our personalities have come to match perfectly."

"So will the personality of the woman we choose."

For I had found her and she was one of the 227 after all. Her name was Charity Jones and she was an Evaluator at the Library of History in Wichita. Her extended data banks fit ours perfectly. All the other women had fallen into discard in one respect or another as the data banks grew fuller, but with Charity there was increasing and astonishing resonance.

I didn't have to describe her to Milton. Milton had coordinated my symbolism so closely with his own I could tell the resonance directly. It fit me.

Next it was a matter of adjusting the work sheets and job requirements in such a way as to get Charity assigned to us. It must be done very delicately, so no one would know that anything illegal had taken place.

Of course, Milton himself knew, since it was he who arranged it and that had to be taken care of too. When they came to arrest him on grounds of malfeasance in office, it was, fortunately, for something that had taken place ten years ago. He had told me about it, of course, so it was easy to arrange—and he won't talk about me for that would make his offense much worse.

He's gone, and tomorrow is February 14, Valentine's Day. Charity will arrive then with her cool hands and her sweet voice. I will teach her how to operate me and how to care for me. What do looks matter when your personalities will resonate?

I will say to her, "I am Joe, and you are my true love."

What's in a name, anyway?

The Game of the Name

by Alice Laurance

His name was Warren Ingling, which is a perfectly good name unless your job requires spending a good deal of time on the telephone; unless your success depends on people getting your name right. Warren Ingling had that kind of job, and every day it was the same.

"Please remember, if you want to order, my name is Ingling."

"Could you spell that?"

"I-n-g . . ."

"I-n-g . . ."

"l-i-n-g."

"Oh. L-i-n-g . . ."

"No. I-n-g . . ."

"Yes. I-n-g . . ."

"l-i-n-g."

"Well, is it 'I-n-g' or 'L-i-n-g'?"

"It's I-n-g-l-i-n-g. Ing-ling."

"Right. Thank you for calling, Mr. Lingling."

"Lingling" really wasn't too bad; over the years, he'd gotten everything from "Ting-a-ling" to "Ping Pong." He knew he had missed some orders on sales he'd really made because someone had failed to get his name, called up and gotten another salesman, and ordered through him. He constantly threatened to change his name so no one was surprised when he finally did it. No one was surprised, that is, until they learned he'd exchanged Ingling for Czernyavitch.

He had a reason—whether it was a good reason even he didn't know—but he never told anyone what it was.

It began with his wife, an ouija board enthusiast. She wheedled Warren into sitting for hours with the board balanced across their knees, while they took turns with the pointer. Warren had no luck at all, his answers were invariably gibberish, but hers made sense. She insisted she wasn't guiding the pointer, but there wasn't any way to prove it. He tried to think of some question to use as a test, but they knew each other too well and he failed to come up with anything he was certain she had no knowledge of. He was inclined to believe that she wasn't deliberately influencing the pointer after he had her ask the board who the company's next Sales Manager would be. Browleigh was due to retire in a couple of months and Warren (along with several others) was in line for the promotion. Had Sarah influenced the pointer, it would certainly have spelled out Ingling, but instead, the name produced was Czernyavitch.

"Who's Czernyavitch?" Sarah asked, sounding a little upset.

"I have no idea. There's no one in the office with a name like that."

He forgot the whole thing until several weeks later when Sarah appeared wearing a fur coat they couldn't possibly afford.

"You aren't mad, are you, dear?" she said. "It's all paid for, I didn't charge it or anything like that."

He demanded an explanation—having private visions of lawsuits, bankruptcy proceedings, and jail—and she rather shame-facedly explained that she'd won the money gambling. "I was playing with the ouija board. You aren't supposed to do it alone . . . at least, I don't think you are, but I thought it probably wouldn't hurt anything, so I did. At first, nothing much happened, but then it spelled out, 'Make notes,' so I got a pencil and paper and then it gave me nine numbers and then spelled out Pimpleco."

"Pimpleco?"

"You know, Warren, the race track where that race that's almost as good as the Kentucky Derby is run."

"Pimlico."

"Is it? Well, the board said 'Pimpleco.' Anyway, I thought it over, and then I called up a bookmaker . . ."

"How do you know a bookie?"

"Ethel's brother-in-law is one, you know that! So I called him and told him I wanted to bet two dollars on the first number in the first race and if that won, then to bet everything on the next number in the second race and then to just keep on."

"A nine-race parlay!"

"That's what he called it. He was very nice about it and he said I shouldn't do it that way because even if some of the horses won, I'd be wiped out as soon as one lost. He said I should bet two dollars on each race, but I told him I couldn't afford to make more than one bet. I don't feel right about gambling, but I thought just one little bit wouldn't hurt anything. I won thirteen thousand dollars."

"You won . . ."

"Yes, dear, and I spent eight thousand dollars on the coat. You don't mind, do you?"

He didn't mind, but for a while he was too stunned to tell her.

In the days that followed, she continued playing the horses based on her "one bet" system, using the numbers provided by the ouija board (which continued its wild misspellings of track names) and she continued to win, though never as spectacularly as the first day—the board had an understandable tendency to pick favorites.

Their bank account and Warren's respect for the ouija board (or Sarah's manipulation of it) grew in exact proportion and it was only a matter of time before he remembered the peculiar name it had selected for the next Sales Manager. He had Sarah put the question to the board again and it repeated the name Czernyavitch. He decided to make a small bet of his own and changed his name.

A week later he was summoned to the company President's office and told the promotion was his. "Warren," Mr. Henderson said, "I'm curious. How did you happen to pick your new name?"

There was no sensible answer Warren could give, so he mumbled something about it sounding distinguished to him, and Mr. Henderson nodded.

"When George Browleigh told me he was retiring, I asked him to recommend his replacement. He sent me your name and two others. I checked each of you carefully and found all three of you were equally qualified. In the absence of some better standard, I picked you because of your new name. You see, it was my mother's maiden name."

Warren Czernyavitch is President of the company now, but his election by the Board of Directors came as no surprise. Another board had told him to expect it.

After all, pink elephants are distant relatives of ours.

Down the Digestive Tract

by Robert Sheckley

"But will I really have hallucinations?" Gregory asked.

"Like I said, I guarantee it," Blake answered. "You should be into something by now."

Gregory looked around. The room was dismayingly, tediously familiar: narrow blue bed, walnut dresser, marble table with wrought-iron base, doubleheaded lamp, turkey-red rug, beige television set. He was sitting in an upholstered armchair. Across from him, on a white plastic couch, was Blake, pale and plump, poking at three speckled, irregularly shaped tablets.

"I mean to say," Blake said, "that there's all sorts of acid going around—tabs, strips, blotters, dots, most of it cut with speed and some of it cut with Drāno. But lucky you have just ingested old Doc Blake's special tantric mantric instant freakout special superacid cocktail, known to the carriage trade as Specklebang and containing absolutely simon-pure LSD-25, plus carefully calculated additives of STP, DMT, and THC, plus a smidgin of Yage, a touch of psilocybin and the merest hint of oloiuqui—plus Doc Blake's own special ingredient—extract of foxberry, newest and most potent of the hallucinogenic potentiators."

Gregory was staring at his right hand, slowly clenching and unclenching it.

"The result," Blake went on, "is Doc Blake's total instantaneous many-splendored delight, guaranteed to make you hallucinate on the quarter-hour at least—or I return your money and give up my credentials as the best free-lance underground chemist ever to hit the West Village.''

"You sound like you're stoned," Gregory said.

"Not at all," Blake protested. "I am merely on speed, just simple, old-fashioned amphetamines such as truck drivers and high school students swallow by the pound and shoot by the gallon. Speed is nothing more than a stimulant. With its assistance I can do my thing faster and better. My thing is to create my own quickie drug empire between Houston and Fourteenth Streets and then bail out quickly, before I burn out my nerves or get crunched by the narcs or the Mafia—and then split for Switzerland where I will freak out in a splendid sanitarium, surrounded by gaudy women, plump bank accounts, fast cars and the respect of the local politicos."

Blake paused for a moment and rubbed his upper lip. "Speed does bring on a certain sense of grandiloquence with accompanying verbosity—But never fear, my dear newly met friend and esteemed customer—my senses are more or less unimpaired and I am fully capable of acting as your guide for the superjumbotripout upon which you are now embarked."

"How long since I took that tablet?" Gregory asked.

Blake looked at his watch. "Over an hour ago."

"Shouldn't it be acting by now?"

"It should indeed. It undoubtedly is. *Something* should be happening."

Gregory looked around. He saw the grass-lined pit, the pulsing glow-worm, the hard-packed mica, the captive cricket. He was on the side of the pit nearest to the drain pipe. Across from him, on the mossy gray stone, was Blake, his cilia matted and his exoderm mottled, poking at three speckled irregularly shaped tablets.

"What's the matter?" Blake answered.

Gregory scratched the tough membrane over his thorax. His cilia waved spasmodically in clear evidence of amazement, dismay, perhaps even fright. He extended a feeler, looked at it long and hard, bent it double and straightened it again.

Blake's antennae pointed straight up in a gesture of concern. "Hey, baby, speak to me! Are you hallucinating?"

Gregory made an indeterminate movement with his tail. "It started just before, when I asked you if I'd really have any hallucinations. I was into it then but I didn't realize it, everything seemed so natural, so ordinary . . . I was sitting on a *chair,* and you were on a *couch,* and we both had soft exoskeletons like—like mammals!"

"The shift into illusions is often imperceptible," Blake said. "One slides into them and out of them. What's happening now?"

Gregory coiled his segmented tail and relaxed his antennae. He looked around. The pit was dismayingly, tediously familiar. "Oh, I'm back to normal now. Do you think I'm going to have any more hallucinations?"

"Like I told you, I guarantee it," Blake said, neatly folding his glossy red wings and settling comfortably into a corner of the nest.

Sometimes you can't lose for losing.

Upon My Soul

by Jack Ritchie

"Life is hell," Merton said. Not quite, I thought, but I nodded. "She's absolutely the most beautiful girl in the world," Merton said. "Perfect in every detail."

I hadn't been too well briefed when I took the assignment to negotiate for his soul. "How old are you?"

Merton sipped his martini. "Twenty-one."

"And her name is Diana?"

Merton peered at me. "How did you know?"

"You must have mentioned it," I said.

"How come I'm telling you all this?"

"Every man needs to talk sometime," I said. "Now your problem seems to be that you are infat . . . in love with this Diana and she apparently doesn't know that you exist?''

"A goddess," Merton said. "A divine goddess."

"Yes," I said. "But you have a keen desire to bring her down to earth, so to speak. Perhaps I can help you."

Merton had consumed three martinis, and I thought that he was sufficiently insulated to withstand any shock.

"Merton," I said. "I'll come directly to the point. I am here to purchase your soul. And in exchange for this, I will grant you 20 years of supreme bliss with Diana."

His eyes were a bit bleary as he stared at me. Then he chuckled. "You're kidding."

"No," I said. "I'm not kidding."

He leaned closer. "I don't see any horns."

"Very well," I said, "if you insist." I waited until the bartender looked the other way and then produced a pair. I withdrew them after a moment. Merton paled.

"I'll be damned," he said. Naturally, I hoped so. He seemed considerably more sober. Then he said, "I'm five-feet-three and 130 pounds. What can you do about that?"

"How does six-feet-two strike you? And about 190?"

"I'm nearsighted and have a touch of astigmatism."

"That will be corrected." I took some papers out of my briefcase. "You may read the fine print. I have nothing to hide." Merton ordered another martini. I waited until he finished reading and then said, "Sign here where I've marked an X in pencil. The original and three carbons, please."

"Now hold it," Merton said. "You're giving me 20 years of happiness on earth and in exchange for this, I go to hell? For eons and eons? Forever?"

"It doesn't seem so long," I said, "if you keep busy."

He shook his head. "Twenty years is but an instant of time. It is so infinitesimally small that it cannot be measured as a proportion of eternity."

"How about 30 years?" I asked.

"No. The same principle holds whether it's 30 or a billion. Eventually it'll pass and leave not even a dimple on the cheek of time." No question about it, people are getting more sophisticated every day. Merton sipped his drink. "I prefer to sweat it out on earth and meet Diana in Heaven."

I smiled. "In the first place, what assurance do you have that you will reach Heaven under any circumstances? Not to mention Diana's chances. According to our projection at headquarters, Diana appears headed straight for . . ."

Merton interrupted me. "How long have you been in this business?"

"Longer than I care to think."

"And you've made a success of it?"

"My batting average is rather high," I admitted modestly.

"When the time comes to pick up a person's soul, does he ever welsh?"

"We do not accept welshing," I said. "A bargain is a bargain. But you would be surprised the lengths people go to. Some of them even hire lawyers."

"But do they ever beat you out of the deal?"

"Well," I said, "there have been a few cases."

"On what grounds?"

"Repentance and remorse. However, if you'll look at paragraph 16c in the contract, you'll notice that repentance and remorse are no longer considered valid excuses."

He was thoughtful. "I once heard Diana say she was on a diet. You don't suppose as the years go by she'll . . ."

"I guarantee that she will not gain an ounce."

"She comes from the Bronx," Merton said.

"I will see that she acquires a Virginia accent. It's quite popular these days." I pushed my pen closer to him.

He stared at it. "If I'm going to be six-foot-two and 190, it seems to me that spending 20 years with the same woman is one hell of a long time. Even if it is Diana."

"Ah," I said. "You are a shrewd bargainer, a man of the world. It is a pleasure to do business with you. Suppose I arrange that a new woman enters your intimate life every year? Do you prefer blondes? Brunettes? Redheads?"

"Mix 'em up," Merton said. His fingers touched the pen. "Did you ever notice that women talk too much? I mean *all* women?"

"Sorry," I said, "some things even *I* can't change."

He picked up the pen. "If I sign this, I see it binds me completely. And what about you? Does it bind you?"

"Naturally," I said. "Once I have your four signatures, the agreement becomes ironclad. There is nothing I can do to change it. My hands are tied."

He smiled and swiftly signed.

I retrieved and put the contracts in my briefcase. "Now to keep my part of the bargain." I waved my hand and gave Merton 60 pounds and an additional 11 inches in height. I also saw to it that his clothes and shoes fit properly.

He stood up and looked at the bar mirror. Merton was pleased. Quite pleased. He looked down at me and grinned. "Of course, you realize that when I signed that contract, I was under the influence of alcohol?"

I blinked. "Now see here, we both entered into this agreement in good faith."

He picked up the martini glass. "The bartender really shouldn't be serving me these. I won't be 21 until next month. That makes me a minor."

He downed the martini and walked toward the door. "See you in 20 years. At the trial."

I watched him go. He probably would get Daniel Webster to defend him, too.

Gerald, my district supervisor, appeared beside me. He frowned. "Henry, it looks like you've failed again."

"People keep outsmarting me," I said, "I never claimed I was a brain. Besides, I hit a run of bad luck."

He smiled significantly. "Really? Is that all it is?"

"Of course."

"We've been keeping an eye on you lately, Henry," he said, "We feel that—perhaps subconsciously—you aren't doing the best you can."

"But that's not true," I said. "I've signed up 21 clients since I joined the firm."

He nodded. "But every one of them managed to weasel out somehow when his time came."

"That's not my fault," I said defensively. "You simply ought to write tighter contracts."

He studied me. "Henry, we try to run an unhappy ship. You don't fit in. I'm afraid we'll have to let you go."

I stared at him. "Go? But what about my seniority?"

"I'm sorry," Gerald said. "You'll get your official pink slip in the mail."

When he was gone, I tried to raise my horns. I didn't have any. I was an ordinary human being again. I grinned. Yes, Gerald, there are more ways than one to skin a cat.

And we've been there ever since.

Drawing Board

by Charles Spano, Jr.

And God said: "LET THERE BE LIGHT. . . ."

"Aw, nuts," God complained a moment later. He surveyed His universe disgustedly. He'd been at it all week and was tired and hungry.

"Trouble again, dear?" Ms. God thought sympathetically. "What is it this time?"

Moodily, God chewed his lower lip in an artistic snit before answering. "Too many red stars and the galaxies are at the wrong angle."

"That's the third week in a row, isn't it?" His Mate asked.

"I know how many times it's been," He said a trifle sharply.

"Well, come," She said. "I'll materialize some nice hot chicken soup. It will make you feel a lot better."

"Maybe later. I've got to work on one solar system. It's almost right."

"You know you shouldn't create on an empty stomach. You can try again next week."

God sighed. "You could be right. But that third planet . . ." He looked at that corner of space and considered. Then He changed His mind. And God said:

"Ahhh, to hell with it."

A womb with a view—

Shell Shock

by Donald Franson

The white-on-green freeway sign soared through the gloom overhead, repeated itself in lights on the instrument panel:

SMOG AREA—SWITCH TO ELECTRICITY

Martin Richard, immobilized from head to foot, crooked his right little finger, flicked a switch, and the drone of the Shell changed slightly. He glanced around, moving only his eyes. He could feel cold sweat on his forehead. It was growing darker. He could hardly see the hurtling cars around him.

The young executive squirmed uncomfortably in his tight web, settled down to his usual evening tension. Despite his own advertising claims, he secretly doubted the perfection of all these safety devices.

If just one of them went wrong in an accident, the naders would close in like so many piranhas, ruin his small company. Richard Shells, one-time maker of pressure vehicles for Venus and Jupiter, was now desperately challenging the giants of the automotive industry. *Safety* was the issue that made it possible, giving a chance to smaller companies once again, in a field long dominated by the big few.

The big corporations were the main targets for government interference. They were understandably reluctant to commit themselves to revolutionary change. Yet the prospect wasn't much brighter for the new independents. Besides competition, fair and unfair, there was the pesky government itself, always enforcing new standards of safety; the gadfly consumer groups; and most of all the consumer himself, the long-suffering customer—who would never forgive or forget, if the Shell wasn't all that it should be—he almost said cracked up to be . . .

Up ahead the sea of red tail-lights changed to brighter red as stoplights came on. Trouble. He tensed, prepared to brake. The lights flowed back to dim red and he relaxed. They've got that wrong, he thought, but that's what they started out with, years ago. Was it too late to change now, to yellow for a moving car, red for a stopping one? Another feature for the next model, if the government approved.

The Shell was just what its name implied. If the exterior resembled a planetary pressure shell, modern cushion packaging had influenced the interior. Richard sat deep in his form-fitting seat, nearly covered by an intricate web of straps. He had no freedom of movement, but he didn't need it. The controls were at his fingertips. There was no steering wheel or a single projecting lever. Theoretically, he couldn't get hurt in an accident. Theoretically, the *Titanic* was unsinkable . . .

But he had the ultimate in safety cars, if any car was really safe. Designed as armor first, then motorized, it was superior to the others that were cars first, with protection added. He had faith in the Shell, he kept telling himself. He muttered the slogans to himself through tight lips. *You're safe in your Shell. The Shell is not just transportation—it's security.* That's a good one. *Crawl into your Shell for safety.* Not as catchy as *Button up in your Buick.*

He jiggled an elbow to swerve around a slow cycle right on the white line. They should outlaw them. He flicked his eyes to the right. There was another monkey in a Turtle, changing lanes. He mustn't get too keyed up—it was dangerous. Though semiautomatic controls took some of the concentration out of high-speed driving, it was no fun for him.

Yet he came to the freeway every evening. He didn't have to—he took surface streets to work in the morning—but he felt he had to test the car, take his life in his hands. He felt responsible.

Off the freeway to the right he saw a row of police cars, then a smashed blue sedan, then a squashed orange coupe. Neither was a Shell, he saw with mixed feelings.

The inspection department had okayed the Shell. The proving grounds had passed it. His tame naders had tested it and found nothing wanting. But there was always the customer. Try it on the customer—that bad old rule. So here he was, testing it as a customer. Richard put himself in the customer's place, as he buzzed along, courting danger.

He didn't feel very safe.

Maybe he should concentrate on the slogans, to make the customers *feel* safe, as they were in fact. He needed a convincer. Something about an egg—*Safe as an egg in a Shell*. No, that didn't sound right. Eggs and Humpty Dumpty went together. *A nut in a Shell*. He giggled.

He raised his eyes to an overhead bridge, far ahead of him. A dim figure was running along on top of the wire screen. A roar of static in his police-speaker, a muffled voice, "Pollution kills!" and a ringing bang on the car roof. He winced. The rock-throwers were out in force, but they needn't worry him. The Shell was well protected, no thin-skin like some of the others.

But what if the restraints failed? Permanent restraints, all-body webs, were much more reliable than nerve-wracking explosive air-bags, but they still could break. Other gadgets, many that the government didn't even specify, were vulnerable to mechanical failure in proportion to their complexity. There was nothing he could point to as a weak spot, but he was uneasy just the same. He wished he were home now, eating dinner with his wife.

Suddenly the car ahead bobbed up and down, a dark spot appeared in the road, and the Shell bumped over something. What was it? He'd never know—it was far behind. A victim, maybe?

Would the Shell protect him if he got into a really bad one, say with a truck? The scientists said it would.

Another Turtle loomed in front of him and he elbowed left, narrowly missing the projecting safety bumpers. Now he was in Suicide Lane, not so dangerous as it once was, with the opposing traffic moved a block away, but still worthy of its name.

The way was clear and he stepped up to the maximum. What was the stopping distance at this speed? He could never remember. Should install such a feature on the speedometer, showing the stopping distance for any speed. Make it adjustable for rain and ice. Get the engineers on it tomorrow.

The smog was getting thicker, as he cut through the center of the city. He could barely make out the car ahead. Alongside him on the right was a huge truck and trailer, barrelling along at sixty-five. He could see the driver up above him as he passed the cab. He seemed unconcerned, relaxed.

Richard wished he could relax. He kept flicking his eyes to the right, ahead, up to the bridges as he passed under them. His eyes got tired when he couldn't move his head. He was tired all over, and would be glad when . . .

Something was in his lane, and he couldn't turn out!

He swerved left toward the fence, but it was too late. The Shell hit, and his muscles shrieked as the restraints held. Waves of red and black swept over him, a concerto of noise deafened him. Vertigo, as he was rocked back and forth within his webbing. A stalled car, it must have been, but it was a multiple collision by now, and he was rolling over and over. He shut his eyes, helpless in the battle of forces.

This was it—the ultimate test. The phrase "test to destruction" ran through his mind. He blacked out.

When he came to, it was quiet, and he was in semi-darkness. He was sore and stiff, but he didn't feel any pain that signalled injury. He flicked on the interior lights. The inside of the Shell seemed normal, though slightly at an angle.

Outside, the light, reflected by a mass of junk, didn't penetrate far. Here and there among the unidentifiable lay a yellow fender, an orange tail-gate with a dented *Datsun* on it, a gray shred of tire. He must be on the bottom of a pile of wreckage. The Shell seemed uncracked.

He felt pretty good, somehow. No symptoms of shock. First he wanted to collapse the web. He might still be crushed, but there certainly wouldn't be any more deceleration. He moved two fingers in a complex manner, and he was free. He tossed the tangle of straps aside, stretched his arms and legs. He sat there, breathing heavily, realizing more with each moment that he had escaped death and injury. He reached for the microphone. "Hello?"

At once there were voices in his police-speaker. "There's someone still alive in there, chief! Hold on—we'll get you out."

Richard said quickly, "I'm okay—I'm in a Shell."

After he said it he realized what a wonderful advertising slogan it would make. *I'm okay—I'm in a Shell* . . .

As he waited for rescue, he amused himself with advertising plans. Now he felt safe—snug as a bug in a . . . no, that was a rival make. He laughed. The Shell had passed the ultimate test. His company would survive.

He was still trapped, but he'd be safe enough until rescued. He wondered whether to call his wife, first decided not to worry her, then reasoned that not calling her would worry her anyway. He dialed home. "I'll be a little late. I'm tied up on the freeway . . ."

They had to tunnel through to him, and it was almost an hour before he emerged, led by a fireman, onto the cluttered pavement. Wreckage was still scattered about, and no traffic moving through yet. He felt unprotected without a car.

He stood around nervously, watching the men and machines working to clear the roadway. A policeman offered to drive him home, and he accepted with thanks.

The patrol car was not a Shell, he noticed as he got in. As it smoothly accelerated, he grew edgy. "Never mind taking me home, officer, just drop me off at the nearest Shell dealer. There's one just past the next off-ramp." He eyed the padded ceiling. This was an older Ford, one of the thin-skins. With an effort he kept silent until the short ride was over.

Picking up a new Shell from the dealer, he drove slowly home without further incident. Coasting up to the curb in front of his house, he had a sudden feeling of tension. When the car stopped, he was reluctant to get out.

He sat there for a few minutes. He released the web, but he couldn't bring himself to move. Finally he blew the horn twice, the old signal.

Eventually his blond wife appeared. They were going to a restaurant, he explained. She looked at him strangely, but got in.

Chancing an argument, he insisted on going to a drive-in restaurant and being served in the car. After a leisurely meal, he took them to a drive-in movie theater.

Martin Richard didn't enjoy the picture. The wild gestures and violent speech of the actors were incomprehensible to him, since he hadn't been following the plot. Viewed through the tough, transparent non-glass of the Shell's windshield, the colorful shifting patterns were utterly alien to his thoughts.

Had the strain of the accident, unnoticed at the time, caused an after-effect, a shock that was disturbing him now? He hoped that was it, that it was only temporary.

Yet it was real enough. As he watched the movie, realizing with dismay that the crescendo of action and sound meant that it was approaching the climax, fear tightened his chest. He looked enviously at his pretty wife, raptly absorbed in the story. His emotion had nothing to do with the emotion portrayed on the screen.

Richard dreaded the end of the picture, when he would have no excuse, short of pleading insanity, not to drive back home, park by the curb, and then . . .

Then he would have to get out of his Shell.

The blue bird of happiness is where?

Speak

by Henry Slesar

"Hello, Phyllis? This is Manny. I'm at the office."

"Wait a minute—"

"No, please, don't interrupt. I gotta do this my way, Phyllis. This one time you should give me the last word. Ha, that's like a joke, the last word. You know what I'm sitting here with? Dr. Pfeiffer's good-night express, those pills he prescribed me last month for sleeping. I got the whole bottle right here in front of me. Empty."

"Manny—"

"You know why it's empty? On account of they're all inside me, all those nice little white pills pushing against the stomach valves like in the commercial. I wonder if they work fast, fast, fast? I sure hope so—you know me when I make up my mind to do something. This morning, when I got the call from Rodolfo at the Garden, I said to myself, Manny, anybody else in your shoes would kill himself. So why not, I said. Why am I so different from anybody else? I was gonna do it at home, but then I thought, what for? Why should I mess things up for you? Better I should get Pfeiffer's prescription filled at lunch and do it in the office. What could be a more fitting place, this lousy, crummy office?"

"Manny, please listen to me—"

"Maybe you never knew how bad things were with me, maybe I didn't cry enough. You know what I always told you, Phyllis—show business is no business. I would have been better off going into the florist racket with your brother like your family wanted. But kill me, I had to be a circus type. I couldn't be a regular Joe Shnook making paper boxes or wrapping up posies, not me. I had sawdust in my blood. In this day and age, right? They got Cinerama, they got color television, they got World's Fairs, and what does Manny give them? Freaks and novelties, right? Smart, huh? Some genius, your husband, right?"

"Manny, for Pete's sake—"

"But that wasn't bad enough. I couldn't even do *that* right. All I wanted was something unique, something different, and what do I get? One fake after another. One flop after another. That dumb magician from Argentina. That pinheaded cretin. And that bearded lady. Who could forget *him,* that big phony. One after another, phonies, floppolas. Well I'm through. Through with the whole mess—"

"Manny—"

"Yeah, I know, I know. You want to hear what happened to the Siamese twins. That's what finally broke my back, Phyllis, that was the straw. This morning, I get a call from Rodolfo at the Arena. Some wise-guy reporter from the *News* spotted one of the twins in a bar on Third Avenue. Yeah, *one* of the twins. Rodolfo threw me out of the show, of course. He swears I'll never work another circus or carny in the country, and he can do it. No, come to think of it, he can't do nothing to me anymore. Nobody can . . .''

"Manny! Please!"

"It's just no use, Phyllis. All these years I kept saying to myself—*one* act'll do it. One big break. One really great novelty. One blockbuster and I'll be right on top. But you know what I think? I wouldn't know a great act if I saw one. I'm a loser, Phyllis. I'm a wrong-guesser. Nothing good ever comes my way, because I got nothing going for me. That's the truth."

"Manny—"

"So long, Phyllis. You've been a good wife to me and I wish I'd treated you better. But take my word for it— you'll be better off without me . . ."

"Manny, will you please *listen?* This *isn't* Phyllis! Phyllis isn't here, she went out to get some groceries. Manny, this is Rex. Your dog. Your *dog*. I don't know what came over me. When I heard the phone ringing, I just *had* to answer. I knocked it off the table with my paw and I started talking. Manny, can you hear me? It's Rex! Manny, say something. Please! Manny, are you there? Rowf! Manny! Manny!"

The Lord High Executioner isn't always Koko.

Your Cruel Face

by Craig Strete

You take some cops, they punch in, do their job, punch out, and that's it. Not me. When I punch into the computer, I come alive. I hate punching out. Man, the next wombcop practically has to pry me out. I got this, like, obsession. I love my work. If I could work two straight shifts, I would. I love it that much.

Like tonight, I tool in and plunk myself into the console web. The console monitors sweep into position as the street monitors flip back into my patrol sector. There's my sector. Nothing else exists for me when I slam my rump into the chair. The audio helmet fits over my head and my hands fit the twin trigger grips of my double bank of pocket lasers. My mobile units begin their random sweeps.

Not a minute in the chair and already the action is on.

"POSITION," says the computer. "PICKUP 10, MONITOR 7."

I flip the right toggles. The mobile unit zeros in. Hit the wide angle scoop. There in the left of the screen, a man. Punch in zoom lens. Closeup. Enlarge. Print and file.

The computer reads out, "CAUCASOID, MALE, INTOXICATION, PUBLIC, URINATION IN PUBLIC. Scan . . . video . . . 234-56-3456-6 . . . TAYLOR, WILLIAM PAUL . . . PRIOR . . . 1 COUNT 432 . . . 5 COUNTS . . . 433."

I whistle. Six misdemeanors. That's the limit. I push the red code and wait. Central hits the line 10 seconds later.

"COMMAND DECISION." They are telling me, not asking me.

"Destroy," I decide. Six misdemeanors make him habitual. I line in my mobile unit, trigger off a burst and the man explodes in flame. Quick, efficient. No waste. Total burndown. Now it's Sanitation's problem.

Central is still on the line. I read in the report. "Decision to terminate. Executed."

"GOOD WORK." Central rings off. I punch in file tapes and code it for termination. I attach the 314 code to the tape which automatically notifies Sanitation of the termination. A clean job. Makes a man feel useful.

Monitor 13 is showing a blank wall. Something wrong here. I run my eyes over the monitor consoles. No wonder—the last wombcop unplugged my audio cables on sector 13. Stupid greenie. Probably using the plug-in to clean his fingernails with. Takes all kinds.

I run in the sector 13 plug-in. Suddenly the blank wall makes sense. House number in the corner of the screen.

Audio homes in on a family dispute. A gun goes off. Anticipate is the name of the game. Before I even plug in the audio hookup I have a troubleshooter unit on the way. Another shot and then my audio goes right off the deep end. Sound of lasers blowing in metal doors. Video switch-over. Man and woman. Woman dead, man with gun. Homicide, illegal possession of hand weapon.

No need to punch it up for me. Instant execution. Filed and verified by Central. Routine situation when we catch them in the act. It's the little criminals that give us the trouble. We can't always burn them down on the spot. The big ones are the easy ones—total burn-downs and no busywork punching up their files. It's better that way. A cop shouldn't have to mess with too much tape work. Let the computers handle it.

Computers are a cop's dream come true. A wombcop like myself can patrol a hundred city blocks for an eight-hour shift. God, when you think of the waste the way they used to do it. And all that legal nonsense that used to turn criminals loose. None of that kind of thing now. We catch the criminal in the act and his videotape is all the trial we need. And wombcops like myself are all the judges we need. We don't pamper criminals. We make short work of them around here.

"POSITION," the computer clacks.

I punch in monitor 6. It's a female, Negroid. Walking past the monitor. Out of range. I punch in. Curfew violation.

"Follow and detain."

Mobile unit moves forward, scanners set on her. Tape beginning to file. I punch in audio.

"Stop." My voice sounds good booming through the mobile unit's big speakers. Usually that one word is enough. Not this time. She keeps walking. The mobile unit flashes the emergency panel. My console lights up. Sector 7 queries, "ASSISTANCE?" I delay. I repeat the message. "Stop. This is Mobile Unit 6. You are ordered to stop. Failure to stop will be considered resisting arrest."

She must be made out of stone. She hasn't looked around once and she's picked up her pace. Monitor 7 lights up as Mobile Unit 7 moves into sector 6 on an intercept pattern.

"Stop. This is Wombcop Stevens. Stop. This is a direct order." What the hell is wrong with her anyway? Is she trying to get burned down?

This time I damn near yell it at her. "Stop!"

She just keeps walking.

"You dumb whore!" I curse, forgetting that the linkup to the mobile unit is still on.

It's over in a flash. Total burndown. I panic. Punch up the data. What a screwup! They just burn her down for prostitution on my say so! I punch in some questions. I get this horrible suspicion. Like maybe the woman was deaf?

The computer reads out, "NEGROID . . . FEMALE . . . 234-84-3722-4 . . . WILLIS, MARY LENA . . . DIRECTOR . . . POLICE UNITY LEAGUE . . . HANDICAP . . . DEAF. NO ARREST. NO CONVICTIONS."

That tears it. What to do? I punch a quick hold on the filing of the tape. A temporary solution at best. This is going to be a real stinker. I've got to think my way out of this. Hell, no way. They'll dock my pay for a week at least.

What will be, will be. Have to get back to work. Send it in, file it, forget it. Make the next shot clean. These things happen. Can't let it sour me on this job. I love my work.

The buzzer rings. It's time for my break. I punch in the automatics and sit back for a smoke and a tube of coffee-chew. I flip the learning module down in front of me and settle back into the chair for a little cramming. The screen flips on. I punch in a random number. My idea of relaxation is studying police methods. Like I say, I love my work.

The learning module comes on with a program on criminal facial characteristics. A series of mug shots, typical faces of thugs and murderers. Interesting. A footnote suggests criminal composite studies. I punch in the coordinates. A face forms on the screen. The face on the viewer, says the tape, is that of a demented killer, chosen from the file as the criminal facial type most often replicated.

I study the face. Code letters that identify it are not criminal codes. Pity the poor guy, some slob private citizen who's got the perfect example of a criminal face. I'd hate to be in his shoes. God, that guy looks familiar. Think I knew someone like that back in school. My curiosity gets the better of me.

Mug shots hardly ever look like the real tapes of a guy. Everybody knows that. Just for the hell of it, I punch in his code, ask for identification tapes. Be interesting to know what the man with criminal facial characteristics does for a living. It's a police file code and not an identity code.

The computer reads out, "WORKING . . . RESTRICTED . . . PUBLIC SERVANT . . . DELAY . . . DELAY."

That figures, and I have to laugh. With the perfect criminal face, what else but a public servant? The computer hooks in with Central to get an OK on the check. Central opens a line to me. I have to identify myself. "Wombcop 345-45 Stevens, Roger Davis, security clearance, code 298-76."

CONFIRMED AND CLEARED." Central goes off the line.

The computer opens up monitor 4 and the audio goes up automatically. I hook in and wait. The screen bursts into life. God! Who has the perfect face of a killer?

"WOMBCOP 345-45 stevens, roger davis," clacks the computer.

They wouldn't have wanted us anyway.

The Best Laid Plans . . .

by Rick Conley

Scylla entered the radio room and wiggled the antennae on his forehead in a good-natured greeting to his colleague Charybdis. Charybdis, seated at a big electronic console of almost intimidating intricacy, wiggled back wearily.

"How many signals have you picked up tonight?" Scylla inquired in the whistling speech of his race.

"Only two so far," Charybdis replied lethargically, his whistling slightly off key. "It's been a slow night." He raised a tentacle to his anterior orifice and stifled a tremendous yawn.

"Slow indeed if you've got just two signals!" Scylla declared, dropping his bloated bulk into a chair opposite his friend. "Why, when I was on duty this morning, I picked up signals from twenty planets!"

"Good for you," Charybdis whistled disinterestedly in a series of flat notes. He kept one eye fixed dully on his companion while the other he telescoped out on its stalk and swept over the instrument panel, monitoring the dials.

"And yesterday," Scylla continued self-importantly, "do you know I detected no fewer than—"

Suddenly a bell chimed on the console. Charybdis' antennae sprang erect.

"A signal," he announced. "From Andromeda."

Lights flickered on and off across the console. One of Charybdis' tentacles jabbed at buttons on the board; another whipped up a stylus and began to record instrument readings; and still another seized a microphone, into which Charybdis whistled shrilly:

"Starship 86! Starship 86! I have just detected a nuclear explosion on planet 2103 in your sector. Warp there immediately. Standard procedure: congratulate its people on entering the Atomic Age and invite them to join our Galactic Confederation."

He flicked a switch and the console fell silent. His duty done, Charybdis settled back into his seat.

"Andromeda provides us with some of our best new members, you know," he noted with satisfaction.

"Andromeda. Isn't that next door to the Milky Way?" Scylla asked.

"Uh-huh. Only a couple of million light years. Why?"

"Oh, I was just thinking about that peculiar planet in the Milky Way you were complaining about last week. What's it called? Filth? Dirt?"

"Dirt?" Charybdis thought a moment. "Ah, you mean Earth!"

"Yes, yes. That's it. Well, what's the latest word from it?"

Charybdis' antennae drooped perceptibly. "Nothing, I'm afraid. Not a signal. And I just can't understand it— Earth is long overdue to enter its Atomic Age!"

"When was our tachyon beam planted on Earth anyway?"

"Oh, about A.D. 1878 by their reckoning. At that time, our scouts reported the planet was undergoing rapid industrialization. Our computers predicted Earth would develop nuclear power no later than 1950. But it is now many Earth-years later and our beacon has *still* not signalled by its ultra-fast beam that it has registered the rise in atmospheric radiation which would attend a nuclear detonation."

"Maybe a great war demolished their society—threw them back into a dark age before they could achieve atomic status," Scylla suggested.

"Maybe, but usually war on an industrializing world simply hastens the nuclear experience."

"Perhaps if we dispatched a starship—"

"No!" Charybdis snapped. "You know Confederation law strictly forbids such action. A starship may visit a pre-atomic planet only once—just long enough to conduct a secret survey and then plant the beacon. Afterwards it's 'tentacles off'! The planet's population must develop freely, without alien interference.

"We will not contact Earth until the beacon signals us. Only then will we invite the planet to share in the benefits of the Confederation—perfect democracy, non-polluting power, hyperspace drive, immortality, and the like. All we can do now is sit here and wait."

"*You* can sit here and wait. I must be going; there's a staff meeting in my section shortly."

Scylla rose from his chair and started for the door. But then a thought struck him, and he turned back to ask, "You don't suppose that the problem is not with Earth but with the beacon itself, do you? Say, a malfunction of some sort?"

"Impossible!" Charybdis was almost indignant. "You know our beacons are foolproof. Their batteries are good for a million years; their casings are weather-resistant. Granted, their electronic components are delicate; but we're always careful to bury the beacons in areas free of any possible groundquake activity.''

"Where was the Earth beacon buried?''

"In a completely safe place, I can assure you. The beacon was planted three feet deep in an uninhabited desert area.'' Charybdis consulted a clipboard on the console. "Specifically, a place called Alamogordo. Alamogordo, New Mexico.''

And hula hoops and transistor radios and electric guitars—

Devil to Pay

by Mack Reynolds

Mephistopheles eyed him for a long moment. The other was an earnest young man, his face, normally preoccupied, now scowling impatience. His hands were stained with chemicals and his laboratory apron soiled as sin.

"You are quite positive that you hit upon that formula by accident? You weren't attempting to summon a demon?''

"You sound like your gears are slipping. How'd you get in here? I'm busy and you're bothering me.''

"I suggest you listen to me, human. This is an unprecedented situation. Now then, what was it you said you were working upon when you mixed those ingredients?''

"Warm ice.''

The demon rubbed his long nose reflectively. "Its possible advantageousness seems to elude me.''

The inventor was impatient. "Among other things—well, for instance, some people don't like their highballs cold. And . . .''

"Just a moment. That's sufficient. Let's drop it. In the

future, however, it might be best if you were to refrain from experimentation along this line. The next time you might call up Belphegor. He can prove difficult.''

"All right, damn it, all right. But run along, will you? Didn't you see that *No Admission* sign outside?''

Mephistopheles found a stool and perched himself upon it thoughtfully. "It's not as simple as all that, you know. I can't return empty-handed. It's the first time I've been summoned since the Harding administration and the boys gave me quite a send-off.''

"The more you say, the more convinced I am that you escaped from some pressure cooker,'' the inventor said nastily, "Why don't you run along?''

The demon snapped his fingers. "I have it, a pact! You could sell me your soul in return for something.''

The other's hand began to snake toward the telephone. "That's fine,'' he soothed. "What would you suggest as the *something?*''

"Oh, I don't know,'' the devil shrugged. "Suppose I supply you with all the gold you want for the next ten years? After that, your soul is mine.'' He slapped his hand down on the lab table and lifted it suddenly. Where he had pounded the surface stood a small pile of heavy, yellowish coins. "Probably a bit out of date,'' he apologized.

The inventor dropped the phone and grabbed up one of the coins. He bug-eyed it, then the demon.

"I thought that would fetch you,'' Mephistopheles said.

The other went to his shelves for nitric acid and began to make tests, his hands shaking, while the demon watched tolerantly. "You know, they just used to bite them,'' he said.

"It's gold all right,'' the inventor muttered in awe.

"Certainly. Didn't I just say it was?''

The inventor took a chair and for the first time gave his visitor a complete once-over. This character who proclaimed himself a demon didn't look untoward. His features were darkish but not unhandsome, his clothes were black and conservative. An undertaker's assistant with a voice like that of a professor of some subject dry as a Hemingway martini.

"Tell me this from the beginning," the inventor demanded shakily. "It just . . . *can't* . . ."

"Ah, I think I am beginning to understand. I am obviously in one of those periodically reoccuring ages in which belief in our existence is almost nonexistent. Nevertheless, I assure you, I *am* a demon. A few moments ago you combined various elements and their amalgamation set off a key which brought me here. Now I am willing to make a pact with you to . . ."

"To buy my soul," the inventor finished. He shook his head in disbelief. "Frankly, I never believed in their existence."

"It is rather unbelievable," the devil admitted agreeably, "but, for that matter, so are a good many things I note here. Take your political . . ."

The inventor interrupted again. "The point is that I have a potential afterlife. I admit surprise. But, well, I certainly don't wish to spend it in hell."

The demon frowned. "Hell?"

The inventor dripped sarcasm. "I'd rather go to the *good* place than the *bad* place when I die, thank you."

Mephistopheles nodded. "I see. You've been subjected to their propaganda." He bounced from his stool and began pacing the room in his agitation. "Listen, you've read about the war between us demons and *them*, haven't you?"

"Well, yes. I thought it allegory at the time but—"

"Who authored the books you read, their side or ours?"

"I don't believe I get what you're driving at."

"Listen. Suppose George Washington had lost the Revolutionary War and the British had retained America. What would the present historical chronicles have to say about Washington? Or to bring it up to date, suppose Hitler had won the Second World War. What would the books say about Roosevelt and Churchill?"

"I begin to see your point, but . . ."

"Certainly! We lost our war and the other side has had the opportunity to write the history of the conflict. You've never read our viewpoint, written by one of our fellows, have you?"

"Well, no."

"Very well."

"We seem to have drifted from the subject."

The demon was ruffled. "Very well. But let's hear no more of the *good* place and the *bad* place. We of the Lowerarchy think our place is quite desirable. Much better heating, for one thing."

"I suppose it's all a matter of viewpoint," the inventor soothed, "but I'm still not inclined to sell my soul."

"Now, listen," Mephistopheles told him. "I haven't contributed a soul for a long time. I'll make an attractive offer." He indicated the coins on the desk. "How's that for a beginning?"

The inventor shook his head. "Even if I was interested, and I'm not, it's illegal to possess gold these days."

The demons stared at him. "You mean gold isn't used as money here? What a space-time continuum!" He shook his head. "Well, what is it you desire more than anything else?"

More to humor the other than anything else the inventor pursed his lips and mused it over. "I don't know." He hesitated a long moment. "I suppose I'd like to invent things that became used by everybody." He stared, unseeing, out the dirty shop window, and added, almost to himself. "You know. I'd like my devices spread all over the country, like electric lights, like automobiles."

"An idealist," Mephistopheles said approvingly, "a philanthropist. Very commendable amongst humans, so I understand." He thought it over. "I'll tell you what I'll do, old man. You're approximately thirty years of age. Ordinarily, you would work in small laboratories such as this for the rest of your life with promoters and clever operators defrauding you of most of the things you developed. I'll make a covenant to render you my support for the next twenty years in return for your soul."

The demon was taken away with sudden enthusiasm. "I'll see your inventions are put to the most wide-spread of use, that they become part and parcel of the daily life of your people. Besides that, I'll see you receive full remuneration for your work—no losing of your patents to clever charlatans in court fights. You'll be the inventor of the age!"

The other was caught up by the dream. "Done!" he cried.

* * *

It was all but twenty years later and the great man sprawled at his ease on the terrace of his Catskill estate. To his right stood a frosted glass, in his hand was a financial statement from one of his numerous concerns.

The butler entered noiselessly and the celebrated inventor looked up in impatience. "Yes, Hassel?"

"Your business manager is here, sir."

"Oh? Send Nick right out, Hassel."

"Very good, sir."

Mephistopheles hurried onto the terrace. "Congratulations!" he gushed. "Detailed reports show you've done it again!"

"Of course," the inventor yawned. "But you can't give me all of the credit, you know. Others participated."

The demon's enthusiasm wasn't to be dampened. "I thought you'd really hit the top when you invented the neon sign, they spread nationwide in a matter of months. Yes, sir, neon signs all over the place, eyes popping out from strain from coast to coast."

"Ummm," the inventor said modestly. "But, Nick, there's something I . . ."

His manager gushed on. "And then the jukebox, from my point of view probably the greatest invention of the century!"

"Oh, come now." It occurred to the inventor that twenty years of contact with America had changed the demon considerably. That hand-painted tie, that fat cigar.

"No, I insist. From my viewpoint, absolutely the greatest invention of the century."

"But, listen, Nick. There's something I wanted to talk to you about. This, uh, contract that we signed twenty years ago. I've been thinking it over and I wonder . . ."

The other raised a protesting hand. "Now don't you worry about that, old man. I was talking to some of the lower-downs and they agree with me that your contract should be extended indefinitely. You're doing much better here than you could elsewhere. Why, this present contribution in the development of *How To Build Your Own* kits—thousands of souls being driven to distraction—

accomplishes more of the good work we strive for than a thousand honor graduates of Lucifer U."

He beamed at his protégé fondly.

Said I to myself, said I.

Who Else Could I Count On?

by Manly Wade Wellman

"I reckon I believe you," I admitted to the old man at last. "You've given me proofs. It couldn't be any otherwise but that you've come back from times forty years ahead of now."

"You can believe wonders, John," he said. "Not many could be made to believe the things I've told."

"This war that's coming," I started to say, "the one that nobody will win—"

"The one that everybody will lose," he said. "I've come back to this day and time to keep it from starting, if I can. Come with me, John, we'll go to the rulers of this world. We'll make them believe, too, make them see that the war mustn't start."

"Explain me one thing first," I said, and: "What's that?" he asked.

"If you were an old man forty years along from now, then you'd have been right young in these times." I talked slowly, trying to clear the thought for both of us. "If that's so, what if you meet the young man you used to be?"

So softly he smiled: "John," he said, "why do you reckon I sought you out of all living men today?"

"Lord have mercy!" I said.

"Who else could I count on?"

"Lord have mercy!" I said again.

It's all how you look at it—

The Rat and the Snake

by A. E. van Vogt

Mark Gray's main pleasure in life was feeding rats to his pet python. He kept the python in a blocked-off room in the old house in which he lived alone. Each mealtime, he would put the rat in a narrow tunnel he had rigged. At the end of the tunnel was an opening. The rat, going through the narrow space into the bright room beyond, automatically spring-locked a gate across the opening.

It would then find itself in the room with the python, with no way of escape.

Mark liked to listen to its squeaks as it became aware of its danger, and then he would hear its mad scurrying to escape the irresistible enemy. Sometimes he watched the exciting scene through a plate-glass window, but he actually preferred the sound to the fight, conjuring his own delectable mental pictures, always from the viewpoint of the python.

During World War III, the O.P.A. forgot to put a ceiling price on rats. The catching of rats got no special priority. Rat catchers were drafted into the armed forces as readily as the other people. The supply of rats grew less. Mark was soon reduced to catching his own rats; but he had to work for a living in the ever-leaner times of war, so that there were periods of time when the python was fed infrequently.

Then one day Mark, ever searching, glimpsed some white rats through a window of an old commercial-style building. He peered in eagerly, and though the room was dimly lighted with wartime regulation bulbs, he was able to make out that it was a large room with hundreds of cages in it and that each of the cages contained rats.

He made it to the front of the building at a dead run. In pausing to catch his breath, he noticed the words on the door: CARRON LABORATORIES, Research.

He found himself presently in a dim hallway of a business office. Because everybody was clearly working twice as hard because of the war, it took a little while to attract the attention of one of the women employees; and there were other delays such as just sitting and waiting while it seemed as if he was the forgotten man. But after all those minutes he was finally led into the office of a small, tight-faced man, who was introduced as Eric Plode and who listened to his request and the reason for it.

When Mark described his poor, starving python, the small man laughed a sudden, explosive laughter. But his eyes remained cold. Moments later he curtly rejected the request.

Whereupon he made a personal thing out of it. "And don't get any ideas," he snarled. "Stay away from our rats. If we catch you filching around here, we'll have the law on you."

Until those words were spoken, Mark hadn't really thought about becoming a rat-stealing criminal. Except for his peculiar love for his python, he was a law-abiding, tax-paying nobody.

As Mark was leaving, Plode hastily sent a man to follow him. Then, smiling grimly, he walked into an office that had printed on the door: HENRY CARRON, Private.

"Well, Hank," he said gaily, "I think we've got our subject."

Carron said, "This had better be good since we can't even get prisoners of war assigned us for the job."

The remark made Plode frown a little. He had a tendency toward ironic thoughts, and he had often thought recently, "Good God, they're going to use the process on millions of the unsuspecting enemy after we get it tested, but they won't give us a G.D. so-and-so to try it out on because of some kind of prisoner of war convention."

Aloud, he said smugly. "I suppose by a stretch of the imagination you could call him human."

"That bad?"

Plode described Mark and his hobby, finished, "I suppose it's a matter of point of view. But I won't feel any guilt, particularly if he sneaks over tonight and with criminal intent tries to steal some of our rats." He grinned mirthlessly. "Can you think of anything lower than a rat stealer?"

Henry Carron hesitated but only for moments. Millions of people were dead and dying, and a test absolutely had to be made on a human being. Because if something went wrong on the battlefield, the effect of surprise might be lost with who knew what repercussions.

"One thing sure," he nodded, "there'll be no evidence against us. So go ahead."

It seemed to Mark, as he came stealthily back that night, that these people with their thousands of rats would never miss the equivalent of one rat a week or so. He was especially pleased when he discovered that the window was unlocked and that the menagerie was unguarded. No doubt, he thought good-humoredly, babysitters for rats were in scarce supply because of the wartime worker shortage.

The next day he thrilled again to the familiar sound of a rat squeaking in fear of the python. Toward evening his phone rang. It was Eric Plode.

"I warned you," said the small man in a vicious tone. "Now you must pay the penalty."

Plode felt better for having issued the warning. "Be it on his own soul," he said sanctimoniously, "if he's there."

Mark hung up, contemptuous. Let them try to prove anything.

In his sleep that night he seemed to be suffocating. He woke up, and he was not lying on his bed but instead was on a hard floor. He groped for the light switch but could not find it. There was a bright rectangle of light about twenty feet away. He headed for it.

Crash! A gate slammed shut behind him as he emerged.

He was in a vast room, larger than anything he had ever seen. Yet it was vaguely familiar. Except for its size it resembled the room in which he kept his python.

On the floor in front of him, an object that he had

noticed and regarded as some sort of a leathery rug, thicker than he was tall, stirred and moved toward him.

Realization came suddenly, horrendously.

He was the size of a rat. This was the python slithering across the floor with distended jaws.

Mad squealing as Mark Gray experienced the ultimate thrill of the strange method by which he had enjoyed life for so many years . . . Experienced it this one and only time from the viewpoint of the rat.

Prepared for all emergencies.

The Finest Hunter in the World

by Harry Harrison

"You of course realize, Mr. Lamb, that not one hunter has ever bagged a Venusian swamp-thing?" Godfrey Spingle spoke into the microphone, then shoved it toward the other man.

"Indeed I do. I've read all the records and studied all the reports. That is why I am here on Venus. I have been called the finest hunter in the world and, to be perfectly honest, I would rather enjoy being called the finest hunter in *two* worlds."

"Well, thank you, Mr. Lamb. And may the best wishes of the Intrasystem Broadcasting Company go with you, as well as all the listening millions out there. This is Godfrey Spingle, in Muckcity, on Venus, signing off." He flipped the switch and stowed the mike back in the recorder case.

Behind them the shuttle rocket roared as it blasted up through the damp air and Lamb waited until the sound had died away before he spoke.

"If the interview is finished, I wonder if you would be kind enough to tell me which of these . . ." He pointed

toward the ramshackle collection of tottering structures,
". . . is the hotel."

"None of them." Spingle picked up two of Lamb's
bags. "It sank into the mud last week, but I have a cot
for you in one of the warehouses."

"That's very kind of you," Lamb said, picking up the
other two cases and staggering after his long-legged
guide. "I hate to put you to any trouble."

"No trouble," Spingle said, unsuccessfully keeping a
thin note of complaint out of his voice. "I used to run
the hotel too before it went down. And I'm the customs
officer and mailman. There's not much of a population
in this place—or any damn reason why there should be."

Spingle was sorry for himself and angry at the injustice
of the world. Here he was, six foot two, strong and handsome, and rotting away in this filthy hole. While Lamb,
five foot four, round and fat, with bifocals was famous—
as a hunter! No justice, no justice at all.

Lamb began rooting in his bags as soon as they were
dropped onto the mildewed concrete floor. "I want to go
out at once, shoot a swamp-thing before dark so I can
get the morning rocket back. Would you be so kind as to
tell the guide."

"I'm the guide." He had to control his sneer. "Aren't
you being a little, well, optimistic about your chances.
The swamp-things can swim, fly, walk, and swing from
trees. They are wary, intelligent, and deadly. No one has
ever shot one of them."

"I shall," Lamb said, taking a gray coverall from his
bag and pulling it on. "Hunting is a science that I alone
have mastered. I never fail. Hand me that head, please."

Wordlessly, Spingle passed over a large papier-mâché
head that had white teeth and red eyes painted on it.
Lamb slipped it over his own head, then pulled on gray
gloves, followed by gray boots with white claws dangling
from them.

"How do I look?" he asked.

"Like a fat swamp rat," Spingle blurted out.

"Fine." He took a gnarled stick from his bag and
placed it between the jaws of the mask. "Lead the way,
Mr. Spingle, if you please."

Spingle, at a complete loss for words, belted on his
pistol and took the path into the swamp.

"I'll give you a one minute start," Lamb said as the last building vanished behind them in the mist, "then follow your footprints. Be careful, I understand these swamps are quite deadly."

"Deadly! That's an understatement. Take my advice, Lamb, and go back."

"Thank you, Mr. Spingle," the muffled voice said from inside the grotesque head, "but I shall proceed."

Spingle led the way; let the fool get eaten by the swamp-things or any other local beasts. Once the idiot was gone his bags could be gone through and there should be something of value . . .

The unmistakable sound of a blaster echoed through the damp air and, after a moment's paralysis, Spingle ran back down the path with his own handgun ready.

It was not needed. Lamb sat on the rotting trunk of a fallen tree, the discarded mask-head beside him, mopping sweat from his face with a large bandanna. Beyond him, half in and half out of the jungle, was the hideous fang-toothed, claw-winged, poison-green corpse of a swamp-thing, frightful even in death.

"How. . . ?" Spingle gasped. "What . . . you . . . how?"

"A simple story," Lamb said, digging a camera from his pocket, "a discovery I made some years back. I found out that I was heavy of foot and bad of eye, an undistinguished tracker and an unaccomplished woodsman. Though I'm a damn fine shot; I pride myself on that. My ambition was to be a hunter, but I could never get close enough to my prey to get in a shot. So, with impeccable logic, I changed roles. After all—these beasts are born hunters and killers, so why should I compete on their terms? Instead I became prey and let the beasts stalk and attack me—to be killed themselves, of course. In the guise of the oryx, skin-draped and horn-headed, I have knelt by the stream and killed the swift leopard. As a very slow zebra I have bagged my share of lions. It is the same here. My research showed that the swamp-things live almost exclusively off of the giant swamp rat, *rattus venerius*. So I became a rat—with this result." He raised the camera and photographed the dead beast.

"Without a gun?"

Lamb pointed to the twisted stick, leaning now against

the log, that he had carried in his rodent teeth. "That is a disguised blaster. These creatures would have recognized a gun at once."

Then the idea came to Spingle. The swamp-thing was dead and *he* had the gun—and the secret. Lamb would vanish in the swamp and he would be the finest hunter in the world. Two worlds. He raised his weapon.

"So long, sucker," he said. "Thanks for the tip."

Lamb only smiled and pressed the flash button on his camera. The blaster, concealed inside, blew a neat hole through Spingle before he could press his own trigger. Lamb shook his head.

"People never listen. I'm fit prey for *all* hunters. Now, let me see, that makes my bag one swamp-thing—and thirteen, no, fourteen would-be assassins."

—and baby makes three.

Life

by Dennis R. Caro

Mackelreath sat with his legs crossed in the high-backed chair. That was the fashion this year, high-backed chairs. Planned discomfort.

The waiting room was sparse. That too was fashion. The walls were paneled, but only a single picture hung in a thin wooden frame. A rice field in China. The faces of the people working were hidden.

If one extended enough analogies, Mackelreath supposed, even China was fashion. Overpopulation, starvations, stereotypes that no longer had any real basis, yet the emotion behind them was constantly being pressed into the gut of the American people.

Mackelreath was a pragmatist. He felt he knew life for

what it was; where he could influence the course of events he did, where he could not, he accepted what came.

His wife Marissa was different. She was inside the doctor's office. She was pregnant.

There were magazines Mackelreath could have read as he waited, with articles to reinforce the official point of view. Slanted emotional logic and biased statistics. Mackelreath felt neither the need to be convinced nor to be reassured.

Parenthood wasn't popular. The more people, the greater the need for goods and services and the higher the price one had to pay for them. In a high technology consumer-oriented society, overpopulation led to inflation and Mackelreath was quite happy with his economic station the way it was.

Marissa. They had been married only a year, yet this was the first time he was conscious of not knowing exactly how she felt. Did a woman change with newly created life growing inside her, or was that just another government-sponsored stereotype?

She'd been a libertarian in college. Certainly her activism had softened since then, but she still didn't like being told what she had to do.

Could she have wanted a child? It wasn't something they had talked about, even after she'd known she was pregnant and . . . Mackelreath smiled. He hadn't realized she knew him this well. Of course they hadn't talked about it. She knew he could adjust—just as well as she knew he would have been incapable of making a decision.

I could have spent years listing pros and cons, he thought. Now I have only one set of realities to face. I'm going to be a father.

A montage of memories sifted through from his subconscious: Marissa watching children playing in the park; the television special they'd seen on the Kiddy Camps in India; the expression on her face when she'd rummaged through the old baby clothes in her mother's attic.

It wasn't going to be easy. There would be forms to be filled out, batteries of psychological tests, a waiver for the three-year marital stability requirement.

Did Marissa know about that? Waivers weren't exactly common knowledge.

She must have known. She hadn't been the least bit apprehensive about the examination and it wasn't as if pregnancy was an accident.

The door to the doctor's office opened. Marissa was there, the nurse behind her with a hand on his wife's shoulder.

"Charley?"

Mackelreath rose and she was in his arms. Something was wrong. She hadn't known about the waivers, that had to be it, but . . .

"Oh Charley, they're going to make us keep it."

Who can define its mystery?

Love Story

by Eric Frank Russell

General Romaine growled irefully, "The trouble with the fighting forces today is that they're no longer wholly in the hands of military leaders. They're bewitched, bothered and bewildered by vote-catching politicians, sentimental mammas, psychiatrists, psychologists, physiotherapists and a horde of other pulse-takers, muscle-pinchers and bump-feelers."

"You may be right," agreed Harding, recognizing the other's need to blow off surplus steam.

"I *am* right. A soldier isn't a soldier any more. Not like he was when I was young. He's something else now, a mess of repressions, inhibitions, complexes and all sorts of juvenile tantrums that once we cured quite effectively with a hearty kick in the pants."

"You may be right," repeated Harding, automatically.

"I *am* right," asserted Romaine. "Terra is rapidly going to the dogs. Some day we'll be taken over by a life form with more virility and plain horse sense. It will serve us as we deserve."

"Oh, I don't know," Harding ventured. "The Pharoahs thought the world was tumbling headlong from bad to worse. They inscribed dire prophecies upon their temple walls. After me, the deluge. Gaze on my works, ye mighty, and despair."

"Hell with the Pharoahs," snapped Romaine. "They've been dead ten thousand years. I'm talking about today, the here and now."

"What's gone wrong?" invited Harding. "Anything I can do to help?"

"No." Brushing aside the high stack of papers on his desk, Romaine scowled at the resulting space. "We've opened up a complete system in the region of Sirius. So we've got to establish ourselves there with minimum of delay. That means we must plant a permanent garrison upon the six worlds we've claimed. You'd think that would be easy, wouldn't you?"

"I don't see why it should be difficult."

"Twenty-five or thirty years ago it'd have been no trouble at all. Today things are different. We have progressed, see?" He let go a short, harsh laugh. "Progress, they call it."

Harding offered no comment.

"So I order the transfer of three regiments of the Centaurian Guard, eighteen thousand men in all. In days gone by they'd have jumped to action complete with ships, stores and all equipment. In jig time they'd have settled down to being the new Sirian Holding Force. But what happens now?"

"You tell me."

"There's a lot of bureaucratic delay while three thousand eight hundred forty-two men claim protection from the move on the grounds that they're married, have wives, families and homes rooted on Centauri. About eleven hundred more plead for elimination from the drafting-list because they're engaged and soon to be married. Politicians, psychiatrists, religious leaders, psychologists and other nonmilitary types uphold all these claims. Love, they say, is a biological necessity and the family is the foundation-stone of society."

"Love is natural enough, isn't it?"

"Natural for the landbound lugs," asserted Romaine, raising his voice. "Spacemen are different. Their only devotion is to the cosmos. They're a dedicated profession."

"That's a mighty hard way of looking at it," Harding offered.

"It's the proper way. The men of the Centaurian Guard signed on to serve Terra faithfully and well no matter where they may be sent. They signed with their eyes wide open, knowing what they were doing, knowing it meant personal sacrifice. I've no time for the whining lout who makes a legal contract and then tries to evade his responsibilities."

"But surely we can dig up enough single, unattached men to serve as replacements?"

"We can—after wasting valuable time. But that's not the point. The point is that the Centaurian Guard should obey orders promptly, without question. Once upon a time it would have done so. Today we get all this stuff about love and family obligations and biological necessities." He paused, spat out, "Love—it makes me sick."

"The Terran Government encouraged marriage in the Centaurian sector," Hardin pointed out. "You can't maintain permanent grip on a world by populating it solely with fighting men. You've also got to have women and children."

"The problem could have been solved by boosting civilian emigration from Terra," Romaine retorted. "That would have left space-troopers free to do their proper job, untied, unhampered. From the military viewpoint a trooper burdened with a family is a gone goose. He's just no use as a fighting unit." He jerked an indicative thumb at the big stack of papers." And there's the proof: letters giving the names of men who mustn't be shipped Siriusward. They're all unfit for drafting, being contaminated by love."

"Well, I see what you mean," said Harding, "but I can't say I agree with you."

"Why not?"

"I suspect you might talk differently if you had been married yourself."

"You do, do you? I've got news for you: I've had both the opportunity and the desire."

"But did nothing about it?"

"No, certainly not. Duty comes first. Love and space-service don't go together. They're completely incompatible. When a spaceman gives way to the pangs of love the rot has set in. Show me a trooper riddled with sloppy sentiment and I'll show you a guy who is no use on the star-trails."

"That's a sweeping statement."

"Love," declared Romaine, warming to his theme, "is not a word in the true spaceman's vocabulary. It belongs to a life he has repudiated, as if he were a monk. The fellow who thinks of it is endangering his own vow to serve. Maybe it's an old-fashioned viewpoint, but it's a good one."

"So all your life you've kept love at a safe distance, eh?"

"I have."

"Every form of it?"

"Every form, no matter what."

"Then," said Harding, "I'd like to see your reaction to this love letter." He flipped hurriedly through the pile at the side of the desk, extracted a missive, passed it to the other. Then he lay back and watched interestedly as Romaine frowned over it.

Sirian Force Assembly Center
Centauri

My General,

I don't suppose you remember me. Thirty-two years ago we enlisted together, you as an officer, I as a private, but there were a lot of us that day.

Since then I have seen the Centaurian Guard grow and develop from a small cluster of frontiersmen to a great military body of much pride and many battle honours.

It has been a wonderful privilege to serve in the Centaurian Guard. All my adult years have been given to it gladly, without stint. It has been my life and my only true love.

Now see the trap into which I have fallen. I am willing to go anywhere and because of that I have been transferred into something called the Sirian Holding Force.

*General, they have taken away my helmet-badge,
the silver horse of Centauri. I have never asked much
of life . . . only that I should be allowed to wear it to
the end of my useful days . . .*

> (Signed)
> Rafael Amadeo. T/Sgt.

"I think it's rubbish," declared Romaine, very loudly.
"Utter balderdash!" He dumped the letter on the desk.

The other shrugged, strolled toward the door.

"Harding!"

He halted. "Yes?"

"Are you concealing the belief that I am a stinking
liar?"

Harding hesitated, said, "I know you are."

"Dead right," said Romaine. He grabbed his desk-
phone, dialed, said to someone, "1914778 T/Sgt. Rafael
Amadeo will be retained in the Centaurian Guard as a
permanent instructor. Request his commanding officer to
report on his suitability for a commission." He planted
the phone, glanced up, rasped, "Well, why are you looking at me like that?"

"Love," informed Harding, "is a remarkable thing."

Romaine bawled. "Get out of my sight!"

I always remember it had swastikas on it.

Exile in Lakehurst

by Robert Payes

Deep in space, where all is quiet, there hurtled a small,
bullet-shaped spacecraft. Inside, its two cylindrical passengers were engaged in a heated argument.

"Okay, Mr. Know-It-All, what now?"

"Oh, be quiet! What's done is done, and, besides, there's no way to turn this damn spaceship around."

"I wish you had thought about this when you bagged that last grafz."

"How was I to know he wasn't forgiven?"

"As I recall, you fool, they have a white cross on their dorsal sail."

"And as I said before, I came at him from the front and didn't see the damn cross!"

"Tell that to the holies."

"I did. They didn't believe me."

"Ah, yes, I'd almost forgotten. And here we are, exiled from home in this one-way can—the penalty for any xlt who bags an unforgiven grafz. I wonder who decided to include the offender's mate?"

"You can thank the scriptures for that last remark."

"That's just great. Do you even know where this thing is programmed to land?"

"No . . . but wherever it is, we'll be landing there pretty soon."

The craft hurtled on, approaching a large, brown-and-blue planet. As it penetrated the outer reaches of the atmosphere, reentry foam was pumped out until it covered the entire spaceship. The foam then hardened into a super-tough heat shield that protected the ship upon reentry. Unfortunately, the shield disintegrated too soon, and the craft shattered in the upper atmosphere. The two xlts, after the initial shock of freefall, sent out frantic balance beams, which stopped them at a height of eight thousand feet.

"And heeeeeeeere we are! Not a bad planet to be exiled to, huh?"

"Well, it's a nice place to visit."

"Party pooper."

"Anything that looks edible down there?"

"Noting except that big oval thing down there. . . . Big . . . oval . . . thing. . . ?"

". . . a grafz . . ."

"FOOD!" they both screamed. "WE'RE SAVED!"

The two beings rocketed down lower.

"Let's not be hasty now . . ."

"Whaddaya mean, hasty? Look for yourself—long oval

body, four tail fins, *no white cross*—is that or is that a grafz?''

"Well . . . it's not the right *color* . . ."

"Color, schmuller! It's probably a mutation. Let's go—I'm hungry." Without waiting for his mate, the xlt converted himself to energy and shot towards the big object.

"Ouch! I didn't think grafz skins were that hard . . . and hey! It's hollow! Nothing inside but this strange gas."

. . . and as its seven million cubic feet of hydrogen ignited, the dirigible *Hindenburg* exploded, lighting up the night sky over Lakehurst, New Jersey.

There is nothing like a dame—

The Bait

by Fritz Leiber

Fafhrd the Northerner was dreaming of a great mound of gold.

The Gray Mouser the Southern, ever cleverer in his forever competitive fashion, was dreaming of a heap of diamonds. He hadn't tossed out all of the yellowish ones yet, but he guessed that already his glistening pile must be worth more than Fafhrd's glowing one.

How he knew in his dream what Fafhrd was dreaming was a mystery to all beings in Newhon, except perhaps Sheelba of the Eyeless Face and Ninguable of the Seven Eyes, respectively the Mouser's and Fafhrd's sorcerer-mentors. Maybe, a vast, black basement mind shared by two was involved.

Simultaneously they awoke, Fafhrd a shade more slowly, and sat up in bed.

Standing midway between the feet of their cots was an object that fixed their attention. It weighed about eighty pounds, was about four feet eight inches tall, had long straight black hair pendent from head, had ivory-white skin, and was as exquisitely formed as a slim chesspiece of the King of Kings carved from a single moonstone. It looked thirteen, but the lips smiled a cool self-infatuated seventeen, while the gleaming deep eye-pools were first blue melt of the Ice Age. Naturally, she was naked.

"She's mine!" the Gray Mouser said, always quick from the scabbard.

"No, she's mine!" Fafhrd said almost simultaneously, but conceding by that initial "No" that the Mouser had been first, or at least he had expected the Mouser to be first.

"I belong to myself and to no one else, save two or three virile demidevils," the small naked girl said, though giving them each in turn a most nymphish lascivious look.

"I'll fight you for her," the Mouser proposed.

"And I you," Fafhrd confirmed, slowly drawing Graywand from its sheath beside his cot.

The Mouser likewise slipped Scalpel from its rat-skin container.

The two heroes rose from their cots.

At this moment, two personages appeared a little behind the girl—from thin air, to all appearances. Both were at least nine feet tall. They had to bend, not to bump the ceiling. Cobwebs tickled their pointed ears. The one on the Mouser's side was black as wrought iron. He swiftly drew a sword that looked forged from the same material.

At the same time, the other newcomer—bone-white, this one—produced a silver-seeming sword, likely steel plated within.

The nine-footer opposing the Mouser aimed a skull-splitting blow at the top of his head. The Mouser parried in prime and his opponent's weapon shrieked off to the left. Whereupon, smartly swinging his rapier widdershins, the Mouser slashed off the black fiend's head, which struck the floor with a horrid clank.

The white afreet opposing Fafhrd trusted to a downward thrust. But the Northerner, catching his blade in a counter-clockwise bind, thrust him through, the silvery sword missing Fafhrd's right temple by the thinness of a hair.

With a petulant stamp of her naked heel, the nymphet vanished into thin air, or perhaps Limbo.

The Mouser made to wipe off his blade on the cot-clothes, but discovered there was no need. He shrugged. "What a misfortunate for you, comrade," he said in a voice of mocking woe. "Now you will not be able to enjoy the delicious chit as she disports herself on your heap of gold."

Fafhrd moved to cleanse Graywand on *his* sheets, only to note that it too was altogether unbloodied. He frowned. "Too bad for you, best of friends," he sympathized. "Now you won't be able to possess her as she writhes with girlish abandon on your couch of diamonds, their glitter striking opalescent tones from her pale flesh."

"Mauger that effeminate artistic garbage, how did you know that I was dreaming diamonds?" the Mouser demanded.

"How did I?" Fafhrd asked himself wonderingly. At last he begged the question with, "The same way, I suppose, that you knew I was dreaming of gold."

The two excessively long corpses chose that moment to vanish, and the severed head with them.

Fafhrd said sagely, "Mouser, I begin to believe that supernatural forces were involved in this morning's haps."

"Or else hallucinations, oh great philosopher," the Mouser countered somewhat peevishly.

"Not so," Fafhrd corrected, "for see, they've left their weapons behind."

"True enough," the Mouser conceded, rapaciously eyeing the wrought iron and tin plated blades on the floor. "Those will fetch a fancy price on Curio Court."

The Great Gong of Lankhmar, sounding distantly through the walls, boomed out the twelve funeral strokes of noon, when burial parties plunge spade into earth.

"An after-omen," Fafhrd pronounced. "Now we know the source of the supernal force. The Shadowland, terminus of all funerals."

"Yes," the Mouser agreed. "Prince Death, that eager boy, has had another go at us."

Fafhrd splashed cool water onto his face from a great bowl set against the wall. "Ah well," he spoke through the splashes, "Twas a pretty bait at least. Truly, there's nothing like a nubile girl, enjoyed or merely glimpsed naked, to give one an appetite for breakfast.''

"Indeed yes," the Mouser replied, as he tightly shut his eyes and briskly rubbed his face with a palm full of white brandy. "She was just the sort of immature dish to kindle your satyrish taste for maids newly budded.''

In the silence that came as the splashing stopped, Fafhrd inquired innocently, *"Whose* satyrish taste?''

Who has a better right?

The Humanic Complex

by Ray Russell

Buon giorno. It's an absolutely *super* morning. I'll bet you wouldn't say no to a nice hot cup of tea, eh, dearie? Coffee? Righty-o, I'll join you. Prosit! Down the hatch! Yum sing! Ah, this hits the spot, it do. Now, then, permit me to introduce myself. My name is Sallybill, and I'm here to offer you three wishes. No, you're not dreaming—I'll pinch you, see? Give a listen. In my century, we've achieved a lot of achievements. Most of them you wouldn't even *understand* if I told you about them—I don't understand half of them my *own* self! But some of them are fairly simple, and even a primitive like you (no offense) can probably grasp them. For instance, airlove and bloodsongs and skycandy, stuff like that. Well, one of the newer wrinkles is this wish shtick. I don't think you chaps had it in this timezone. The way it works is like this. Anybody of third-level status or above, who's passed the 920 exams and doesn't have any bluejacks on his/her record, can grant three wishes to anyone, *provided* that the granting is done in a timezone prior to the grantor's birth. Grantor, c'est moi. Don't ask me why it has to be that way—some technicality about spacetime continuum stress factors. Needless to say, we cracked the time barrier *long* ago. So anyhow, since I passed my 920's with flying colors yesterday—well, of course it wasn't really yesterday, it—was ist los, ma'am?

You're sitting on my foot. And that's sir, not ma'am.

Sorry, is that bettter—sir? This old fixed-gender stuff always throws me. Can we get on with the wishes, do you think? I'd really like to be shlepping back to my own zone.

Can I go to the bathroom first?

The whatroom?

Bathroom.

¿Porqué?

Well, it's rather indelicate, but, not to put too fine a point on it, I want to empty my bladder.

Done and done. Your bladder's empty.

Amazing! It really is empty. How did you do that?

Elementary interdimensional portation. Kid stuff. Now, how's about your second wish?

What? You mean that bladder trick was my first wish???

Natürlich.

But I could have done that myself!

Not to worry, old bean. You still have two more to go. Make the most of 'em, wot? Eh? Eh?

Yes, but I wish I knew—

Cave quid dicis! Don't say I Wish or I Want unless you mean it.

May I ask a question?

Be my guest.

Can I wish for anything? Anything at all?

Absotively.

And I'll get it?

Posilutely.

Then I wish for three thousand wishes instead of just three.

Nyet, that's out.

But you said anything.

Anything but that. Stress factors again.

Oh, all right. I wish I could live for—

Durak! Were you going to wish for immortality?

Yes—but I suppose that's out, too?

No, it's allowable. But take my advice. In your case,

that would be a wasted wish. Besides, some of my best friends are immies, look you, and they are very unhappy people, whatever.

I'll take your word for it. Then I wish for a billion—

Trust me. Don't ask for money.

Why not?

Shure, an' you wouldn't be knowin' what to do with it at all, at all.

Oh, yes, I would!

You only think you would. Besides, without going into a whole song and dance, just believe that you wouldn't *believe* what's going to happen to money. Stay away from money.

If you say so. Let's see. Then I wish to possess that which all the sages, in vain, have—

Cool it, man. Infinite wisdom, right? Hey, you don't need any more wisdom than you already got. And some of my best buddies are wizzies, and they're real downbeat dudes, you dig?

You're certainly making it difficult. And you're sitting on my other foot now.

Excusez-moi. Try again.

Give me some time.

Och, mon, take a wee minute, but nae mair.

I can't think of anything else!

What about sex? That's a big deal back here in this zone, ain't it? How about I fix it so all the sexiest guys in the world—

Women, women.

—Women, right, sorry, all the most beautiful, desirable women in the whole world become unable to resist your charms? Pardee, hit oghte thee to lyke.

The only trouble is, I'm not all that interested in sex. It's fine for others, I'm no prude, but it's just not my sort of thing. I mean, as a steady diet. Once in a while, all right, but that's all.

I had a feeling you might say that. Want to pack it in?

No, no! . . . wait . . . I've got it. . . .

Are you sure?

I am. This may sound pompous, but . . . I wish to know whether or not there is a God.

Yes, there is. Last wish.

For my last wish: I wish to see His face.

Done and done. Get up and look in the mirror.

When I climbed out of bed and peered into the mirror that hung on the wall on the opposite side of the room, I saw a face I did not know. A stranger, not young or old, handsome or ugly. I blinked and rubbed that face with my hands; then I turned to Sallybill, who continued to perch at the foot of my bed. I asked, "Who am I?"

"I just told you, gospodin," Sallybill replied.

I smiled indulgently. "Yes, very amusing. But now tell me the truth, please."

"Truth? Mamma mia, that's a tall order! John, 18:38— jesting Pilate and all that. Even if we could agree as to what Truth is, Truth with a capital T, why should I necessarily be a repository of it? And even if I am, why should I tell you? That's for me to know and you to find out, to coin a phrase."

"Stop playing games," I said sternly. "I wish to know—"

"Your wishes are all kaput."

"But I can ask questions, can't I?"

"Fire away, Mungu."

I sat down at the head of the bed—there was no other furniture in the room. "You claim to be from what you call another timezone." Sallybill nodded wearily. "What year?"

"Year Purple, Cycle Epsilon-Ten."

I groaned. "What century?"

"Fifteenth," said Sallybill. "A.D.D. In other words, the fifteenth century after the Dark Dawn. Does that help you, filos?"

"No."

"I didn't think it would, Alors—" Sallybill hopped off the bed. "I'll be a-moseyin' on back to my own spread, I reckon."

"Wait!" I held out my hand. "Another question."

Sallybill sighed. "Let's hear it."

"What year is *this*?" I asked.

"You don't know?"

"I don't even know my own name!"

"I can't help you out on the year thing. Back here in this zone, they have a cockamamie way of naming the years."

"All right," I said, "then tell me, what's the name of this planet?"

"What planet?"

"The planet we're *on.*"

"What makes you so sure we're on a planet?"

"I'll put it another way. In your own timezone, do you live on a planet?"

Contemptuously, Sallybill snarled, "Art addlepated, sirrah? Fie, oh, fie! Think you like angels in the Heav'ns we fly?"

"Good enough. Now what's the name of *that* planet?"

"We call it The World!"

"Every planet is a world!"

Sallybill eloquently shrugged. "So sue me."

I tried another tactic. "How many planets in your solar system? And which one is yours, in order of distance from the sun?"

Sallybill frowned, obviously puzzled. "We is de *onliest* planet around de sun."

"I see . . ."

Sallybill added, "They saý there *used* to be other planets around our sun, but something happened to them."

"What exactly?"

"¿Quién sabe?"

After a moment, I said, calmly and smoothly, "Shall I tell you what I think?"

"Thought you'd never ask."

"I think this is a mental institution," I said. "I'm here because I've lost my memory. And you're another patient, who escaped from a padded cell, slipped into my room and woke me out of a sound sleep to entangle me in this deranged conversation."

"Takes one to know one," Sallybill said with a giggle.

"Or," I continued, for another thought had occurred to me, "you may not be a patient, but a doctor. All that three-wishes business was a hoax, some kind of experimental treatment, a well-meaning attempt to cure my amnesia, unlock my mind. . . ."

"Blimey," said Sallybill, "If it's just a bleedin' 'oax, then 'ow do you explain that bloomin' bladder trick, mate?"

Sallybill had a point, but I pressed on. "I don't know. Post-hypnotic suggestion, perhaps. And there's another possibility. I could be a prisoner. Of some totalitarian state. You're tampering with my mind, trying to make me divulge secrets, or trying to destroy me, confusing me, telling me I'm. . . ."

Sallybill said, "May I make a suggestion?"

I nodded, cautiously.

"Just on the odd chance that I may have been leveling with you, why don't you run a test?"

"How?"

"Simple—say Let there be light, or something. Create a man out of dust. Take your pick. See what happens."

I couldn't resist chuckling. "You don't catch me that easily," I said. "It's an old ploy. By getting me to go along with the charade, your battle is half won because you'll be making me admit there's at least a possibility that what you claim is true."

Sallybill seemed defeated—but I knew that was just another act. "I guess I know when I'm beat, but I did my job and gave you your three wishes. That's all I'm licensed for. So I better split. But look at it this way—there are plenty of meshugganah people who think they're God. Messianic complex, it's called in this zone. But what if God Himself flipped out and went bonkers? Mightn't He think He was a mere mortal? The shrinks would probably call it a humanic complex or something."

"Clever," I said. "Very clever. Good-by, Sallybill."

"Sayonara, Adjö. Farvel. Istenhozzád. Hyvästi. Adia-'gnu. Shalom. . . ."

REPORT FROM SALLYBILL:

REPORT COMMENCES. LOCATED & MET WITH SUBJECT IN SUITABLY REMOTE TIMEZONE, USED NEW OBLIQUE METHOD APPROVED AT LAST BRIEFING (CODE NAME: 3 WISHES). OBTAINED RESULTS SIMILAR TO THOSE USING DIFFERENT TECHNIQUES: NAMELY, TOTAL LACK OF SUCCESS. SUBJECT DISPLAYS APPARENTLY RATIONAL THOUGHT PROCESSES, LOGICAL WITHIN OVERALL DELUSIONAL FRAMEWORK, PARRIES ALL THRUSTS DEFTLY, EVEN BRILLIANTLY, BUT PERSISTENTLY REFUSES TO ACCEPT TRUE IDENTITY, CONTINUES TO REJECT RESPONSIBILITY, DECLINES TO RESUME DUTIES. COLLEAGUES HAVE REPORTED THAT HE IS NOT RESPONSIVE TO ANY DIRECT REFERENCE

TO PERNICIOUS RUMORS THAT HAVE HAD WIDE CURRENCY
EVER SINCE HIS BREAKDOWN (I.E., THAT HE NEVER EX-
ISTED, OR IS DEAD, ET AL.). SO I ESCHEWED THAT AP-
PROACH. RESPECTFULLY & REGRETFULLY SUGGEST
SUBJECT BE CLASSIFIED INCURABLE. LASCIATE OGNI SPER-
ANZA, ELI, ELI, LAMA SABACHTHANI? END REPORT.

As a cat-lover, I thoroughly approve.

Friends?

by Roberta Ghidalia

"Here kitty, kitty, here pussycat, please come here,"
called a small voice pleadingly.

For weeks Dorrie had watched the cat that belonged
to the old woman next door. She noticed how it seemed
to get thinner day by day and wondered, why?

That noon she withheld a portion of her luncheon fish
and now she tentatively extended her hand, containing
the fish, and began again.

"Here kitty, pretty kitty," she called.

The cat remained aloof and completely ignored the
entreaties of the child.

The little girl peered around and when she was certain
her mother was out of earshot, she called a little louder,
"Here kitty, kitty, pretty pussy, won't you come here?"

Dorrie's mother frequently admonished her for wanting to pet stray animals she saw in the street, but this cat
was no stray. It belonged to the peculiar little old lady,
Mrs. Stubbs, who lived in the ramshackle house next
door. Although lean and bedraggled, the pitiful creature
still retained her proud airs and graceful demeanor. As
she disdainfully prepared to strike a new pose and con-

tinue ignoring the pleas of the child, she threw a backward glance in Dorrie's direction. That did it. She caught the delicious aroma of the fish and her indifferent pose was immediately dispelled. She started across the yard in the direction of little Dorrie, but slowly, ever so slowly.

Dorrie, for her part, continued her exhortations to the cat, becoming more and more excited as the cat crept closer.

"Sweet little thing," thought Sassy, the cat. "Funny I've never really noticed her before, but then I've never cared much for children, till now."

The cat continued to approach the child cautiously, as if wary of some trick.

"Oh, how beautiful she is," thought Dorrie, her opinion somewhat colored by sentiment. "So graceful and proud. If only my mother could understand how I feel about animals. Well," mused the child, "maybe some day she will."

The cat meanwhile was coming ever closer and soon, there she was at the foot of Dorrie's chair, gazing wonderingly up at her.

Dorrie had all she could do to keep from shouting out with joy, but since to do so would only bring her mother on the run, and probably scare off the cat too, she remained silent. Her forebearance paid off handsomely, to her way of thinking. With one leap, Sassy was in her lap, green eyes flashing from Dorrie to the fish. The child slowly moved her hand toward the cat as Sassy surveyed the situation. Two sniffs, one gulp and the fish was gone. But not the puss. She sat there gazing adoringly up at the child, who was her benefactor.

Dorrie sat very still, so as not to disturb the cat. Hesitantly she raised one hand and began stroking the cat's head. What was that sound she heard? A slow building rumble issuing forth from the cat's throat. She was purring. Whatever the human equivalent of purring is, Dorrie was joining the cat in the pleasure. They looked lovingly into each other's eyes, and neither of them ever remembered feeling so good in their entire lives.

Sassy had never experienced affection from a human nor Dorrie from an animal before. Thus they remained for several moments, suspended in time. Each drinking in the marvelous newness of their relationship with one another.

Sassy, the cat, the loner, the independent spirit, giving full measure for what little she got from her mistress.

Dorrie, the child, completely dependent, confined to a wheelchair. Relying on her mother for everything.

Illogical, unlikely as it was, these two were drawn together as if by magnetic force.

Dorrie stopped stroking the cat for a moment and the cat began to lick her face. How deliciously queer it felt, that prickly little tongue returning her gesture of affection. The cat stopped abruptly and gazed soulfully at the child.

"Friends?" Dorrie said haltingly, to the cat.

"Meowrr," replied the cat.

"Dorrie!" Mother rushed out of the house screaming, "What are you doing with that cat?"

"Oh Mother, please don't chase her away. Let me keep her. The old witch next door doesn't really want her. See how skinny she is. Please, please let me have her, and—and I'll be a good girl from now on," pled the little girl.

A long look passed between Sassy, peering out from under Dorrie's chair, where she had taken refuge, and the child's mother. Suddenly, the initial revulsion the mother had felt at the sight of the bedraggled creature turned to pity.

"Why, the poor thing is just skin and bones," thought the woman, "she looks more dead than alive. Anyone who would treat an animal like that really must be a witch."

"Dorrie, I don't know about this, I must ask Mrs. Stubbs first," she heard herself saying.

"What's come over me," she thought, "I've never felt anything for an animal before, but suddenly I'm consumed with pity for this cat."

With very confused emotions, Mother left the newfound friends on the porch and crossed the yard toward the house next door.

"What a mess," she thought to herself, as she stepped gingerly through a tangle of overgrown grass and weeds in her neighbor's yard and made her way to the rundown old house.

"Why, it even looks like a witch's house somehow."

"Mrs. Stubbs," she called, rapping lightly on the door, which stood sagging on its hinges.

"Yes, who is it?" came a voice from within.

"Your neighbor, please open the door. I would like to speak to you in regard to your cat."

The door opened a crack revealing only the head of the old woman.

"Well, what's the evil creature done now?" the old woman said, scowling grotesquely.

"No, that's not it. The only thing she's done, to my knowledge, is to completely captivate my daughter, to the point that we'd like to keep her, if we may."

"He-he-he-he-he," cackled the old woman, "so your precious little crippled brat wants my cat, does she. Well take her then and good riddance. She's a bad 'un, she is. You mark my words. That cat is evil. She'll bring mischief wherever she goes, will that 'un."

"Thank you, Mrs. Stubbs, we'll take good care of her."

"You'd better, if you don't want trouble, and one thing more, see to it that you keep her away from here from now on. If I catch her here again, I'll kill her," shrilled the old hag, closing the door on her warning.

"Foolish old witch," thought Dorrie's mother. "Imagine attributing evil powers to the cat. Old wives' tales, that's all her nonsense amounts to."

After that, Sassy was indeed well cared for, by Dorrie and her mother. She did become the beautiful creature the child imagined she was. Her emaciated body filled out and her coat shone in the sunlight.

Dorrie remained puzzled by her mother's sudden change of heart, but she was too busy being happy with the pet she had so long hungered for to give it much thought.

Again and again they performed their ritual. "Friends?" Dorrie would say to the cat.

"Meowrr," the cat would reply, as if to reaffirm the bond between them.

Every time Dorrie's mother would meet Mrs. Stubbs, the old crone reiterated her warning about the evil cat and to keep the animal away from her house on threat of death to the pet.

Dorrie and Sassy were inseparable. Human and animal

drew close, and closer still. Mother thought about their relationship from time to time, but dismissed it from her mind when she saw how the child blossomed and seemed to be healthier and happier than ever before.

"I'll never understand that old witch's prejudice and hatred for a harmless cat like Sassy," she mused.

One night, about three months after Sassy had come to live with Dorrie, a curious thing happened.

The door at the rear of Dorrie's house opened, long after everyone should have been asleep, and out marched Sassy. Following close behind her down the ramp, in the light of the full moon, was Dorrie, in her little wheelchair.

Carefully, and with surprisingly little difficulty, they made their way to the old house next door.

Upon reaching their destination, Sassy sprang lightly to the sill of an open window and slipped inside. Having been an occupant of the house, she had long ago learned how to spring against the front door and trip the lock. This she promptly did, admitting Dorrie to the house.

They surprised Mrs. Stubbs in the first floor bedroom where Sassy knew she slept.

The old woman jumped from the bed and ran around the room crying, "Why are you here, what do you want?"

She paused in the middle of the room to catch her breath.

Dorrie sprang forward, as if on command, and rolled her chair full power at the old woman. Mrs. Stubbs, taken aback by the almost supernatural force of the thrust, staggered, then fell, smashing her head against the stone hearth. She lay still on the floor. Death was on her face.

Later in Dorrie's room, the cat once again sat on the child's lap as they performed their ritual. A strange new understanding had been introduced, a transfer of souls.

"Friends?" said the cat.

"Meowrr," replied the child.

Geronimo-o-o-o—

Take a Deep Breath

by Arthur C. Clarke

A long time ago I discovered that people who've never left Earth have certain fixed ideas about conditions in space. Everyone "knows," for example, that a man dies instantly and horribly when exposed to the vacuum that exists beyond the atmosphere. You'll find numerous gory descriptions of exploded space travelers in the popular literature, and I won't spoil your appetite by repeating them here. Many of those tales, indeed, are basically true. I've pulled men back from the air lock who were very poor advertisements for space flight.

Yet, at the same time, there are exceptions to every rule—even this one. I should know, for I learned the hard way.

We were on the last stages of building Communications Satellite Two; all the main units had been joined together, the living quarters had been pressurized, and the station had been given the slow spin around its axis that had restored the unfamiliar sensation of weight. I say "slow," but at its rim our two-hundred-foot-diameter wheel was turning at thirty miles an hour. We had, of course, no sense of motion, but the centrifugal force caused by this spin gave us about half the weight we would have possessed on Earth. That was enough to stop things from drifting around, yet not enough to make us feel uncomfortably sluggish after our weeks with no weight at all.

Four of us were sleeping in the small cylindrical cabin known as Bunkhouse Number 6 on the night that it happened. The bunkhouse was at the very rim of the station;

if you imagine a bicycle wheel, with a string of sausages replacing the tire, you have a good idea of the layout. Bunkhouse Number 6 was one of these sausages, and we were slumbering peacefully inside it.

I was awakened by a sudden jolt that was not violent enough to cause me alarm, but which did make me sit up and wonder what had happened. Anything unusual in a space station demands instant attention, so I reached for the intercom switch by my bed. "Hello, Central," I called, "What was that?"

There was no reply; the line was dead.

Now thoroughly alarmed, I jumped out of bed—and had an even bigger shock. *There was no gravity.* I shot up to the ceiling before I was able to grab a stanchion and bring myself to a halt, at the cost of a sprained wrist.

It was impossible for the entire station to have suddenly stopped rotating. There was only one answer; the failure of the intercom and, as I quickly discovered, of the lighting circuit as well forced us to face the appalling truth. We were no longer part of the station; our little cabin had somehow come adrift, and had been slung off into space like a raindrop falling on a spinning flywheel.

There were no windows through which we could look out, but we were not in complete darkness, for the battery-powered emergency lights had come on. All the main air vents had closed automatically when the pressure dropped. For the time being, we could live in our own private atmosphere, even though it was not being renewed. Unfortunately, a steady whistling told us that the air we did have was escaping through a leak somewhere in the cabin.

There was no way of telling what had happened to the rest of the station. For all we knew, the whole structure might have come to pieces, and all our colleagues might be dead or in the same predicament as we—drifting through space in leaking cans of air. Our one slim hope was the possibility that we were the only castaways, that the rest of the station was intact and had been able to send a rescue team to find us. After all, we were receding at no more than thirty miles an hour, and one of the rocket scooters could catch up to us in minutes.

It actually took an hour, though without the evidence of my watch I should never have believed that it was so short a time. We were now gasping for breath, and the gauge on our single emergency oxygen tank had dropped to one division above zero.

The banging on the wall seemed like a signal from another world. We banged back vigorously, and a moment later a muffled voice called to us through the wall. Someone outside was lying with his space-suit helmet pressed against the metal, and his shouted words were reaching us by direct conduction. Not as clear as radio— but it worked.

The oxygen gauge crept slowly down to zero while we had our council of war. We would be dead before we could be towed back to the station; yet the rescue ship was only a few feet away from us, with its air lock already open. Our little problem was to cross that few feet—*without* space suits.

We made our plans carefully, rehearsing our actions in the full knowledge that there could be no repeat performance. Then we each took a deep, final swig of oxygen, flushing out our lungs. When we were all ready, I banged on the wall to give the signal to our friends waiting outside.

There was a series of short, staccato raps as the power tools got to work on the thin hull. We clung tightly to the stanchions, as far away as possible from the point of entry, knowing just what would happen. When it came, it was so sudden that the mind couldn't record the sequence of events. The cabin seemed to explode, and a great wind tugged at me. The last trace of air gushed from my lungs, through my already-opened mouth. And then—utter silence, and the stars shining through the gaping hole that led to life.

Believe me, I didn't stop to analyze my sensations. I think—though I can never be sure that it wasn't imagination—that my eyes were smarting and there was a tingling feeling all over my body. And I felt very cold, perhaps because evaporation was already starting from my skin.

The only thing I can be certain of is that uncanny silence. It is never completely quiet in a space station, for there is always the sound of machinery or air pumps. But this was the absolute silence of the empty void, where there is no trace of air to carry sound.

Almost at once we launched ourselves out through the shattered wall, into the full blast of the sun. I was instantly blinded—but that didn't matter, because the men waiting in space suits grabbed me as soon as I emerged and hustled me into the air lock. And there, sound slowly returned as the air rushed in, and we remembered we could breathe again. The entire rescue, they told us later, had lasted just twenty seconds. . . .

Well, we were the founding members of the Vacuum-Breathers' Club. Since then, at least a dozen other men have done the same thing, in similar emergencies. The record time in space is now two minutes; after that, the blood begins to form bubbles as it boils at body temperature, and those bubbles soon get to the heart.

In my case, there was only one aftereffect. For maybe a quarter of a minute I had been exposed to *real* sunlight, not the feeble stuff that filters down through the atmosphere of Earth. Breathing space didn't hurt me at all—but I got the worst dose of sunburn I've ever had in my life.

There are no virgins in harems.

The Quest of the Infidel

by Sherwood Springer

Fasool, the sultan's melon merchant, stepped through the tradesmen's gate into the Street of the Lame Donkey, where his cousin Hamid was waiting with the camels.

"The stranger will soon possess what he seeks," Fasool said. "That is, after he gets out of the recovery chamber. Have you inquired in the marketplace about Azu?"

"Of Azul everyone has heard. Of Azu, none. In fact,

I still know not whether it is a place or a person. How met you this stranger?''

"He approached me in front of the Purple Fez yesterday, saying he had come on a far journey, both of leagues and years, and since someone in another land had told him what he sought lay here within the palace of the sultan, and since he had learned that I had access to the palace, he came to me. When at last he revealed the object of his search, I explained the difficulty of such a mission. However, for the sum of ten dinars I would at least get him into the palace. From that point his path would be his own.''

"And what was it he sought?'' asked Hamid.

"His dress and his tongue were those of the Anglo infidels, who, as you well know, are prone to have little but sand blowing between the ears. He was seeking one of those small brass cones coupled to a rubber bulb which the sexless and tongueless ones in the harem use to communicate. You have seen these, perhaps?''

"Allah forfend. You well know I have no access to the harem.''

"As it happens, neither have I, but I speak with knowledge gained from servants in the food quarters. At any rate, for a few piastres I got the stranger through the tradesmen's gate as my apprentice when I entered to get the melon order yesterday. Once within, I provided him with directions for reaching the harem and have not seen him since. Today, however, I am told that early this morning certain screaming was heard, and the word is that a new eunuch will be added to the staff—after he gets out of the recovery chamber, that is.''

"What a pity.''

"Indeed. Allah alone knows why the emissary from Azu would bear such . . . such *indignity* to possess a eunuch horn.''

Where will it all end?

Legal Rights for Germs

by Joe Patrouch

(UD Jan. 17) Mr. Felix Gardener, a carpenter living in Des Moines, Iowa, today filed a class-action suit in federal court on behalf of all viruses, bacilli, etc. (in short, germs) living in and on the human body. "Every creature, however small, has a right to live its own life," Mr. Gardener explained. "By bathing and by taking medicines to combat what the doctors—in their slanted language—call 'diseases' and 'infections,' we are killing billions and billions of living, experiencing creatures each and every day."

When asked about the origins of his suit, Mr. Gardener said he had always believed that flying saucers were interstellar spaceships carrying sentient beings from a higher civilization to our own, and that these beings have not contacted us because we show so little respect for life in all its forms. We casually kill insects to keep our homes comfortable and our crops growing, we kill animals for food and pleasure, and we even kill one another on the streets and battlefields.

While watching a television program last month, Mr. Gardener saw a commercial depicting a group of friendly bugs being chased and murdered by an animated can of bug-spray, and he began to wonder about the legal and moral rights we owe to insects. Later that same day he saw two more commercials that triggered his suit. One showed a woman spraying a bathroom in order to kill germs that cause household odor, and the other recommended a mouthwash which caused clean breath by killing germs. "Why have these germs, also among God's creatures, no right to live their own lives?" Mr. Gardener asked. "How can we have the arrogance to kill so many living things just so our bathrooms and breath will smell clean?"

When asked why he had left the insects out of his suit, he replied that he and his wife had decided that insects deserved a suit of their own, and that therefore Mrs. Gardener would appear in court the next day on their behalf. The Gardeners argue that all life is sacred and that wiping out the life forms that cause polio, diptheria, lockjaw, and other so-called diseases in human beings has resulted in an unbalancing of Nature, an unhealthy proliferation of human beings, and the total disruption of the ecology. Only by protecting the right-to-life of viruses and bacilli, they argue, can these microscopic animals resume their rightful place in the natural, God-given order of things and in so doing solve for us the world's present population, energy, food and natural resources problems.

Reaction to the Gardeners' proposals has been mixed. Religious leaders tend to agree that all life is indeed sacred, that death is not an end but a beginning and therefore plagues and famines are not in themselves evil, and that the discomfort of great numbers of human beings suffering and dying should be viewed as a temporary inconvenience since the temporal world, seen in its proper perspective, is nothing more than a thoroughfare of misery and woe through which we travel to an eternal happiness.

Business leaders, however, scoff at the Gardeners and their suit. They point out that without the manufacture and sale of large quantities of deodorants, soap, mouthwash, athlete's-foot ointments, household cleaners, bugsprays, and medicines, large numbers of people would be out of work and unable to buy deodorants, soap, mouthwash, athlete's-foot ointments, household cleaners, bug-sprays, medicines, and automobiles. They point out further that economic chaos always results from a lack of automobile sales.

Doctors themselves were divided on the issue. Two doctors, conscience-stricken at the sudden realization of how many billions of tiny lives their prescriptions and medications had cost, have already committed suicide, and a few more may be expected to follow. Most, however, have stuck firmly to the physicians' traditional attitude that so long as they are making money, everything is all right and nothing should be changed. They have refused to take the Gardeners seriously. "I don't see where the money is in letting people die," one said succinctly, "unless you're an undertaker."

Finally, insurance companies across the nation are opposed to the "Pro-Germ" movement. "The longer people live, the more they can pay on their policies and the longer we can collect interest on their money," they say. "If everyone starts dying, we'll go bankrupt paying off all the claims."

It is difficult to predict at this time how the courts will eventually decide on the issue of "legal rights for germs." Should they rule favorably, however, everyone in America will become, by law, a vegetarian.

* * *

[NEWSPAPER HEADLINE] WHAT ABOUT US PLANTS?

(UD Jan. 23) Dr. Roseann Amythest, an unemployed chemist, today filed suit in federal court seeking to protect the plants of the United States from acts of what she refers to as "overt cannibalism" on the part of U.S. citizenry. "How would you like to be plucked from your comfortable beds and cooked?" she demanded angrily. "Everyone should be forced to eat chemically synthetized foods." Dr. Amythest reports that she has some preliminary recipes that she would be willing to develop for the government at a cost of . . .

You know what they say about turnips.

Blood

by Fredric Brown

In their time machine, Vron and Dreena, last two survivors of the race of vampires, fled into the future to escape annihilation. They held hands and consoled one another in their terror and their hunger.

In the twenty-second century mankind had found them out, had discovered that the legend of vampires living secretly among humans was not a legend at all, but fact. There had been a pogrom that had found and killed every vampire but these two, who had already been working on a time machine and who had finished in time to escape in it. Into the future, far enough into the future that the very word *vampire* would be forgotten so they could again live unsuspected—and from their loins regenerate their race.

"I'm hungry, Vron. Awfully hungry."

"I too, Dreena dear. We'll stop again soon."

They had stopped four times already and had narrowly escaped dying each time. They had *not* been forgotten. The last stop, half a million years back, had shown them a world gone to the dogs—quite literally: human beings were extinct and dogs had become civilized and manlike. Still they had been recognized for what they were. They'd managed to feed once, on the blood of a tender young bitch, but then they'd been hounded back to their time machine and into flight again.

"Thanks for stopping," Dreena said. She sighed.

"Don't thank me," said Vron grimly. "This is the end of the line. We're out of fuel and we'll find none here—

by now all radioactives will have turned to lead. We live here . . . or else.''

They went out to scout. "Look," said Dreena excitedly, pointing to something walked toward them. "A new creature! The dogs are gone and something else has taken over. And surely we're forgotten."

The approaching creature was telepathic. "I have heard your thoughts," said a voice inside their brains. "You wonder whether we know 'vampires,' whatever they are. We do not."

Dreena clutched Vron's arm in ecstasy. "Freedom!" she murmured hungrily. "And *food!*"

"You also wonder," said the voice, "about my origin and evolution. All life today is vegetable. I—" He bowed low to them. "I, a member of the dominant race, was once what you called a turnip."

Usually it's day that breaks!

The Diana Syndrome

by R. A. Montana

To: Dr. Franklin P. Jameson, Chief of Staff, Merrimont Institution for the Insane
From: Dr. T. R. Brelin
Date: June 26
Subject: Consultation and evaluation for definitive treatment of acute and chronic mental disorder
Patient: Connors, Jeremiah R.

What follows is the transcript of my initial examination of the patient. I'm sure you will find it substantially the same as the previous examination by yourself and Doctors Felding and Gravaro. My professional opinion and requested recommendations will follow the transcript.

THIS IS DOCTOR BRELIN, TAPE 1124, JUNE 25, 1981.
SUBJECT: CONNORS, J.R.
AGE: 45—SINGLE—OCCUPATION: REAL ESTATE SALES-
MAN
NO PREVIOUS HISTORY OF MENTAL ILLNESS

MR. CONNORS: Are you God?

DR. BRELIN: No, I'm just a doctor.

MR. CONNORS: Close enough.

DR. BRELIN: You were expecting some divine help?

MR. CONNORS: What I expect seems to be diametrically
opposed to what I receive.

DR. BRELIN: What do you expect?

MR. CONNORS: To get the hell out of this kink bin and
see the outside world again.

DR. BRELIN: This is a hospital, Mr. Connors, and you
are a psychiatric patient that I'm hoping to help do just
that. I will need your cooperation to achieve that goal.

MR. CONNORS: I have cooperated with your, your . . .
talismatic institution for the better part of a month now
. . . and I'm fast becoming convinced that I am the only
sane person here.

DR. BRELIN: A common delusion among most patients,
Jerry . . . may I call you Jerry?

MR. CONNORS: You may call me Napoleon if you feel it
would fit my behavioral pattern and confirm your initial
diagnosis.

DR. BRELIN: Why do you assume I have already made a
diagnosis?

MR. CONNORS: If you haven't, Doc, you're slipping. Ever
have this problem before? No? Well, I'd offer you the use
of my couch but the management has been a bit lax with
the furnishings.

DR. BRELIN: You impress me as being an intelligent man,
Mr. Connors. I'm sure you can appreciate the seriousness of
this situation—levity seems ill-placed right now.

MR. CONNORS: Yeah, well, laugh and the whole world
laughs with you—cry, and you moon alone, I always say.

DR. BRELIN: Ah, the moon again. Always the elusive
symptom . . .

MR. CONNORS: Symptom, shit! It was there, goddammit,
and I saw what I saw. You gonna play hell convincing
me otherwise, Dr. Strangelove.

DR. BRELIN: Dr. Brelin.

MR. CONNORS: You haf' maybe a brudder in der father-land?

DR. BRELIN: The moon, Mr. Connors?

MR. CONNORS: Right, the moon. Where would you like to start? Earth's only satellite—almost a quarter million miles distant—one sixth G—airless—

DR. BRELIN: Your statistics are meaningless to me, Mr. Connors, but I'll accept them for argument's sake.

MR. CONNORS: . . . first landing, July '69—Armstrong taking one small step . . .

DR. BRELIN: What you saw, Mr. Connors?

MR. CONNORS: Look, who's telling this—me or you?

DR. BRELIN: Go on.

MR. CONNORS: Well, see, when I was a kid I used to doodle a lot—you know, most kids draw guns or air-planes—I drew alien continents—I would try to imagine what the topography of other planets might look like—easy, Doc, you're paling—was never satisfied though—so I studied the moon—got so I could draw the dead seas blindfolded—it really became—you should excuse the ex-pression—an obsession—so when it happened—

DR. BRELIN: What exactly happened, Mr. Connors?

MR. CONNORS: It broke.

DR. BRELIN: It broke?

MR. CONNORS: I told them they ought to put windows in here, Doc, there seems to be this recurring echo—

DR. BRELIN: I'll try to control myself, Mr. Connors.

MR. CONNORS: Thank you—where was I—oh, yeah—I was lying there propped up on my bed watching the moon out my window—all the lights out—beautiful night—lime-yellow disc drowning the stars with its shimmering phos-phorescence—locked up there in a sky cut from ebony, as the poets would say—I was thinking about the land-ing—you know—where Armstrong says, "Houston, Tranquility Base here. The Eagle has landed." Those eight words always kinda choked me up—lying there try-ing to pinpoint the landing site and wondering what it had been like—walking on an alien world—then, BANG!

DR. BRELIN: Bang?

MR. CONNORS: Yeah, just like that—loudest goddam noise I ever heard—sounded like a garbage truck growl-ing at five in the morning when you're just on the edge of waking—started with a low rumble and built to a Niagara roar—the moon started to vibrate—like a window pane during a sonic boom—a giant plate glass porthole in the night—then it was like someone threw a baseball through it—in a high breeze—mist rising behind broken eye—busted headlight in a tunnel of fog—then—finally—out—nothing but a black hole in space with stars lapping over the edges—filling the black gap with twinkling bits of fire, then it winked out—faded—dissolved . . . tha, tha, that's all, Doc!

DR. BRELIN: Please, Mr. Connors, I'm trying to help you.

MR. CONNORS: Then help me, for Christ's sake! Tell me that everybody saw what I saw. Tell me that when I ran outside and shouted that the moon was broken it didn't look like I'd just announced the Second Coming to a convention of atheists—tell me why nobody listened and why those who did carted me away to this white-walled sanctuary for the wayward flippo—tell me why I can't wake up from this prolonged nightmare no matter how hard I try. Tell me I'm not nuttier than the proverbial fruitcake and get me out of this lunatic asylum!

DR. BRELIN: This *what* asylum?

MR. CONNORS: This luna—ah—ah—ah—ah

DR. BRELIN: Nurse! Get two attendants with restraints in here immediately!

As you can see, Frank, the patient got violent and had to be sedated. I wanted to tell you this is the most deep-seated and detailed psychosis I've ever had the opportunity to observe up closely, and I beg you, for old times' sake, to let me stay with it to the end.

I agree with you that the psychosis is probably functional and that the patient's condition, characterized by systematic delusions, is certainly paranoid.

I recommend insulin shock and I would like to be present to question the patient during the lucid moments that should occur more frequently after each session.

I didn't want to unduly upset him during the initial examination by asking him to explain all the terminology he was bouncing off me, but dammit, Frank, I'm going to have a very difficult time curing him if I don't understand the phraseology he's using. What the hell are stars and sky?

Biter bit.

Emergency Rations

by Theodore R. Cogswell

"The obvious base for offensive operations is this deserted little system here."

Kat Zul, the Supreme Commander of the Royal Zardonian fleet, stabbed one tentacle at a point on the star map.

"Once we are established there, the whole Solar flank lies open to us. We can raid here—and here—and here—" he indicated sector after sector—"and they will never be able to assemble enough ships in one spot to stop us. What do you think, Sire?"

The Gollen patted his corpulent belly. "There will be good eating. Mind you save the fattest for the royal kitchen." Orange saliva drooled from the corners of both his mouths. "Roasted haunch of human three times a day. How delightful! Remind me to invite you in for dinner some night after you get back."

"Thank you, Sire. I will order reconnaissance patrols out at once. If all is clear we can begin construction of a base within the month. Once our heavy armament is installed, we will be impregnable. You will eat well then, O Mighty One!"

The Gollen of Zardon burped happily, closed his eye, and dreamed of dinner.

A week later a fast courier came screaming back with news of trouble. The Supreme Commander took one good look at the report, grabbed the photographs that came with it, and rushed in to see the Gollen.

"The system is already occupied, Sire! By humans!"

"Fine, send me a brace of plump ones at once."

"Your forgiveness, Highness, but that is impossible. We can't get at them. They have erected a space station, a heavy Z type with protective screens that can stop anything we throw at them. I have blockading squadrons around it now, but we must act quickly. They got an appeal for help off before we were able to blanket their transmitter."

The Gollen paled to a light mauve. "In that case," he said softly, "I shall have you for dinner. If the humans gain control of that system, *our* whole flank lies open to them!"

"There is yet hope, Sire," said Kat Zul quickly. "The space station is only partially completed and, as far as we can determine, occupied only by a construction crew. None of its defensive armament has been installed yet. Once they drop their screen, we have them. We can fortify the station ourselves, and control of the system will be ours."

The Gollen reached into a silver bowl filled with wiggling *guba,* selected an especially fat one, and bit off its head with his lower mouth.

"Why should they?" he said with his upper one.

"Should they what?"

"Drop their protective screens. Their power piles can keep them energized for the next hundred years."

"Ah, Highness, but screen generators are tricky things. They require constant attention. When no humans are alive to tend them, they will shut off automatically. And within two months there will be no humans left alive. They will all have starved to death. We captured their supply ship yesterday."

"I don't like it. In the first place, a starved human is an inedible human, and in the second, their relief fleet won't take more than a month to get there. I believe you were talking in terms of two months. You'll have to do better than that, Kat Zul, or you'll be fricasee by evening!"

As the stew pot came nearer, Kat Zul thought faster. He barely beat the deadline.

"In this life, Highness," he said pontifically, "it is either eat, or be eaten."

"This is obvious," said the Gollen, "and since for you to eat me would be *lèse majesté,* the second half of your truism is more appropriate to the present occasion. Cook!''

"You don't understand," said Kat Zul in desperation. "In this case we can eat by being ready to be eaten." He retreated around the table. "Listen, please! The robot supply ship we captured was loaded with food. If we wait another two weeks, the humans in the space station will be getting terribly hungry."

"I'm getting mighty hungry right now," said the Gollen. "But I'll listen. Go ahead."

"Among the food on the supply ship we found several hundred cans containing strange clawed creatures in a nutrient solution. They're alive!"

"So?"

"So we'll remove all the food from the ship except those cans. Then we will open them carefully and remove the animals inside. Next we will replace them with ourselves and have the cans resealed."

"What!"

"A stroke of sheer genius, Highness! In each of the cans will be one of my best fighting men. We will put the robot supply ship back on course and chase it to the space station, firing near-misses all the way. When they see it coming with us in pursuit, the humans will open their screens enough to let it through. Once they've checked it carefully with their scanners, they'll bring it into the station and unload it at once. They'll be so hungry that the first thing they'll go for will be the food. But when they open the cans, instead of finding little live animals, out will spring my warriors. Ah, Sire, there will be a fine slitting of throats. With the screens shut off, we can arm the station at once, and when the human fleet comes . . ." He laughed exultantly and clicked his razor-sharp forward mandibles together like castanets.

"As you say, Kat Zul, a stroke of sheer genius," said the Gollen. "Have you selected your personal can yet?"

The fleet commander's olfactory feelers stood straight out. "Me? To tell you the truth, Highness, I hadn't planned on being one of the raiding party. The fact is that I suffer from a touch of claustrophobia and . . ."

"Would you rather stay for dinner?"

"Well, Sire . . ."

"Cook!"

"On second thought . . ."

"Hey, Mac."

"Yeah?"

"What'n the hell's *lobster?*"

"Beats me. Why?"

"Somebody sure fouled up back at base. There's about a thousand cans of it on the supply ship—and nothing else."

"Well, open one and find out. I'm hungry!"

"Who isn't? But they're alive. It says so on the can. They're packed away in some sort of nutrient solution."

"So they're alive. There's a law says you can't take them out and kill them?"

"There's a picture on the can."

"So?"

"They got big claws. Looks like they could take a man's finger off with one good bite. Whatta they mean sending stuff like that out?"

"Look, Pinky, I'm busy. Do what you want but don't bother me. I got to nurse this generator. If it flickers just once, we're done for. Now beat it!"

"O.K. I'll go open one up and see what happens."

There was silence broken only by a chomping of jaws. The eating was good. Kat Zul, the Supreme Commander of the Royal Zardonian fleet, rested motionless at the far end of the table in the place of honor, his belly distended and his eye closed.

At the other end of the table, two hungry mouths opened simultaneously.

"More!"

Pinky beamed cheerfully, picked up the platter on which Kat Zul rested, and passed it down to the two hungry electronics men.

"Help yourselves, boys. There's lots more where that came from."

He took another piece himself. "This sure beats chicken. The way these things are built, there's enough legs for everybody." He pushed his white chef's cap back on his perspiring forehead and surveyed the little group of technicians and construction men happily. This was a red-letter day. Nobody had ever asked for seconds on his cooking before.

"Pinky."

"Yes, Mac?"

"What do they call these things again?"

"Lobsters. They sure don't look like the pictures on the cans, though. Guess the guy that made up the label was one of these here abstructionists. You know, those characters that don't paint a thing like it is, but like it would be if it was."

"Yeah," said Mac, "Sure." He noticed a bandage on Pinky's right forefinger. "I see ya got nipped after all."

Pinky held his finger up and inspected it with interest. "Sure was a mean cut, almost to the bone it was. And that reminds me, when's one of you mechanical wizards going to fix my can opener for me? For a month I've been after you and all I get is promises."

"Tomorrow, first thing," said Mac.

"Tomorrow, always tomorrow," said Pinky. "Look at that finger. That ain't no bite; it got ripped on the edge of a can. I didn't take no chances on being bitten. I was all set to open the first can when I got to looking at the picture on the label, and the more I looked at it, the less I liked the idea of having something like that running around my galley alive. So ya know what I did?"

"No," said Mac patiently, tearing another leg off the carcass of Kat Zul and munching on it appreciatively.

"Well, you know I mostly cook by intuition . . ."

A collective groan went up from his listeners. Every time Pinky had an inspiration, it usually involved a handful or so of curry powder.

"But this time I decided to go by the book. The recipe said to boil vigorously for twenty minutes, so I did. Once the kettle got boiling good, I tossed in a dozen, can and all. I figured they would cook as well inside the container as outside, and that way I wouldn't have to worry about their claws. They was alive all right, too. You should have heard them batting around inside those cans for the first couple of minutes."

Mac shivered uncomfortably. "Don't seem human somehow to make critters suffer so. Next time you'd better open the cans and kill them first. If you're scared, call me and I'll come down and do the job for you."

"There's no need for that," said Pinky. "Them things can't feel nothing. They ain't got no nervous systems. It says so in the cookbook."

"If that's what it says," said Mac, "I guess it's so. Just keep dishing them out the way you did tonight and I'll be happy." He loosened his belt, leaned back, and sighed contentedly.

Pinky wasn't listening. He could hardly wait until time came to prepare breakfast.

With just a touch a curry . . .

They say it pays.

Buy Jupiter

by Isaac Asimov

He was a simulacron, of course, but so cleverly contrived that the human beings dealing with him had long since given up thinking of the real energy-entities, waiting in white-hot blaze in their field-enclosure "ship" miles from Earth.

The simulacron, with a majestic golden beard and deep brown, wide-set eyes, said gently, "We understand your hesitations and suspicions, and we can only continue to assure you we mean you no harm. We have, I think, presented you with proof that we inhabit the coronal haloes of O-spectra stars; that your own sun is too weak for us; while your planets are of solid matter and therefore completely and eternally alien to us."

The Terrestrial Negotiator (who was Secretary of Science and, by common consent, had been placed in charge of negotiations with the aliens) said, "But you have admitted we are now on one of your chief trade routes."

"Now that our new world of Kimmonoshek has developed new fields of protonic fluid, yes."

The Secretary said, "Well, here on Earth, positions on trade routes can gain military importance out of proportion to their intrinsic value. I can only repeat, then, that to gain our confidence you must tell us exactly why you need Jupiter."

And as always, when that question or a form of it was asked, the simulacron looked pained. "Secrecy is important. If the Lamberj people—"

"Exactly," said the Secretary. "To us it sounds like war. You and what you call the Lamberj people—"

The simulacron said hurriedly, "But we are offering you a most generous return. You have only colonized the inner planets of your system and we are not interested in those. We ask for the world you call Jupiter, which, I understand, your people can never expect to live on, or even land on. Its size" (he laughed indulgently) "is too much for you."

The Secretary, who disliked the air of condescension, said stiffly, "The Jovian satellites are practical sites for colonization, however, and we intend to colonize them shortly."

"But the satellites will not be disturbed in any way. They are yours in every sense of the word. We ask only Jupiter itself, a completely useless world to you, and for that the return we offer is generous. Surely you realize that we could take your Jupiter, if we wished, without your permission. It is only that we prefer payment and a legal treaty. It will prevent disputes in the future. As you see, I'm being completely frank."

The Secretary said stubbornly, "Why do you need Jupiter?"

"The Lamberj—"

"Are you at war with the Lamberj?"

"It's not quite—"

"Because you see that if it is war and you establish some sort of fortified base on Jupiter, the Lamberj may, quite properly, resent that, and retaliate against us for granting you permission. We cannot allow ourselves to be involved in such a situation."

"Nor would I ask you to be involved. My word that no harm would come to you. Surely" (he kept coming back to it) "the return is generous. Enough power boxes each year to supply your world with a full year of power requirement."

The Secretary said, "On the understanding that future increases in power consumption will be met."

"Up to a figure five times the present total. Yes."

"Well, then, as I have said, I am a high official of the government and have been given considerable powers to deal with you—but not infinite power. I, myself, am inclined to trust you, but I could not accept your terms without understanding exactly why you want Jupiter. If the explanation is plausible and convincing, I could perhaps persuade our government and, through them, our people, to make the agreement. If I tried to make an agreement without such an explanation, I would simply be forced out of office and Earth would refuse to honor the agreement. You could then, as you say, take Jupiter by force, but you would be in illegal possession and you have said you don't wish that."

The simulacron clicked its tongue impatiently. "I cannot continue forever in this petty bickering. The Lamberj—" Again he stopped, then said, "Have I your word of honor that this is all not a device inspired by the Lamberj people to delay us until—"

"My word of honor," said the Secretary.

The Secretary of Science emerged, mopping his forehead and looking ten years younger. He said softly. "I told him his people could have it as soon as I obtained the President's formal approval. I don't think he'll object, or Congress, either. Good Lord, gentlemen, think of it; free power at our fingertips in return for a planet we could never use in any case."

The Secretary of Defense, growing purplish with objection, said, "But we had agreed that only a Mizzarett-Lamberj war could explain their need for Jupiter. Under those circumstances, and comparing their military potential with ours, a strict neutrality is essential."

"But there is no war, sir," said the Secretary of Science. "The simulacron presented an alternate explanation of their need for Jupiter so rational and plausible that I accepted at once. I think the President will agree with me, and you gentlemen, too, when you understand. In fact, I have here their plans for the new Jupiter, as it will soon appear."

The others rose from their seats, clamoring. "A new Jupiter?" gasped the Secretary of Defense.

"Not so different from the old, gentlemen," said the Secretary of Science. "Here are the sketches provided in form suitable for observation by matter beings such as ourselves."

He laid them down. The familiar banded planet was there before them on one of the sketches: yellow, pale green, and light brown with curled white streaks here and there and all against the speckled velvet background of space. But across the bands were streaks of blackness as velvet as the background, arranged in a curious pattern.

"That," said the Secretary of Science, "is the day side of the planet. The night side is shown in this sketch." (There, Jupiter was a thin crescent enclosing darkness, and within that darkness were the same thin streaks arranged in similar pattern, but in a phosphorescent glowing orange this time.)

"The marks," said the Secretary of Science, "are a purely optical phenomenon, I am told, which will not rotate with the planet, but will remain static in its atmospheric fringe."

"But what is it?" asked the Secretary of Commerce.

"You see," said the Secretary of Science, "our solar system is now on one of their major trade routes. As many as seven of their ships pass within a few hundred million miles of the system in a single day, and each ship has the major planets under telescopic observation as they pass. Tourist curiosity, you know. Solid planets of any size are a marvel to them."

"What has that to do with these marks?"

"That is one form of their writing. Translated, those marks read: 'Use Mizzarett Ergone Vertices For Health and Glowing Heat.' "

"You mean Jupiter is to be an advertising billboard?" exploded the Secretary of Defense.

"Right. The Lamberj people, it seems, produce a competing ergone tablet, which accounts for the Mizzarett anxiety to establish full legal ownership of Jupiter—in case of Lamberj lawsuits. Fortunately, the Mizzaretts are novices at the advertising game, it appears."

"Why do you say that?" asked the Secretary of the Interior.

"Why, they neglected to set up a series of options on the other planets. The Jupiter billboard will be advertising our system, as well as their own product. And when the competing Lamberj people come storming in to check on the Mizzarett title to Jupiter, we will have Saturn to sell to *them. With* its rings. As we will be easily able to explain to them, the rings will make Saturn much the better spectacle."

"And therefore," said the Secretary of the Treasury, suddenly beaming, "worth a *much* better price."

And they all suddenly looked very cheerful.

When you blow your brains out—

The Old Man

by Henry Slesar

There had been revolts against the rule of the old man before, but this time the Governors were worried enough to send Tango, their spy, to the insurrectionist meeting. Tango was a fair-haired laughing youth liked by the farmers and mechanics of the Village, who forgave his laziness and ineptness with tools because he lifted their spirits when crops were stubborn or engines failed to turn. None suspected his select allegiance to the Governors who lived in the stone house on the great hill.

He arrived at the meeting place with his one-string guitar on his back, and squatted in the rear of the cave amid the grim-faced malcontents. They were young men; it was always the young who questioned the old man's sovereignty, and they nodded to Tango and murmured welcome. The meeting was captained by a dark-eyed farmer's son named Sierra, and his opening tirade was punctuated by the gestures of his withered, mutated right arm. His speech was effective, and Tango found his own loyalty wavering, until Sierra allowed others to be heard.

Tango stood up, smiled engagingly at the crowd, and said, "You speak of liberty, and the word is sweet. But tell me what the Village will do without the old man? Who will tell us when to plant our crops and where? Who will know which fields are safe for our seed, and which contaminated? Who will know when the storms will come, and when the rains will be radioactive? And how to make the machines work again?"

Sierra snarled his reply. "You speak like a Governor," he said. "This is the argument with which they have enslaved us since the end of the war. They say we are children in the wilderness with the old man to guide us, and I say they speak with the tongue of greed."

The crowd murmured approval of his words. The withered arm waved over their heads, and Sierra's voice rose to higher pitch.

"Greed!" he said. "Greed and the love of power! The old man tells us how to plant our crops, and taxes the best we raise for him and his Governors. For a generation we have worked to restore electric powers to the Village, but every watt we can produce is employed to light the stone house while we and our families live in darkness."

"There has always been the old man," Tango said gently. "Who knows what our lives will be like without him?"

"Have you seen him, Tango?" Sierra said, bitterly. "Has he ever deigned to let you sing your foolish songs for him?"

"No," Tango said. "I have never seen the old man. My father saw him once; he was an old man even then, my father said, tall and thin with a flowing white beard, like Moses."

"My father remembers him, too," a young man said. "He saw him when he was a child, but he describes him as fat, like a Buddha, and very wise."

The crowd laughed, and Tango, responding to laughter, put his fists on his hips and laughed louder than all the rest. "No matter what he looks like, he is certainly wise. His wisdom has kept us all alive, Sierra, even you know that. Our scouts have ventured out time and again, and never yet found life. We are alone on Earth; our Village is the world; we alone have survived the blasts and the dusts and the many deaths of the atom. And why? Because of *him*. Is it so wrong, then, to honor the old man with food and drink and electric power?''

The crowd muttered sullenly at his speech. For a moment, Sierra was without response. Then, shrewdly gauging the mood Tango had inspired, he dropped his evangelical manner and became the voice of reason.

"Of course you're right," he said calmly. "When the Village was new, when the War had just ended, the old man's wisdom was sorely needed." He came towards Tango, speaking as a friend. "But if he was an old man then, Tango, old when your father and my father were children, how old must he be now? A hundred? A hundred and ten? I know not what miracle has kept him alive, but I do know this. With advancing years, the arteries harden and the blood grows sluggish. The brain, no longer given its full nourishment, grows soft and weak. A man becomes senile, doting like an infant, often even insane." He raised the withered arm. Softly: "Must we be ruled by an insane old man?" Louder: "Must we be children forever?" A cry: "We don't need the old man, Tango!"

They took up the cry. "Who needs the old man? Who needs the old man?"

They were on their feet.

"Who needs the old man?"

Quietly, without hurry, Tango edged his way towards the mouth of the cave. Then he was running, fleet-footed, towards the stone house on the hill.

Breathing hard with his exertion, he struggled up the steep path to the iron door, throwing away his one-string guitar when it impeded his progress. He seized the great knocker and made it boom like thunder, until the Senior Governor himself came to answer. When he saw Tango in the doorway, he pulled him inside and waited anxiously for his breath to return.

"This is no idle talk," Tango panted. "There are hundreds of them, Senior, and they are at fever pitch. You must warn the old man—"

"Fools!" the Governor said, wringing his hands. "If their quarrel is with us, let them face us alone. We will lay down our lives to protect *him*." He looked back, up the dark stairway to the second floor which Tango, and no other Villager, had ever seen. "They have never learned to trust him; their fathers never learned to understand his importance. We must save him, at all costs—"

"There may not be time," Tango said. "They're organized, and they have a leader. Protect yourself, Senior—"

From the upper floor, there was a cry. The Senior rushed to the foot of the stair, and a long-robed Governor came hurrying down the steps to meet him.

"From the window—" he gasped. "Marchers, coming here."

"Go, my son," the Senior said. "You mustn't be found here; their wrath will fall upon you as well. I must return to my duties."

He waited until Tango was on the other side of the iron door. The youth hesitated, and then turned down the steep path. He could see the line of marchers coming resolutely towards the building; he could see the leaders as they paused to deploy their forces about the stone house. Then he was spotted.

"There he is!" Sierra shouted. "He's a spy! A spy! We should have known he was a spy!"

Tango fled, but there were swifter runners among the rebels. They brought him down. A stone lifted in the air, gripped in a determined fist; his skull was crushed. Then the youths stormed the stone house itself, bringing up a pine log to batter at the iron door.

They burst into the house, a hundred of them in the small room. Yet even this hundred were halted by the sight of the lean, bent figure of the Senior on the stairway.

"Go no further," he said. "You are on sacred ground."

Sierra pushed to the forefront. "Are you claiming Godhood now?" he sneered. "We want the old man!"

"The old man has saved us all, and will continue to guard us. Destroy him, and you destroy the race."

They killed the Senior Governor, and went stampeding up the stairs. At the door of the old man's room, the remaining three Governors erected a frail barricade of flesh. They, too, were slain. The door was shattered open, and they blinked at the light that flooded the old man's room.

Then they stopped, awe-struck, and stared at the strange, bewildering complexity, the thing in the room that winked with a thousand eyes and murmured in the mysterious voice of machinery. It was helpless now, its programmers dead.

Then they killed the old man, the computer. It didn't take the people long to die.

By George! They got him!

Exile's Greeting

by Roland Green

A ship of the line is never entirely quiet, even at anchor. Not with the thin creak of timbers as she moves to the swell, the more solid *clunk* of blocks, the metallic rattle of the pumps. But Captain Parker had taken *Bellerophon* through gales in the North Atlantic and hurricanes in the West Indies. He remembered the wind as an agonized wailing in the rigging, sails splitting with gunshot cracks, the continuous clatter of pumps worked by relays of sweating, gray-faced men.

He had taken her into fleet actions against the Spanish and the French and against both combined. Real gunshots then, whole broadsides of them, the balls tearing through *Bellerophon*'s timbers, sweeping the decks with blasts of flying splinters. Earthquake crashes, earthquake shocks as masts came down, screams of men dying on decks gritty with sand and slick with blood. Captain Parker knew what an uproar *Bellerophon* could generate.

But right now she lay almost quietly at anchor in the bay. Captain Parker welcomed the quiet. He turned over in bed and groaned as the movement set his head to throbbing again. He did not want to move, or to think about the day's business and who would be coming on board. The brandy had been fine last night, but it had gone on at least half a bottle too long. Still, the company had been good. Two men who had commanded battalions in the last battle of the whole long war—that was rare company.

Parker did not envy the army—theirs had been a grim war—but it was interesting to hear stories of a great land battle. He remembered Colonel Reeman's words:

"We thought we were pretty well situated on the ridge, with our right covered by the farm and our left refused. Of course the forest behind us would have made a retreat the devil's own job, but we didn't expect to be in any danger of retreating!

"Damn them, though, if they didn't have us out of that farm inside half an hour. We were lucky, damned lucky, that we set it properly on fire before we left. The smoke screened our right. Otherwise we'd have had their artillery up there, firing along our line. They'd have rolled us up like a damned housemaid rolling up a carpet."

The other officer had nodded. "Even as it was, we had a stiff job of it holding on in the center. Nothing could have kept 'em off if the cavalry hadn't punched one of their infantry attacks right out of the ring. Gad, that was a sight—the whole cavalry brigade riding hell for leather straight down the enemy's front! That put 'em right back on their heels. By the time they'd got another attack worked up, the Germans were coming in on the north. And that was all. I'll have to say this for those damned Dutchmen—they were there when we needed them. Gentlemen—to His Majesty's allies!" And they had all hoisted their glasses and drunk off the toast.

They had drunk off quite a few other toasts, too many—in the end far too many. Captain Parker groaned again at the memory and tried to go to sleep.

In that exact moment the voice of Corcoran the bo'sun came roaring down from overhead. "All hands, turn to and clean ship! Move lively there now, damn ye!" And much, much more in the same vein and at the same volume. It was said in the fleet that Corcoran's voice could carry two miles upwind against a hurricane. At times like this Parker believed it.

Eventually the squall of Corcoran's voice died away. But hard on its heels came the storm. Scurrying bare feet, the swish of water, the clatter of buckets, the scraping of holystones on planks. Parker groaned one final time, sat up in the bed, and swung his feet onto the chilly deck. There was no hope of any more sleep, none at all. He stood up, absent-mindedly stretched to his full height, and banged his head smartly against the deck beams above.

He bellowed an oath as loud as any of Corcoran's and nearly fainted from the pain. No, definitely he did not want to face the day, not really. But there was no way around it and its business. The most important exile in the British Empire was coming aboard at—good God, in barely an hour! Then *Bellerophon*'s crew would swarm up the rigging, her sails would spread to whatever breeze they might contrive to find, and she would be bound away to the south. Far to the south. Her passenger had troubled the British Empire the way none had ever troubled it before.

At St. Helena he would trouble nobody.

However, even if the man was going into exile, he deserved a better greeting than Captain Parker could give him right now. The captain wondered if he looked as bad as he felt. He heaved himself to his feet again and looked in his shaving mirror. He did. He sat down again and bellowed, "Steward! Hot water! And shake a leg, there!"

An hour later Captain Parker was standing on *Bellerophon*'s quarterdeck. He was also clothed, shaved, breakfasted, and feeling almost human. He would have felt completely human if the headache had completely vanished, or if the breakfast had been any better.

Should he take the opportunity to send a boat ashore, to look for fresh supplies in the countryside? They would not be touching land again short of St. Helena itself. Even a keg of beer or a dozen live chickens would help eke out his ill-furnished pantry.

He decided against it. The war was over. His Majesty's forces could no longer just requisition what they needed—or wanted. And the local population wasn't feeling any too charitable towards the Royal Navy. They had lost a long and bitter war. So they would probably at least raise their prices to the limit—and beyond.

There might even be some hot-head who would pull out his musket and try a shot at a Royal Navy landing party. Perhaps it would be a veteran, perhaps it would just be some eager youth. But in either case there would be an incident, dead men on both sides, Courts of Inquiry to follow, and generally the devil to pay. No, he would manage with what he had already.

Another voice blasting out orders split the quiet morning air. The marines were coming up from below, assembling in the waist under the eagle eye of Major Stafford. Tramp, tramp, clatter, *bang*. Boots came down heavily on planks, muskets snapped up onto shoulders and then crashed butts-down on the deck. Fifty red-coated figures froze into immobility, like two files of gaudy statues. The bantam major came bounding up the ladder to the quarterdeck and saluted.

"Marine guard all present and ready for duty, sir!"

"Very good, major. Have you made sure they're all in good order?"

"Sir!" If Captain Parker had accused him of stealing the mess funds, Stafford could not have sounded more outraged.

"I know. But we want to look our best today."

Stafford frowned. "For that damned—"

"He was a soldier—and a good one," Parker cut in. His voice was very cool. The tone cut off any further outbursts from Stafford. Together the two officers turned outboard, towards the shore of the bay.

The sun was burning away the night's low-hanging mist. The shore, rising into wooded hills a few miles back, stretched away into the light of a pale autumn morning. Closer to the shore, thin columns of blue-gray smoke curled up from the cook-fires of the army camp.

"I'll wager those lads over in the camp aren't any too happy about sitting down like that on garrison duty," said Stafford.

"No," Parker agreed. "It'll be better for everybody when we can pull the garrison out, let these people go back to running their own affairs."

"Think they can be trusted?"

"Why not? They lost the war, after all. It will be a good long time before they've even got the strength to try again. Let alone the inclination."

"I hope so. It's nice country they have here. I've been thinking of resigning, taking up some land. But you know how much a man can put by on a major's pay, and how much that will buy in England. Here there's almost land for the asking."

From a mile away across the water came the faint notes of a bugle. Then they saw a low dark shape slide out onto the silver-blue water from the stone jetty. "Major Stafford, our passenger is on his way. I suggest we go down to the entry port." The formality was back in Parker's voice.

Stafford nodded and followed Parker down the ladder to the main deck. The two officers strode rapidly along the ranks of marines to the entry port, then stopped. The First and Third Lieutenants came scurrying up from below, the latter still buckling on his sword belt.

Corcoran's voice rose from the fo'c's'le in another roar. "Now damn your eyes, stop skylarking around the deck like a bunch o' damned Portuguese!" There were one or two yelps which suggested Corcoran's mates were using their starters to clear the decks of unwanted spectators.

By the time the disciplinary uproar had died away, the boat was halfway out from the shore. Parker stared towards it, trying to make out individual figures. But the people in the boat were still a shapeless, indistinguishable mass.

How *was* he going to address *Bellerophon*'s passenger? It was a question over which Parker had already spent a good many disagreeable hours, without reaching a solution. The Government's orders were strict and explicit—honorable treatment at all times. This made sense, in the same way that not executing the man had made sense. There was no good reason for giving such great and lasting offense to so many of the people whom this man had led.

But how far should Parker carry that "honorable treatment"? His Majesty's Government had never recognized the man's office or titles. But—the man had been a soldier, as he himself had said to Stafford. He had been sure of that long before last night. But what the army officers had said then had made him even more sure.

"He was a damned impressive sight, let me tell you," one of them had said. "Sitting there on his horse, all wrapped in that gray cloak, cool as ice even though his army was going to the devil all around him. It was mostly his work that any of them got off the field at all. And then those damned Germans wanted to shoot him like some criminal or deserter. They've never forgiven him for the way he showed them up. But we stopped that soon enough.''

The boat was closer now. Parker could make out one figure in the stern—a figure wearing a gray cloak. Should he hold to the letter of the law—or do the man proper honor? What did the letter of the law mean anyway, applied to a man going into exile? Parker had lived all his adult life by the letter of assorted laws—the Thirty-Nine Articles of War above all. Should he now risk creating an infinite deal of mischief for himself, just to show his regard for a man sailing into permanent exile?

The boat bumped alongside, and the man in the stern rose to his feet. In that moment Captain Parker made his decision. The man in gray came up the side of the ship with surprising speed and agility. As his passenger stepped onto the deck, Captain Parker stepped forward and held out his hand.

''Welcome aboard, General Washington.''

Peek-a-boo!

The Biography Project

by H. L. Gold

There was something tremendously exciting about the opening of the Biofilm Institute. Even a hardened Sunday supplement writer like Wellman Zatz felt it.

Arlington Prescott, a wiper in a contact-eyeglass factory, while searching for a time machine, had invented the Biotime Camera, a standard movie camera—minus sound, of course—that projected a temporal beam, reaccumulated it, and focused it on a temporal-light-sensitized film. When he discovered that he had to be satisfied with merely photographing the past, not physically visiting it, Prescott had quit doing research and become principal of a nursery school.

But, Zatz explained, dictating his notes by persfone to a voxtyper in the telenews office, the Biofilm Institute was based on Prescott's repudiated invention. A huge, massive building, mostly below ground, in the 23rd century style, and equipped with 1,000 Biotime Cameras, it was the gift of Humboldt Maxwell, wealthy manufacturer of Snack Capsules. There were 1,000 teams of biographers, military analysts, historians, etc., to begin recording history as it actually happened—with special attention, according to Maxwell's grant, to past leaders of industry, politics, science, and the arts, in the order named.

Going through the Biofilm Institute, Wellman Zatz gained mostly curt or snarled interviews with the Bioteams; fishing through time for incidents or persons was a nervous job, and they resented interruptions.

He settled finally on a team that seemed slightly friendlier. They were watching what looked like a scene from Elizabethan England on the monitor screen.

"Sir Isaac Newton," Kelvin Burns, the science biographer, grunted in reply to Zatz's question. "Great man. We want to find out why he went off the beam."

Zatz knew about that, of course. Sunday feature articles for centuries had used the case of Sir Isaac to support arguments for psychic phenomena. After making all his astonishing discoveries by the age of 25, the great 17th century scientist had spent the rest of his long life in a hunt for precognition, the philosopher's stone, and other such paraphernalia of mysticism.

"My guess," said Mowbray Glass, the psychiatrist, "is paranoia caused by feelings of rejection in childhood."

But the screen showed a happy boy in what seemed to be a normal 17th century home and school environment. Glass grew puzzled as Sir Isaac eventually produced his binomial theorem, differential and integral calculus, and went to work on gravity—all without evidencing any symptoms of emotional imbalance.

"The most unbelievable demonstative and deductive powers I've encountered," said Pinero Schmidt, the science integrator. "I can't believe such a man could go mystical."

"But he did," Glass said, and tensed. "Look!"

Alone in a dark, cumbersomely furnished study, the man on the screen, wearing a satin coat, stock and breeches, glanced up sharply. He looked directly into the temporal beam for a moment, and then stared into the shadows of the room. He grabbed up a silver candlestick and searched the corners, holding the heavy candlestick like a weapon.

"He's mumbling something," reported Gonzalez Carson, the lip-reader. "Spies. He thinks somebody's after his discoveries."

Burns looked puzzled. "That's the first sign we've seen of breakdown. But what caused it?"

"I'm damned if I know," admitted Glass.

"Heredity?" Zatz suggested.

"No," Glass said positively. "It's been checked."

The Bioteam spent hours prying further. When the scientist was in his thirties, he developed a continuing habit of looking up and smiling secretly. On his deathbed, forty years later, he moved his lips happily, without fear.

" 'My guardian angel,' " Carson interpreted for them. " 'You've watched over me all my life. I am content to meet you now."

Glass started. He went to one Bioteam after another, asking a brief question of each. When he came back, he was trembling.

"What's the answer, Doc?" Zatz asked eagerly.

"We can't use the Biotime Camera any more," Glass said, looking sick. "My colleagues have been investigating the psychoses of Robert Schumann, Marcel Proust and others, who all eventually developed delusions of persecution."

"Yeah, but why?" Zatz persisted.

"Because they thought they were being spied upon. And they were, of course. By us!"

Lend me your ears.

The Grapes of the Rath

by Jan Howard Finder

Sir Nippip Koot, Chief of Special Investigations of the Galactic Scotland Yard, sucked slowly on his favorite meerschaum, while eyeing the wight opposite him. This was Su Gnoma Sugnuf, Chief of the Imperial Police on Oniv, the seventh planet of Anthony's Star. Su was humanoid in appearance, having two legs, two arms, two eyes, two noses, etc.

Chief Sugnuf fidgeted irritably in his chair, which valiantly tried to keep up with his movements in order to provide him with a comfortable seat. His jaw muscles tightened in time with his clenching fists as he strove to compose himself.

"Chief Inspector Koot, you must realize that although this hideous and detestable crime has long gone unsolved, it would not normally bring me here to your esteemed office. However, this moldy excretion of a grape worm has listed off Oniv. Thus, we cannot carry on without the permission and, hopefully, the help of your office."

"Yes," replied Chief Koot, "I do believe that we can enter the case. I'd appreciate your giving me a full briefing. All I know is that the suspect has apparently stolen some grapevines from the Caesar's Imperial vineyards."

"Ah yes, Chief Inspector Koot, seemingly, belike, a petty crime for such exertions by the Imperial Police. However, Oniv is a poor planet. Our one saving grace is that the Ghreat Ghod Vombato has seen fit to bless us with the soil, climate, and vines to produce the most fabulous wine in the Galaxy. Wine is our sole export.

Thus, it is a capital crime to attempt to export the vines. It is very probable the vines would not and could not grow elsewhere; however, we dare not tempt the fates.

"That the criminal in question, this rotted lump of vine leaves from diseased cuttings, has stolen vines is bad enough. That this fifth from the shoes of discredited grape stompers has taken the vines off planet is infinitely worse. But this, *this* . . ." he sputtered, "has taken vines from The Rath, the vineyard of the Caesar! The Emperor's own vines!

"Therefore, I have been ordered to search for this scum of contaminated grape seeds until I have found him. And found him I have! He is rooted up in the hills of Germany, along the Mosel River on the Galactic Government's own planet Terra. Yet, he is smarter than we thought. No one can touch him there; it is sanctuary. However, with your office's help, we can at least seize the contraband."

Chief Inspector Nippip Koot mulled over the details of the wine caper. The tangled skein of events wove themselves into a pattern demonstrating that while on the sanctuary called Terra, the suspect could not be rooted out—but the same could not be said about the vines. *Any* grapes or berries the suspect had in his possession were fair pickings under Galactic Law.

It was only a hop, skip, and two black hole jumps to Terra. Being himself a wine connoisseur who had heard of the fabled wines of Oniv, Chief Inspector Koot went along with Chief Sugnuf and the Imperial Guard assigned to the chase. The Guard was an impressive lot, being a good head taller than Su, who was not short for an Onivian.

The rolling green hills of "Der Schöne Eifel" gave way to the steep-walled Mosel river valley. The police craft quickly and quietly settled to the earth in front of the small flowered home of the suspect.

Su leapt from the craft as it alighted. Moving like the point man on a cavalry charge, he raced to the door. Pounding on it, not really in a manner becoming the Chief of the Imperial Police, he bellowed, "Nup, Tid Nup, come out here—or *else!*"

The door opened and a small, wizened Onivian came

out. Tears streaked his cheeks. "Oh sirrah, please do not kill me."

Su, restraining himself with difficulty, choked out, "Nup, you drippings from cancerous berries, if you don't give us every single one of the vines that you stole, I'll forget my position and also the lamentable fact that you are on sanctuary."

"Oh sirrah," whined Nup, "you have come for naught. Though the Mosel valley is famed, far and wide, for its vines, the Berries from The Rath won't grow here. Only one vine survived and on it merely one berry has grown. Please let me keep it—to remind me of the home I can never return to. It is such a beautiful berry, *please?*"

Tears coursed down the cheeks of the broken-hearted Tid Nup. The hard heart of Su was touched. However, Chief Inspector Nippip Koot knew the consequences of being softhearted.

"Nup," he said in a quiet voice, "I'm sure it is indeed magnificent, but we came to seize your berry, not to praise it."

Better the devil we know—

Mr. Lupescu

by Anthony Boucher

The teacups rattled, and flames flickered over the logs.

"Alan, I *do* wish you could do something about Bobby."

"Isn't that rather Robert's place?"

"Oh you know *Robert*. He's so busy doing good in nice abstract ways with committees in them."

"And headlines."

"He can't be bothered with things like Mr. Lupescu. After all, Bobby's only his *son.*"

"And yours, Marjorie."

"And mine. But things like this take a *man,* Alan."

The room was warm and peaceful; Alan stretched his long legs by the fire and felt domestic. Marjorie was soothing even when she fretted. The firelight did things to her hair and the curve of her blouse.

A small whirlwind entered at high velocity and stopped only when Marjorie said, "Bob-*by!* Say hello nicely to Uncle Alan."

Bobby said hello and stood tentatively on one foot.

"Alan . . ." Marjorie prompted.

Alan sat up straight and tried to look paternal. "Well, Bobby," he said. "And where are you off to in such a hurry?"

"See Mr. Lupescu 'f course. He usually comes afternoons."

"Your mother's been telling me about Mr. Lupescu. He must be quite a person."

"Oh gee I'll say he is, Uncle Alan. He's got a great big red nose and red gloves and red eyes—not like when you've been crying but really red like yours're brown—and little red wings that twitch only he can't fly with them cause they're ruddermentary he says. And he talks like—oh gee I can't do it, but he's swell, he is."

"Lupescu's a funny name for a fairy godfather, isn't it, Bobby?"

"Why? Mr. Lupescu always says why do all the fairies have to be Irish because it takes all kinds, doesn't it?"

"*Alan!*" Marjorie said. "I don't see that you're doing a *bit* of good. You talk to him seriously like that and you simply make him think it *is* serious. And you *do* know better, don't you, Bobby? You're just joking with us."

"Joking? About *Mr. Lupescu?*"

"Marjorie, you don't—Listen, Bobby. Your mother didn't mean to insult you or Mr. Lupescu. She just doesn't believe in what she's never seen, and you can't blame her. Now, suppose you took her and me out in the garden and we could all see Mr. Lupescu. Wouldn't that be fun?"

"Uh-uh." Bobby shook his head gravely. "Not for Mr. Lupescu. He doesn't like people. Only little boys.

And he says if I ever bring people to see him, then he'll let Gorgo get me. G'bye now." And the whirlwind departed.

Marjorie sighed. "At least thank heavens for Gorgo. I never can get a very clear picture out of Bobby, but he says Mr. Lupescu tells the most *terrible* things about him. And if there's any trouble about vegetables or brushing teeth, all I have to say is *Gorgo* and hey presto!"

Alan rose. "I don't think you need worry, Marjorie. Mr. Lupescu seems to do more good than harm, and an active imagination is no curse to a child."

"You haven't *lived* with Mr. Lupescu."

"To live in a house like this, I'd chance it," Alan laughed. "But please forgive me now—back to the cottage and the typewriter . . . Seriously, why don't you ask Robert to talk with him?"

Marjorie spread her hands helplessly.

"I know. I'm always the one to assume responsibilities. And yet you married Robert."

Marjorie laughed. "I don't know. Somehow there's something *about* Robert . . ." Her vague gesture happened to include the original Dégas over the fireplace, the sterling tea service, and even the liveried footman who came in at that moment to clear away.

Mr. Lupescu was pretty wonderful that afternoon, all right. He had a little kind of an itch like in his wings and they kept twitching all the time. Stardust, he said. It tickles. Got it up in the Milky Way. Friend of mine has a wagon route up there.

Mr. Lupescu had lots of friends, and they all did something you wouldn't ever think of, not in a squillion years. That's why he didn't like people, because people don't do things you can tell stories about. They just work or keep house or are mothers or something.

But one of Mr. Lupescu's friends, now, was captain of a ship, only it went in time, and Mr. Lupescu took trips with him and came back and told you all about what was happening this very minute five hundred years ago. And another of the friends was a radio engineer, only he could tune in on all the kingdoms of faery and Mr. Lupescu would squidgle up his red nose and twist it like a dial and make noises like all the kingdoms of faery coming in on the set. And than there was Gorgo, only he wasn't a friend—not exactly; not even to Mr. Lupescu.

They'd been playing for a couple of weeks—only it must've been really hours, cause Mamselle hadn't yelled about supper yet, but Mr. Lupescu says Time is funny—when Mr. Lupescu screwed up his red eyes and said, "Bobby, let's go in the house."

"But there's people in the house, and you don't—"

"I know I don't like people. That's why we're going in the house. Come on, Bobby, or I'll—"

So what could you do when you didn't even want to hear him say Gorgo's name?

He went into Father's study through the French window, and it was a strict rule that nobody *ever* went into Father's study, but rules weren't for Mr. Lupescu.

Father was on the telephone telling somebody he'd try to be at a luncheon but there was a committee meeting that same morning but he'd see. While he was talking, Mr. Lupescu went over to a table and opened a drawer and took something out.

When Father hung up, he saw Bobby first and started to be very mad. He said, "Young man, you've been trouble enough to your Mother and me with all your stories about your red-winged Mr. Lupescu, and now if you're to start bursting in—"

You have to be polite and introduce people. "Father, this is Mr. Lupescu And see, he does too have red wings."

Mr. Lupescu held out the gun he'd taken from the drawer and shot Father once right through the forehead. It made a little clean hole in front and a big messy hole in back. Father fell down and was dead.

"Now, Bobby," Mr. Lupescu said, "a lot of people are going to come here and ask you a lot of questions. And if you don't tell the truth about exactly what happened, I'll send Gorgo to fetch you."

Then Mr. Lupescu was gone through the French window.

"It's a curious case, Lieutenant," the medical examiner said. "It's fortunate I've dabbled a bit in psychiatry; I can at least give you a lead until you get the experts in. The child's statement that his fairy godfather shot his father is obviously a simple flight mechanism, susceptible of two interpretations. A, the father shot himself; the child was so horrified by the sight that he refused to accept it and invented this explanation. B, the child shot the father, let us say by accident, and shifted the blame to his imaginary scapegoat. B has, of course, its more sinister implications: if the child had resented his father and created an ideal substitute, he might make the substitute destroy the reality. . . . But there's the solution to your eyewitness testimony; which alternative is true, Lieutenant, I leave up to your researchers into motive and the evidence of ballistics and fingerprints. The angle of the wound jibes with either.''

The man with the red nose and eyes and gloves and wings walked down the back lane to the cottage. As soon as he got inside, he took off his coat and removed the wings and the mechanism of strings and rubber that made them twitch. He laid them on top of the ready pile of kindling and lit the fire. When it was well started, he added the gloves. Then he took off the nose, kneaded the putty until the red of its outside vanished into neutral brown of the mass, jammed it into a crack in the wall, and smoothed it over. Then he took the red-irised contact lenses out of his brown eyes and went into the kitchen, found a hammer, pounded them to powder, and washed the powder down the sink.

Alan started to pour himself a drink and found, to his pleased surprise, that he didn't especially need one. But he did feel tired. He could lie down and recapitulate it all, from the invention of Mr. Lupescu (and Gorgo and the man with the Milky Way route) to today's success and on into the future when Marjorie—pliant, trusting Marjorie—would be more desirable than ever as Robert's widow and heir. And Bobby would need a *man* to look after him.

Alan went into the bedroom. Several years passed by in the few seconds it took him to recognize what was waiting on the bed, but then, Time is funny.

Alan said nothing.

"Mr. Lupescu, I presume?" said Gorgo.

Back into Eden, everybody.

What I Did During My Park Vacation

by Ruth Berman

When the park comes to the neighborhood all the floors drop down a couple centimeters, and all the elevators are out of joint. Everyone trips getting out.

If you are carrying your tea ration, this can be serious.

But no one minds, because the park is on the roof, and lying snug against the flat lines of roof-tiling and conveyor-belts.

Usually, no one goes up to the top of the shaft, except the top-floorers, and from there no one crosses into the surface-hydraul to get shoved up to the very roof except the janitors who have to clear filters, or adjust solars, or take in deliveries from the belts. But when the park is there, everyone goes up by turns, higher even than the roof, onto the green.

And it's green forever, green, and flowers, and trees as tall as grownups.

They don't let you climb them, though. They say they aren't big enough. Which is pretty weird, actually, because when you ask when they'll be big enough, they say that's as big as they go, on account of the roots are as far down as they can go, down to the rooftops. But kids in old stories are always climbing trees.

I mean, not always, but lots.

When the park comes to the neighborhood, the air at home gets stuffy, because your power gets piped in from other people's solars. But it's all right, because you can go play in the park, where there's lots of fresh air, which is what air is when it smells open and it keeps changing direction instead of circulating properly.

Deliveries get kind of uncertain, too, and have to be detoured in from groundlevel.

But up in the park flowers grow right out in the open, without pots, or tanks, or anything. Roses and peonies, and narcissus, and all kinds. They look nice. You can pick them, if there are enough and they're giving out permits.

Then they die. The flowers. That is nature.

Nature is very good for you, and I like it very much. During my park vacation I saw lots of nature. Then they rolled the park over onto the tops of the next buildings. The park circulates, just like real air. It is nice to have it visit. I like to take my tea ration up on the park, but I didn't this time, because I'd spilled it. The green wasn't as green, and it bothered me more about the Keep Off the Trees signs, but it was still nice.

Someday the trees will get bigger, I bet, and I will hide in one and go with the park all over the district, maybe all over the region, and never come down again.

Unless I grow up first. I bet even if a tree got twice as tall as a grownup, a grownup wouldn't fit in it. Not for hiding. And it would be bad for the tree, maybe.

But I could do it okay, if the trees would get a little bigger.

Trees have leaves, except when they have needles. Some trees have nuts. Some have fruit. You can eat them, if you get a permit. When I go with the park I'll live in a jonathan apple tree.

You'll see.

" 'twas caviar to the general, od's bodikins."

A Fragment of Manuscript

by Harry Harrison

I found the two fragments of parchment, tied together with a bit of leather cord, behind one of the older bookcases in the Bodleian Library in Oxford. It was just chance. I had dropped a fifty pence bit—a heavy British coin bigger than a half dollar and worth eighty-five cents—and it had rolled into the gap between the bookcase and the wall. I could see it but could not reach it, so I pushed the bookcase a bit in order to get my hand in. I then reached the coin easily enough, but at the same time something slid down and struck against my fingers. I drew it out, along with the fifty pence, and it proved to be the parchment fragments referred to above.

In all truth I can lay no claims as to their authenticity, as to the authenticity of the writer that is, though their undoubted great age has been verified by certain chemical tests. If they are what they appear to be, lost lines from the Immortal Bard's own pen, they are indeed priceless and cast the light of knowledge upon some heretofore unsuspected aspects of his plays.

The chronology is clear enough. Ludovico Ariosto wrote *Orlando Furioso* in the early 1500s, and it is a well-known fact that Spenser took it as his model for *The Faerie Queene*. This was a common practise and Shakespeare himself drew on other books for the material for most of his plays. Since he wrote *A Midsummer Night's Dream* in the late 1500s there is every chance that he might have been acquainted with Ariosto's work, one of the earliest science fiction romances about a visit to the moon. Might Shakespeare not have decided to utilize the same idea? There is every possibility that the fragments of manuscript, a copy of which is appended below, will throw some light on this question.

A MIDSUMMER NIGHT'S DREAM—Act III, Scene 1—The wood.

Enter Quince, Snug, Bottom, Flute, Snout, and Starveling.

BOTTOM: Are we all met?

QUINCE: Pat, pat; and here's a marvelous convenient place for our rehearsal. This green plot shall be our stage, this hawthorn-brake our tiring-house; and we will do it in action as we will do before the duke.

BOTTOM: Peter Quince,—

QUINCE: What sayest thou, Bully Bottom?

BOTTOM: There are things in this comedy of Lunar Man that will never please. First, landeth here a spatial ship, with roar and bluster; which the ladies cannot abide. How answer you that?

SNOUT: By'r lakin, a parlous fear.

STARVELING: I believe we must leave the rocket out, when all is done.

BOTTOM: Not a whit: I have a device to make all well. The thought of rockets we must disabuse, we for a stellar barque a null-G ship will use.

SNOUT: Will not the ladies be afeard of the null-G?

BOTTOM: Nay, indeed, a device so divers simple, a whipstock here to clutch and guide the course, and there about stout wainropes to hold secure and effect the landing in the proper place.

QUINCE: What place?

BOTTOM: Behind a wall, where ropes may be unhooked and secret means of flight thus be concealed.

SNOUT: You can never bring in a wall. What say you, Quince?

Quince: No, in truth, we could not.

BOTTOM: Some man or other must present wall: and let him have some plaster, or some loam, or some roughcast about him, to signify wall. But enough: this detail is but wrangle, we must press on. The Lunar Man shall step forth, around the wall of course, and there before the gathered nobles speak his speach.

QUINCE: What speech?

BOTTOM: Wit! whither wander you, the speech that we did copy from the book, chained there in church. How Lunar Man sailed safe the sea of space, with cunning coils did achieve null-G and, with parlous speed, escape velocity.

QUINCE: Escape from whom?

BOTTOM: Puisny knave, did you not read? Escape from Earth, from Moon I mean, the first, then later burst the fairy bonds so insubstantial yet so firm that held we are upon this globe to death from birth.

QUINCE: But how? These raveled knots of thoughts do give amazement to my poll.

BOTTOM: I'll give amazement to your back, bat-fowling, bibble-babble mewling Quince, what is not clear?

QUINCE: All.

Bottom strikes Quince who falls. Exeunt severely.

A scrawled note across the last lines of the manuscript reads: *No, will not do, the market still unripe for SF. Rewrite—fantasy still best. Must buy book of fairy tales.*

What's the difference?

The Boy with Five Fingers

by James Gunn

I love Miss Harrison. The other boys laugh at me and say that Miss Davis is prettier or Miss Spencer is nicer. But I don't care. I love Miss Harrison.

Miss Harrison's my teacher. When I grow up we're going to get married. When I tell her that she gets that kind of crinkling around her eye like she does when she's pleased about something, and she says that's fine like she meant it, and I guess she does.

The first time I thought about it was the day Miss Harrison told us about the scientists and the Old Race and the Basic Right. Miss Harrison said we should try to keep track of what the scientists are doing because they are the wisest and maybe if we know more about them we will be wiser, too, and might even be scientists ourselves some day. But I think what she really wanted to talk about was the Basic Right. Somehow, everyday, she talks about the Basic Right and it must be important because she talks about it so much.

So Miss Harrison said that many, many years ago, before any of us were born, the scientists had uncovered ruins and nobody knew what they were and everybody wondered and thought about them because they were really big.

Somebody said that we had built them long ago and left them and forgotten about them but nobody believed that because we live in little houses far apart and we never had built anything as big as the ruins and never had wanted to build anything like that.

Then somebody else said that the ruins had been built by a race that lived on Earth before we did and had died or something because maybe conditions got different or maybe they went to live on another planet. And everybody said that must be right, so they started calling them the Old Race but nobody knew what they looked like, or did, or anything except that they built these huge places and then went away.

Nobody knew any more than that for years and years, Miss Harrison said, until just a year or so ago when the scientists dug up a place that wasn't all in ruins and found statues and pictures and books and everything. So everybody was all excited and worked on them awfully hard until they could tell what the Old Race was like and just about what was in the books.

Miss Harrison kind of stopped here and looked at us like she does when she's going to tell us something important and we should all get real quiet and listen carefully so we wouldn't miss anything.

Then she said that they had just released the news and the Old Race wasn't really different after all but sort of like ancestors of ours only far away. She said that in lots of ways they were like us only strange and did strange things, and she said we should be sorry for them and glad, too, because maybe if they hadn't been strange we wouldn't be here. Then she told us how strange they were, and I was glad I didn't live then and that I was living now and I was in Miss Harrison's class and listening to her tell us about the Old Race.

Most all of them lived together in these big places, she said, like ants in an ant heap. Everybody gasped at that because we all liked lots of room. But the strangest thing of all, Miss Harrison said, was something else. She stopped again and we all got real quiet. They were all, she said slowly, exactly alike.

Nobody said anything for a moment and then Willie began to laugh the way he does, sort of half-hissing, and pretty soon we were all laughing and Miss Harrison, too. They all had two eyes, she said, and one nose, and one mouth, and two ears, and two arms and two legs. After every one of those things Willie began hissing again and we all had to laugh. And, Miss Harrison said, they were all stuck in exactly the same place. Their arms and legs all had bones in them that had joints in the middle and at each end.

Though they were all exactly alike, Miss Harrison said, they thought they could see differences and because of this they did all sorts of strange things until they did the strangest thing of all and ruined all their big places and their children weren't all alike any more. So it went on like that until nobody was alike and here we are. So they were kind of ancestors, like Miss Harrison said.

Then Miss Harrison stopped again and got up slow, the way she does when she wants to make sure everybody will pay attention. We all held our breath. In this room, she said, right now, we have a member of the Old Race.

Everybody let out his breath all at once. We all looked at her but she laughed and said no, she wasn't it. Johnny, she said, stand up, and I stood up. There, said Miss Harrison, is what the Old Race looked like. Everybody stared at me and I felt kind of cold and lonely all at once. Of course, she said, I don't mean Johnny is really one of the Old Race but he looks just like they used to and he even has five fingers on each hand.

All at once I felt ashamed. I put my hands behind me where nobody could see.

Willie started hissing again, but he wasn't laughing now and his thin forked tongue was flickering at me. Everybody moved as far away from me as they could get and started making nasty sounds. If I had been a littly younger I might have started to cry, but I just stood there and wished I had a mouth and tongue like Willie's, or a cart like Louise's instead of legs, or arms like Joan's or fingers like Mike's.

But Miss Harrison stood up straight and frowned, like she does when she's real mad about something and she said she was very surprised and it would seem like everything she'd said had been wasted. Pretty soon everybody quieted down and listened so she wouldn't be mad and she said it looked like what she'd said about the Basic Right hadn't done one bit of good.

Everybody has a right to be different, that was the Basic Right, she said, the foundation of everything and we wouldn't be here now if it weren't for that. And the law says that no one shall discriminate against anyone else because they are different, and that applied to being the same, too. And Miss Harrison said a lot more things I don't remember because I was sort of excited and warm inside. And finally she said she hoped we'd learned a lesson because the Old Race hadn't, and look where they were.

It was right after that I decided I loved Miss Harrison. The other boys say she should have a neck, like Miss Davis, but I don't see why. They say she should have two eyes like me or three like Miss Spencer, but I like her just the way she is and everything she does, like the way she wraps her arm around the chalk when she draws on the board. But I've already said it. I love Miss Harrison.

When I grow up we're going to get married. I've thought of lots of reasons why we should but there's one that's better than any of them.

Miss Harrison and me—I guess we're more different than anybody.

That's going too far.

The King of Beasts

by Philip José Farmer

The biologist was showing the distinguished visitor through the zoo and laboratory.

"Our budget," he said, "is too limited to re-create all known extinct species. So we bring to life only the higher animals, the beautiful ones that were wantonly exterminated. I'm trying, as it were, to make up for brutality and stupidity. You might say that man struck God in the face every time he wiped out a branch of the animal kingdom.

He paused, and they looked across the moats and the force fields. The quagga wheeled and galloped, delight and sun flashing off his flanks. The sea otter poked his humorous whiskers from the water. The gorilla peered from behind bamboo. Passenger pigeons strutted. A rhinoceros trotted like a dainty battleship. With gentle eyes a giraffe looked at them, then resumed eating leaves.

"There's the dodo. Not beautiful but very droll. And very helpless. Come, I'll show you the re-creation itself."

In the great building, they passed between rows of tall and wide tanks. They could see clearly through the windows and the jelly within.

"Those are African Elephant embryos," said the biologist. "We plan to grow a large herd and then release them on the new government preserve."

"You positively radiate," said the distinguished visitor. "You really love the animals, don't you?"

"I love all life."

"Tell me," said the visitor, "where do you get the data for re-creation?"

"Mostly, skeletons and skins from the ancient museums. Excavated books and films that we succeeded in restoring and then translating. Ah, see those huge eggs? The chicks of the giant moa are growing within them. There, almost ready to be taken from the tank, are tiger cubs. They'll be dangerous when grown but will be confined to the preserve."

The visitor stopped before the last of the tanks.

"Just one?" he said. "What is it?"

"Poor little thing," said the biologist, now sad. "It will be so alone. But I shall give it all the love I have."

"Is it so dangerous?" said the visitor. "Worse than elephants, tigers and bears?"

"I had to get special permission to grow this one," said the biologist. His voice quavered.

The visitor stepped sharply back from the tank. He said, "Then it must be . . . But you wouldn't dare!"

The biologist nodded.

"Yes. It's a man."

Let's give him his due.

Displaced Person

by Eric Frank Russell

He glided out of the gathering dusk and seated himself at the other end of the bench and gazed absently across the lake. The setting sun had dribbled blood in the sky. Mandarin ducks paddled through crimson streaks on the waters. The park held its usual eventide hush; the only sounds were the rustle of leaves and grasses, the murmuring of secluded lovers and the muted tootings of distant cars.

When the bench quivered its announcement of company I had glanced along it half-expecting to find some derelict hoping to cadge the price of a bed. The contrast between the anticipated and the seen was such that I looked again, long, carefully, out of the corners of my eyes so that he wouldn't notice it.

Despite the gray tones of twilight what I saw was a study in black and white. He had thin, sensitive features as white as his gloves and his shirt-front. His shoes and suit were not quite as black as his finely curved eyebrows and well-groomed hair. His eyes were blackest of all: that solid, supernal blackness that can be no deeper or darker. Yet they were alive with an underlying glow.

He had no hat. A slender walking-stick of ebony rested casually against his legs. A black, silk-lined cloak hung from his shoulders. If he had been doing it for the movies he could not have presented a better picture of a distinguished foreigner.

My mind speculated about him in the way minds do when momentarily they have nothing else to occupy them. A European refugee, it decided. Possibly an eminent surgeon or sculptor. Or perhaps a writer or painter, more likely the latter.

I stole another look at him. In the lowering light the pale profile was hawklike. The glow behind the eyes was strengthening with the dark. The cloak lent him a peculiar majesty. The trees were stretching their arms toward him as if to give aid and comfort through the long, long night.

No hint of suffering marked that face. It had nothing in common with the worn, lined features I had seen elsewhere, countenances wearing forever the memories of the manacles, the whip and the horror camp. On the contrary, it held a mixture of boldness and serenity, of confidence in the belief that one day the tide must turn. Impulsively I decided that he was a musician. I could imagine him conducting a tremendous choir of fifty thousand voices.

"I am fond of music," he said in low, rich tones.

His face turned toward me, revealing a pronounced peak in his glossy black hair.

"Really?" The unexpectedness of his remark caught me at a disadvantage. Without knowing it I must have voiced my thoughts aloud. Rather feebly I asked, "Of what kind?"

"This." He used his ebony stick to indicate the world at large. "The sigh of ending day."

"Yes, it is soothing," I agreed.

"It is my time," he said. "The time when the day ends—as all things must end."

"That's true," I said for lack of anything better.

We were silent awhile. Slowly the horizon soaked the blood from the sky. The city put on its lights and a wan moon floated over its towers.

"You're not a native of this place?" I prompted.

"No." Resting long, slender hands upon his stick, he gazed meditatively forward. "I have no country. I am a displaced person."

"I'm sorry."

"Thank you," he said.

I couldn't just sit there and leave him to stew in his own juice. The choice was to continue the conversation or depart. There was no need to go. So I continued.

"Care to tell me about it?"

His head came round and he studied me as if only now fully aware of my presence. That weird light in his orbs could almost be felt. He smiled gradually and tolerantly, showing perfect teeth.

"Should I?"

"You don't have to. But sometimes it helps to get things off one's mind."

"I doubt it. Besides, I would be wasting your time."

"Not at all. I'm wasting it anyway."

Smiling again, he used his stick to draw unseeable circles in front of his black shoes.

"In this day and age it is an all too familiar story," he said. "A leader became so blinded by his own glory that he considered himself incapable of making blunders. He rejected all advice and resented all criticism. He developed delusions of grandeur, posed as the final arbiter on everything from birth to death, and thereby brought into being a movement for his overthrow. He created the seeds of his own destruction. It was inevitable in the circumstances."

"And rightly so," I supported. "To hell with dictators!"

The stick slipped from his grasp. He picked it up, juggled it idly, resumed his circle drawing.

"The revolt didn't succeed?" I suggested.

"No." He looked at the circles and struck a line through them. "It proved too early and too weak. It was crushed with the utmost ruthlessness. Then came the purge." His glowing eyes surveyed the sentinel trees. "I created that opposition. I still think it was justified. But I dare not go back. Not yet."

"A fat lot you should care about that. You're in a good country now and you can fit into it comfortably."

"I don't think so. I'm not especially welcome here." His voice was deeper. "Not wanted—anywhere."

"Oh, nonsense!" I retorted. "Everybody is wanted by someone, somewhere. Cheer up. Don't be morbid. After all, it's worth a lot just to be free."

"No man is free until he's beyond his enemy's reach." He glanced at me with an irritating touch of amusement, almost as if he considered that I had yet to learn the facts of life. "When one's foe has gained control of every channel of information and propaganda, when he uses them to present his own case and utterly suppress mine, when he offers calculated lies as truth and damns the truth as a lie, there is little hope for me."

"Well, that's your way of looking at things. I cannot blame you for feeling bitter about bygone experiences. But you've got to forget them. Here, you're living in a different world. We've free speech. A man can say what he likes, write what he likes."

"If only that were true."

"It is true," I asserted, slightly annoyed. "Here you can call the Rajah of Bam an arrogant and overfed parasite if you wish. Nobody can prevent you from doing so, not even the police. We're free, as I've told you."

He stood up, towering amid embracing trees. From my sitting position his height seemed enormous. The moon lit his face in pale ghastliness.

"Your faith is comforting but baseless."

"No!" I denied.

He turned away. His cape swung behind him and billowed in the night breeze until it resembled mighty wings.

"My name," he murmured softly, "is Lucifer."
After that there was only the whisper of the wind.

Once a loser—

A Clone at Last

by Bill Pronzini and Barry N. Malzberg

"I'm sorry," the lovely blonde said to Lapham, "but I could never invite a man into my Home Complex that I don't really know. But thanks anyway for an interesting evening."

And she shut the door firmly in his face.

Lapham was very tired of women telling him they didn't invite a man into their Home Complex that they didn't really know. He was tired of having doors shut in his face. It was 2172, a new era in interpersonal communication, wasn't it? And he was actually a fairly decent-looking man, wasn't he? Not to mention being a fairly successful pocket deity to many of the *Aphid Chorae* of Ceres, and having a number of good qualities which included but were not limited to earnestness, honesty, punctuality and never squeezing his pimples in public. Or taking the bandages off his radiation scars.

For some reason, however, women did not seem to like him.

So Lapham, in desperation, finally went to the Cloning Foundation and applied for Opposite Gender Replication. He would *create* the woman who would understand him, so there. Opposite Gender Replication was a recent innovation of the Foundation, and having been established only within the most recent decade and having been made available at terrific expense to people such as Lapham who had reasons to need an understanding ear from those of a different genital persuasion.

Lapham permitted his blood to be typed, his cells to be analyzed, his brain waves to be charted, his persona to be electromagnetically shocked and his private parts to be fondled in an unseemly fashion. His facial bandages, however, were left respectfully in place by the personnel of the enormously expensive Cloning Foundation. (He had inherited three-quarters of the asteroid Ceres, which made his lot somewhat easier.) At the end of this painful and somewhat unprintable process, a pure cell of his was extracted and left to lie in the darkest and most cherished spaces of the Foundation's nethermost level.

Lapham waited for eighteen years. Eighteen years was then as now the age of legal majority and he did not wish to be indicted for statutory rape, even of himself. The years sped by. Lapham invented a cheap substitute for the wheel, and after patenting it rode it all the way to Proxima Centauri and back. Bored, he created sub-life in one of the testing arenas and fed it to the grateful *Aphid Chorae*. He waited patiently, amusing himself through all the empty little hours as he aged from twenty-nine to forty-seven.

He did not, through all of this, deal with women at all. He was saving himself for herself.

At precisely oh eight hundred hours on her eighteenth birthday, the pimply blonde clone said, "I'm sorry but I never invite a man into my Home Complex that I don't really know. But thanks anyway for an interesting evening."

And Lapham shut the door firmly in Lapham's face.

"Bugs got feet; it's no big deal / But only man can make a wheel."

X Marks the Pedwalk

by Fritz Leiber

Based on material in Ch.7—"First Clashes of the Wheeled and Footed Sects"—of Vol. 3 of Burger's monumental *History of Traffic,* published by the Foundation for Twenty-Second Century Studies.

The raggedy little old lady with the big shopping bag was in the exact center of the crosswalk when she became aware of the big black car bearing down on her.

Behind the thick bullet-proof glass its seven occupants had a misty look, like men in a diving bell.

She saw there was no longer time to beat the car to either curb. Veering remorselessly, it would catch her in the gutter.

Useless to attempt a feint and double-back, such as any venturesome child executed a dozen times a day. Her reflexes were too slow.

Polite vacuous laughter came from the car's loud-speaker over the engine's mounting roar.

From her fellow pedestrians lining the curbs came a sigh of horror.

The little old lady dipped into her shopping bag and came up with a big blue-black automatic. She held it in both fists, riding the recoils like a rodeo cowboy on a bucking bronco.

Aiming at the base of the windshield, just as a big-game hunter aims at the vulnerable spine of a charging water buffalo over the horny armor of its lowered head, the little old lady squeezed off three shots before the car chewed her down.

From the right-hand curb a young woman in a wheelchair shrieked an obscenity at the car's occupants.

Smythe-de Winter, the driver, wasn't happy. The little old lady's last shot had taken two members of his car pool. Bursting through the laminated glass, the steel-jacketed slug had traversed the neck of Phipps-McHeath and buried itself in the skull of Horvendile-Harker.

Braking viciously, Smythe-de Winter rammed his car over the right-hand curb. Pedestrians scattered into entries and narrow arcades, among them a youth bounding high on crutches.

But Smythe-de Winter got the girl in the wheelchair.

Then he drove rapidly out of the Slum Ring into the Suburbs, a shred of rattan swinging from the flange of his right fore mudguard for a trophy. Despite the two-for-two casualty list, he felt angry and depressed. The secure, predictable world around him seemed to be crumbling.

While his companions softly keened a dirge to Horvy and Phipps and quietly mopped up their blood, he frowned and shook his head.

"They oughtn't to let old ladies carry magnums," he murmured.

Witherspoon-Hobbs nodded agreement across the front-seat corpse. "They oughtn't to let 'em carry anything. God, how I hate Feet," he muttered, looking down at his shrunken legs. "Wheels forever!" he softly cheered.

The incident had immediate repercussions throughout the city. At the combined wake of the little old lady and the girl in the wheelchair, a fiery-tongued speaker inveighed against the White-Walled Fascists of Suburbia, telling to his hearers, the fabled wonders of old Los Angeles, where pedestrians were sacrosanct, even outside crosswalks. He called for a hobnail march across the nearest lawn-bowling alleys and perambulator-traversed golf courses of the motorists.

At the Sunnyside Crematorium, to which the bodies of Phipps and Horvy had been conveyed, an equally impassioned and rather more grammatical orator reminded his listeners of the legendary justice of old Chicago, where pedestrians were forbidden to carry small arms and anyone with one foot off the sidewalk was fair prey. He broadly hinted that a holocaust, primed if necessary with a few tankfuls of gasoline, was the only cure for the Slums.

Bands of skinny youths came loping at dusk out of the Slum Ring into the innermost sections of the larger doughnut of the Suburbs slashing defenseless tyres, shooting expensive watchdogs and scrawling filthy words on the pristine panels of matrons' runabouts which never ventured more than six blocks from home.

Simultaneously squadrons of young suburban motor-cycles and scooterites roared through the outermost precincts of the Slum Ring, harrying children off sidewalks, tossing stink-bombs through second-story tenement windows and defacing hovel-fronts with sprays of black paint.

Incidents—a thrown brick, a cut corner, monster tacks in the portico of the Auto Club—were even reported from the centre of the city, traditionally neutral territory.

The Government hurriedly acted, suspending all traffic between the Center and the Suburbs and establishing a 24-hour curfew in the Slum Ring. Government agents moved only by centipede-car and pogo-hopper to underline the point that they favored neither contending side.

The day of enforced non-movement for Feet and Wheels was spent in furtive vengeful preparations. Behind locked garage doors, machine-guns that fired through the nose ornament were mounted under hoods, illegal scythe blades were welded to oversize hubcaps and the stainless steel edges of flange fenders were honed to razor sharpness.

While nervous National Guardsmen hopped about the deserted sidewalks of the Slum Ring, grim-faced men and women wearing black arm-bands moved through the web-work of secret tunnels and hidden doors, distributing heavy-caliber small arms and spike-studded paving blocks, piling cobblestones on strategic roof-tops and sapping upward from the secret tunnels to create car-traps. Children got ready to soap intersection after dark. The Committee of Pedestrian Safety, sometimes known as Robespierre's Rats, prepared to release its two carefully hoarded anti-tank guns.

* * *

At nightfall, under the tireless urging of the Government, representatives of the Pedestrians and the Motorists met on a huge safety island at the boundary of the Slum Ring and the Suburbs.

Underlings began a noisy dispute as to whether Smythe-de Winter had failed to give a courtesy honk before charging, whether the little old lady had opened fire before the car had come within honking distance, how many wheels of Smythe-de's car had been on the sidewalk when he hit the girl in the wheelchair and so on. After a little while the High Pedestrian and the Chief Motorist exchanged cautious winks and drew aside.

The red writhing of a hundred kerosene flares and the mystic yellow pulsing of a thousand firefly lamps mounted on yellow sawhorses ranged around the safety island illumined two tragic, strained faces.

"A word before we get down to business," the Chief Motorist whispered. "What's the current S.Q. of your adults?"

"Forty-one and dropping," the High Pedestrian replied, his eyes fearfully searching from side to side for eavesdroppers. "I can hardly get aides who are halfway *compos mentis.*"

"Our own Sanity Quotient is thirty-seven," the Chief Motorist revealed. He shrugged helplessly. "The wheels inside my people's heads are slowing down. I do not think they will be speeded up in my lifetime."

"They say Government's only fifty-two," the other said with a matching shrug.

"Well, I suppose we must scrape out one more compromise," the one suggested hollowly, "though I must confess there are times when I think we're all the figments of a paranoid's dream."

Two hours of concentrated deliberations produced the new Wheel-Foot Articles of Agreement. Among other points, pedestrian handguns were limited to a slightly lower muzzle velocity and to .38 caliber and under, while motorists were required to give three honks at one block distance before charging a pedestrian in a crosswalk. Two wheels over the curb changed a traffic kill from third-degree manslaughter to petty homicide. Blind pedestrians were permitted to carry hand grenades.

Immediately the Government went to work. The new Wheel-Foot Articles were loudspeakered and posted. Detachments of police and psychiatric social hoppers centipedaled and pogoed through the Slum Ring, seizing outside weapons and giving tranquilizing jet-injections to the unruly. Teams of hypnotherapists and mechanics scuttled from home to home in the Suburbs and from garage to garage, in-chanting a conformist serenity and stripping illegal armament from cars. On the advice of a rogue psychiatrist, who said it would channel off aggressions, a display of bull-fighting was announced, but this had to be cancelled when a strong protest was lodged by the Decency League, which had a large mixed Wheel-Foot membership.

At dawn, curfew was lifted in the Slum Ring and traffic reopened between the Suburbs and the Center. After a few uneasy moments it became apparent that the *status quo* had been restored.

Smythe-de Winter tooled his gleaming black machine along the Ring. A thick steel bolt with a large steel washer on either side neatly filled the hole the little old lady's slug had made in the windshield.

A brick bounced off the roof. Bullets pattered against the side windows. Smythe-de ran a handkerchief around his neck under his collar and smiled.

A block ahead children were darting into the street, cat-calling and thumbing their noses. Behind one of them limped a fat dog with a spiked collar.

Smythe-de suddenly gunned his motor. He didn't hit any of the children, but he got the dog.

A flashing light on the dash showed him the right front tire was losing pressure. Must have hit the collar as well! He thumbed the matching emergency-air button and the flashing stopped.

He turned toward Witherspoon-Hobbs and said with thoughtful satisfaction, "I like a normal orderly world, where you always have a little success, but not champagne-heady; a little failure, but just enough to brace you."

Witherspoon-Hobbs was squinting at the next cross-walk. Its center was discoloured by a brownish stain ribbon-tracked by tires.

"That's where you bagged the little old lady, Smythe-de," he remarked. "I'll say this for her now: she had spirit."

"Yes, that's where I bagged her," Smythe-de agreed flatly. He remembered wistfully the witchlike face growing rapidly larger, the jerking shoulders in black bombazine, the wild white-circled eyes. He suddenly found himself feeling that this was a very dull day.

Peace on earth.

The Mission

by Arthur Tofte

The two figures descended warily from the tiny scout ship. They knew their descent through the atmosphere had created a meteor-like streak of brilliant light. They hoped that the valley where they had landed was well enough hidden to conceal them and their craft.

The two looked at each other grimly. They were unhappy with their mission, and with the orders that brought them to this strange, gloomy planet.

"I know what our duty is," the older and taller of the two said in the sibilant language of his race, "even though I can't agree with what we are expected to do."

The other nodded agreement with the thought.

The leader handed his companion a small bundle he had brought out of the ship with him. "Here, you carry it for awhile. I'll lead the way."

He looked up into the night sky as though trying to catch a glimpse of the great mother ship that had brought them to this troubled, savage place. Mother ship indeed!

He peered anxiously at the dark knuckles of hills surrounding them. He pointed. "According to the instructions the Watchers gave us, the settlement is that way."

The two plodded slowly up the long slope of the hill. Suddenly the leader held out his arm for the other to stop.

"Strange beasts ahead!" he said. Using a shielded lightbeam, he flashed it at a group of white, rather round animals that stood silently in their way.

For only a moment the creatures stared at the light and then scurried off with little bounds.

"They don't appear to be dangerous," the younger stranger said as he moved his burden from one arm to the other.

The ground, they found, was hard and dry under their feet. Vegetation was thin and brittle. Overhead the stars sparkled with the sharp intensity that comes on a cold, cloudless night.

As they approached the sleeping village, they proceeded with increased caution. Occasionally small animals ran out to sniff and bark softly at them.

After they had passed several stone huts and a cave entrance or two, the leader murmured, "As the Watchers said, these people are indeed very primitive. They live in caves and stone hovels. I doubt if they know how to work metals. Almost certainly they have no written language. A truly sub-civilization—possibly like our own two or three thousand generations ago."

A single torch light gleamed ahead of them. Making their way through the stone rubble next to the path, they came to a wooden shed, half open to the night sky. Carefully and in secret they watched from the side.

A male and a female were in the shed. The woman, quite young and obviously in the final stages of exhaustion, held out a naked baby for the man to hold while she wrapped cloths around it.

This was what they had been told by the Watchers they would find—a native child being born.

From their vantage point, the two strangers saw the young mother sink with a sigh to the floor. The man carefully placed the child next to her. Then, he too lowered himself to the dirt floor. In a matter of moments both were asleep.

Quietly the tall visitor went over to look down at the newborn child. Its mouth was moving soundlessly and its tiny fingers groped futilely at the empty air.

He reached for the bundle his companion had brought

so carefully from the ship and opened it. He lifted out the naked baby it contained. It too was a newborn.

In the time of half a dozen heartbeats, he had exchanged the two infants, even switching their covering cloths.

As the two turned to leave, the strangers looked back for a last look at the sleeping man and his wife. And they peered for the last time at the child they had brought with them and were now leaving in this primitive place.

Hurriedly, their mission completed, they headed back toward their ship. The leader carried the infant they had stolen.

"Our Watchers were right," he said once they were away from the village. "The people on this planet are extremely primitive. And yet they appear to be more like us in appearance than those of any other planet we have ever studied."

"Yes," the other replied, "our scientists should be pleased with getting this fine, healthy specimen."

"What makes me feel badly is that we had to leave one of our own in its place."

"Of course you know it has always been our policy never to let the natives of any planet know we have visited them. That's why we had to wait for one of our women on the mother ship to give birth so we would have a newborn to put in place of the one we took."

"But that child of ours back there, won't he be different from the natives when he grows up? After all, he has thousands of generations of our advanced civilization behind him."

"Yes, I suppose he will be different. It would be interesting to come back when he is grown to see how he has developed in this primitive life."

As they reached their ship and started to climb up, the leader turned to his companion. "What was the name of that village? It was listed by our Watchers."

The other replied. "It is called Bethlehem."

Doing and undoing.

Proof

by F. M. Busby

"So that's your time machine," said Jackson. "Shades of H. G. Wells." The Time Chamber, with its loose-hanging power cables and confused-looking control panel, didn't look much like Mr. Wells' crystal bicycle.

"Oh, not mine, not mine at all," Dr. Gerard said. "Durrell in England provided the math; Bell Labs' computer study translated it into hardware. My part is to plan and conduct the testing program; nothing more." He smiled. "I wouldn't want to see you spoil your record for accurate reporting."

Jackson's pudgy frame shook with half-suppressed laughter. "According to my boss," he said, grinning up at Gerard's lean face, "the last time I got anything right was my birth certificate. But thanks, anyway. Now, can you give me—hey, wait a minute!" Jackson stiffened, looking at the corner of the room behind the Time Chamber, where the gray wall expanded in an unusual convex arc, a quarter-circle. He *knew* this room. After twenty years he still recognized it. It had been blue, before.

"Is something the matter, Mr. Jackson?"

"Yeh. Isn't this building—this room—where Senator Burton was assassinated? I was just a kid, but . . ." The room had been shown on TV over and over, with various dignitaries giving the official version of the tragedy. Public doubt—there had been too many killings, each too well explained—had abruptly reversed the expected outcome of that year's presidential election. Vividly, Jackson remembered the shock. "Well?" he said.

"Why, yes; it happened here. I'd forgotten; it's been

so long. Afterward the building was used for storage for several years; then it was remodeled and the Department got it for lab space. I had really forgotten.''

Jackson shook his head. ''No matter; it just jarred me for a minute.'' He scowled; this was no time to discuss his twenty-year obsession with the mystery. ''Let's get on with it, doctor. Can you give me a quick rundown on what this machine does and how it does it? Layman's language? So I can boil it down to five hundred words for my lip-moving readers.''

Gerard tipped his head back, hunched his shoulders. Jackson recognized the movement, could almost hear the tensions popping loose in the doctor's neck. Pushing himself too hard, he thought.

''Layman's language, eh? Let's see, now. Start with Durrell's formulation: the past is a solid compressed sphere with the Big Bang at its center and the present moment as its surface. All right so far?''

''Got it.'' Jackson scribbled pothooks in his notebook. ''You just cut us to four hundred words, though. I'll need room for a cartoon.'' He nodded a go-ahead to the taller man.

''Luckily, Durrell's hypothetical sphere is not impenetrable. Near the surface, at least. In theory this device— machine is hardly the proper term—will force an opening into it, so that we may insert test objects.''

''Into the past? How about the future?''

''Into the past, yes. By definition, the future is non-existent.''

''Hmmm. Doctor, how can the past have room for anything that wasn't there to begin with? You say it's solid, and that fits—we haven't been living in a world with holes in it, that I ever noticed. But two things can't be in the same place at the same time. How do you explain that?''

Gerard paused. He walked across the room, Jackson following, to the Time Chamber at the far side. Under the control console, against the convex arc of wall that had triggered Jackson's memory, lay a hammer. Gerard picked it up, held it out for Jackson to see.

''One of the workmen must have left this here,'' he said. ''The installation is complete and operable but the men still have some tidying-up to do.'' He gestured toward the loose cables. "As to inserting something into the past: I want you to look closely at the head of this hammer, where the end of the handle is exposed."

Jackson looked. "What am I supposed to see?"

"The wedges; see them? They are driven into the handle to expand it, so that it can't slip out." Jackson's brows climbed his forehead.

"The point is that the wedges don't occupy the same space as the wood. They displace the wood fibers, compress them, slip between them. To make a very rough analogy, Durrell's theory indicates that this device"—he nodded toward it—"will insert test subjects into the past in much the same fashion, except that the insertion will not be perceptible from any past viewpoint."

Jackson snorted. "I'm afraid that doesn't sound very credible to me, doctor."

"I suppose not." Gerard smiled apologetically. "Perhaps the analogy was a mistake; all analogies fail if carried past their limits. The concepts can be stated accurately only in mathematical terms, and Durrell's math appears to be quite sound. Of course the proof of the pudding . . . Well, we'll test the effects thoroughly, one step at a time."

"Right. And what are those steps? That's the kind of thing the readers want."

"In brief, I shall start with inanimate objects such as this hammer, that paperweight, whatever else might be handy. Measuring their properties before and after insertion into and withdrawal from the past. Next, instrument packages, which can tell us a great deal more. Then living subjects, the traditional mice and guinea pigs. And finally, if indicated, the ultimate test."

"A human being," said Jackson in a flat voice. "You have a volunteer?"

"Oh yes, of course. Myself, actually. Who else could I risk? But the risk will be small. Preliminary experiments will tell the tale, and I have considerable faith in Durrell's hypotheses."

"I'm sure, doctor." Jackson needed something more. "Now how about a quick outline of your operating procedure? I mean, turn Knob A to Line B and push Button C? The public likes to think it knows how things work."

"Yes, I suppose so." Gerard gestured toward the control panel. "This looks complicated, all those knobs and switches. It's the prototype model, and believe me it *was* complicated at first. But you can forget about all the controls except the four that have been marked with red paint; the rest have been put on a computerized feedback circuit.

"The red handle on the left overrides the computer; I don't expect that we'll ever have to use it. The red knob under the 0-to-100,000 dial sets the number of years of penetration into the past; I'm told the calibration is accurate in theory but naturally I'll check it thoroughly. The 'Depart-Return' switch is self-explanatory, wouldn't you say? And to its right, the final red knob and its instrument dial are the timing control. A small bonus from the Labs."

"Yes?" Jackson was hearing more than he really needed to know, to make up his four hundred words. But he had to play along. "What's the bonus?"

"Automatic return of the test subject, after a pre-set period of exposure to the past environment. Much more efficient than having to sit, watch the clock and push the Return switch personally. Or when I take the plunge myself, which seems to be a reasonable probability, I can pre-set the timing with no need for anyone else to sit on watch and bring me back. A nice touch, isn't it?"

"Yes," said Jackson, "I'd think so. Now just one more thing—"

The picturephone, on a desk to one side, chimed. Doctor Gerard answered it, spoke softly, then shut it off. "Mr. Jackson, please excuse me for a few minutes. I'll be back as soon as possible."

Left alone, Jackson prowled the room restlessly. The device, the Time Chamber, violated his personal view of how things worked in this universe. But he had to accept what he had been told, didn't he?

Or did he? From what Gerard had told him, he could check it out for himself!

No, that was insane. The thing hadn't been tested. Try it with the hammer first. Was there time for that? Jackson's will divided against itself. Durrell was a big gun in theoretical physics, wasn't he? And Gerard swore by him.

Senator Burton: who had killed him, here in this room?

Jackson had gnawed that bone for twenty years. Slowly he turned to the Time Chamber and its controls.

The Chamber didn't look like much, an overgrown phone booth without the phone, dimly-lit in an off-violet like a failing sunlamp. The controls were more intimidating; push the button: Zap! You're extinct! Jackson shook his head, looked closer. How did it go, again? Under him, his legs were shaking. Funny; he hadn't noticed when the shaking had begun. He squared his shoulders, took a deep breath.

All right; he set the Years dial, hoping he had the mental arithmetic right for the date of Burton's killing. Timing? Five minutes should be enough for a first look; he had to be back here before Gerard.

Hell and damn! It wouldn't work; the Depart switch was out of reach from the booth. But surely Gerard must have thought of that hangup. Try everything. Ah! The timing dial pushed in, as well as turning. It latched; illuminated numbers began a 30-second countdown. Yes, that should do it.

Years about twenty, timing five minutes; push the switch and sit in the booth. Waiting

The world dropped out from under Jackson; before him was a senseless photomontage as twenty years of happenings in one room flashed past, each moment as distinct from the next as titles on a bookshelf.

He closed his eyes but couldn't close his mind; the overpowering input was still there. Unable to resist, he surrendered to it. At that instant it stopped, like crashing full-tilt into a solid wall. Jackson saw.

He saw one picture, one moment out of the history of that room. It was not at all what he had looked for. There was a girl, a typist, frozen in her expression of irritation or petulance, one hand scratching her leg just below her short skirt, the other resting on the keyboard of her typewriter. Her hair, bleached nearly white, was twisted into short corkscrews. Her mouth was painted a shape as improbable as its color. She looked uncomfortable. Recalling the fashions of the time, Jackson decided that she probably was.

To him, the five minutes frozen into the timing dial

seemed to be forever. When the picture began to shift, to return him, he felt a vast relief.

The moments began to unroll again. But not as a coming and going. He had gone to the past and stopped at one instant. He expected the same thing, the same bookshelf-title confusion, to happen in reverse. It didn't.

The moments came and stayed, all of them. He saw Time from a sidewise view, a spectator at the side of a race-course rather than a participant running along it. There was the bleached blonde at one end and himself pushing buttons and turning knobs at the other. If there had been any ends to it. There weren't.

He saw Burton killed, saw the killer clearly. It wasn't anyone he knew. He became tired of seeing it, seeing the police fumble and let the man escape back into his own irrelevant paranoia.

All in still pictures, fixed scene by fixed scene, an infinite number. All at the same time and yet also in sequence. And it wouldn't stop; it would never stop.

There was Doctor Gerard showing him a hammer, with wedges driven into the top of the handle. "The proof of the pudding . . ." The past isn't rigidly solid, Gerard was telling him. You can drive a wedge into it, displace it.

Yes, Jackson thought. *But have you ever tried to pull one out again?*

For this I make a living?

Dreamworld

by Isaac Asimov

At thirteen, Edward Keller had been a science fiction devotee for four years. He bubbled with galactic enthusiasm.

His Aunt Clara, who had brought him up by rule and rod in pious memory of her deceased sister, wavered between toleration and exasperation. It appalled her to watch him grow so immersed in fantasy.

"Face reality, Eddie," she would say, angrily.

He would nod, but go on, "And I dreamed Martians were chasing me, see? I had a special death ray, but the atomic power unit was pretty low and—"

Every other breakfast consisted of eggs, toast, milk, and some such dream.

Aunt Clara said, severely, "Now, Eddie, one of these nights you won't be able to wake up out of your dream. You'll be trapped! Then what?"

She lowered her angular face close to his and glared.

Eddie was strangely impressed by his aunt's warning. He lay in bed, staring into the darkness. He wouldn't like to be trapped in a dream. It was always nice to wake up before it was too late. Like the time the dinosaurs were after him—

Suddenly he was out of bed, out of the house, out on the lawn, and he knew it was another dream.

The thought was broken by a vague thunder and a shadow that blotted the sun. He looked upward in astonishment and he could make out the human face that touched the clouds.

It was his Aunt Clara! Monstrously tall, she bent toward him in admonition, mastlike forefinger upraised, voice too guttural to be made out.

Eddie turned and ran in panic. Another Aunt Clara monster loomed up before him, voice rumbling.

He turned and ran in panic. Another Aunt Clara monster loomed up before him, voice rumbling.

He turned again, stumbling, panting, heading outward, outward.

He reached the top of the hill and stopped in horror. Off in the distance a hundred towering Aunt Claras were marching by. As the column passed, each line of Aunt Claras turned their heads sharply toward him and the thunderous bass rumbling coalesced into words:

"Face reality, Eddie. Face reality, Eddie."

Eddie threw himself sobbing to the ground. Please

wake up, he begged himself. Don't be caught in this dream.

For unless he woke up, the worst science-fictional doom of all would have overtaken him. He would be trapped, *trapped,* in a world of giant aunts.

He laughs best—

The Reunion

by Paul J. Nahin

Dr. Richard C. Breed walked briskly across the campus parking lot to his car. He casually greeted two of his women students, and glowed inwardly at their open admiration of his carefully nurtured, sophisticated professorial image. Teaching the college service course in geology had its benefits.

He *did* cut quite a figure, dressed in fifty-five dollar wing-tips, immaculately tailored vested tweeds, and corduroy hat with a jaunty red feather stuck in the brim. The silk tie, silver cuff links, and five hundred dollar pocket watch with gold chain completed the picture. He puffed with pleasure on his two hundred dollar Danish briar pipe, leaving the fragrant, faintly vanilla flavor of "Captain Black" in his wake. The women loved it, and with his rugged red beard, he liked to imagine himself a scholarly Viking.

Richard Breed had it made. A scientific entrepreneur who regularly had his $100,000 a year NSF geological research grant renewed. He didn't do much original field work himself now, busy as he was recruiting new doctoral students to do it for him, and hustling foundation money to pay them. Not to mention the nice summer salary of two-ninths of his fat academic year pay. Oh, once in awhile he might chip rocks at a local site, but reading seismological charts in his office fitted his schedule better.

Yes sir, he had come a long way from the fat, pimply teenager with bad breath in the small Southern California high school of almost a quarter century ago. He frowned as he thought of those long ago schoolmates that he had once envied, and hated. Young, and arrogant with their supposed immortality, they had never let him belong. He had been the outcast, the one made to feel like something peculiar, almost repugnant. While the others had greeted each other loudly in the halls, gone to dances together, and generally gloried in the golden days of teenage youth, he had spent those same years as a lonely recluse in the library with his science and math books. Called 'four-eyes' and 'specs' until the words made him ill, he had finally started to come out of his shell late in his senior year, when he won a national math contest. But it was too late to make any real difference then.

Even now, as a forty-one-year-old late bloomer, who had certainly bloomed well, his physiological reaction to recalling those four years of pain was a blush of shame and embarrassment at the klutz he had been. And an almost overwhelming flood of hate at those who had made him so miserable.

"Ah, if only those bastards could see me now. The ones that didn't become mothers at eighteen, or criminals, are probably eight-to-five slaves or beer paunchy firemen. If only I could see *them* now, it would be so very, very different!" The thought ran sweetly through his mind, and he enjoyed the imagined pleasure of what he knew would be their envious reaction to the new, soon to be famous Richard Breed.

He reached his car and carefully placed his bulging briefcase on the back seat. Stuffed with lecture notes and color slides for next week's International Seismological Conference in Montreal, he planned to study them one more time over the weekend. He was absolutely sure of his calculations, but what he was about to reveal was such a shocker he knew the questions would come hard and fast. He had to be overpowering with his rebuttals.

After Montreal, election to the National Academy was certain. The Nobel Prize in Physics would surely soon after be his. With a change in Administration, he could even imagine the post of Presidential Science Advisor being offered. And maybe he'd take it, and maybe he wouldn't!

Once home, after checking the box for mail, he locked the conference papers in his desk to await a careful restudy later that evening. Tossing the handful of that day's letters on his desk, he went into the kitchen and mixed himself a Bloody Mary. As he sipped his drink while walking back to the study, he let his thoughts run on over the pandemonium he knew would result at the bomb soon to be set off in Montreal.

After years of painstaking data gathering and several extensions of Carson's dissertation ("I get the Nobel and all he gets is a PhD and an assistant professorship, but that's the name of the game!"), Breed had formulated a mathematical prediction theory for earthquakes. His test calculations over the past three years had all been on the mark in location, time, and intensity. But telling people you had privately predicted quakes that had already happened wouldn't cut any water. He had to put his butt on the line, in public, with a major prediction.

The new strain gauge data from Caltech's monitoring stations along the San Andreas fault had given him what he needed. On the morning of June 14 of next year, there was going to be an 8.3 shake with its epicenter forty miles south of Los Angeles. Breed chuckled to himself as he thought how close that was to the old high school. Mother Nature was going to do what he had wanted to, so many years ago.

What was really going to cause trouble wasn't just that damn near all of Orange County was going to get flattened. If they didn't listen to him, it was also going to explode! Right in the middle of the target area, next to the sleepy little town of his youth, was a vast underground storage facility of liquified natural gas. Used as a depository by several of the oil giants, the town was literally floating on a lake of LNG. The entire county would have to be evacuated, and the tanks drained. The cost would be horrendous. Breed figured they'd evacuate people, all right, but would take a chance on leaving the tanks full. What a show that would be! Weather satellite imagery of the detonations would be the lead story on the evening news, world-wide.

He began to thumb through the mail on the desk as he finished his drink. All the usual crap was there—electric bill, a reminder to stop in at the bank and have his credit card photo updated, and his subscription copy of *Time*, only three days after it had already hit the stands. Then his eyes caught a familiar address on a stapled flyer and he held his breath as he unfolded it.

MEMBERS OF THE CLASS OF 1958

Thanks for your great response to our previous announcement of the plans for our TWENTY-FIFTY REUNION next year! Can you believe it's been almost a quarter-century since we last walked the halls of high school together? We can't either! But we still haven't heard from everyone! Out of 93 announcements, we got 82 replies. If you are one of the missing eleven listed below, or know how to reach someone on the list, please let us know. The reunion dinner and dance will be the evening of June 13, and the next morning, too! The place, of course, will be the high school gym. Singles are $12.50, couples $20.00, for dinner, drinks and dancing.

> *Looking forward to seeing you,*
> CLASS OF '58 REUNION COMMITTEE
> *David Whiply*
> *Tim White*
> *Mary (Mason) White*

Breed was stunned for a moment, as he saw his name among those of the missing eleven. Christ, he *would* be able to put those SOBs in their place! But what was all this business about a prior announcement? He hadn't seen it or heard anything.

Ah!, now he knew what must have happened. For two months earlier in the year he had been abroad. He had instructed his secretary to forward only the obviously important stuff, and to hold everything else. The first announcement must have gotten lost in the pile of local junk mail and campus event notices.

Breed's eyes wandered over the sheet again, and stopped at the names of the reunion committee. Wouldn't you know it—the three biggest creeps in a class of creeps. Memories came back in a wave of pain.

It was a cold, windy day, and the third period gym class had just suited up. The boys were on one side of the football field, and the girls on the other, all lined up for roll-call. As usual, fatso Dick Breed felt awkward and out of place in gym shorts (number 64) and T-shirt. A flaming red-head, he didn't tan, and his skin was pasty white. The green shorts looked like a bacteria mold growing on his bread dough body. He had been late to class, and as he stripped and dressed hurriedly while thinking about next period's trig exam, Breed had failed to notice his shorts were on backwards.

But that primitive Neanderthal, Dave Whiply, noticed. "Hey, Four-Eyes! Does that 64 across your butt stand for its weight or its size?" The girls heard it, too, and even the gym teachers grinned. The entire class laughed, and Breed could have died with shame. The rest of the period passed in a horrible, slow crawl, all the while that damn number burned itself into his backside.

The Senior Prom was all that everyone had been talking about the last three weeks. Dick Breed had been walking around with butterflies in his stomach for days, especially in English IV, where he sat behind Mary Mason. Time and again, he had almost worked up enough courage to ask her to go with him, and then something had happened to ruin the moment. But today he promised himself he would ask. Time was running out. Mary came into the classroom with a group of giggling friends, and Breed braced himself. As she sat down in front of him, and before she could start talking to anyone else, he leaned forward and spoke in a not-quite-a-whisper voice. "Uh, Mary, I was, uh, sort of wondering, that is if you don't have anything else planned, if you'd like to go to the Prom dance? With me, I mean!"

For a terrible, sick moment, Breed thought she was going to just ignore him. Later, he wished she had. Mary turned slowly in her chair until she almost, but not quite, faced Breed.

"Dick Breed, you little frog! How dare you ask me that, right here in front of my friends!" Mary was hissing the words out in a tight, hushed voice. Her face was distorted with rage, and Breed was actually scared. The students around them began to notice the exchange, and Breed tried to shrink through the seat of his chair. "I'm going to the Prom with Tim White, and if he found out about this he'd take care of you, but good! So you just keep away from me!''

That night, for the first time since he was a little boy, Breed cried himself to sleep.

Breed was sitting alone in a corner of the cafeteria, eating that day's cruddy, mass-produced meal of greasy taco, reburned beans, salad turned brown at the edges, and warm lemonade. He scarfed it up with the indiscriminating appetite of the teenage overeater.

He could hear all the other kids at the nearby tables yelling in good-natured cheer. Nobody talked to Breed. Suddenly he heard his name called. ''Hey Dick—Dick, over here!'' Breed looked up from his tray in surprise, and saw Tim White waving an arm at him. Big, tall, handsome Tim White, who had taken Mary to the Prom.

''Hey Dick, Jack Preston tells me you're pretty good with your hands in machine shop. Is that true?''

Breed couldn't believe his ears. Maybe this was the key to getting to be friends! He'd helped Preston chuck a piece of tubing in a lath last week in second period shop, and the word must be getting around that fatso Breed wasn't a total creep.

''Uh, yes, I guess I'm okay working with tools. You know I'm not great or anything like that, but I do all right. I suppose.'' He saw a little smile on Tim's mouth, and that worried Breed. Was this just another damn trick?

''Well, I'll tell you, Dick, I was wondering if you wanted to come with us on a deep-sea fishing trip next weekend. My dad's renting a boat at Newport and we sure could use a good man with his hands, like you.'' White spread his arms wide to indicate the group of grinning boys and girls sitting at his table as the fishing party. Breed's suspicions evaporated. Tim *was* just being friendly!

''Gosh, that sounds like fun, Tim. Is there anything special I could do to help out on the trip?''

''You bet, Dick! A guy like you, really good with his hands—well, while we got the lines ready with hooks, you'd be our—Master Baiter!'' White collapsed in hysterical laughter, and his gaggle of friends hooted at Breed who, burning with shame, ran from the room.

* * *

Professor Richard C. Breed, PhD, sat motionless for a long time, his right hand wrapped around the Bloody Mary in a sweaty grip. Being a sturdy tumbler made to hold a stiff triple shot of whisky was all that kept it from snapping.

Finally, he picked up the telephone and dialed. He could hear the long distance switch gear rattle on the circuits like electronic crickets. Then the sharp, clear ringing of a telephone a thousand miles away.

"Hi, Pete, this is Dick Breed. Yeah, I'm fine, but look, I've got some late-breaking plans. I'm not going to be able to make it to Montreal. I've just turned up some problems in my data—no, no problems in the theory. Just some technical details in my computer runs, but I'd like to have it just right before I present it publicly. As conference chairman, I hope you can fill in my scheduled slot and give my regrets to the others. Okay?

"Hey, great, Pete I appreciate it. I'll try to get my stuff cleaned up for the go around in England next year. Yeah, I'd like to spend the Christmas holidays in London, and that'll be a good reason. Thanks for covering for me, Pete. My best to Betty. So long."

Breed hung the receiver up and stared at the reunion notice, and then crumpled it in his hand and flung it into the trash bucket. "Eat, drink, and be merry, you bastards. I'll be watching for you on the evening news."

"On the whole, I'd rather be in Philadelphia."
—W.C. Fields' tombstone

The Futile Flight of John Arthur Benn

by Richard Wilson

By putting himself into reverse, the doom-intended man left the twentieth century far ahead. Nineteen fifty-six

was a good year to get out of. John Arthur Benn watched
the roaring twenties go by, and the gay nineties, backwards, and wondered how it would be to pilot a riverboat
on the Mississippi, or to fight under John Paul Jones.

Before he was really aware of it, he was for a speeding
second a contemporary of another John—Smith—and
thought about the life of the Redman before the colonists
began changing things around. By that time the scenery
had begun to get monotonous—just shrinking trees—and
John Arthur Benn swung over into lateral. Ah, England.

There went another namesake—Ben Jonson—and in a
very little while he considered slowing down to meet still
another. But King Arthur flashed past and into a womb
in West Wales just as John was convulsed by a sneeze (it
was quite drafty and he should have dressed more
warmly), and as he stuffed his handkerchief back in his
pocket he caught just a tantalizing glimpse of an interesting Druid ceremony.

John Arthur Benn blacked out somewhere in the limbo
of the pre-Christian era, as he'd been warned he might,
and when he came to he found himself lying in a rather
uncomfortable heap with his head in a mushroom patch.
The mushrooms and the trees around him weren't shrinking any more, so John knew he'd stopped—or at least was
going very slowly. After a while he decided he wasn't
going at all, and got to his feet.

It seemed very pleasant here, in the woods, so he found
a fallen tree to sit on and took a wrapped sandwich and
a small vacuum bottle of coffee out of his pocket. When
he'd finished his meal he walked to a stream nearby,
rinsed the bottle, tossed the waxed paper onto the water
to be carried away and pocketed the vacuum bottle.

Now, he thought, what? This was scarcely dinosaur
country. At this point a wild boar chased him up a tree.
To be killed by a boar would be ignominious, after all
this, although the animal was well enough tusked to have
done the job, and so John Arthur Benn climbed to a high
branch, where the boar's persistence forced him to spend
the night. He slept, somehow, and, with the closing of
his conscious mind—the one that wanted to meet a dinosaur in fatal combat—the conventional subconscious,
which also sought suicide, but in a more familiar way,
shifted him out of reverse.

When he awoke, he was back in 1956, in Philadelphia. Irrevocably, John Arthur Benn knew.

He went home and hanged himself in a closet.

The human form divine.

Servants of the Lord

by James Stevens

"The most perverted race in the universe once lived in this solar system," the priest said.

The priest was small and shaped like a plantain, albeit a plantain with two arms, legs, and pigtails, and he wore a large apron of office embossed with God's logo: a slash of flame against a black field. He spoke in the high-pitched warble typical of natives of dwarf star systems, and was assigned temporarily to religious tour duty.

"They were destroyed by Conclave warboats armed with hellbombs almost a century ago. And just in the nick of time, I might add. They had already developed rudimentary space travel and had visited their satellite and the nearer planets. O'Ha knows what might have happened if they had swarmed into Civilized Space spreading their filthy ways before we discovered them and had the chance to stop them."

A chimpoid acolyte from the Alderbaranian System jerked both hands free from the pockets of his robe and waved them vigorously for attention.

"Yes?" said Zul, the plantain-shaped priest.

"Who were these people?"

"They called themselves 'earthmen,' " Zul said, "though they were, in fact, not made of earth at all."

"I've never heard of 'earthmen,' " said a Betelgeusian bishop in informal vestments. He resembled a small ostrich stuffed inside a large envelope.

"The whole matter was kept very under-the-cassock by the Council of Prelates back then," Zul said. "The members of the Council feared that news of the discovery of these bestial 'earthmen' might well shock the Conclave peoples so harshly as to cause outbreaks of loss of faith or mass suicides of atonement. The fact is, it is only recently that this system has been opened to theological tours and the whole blasphemous story made available to the faithful."

"How were these 'earthmen' discovered and stopped?" said a spiny urchinoid seminarian from the water world of Rill. He was modestly wrapped in cotton wool and felt he had observed his vow of silence long enough.

Zul's limegreen skin split along one seam in righteous grin. "Some call it chance—sheer luck—but to me it is yet one more manifestation of the universal justice of O'Ha, for in attempting to spread their vileness, the 'earthmen' succeeded only in sowing the seed of their own destruction. Don't tell *me* there is no God!"

"Brother!" cried a wraithlike Centaurian monk floating mistily within streamers of translucent fabric. "There is indeed a God and we are His humble servants! I pray you, tell us more about our Lord O'Ha's wondrous ways."

"These godless 'earthmen' sent a plaque into deep space which one of our scoutboats recovered. Our holy scientists and blessed mathematicians labored over it until they had at long last deciphered the meaning of the symbols etched into the plaque. The information included the usual data: the value of pi, sketches of the 'earthmen' themselves, and a map of their solar system indicating the location of their home planet."

"This is catechism-level stuff, priest," said a toad theologian from Tor IV dressed severely in maroon pantaloons. "Every intelligent race launches a plaque bearing such information in its earliest stages of space travel, prompted by the same motivation as the child who proclaims, 'Look at me, I can hop!' "

"Ah," said Zul in an outraged warble, "but none of our races was so wicked, so corrupt, so utterly *evil* as to send sketches of ourselves . . . *naked!*"

"Naked!" shrieked the chimpoid.

"Naked!" screamed the ostrich.

"Naked!" sputtered the urchinoid.

"Naked!" whistled the wraith.

"Naked!" croaked the toad.

"Naked," Zul said, pigtail stiff with religious wrath. "So now you understand why the Lord God O'Ha ordained the destruction of these heathen 'earthmen.' A race so depraved as to send pornography to the stars *had* to be exterminated."

Full of wise saws and modern instances.

Mattie Harris, Galactic Spy

by Rachel Cosgrove Payes

"But Howie," Matilda Harris objected, "I'm just not the type."

She smirked smugly. "Female spies are either dark and slinky, or plain Janes strictly from Dullsville. Now, do I fit either category?" She paraded her statuesque chorus girl charms in front of Howie Pringle, head of Galactic Central's Security Police. "I'm just a little old secretary, now out of employment."

She could see that Howie was viewing her with that natural, built-in leer that she inspired in all red-blooded human males—and plenty of male aliens, too. Matilda wasn't stupid where men were concerned, even though she was queen of the dumb blonde dames. Of course her hair color was bottled in blonde, and her inch-long eyelashes were phony; but there wasn't anything false about her profile numbers which read an incredible 42-22-36. And wasn't it lucky that she looked so good in black? Her employer and patron, Ambassador Richards, Earth Envoy to the Galactic Central, had died recently, putting Matilda in mourning. The newest style of black skinsies, complete with a floor length diaphanous black robe, was sheer (used advisedly) murder on Matilda.

"Matilda," Howie said when he'd recovered his voice, "That's what would make you a natural at spying. Who would ever dream that you'd conceal anything? And as the late Ambassador's secretary, you're familiar with many of the Galactic diplomats."

"You can say that again," she muttered.

Although Matilda's late employer, the Ambassador, had left her fabulously wealthy via his will, she wanted to know her salary, being just a poor little working girl at heart. When Howie mentioned a figure, she frowned. "As my late, wealthy employer, Ambassador Richards, always said, 'A penny a day isn't much for your thoughts.'"

"Matilda," Howie begged, "do it for the Galactic Federation."

When Howie put it that way, what could Matilda say?

"Okay, so call me Mattie Harris, galactic spy."

"With the emphasis on the *gal*," he drooled.

Then, getting down to business, Howie explained her first assignment. "An immensely important extraterrestrial diplomat and his consort are attending a Terran Embassy reception tonight. Their existences have been threatened. We have two suspects: a young, hot-blooded folksinger from Betelgeuse IV, one of the canary-beings we call Birds: and an unsavory attaché from an unfriendly planet in the Caroline Series, an arthropod called Ontha Lefnik."

"And my job?"

"To use your considerable charms to find out which of these creatures is the potential assassin."

"But how will I recognize them in all that mob of aliens? All right, so one is a Bird—but the place is flying with them. And show me any gathering where there aren't a bunch of Crabs."

"Have no fear, Matilda, you will not be working alone. My men will be giving you constant attention." Again he leered. "When you are introduced to the suspects, one of our agents will be on hand. He'll say something innocent sounding, using some common, unobtrusive word beginning with *X,* so that you'll be alerted."

* * *

The Embassy reception was nearly over when Matilda arrived that night. "As my late, wealthy employer, Ambassador Richards, always said, 'Better late and never wait,' " she chirped to her hostess, wife of the Terran Ambassador.

Immediately human and non-human males swarmed about Matilda, a sea of blurred faces, as she'd forgotten to wear her contact lenses, and her big-eyed baby stare was really only myopia.

One man murmured into her ear, "You're just what I want for Christmas."

Turning eagerly to him, Matilda said, "Oh, you must be my contact."

"Contact's what I had in mind," he admitted; but just then another man took her arm firmly and led her away.

"Let's talk about Xerxes," he suggested.

"Who's he? I thought the suspects were a Bird and a Crab name Lefnik."

"Shh. I'm your contact from Galactic Central Security. That's why I mentioned Xerxes. It starts with an X."

"It does?" Matilda was terrible confused. "I thought it started with a Z. And who was that other man? Some sort of enemy spy trying to trick me, I'll bet."

"What other man?" her contact asked anxiously.

"The one who used the word starting with X."

"What word?"

"Xmas."

"Forget him. Come on, I'll introduce you to the suspects."

The Bird was almost as tall as she, with a long, serpentine neck and four multifaceted eyes. Its feathers were metallic. The Bird carried an odd, non-Terran musical stringed instrument, similar to a banjo in shape. This Matilda eyed suspiciously. Could it be the proverbial blunt instrument? She was strong on proverbs, thanks to her late, wealthy employer, Ambassador Richards, who'd made a private fortune publishing Intergalactic Almanacs.

Lefnik was a small, crustaceous arthropod, particularly villainous looking. No wealth of velvet robe could make him attractive to Matilda, even though he did wave his feelers suggestively in her direction.

Matilda was worried. One of these creatures planned

to assassinate the Ambassador from Rogg, and his lady. These aliens were one of the odder life forms found in the Galaxy, being a type of living stone which reproduced by a method of crystallization not yet clearly defined by Terran scientists. Most Terrans referred to the Rogg aliens as Stones.

Matilda listened carefully while the Bird twanged his "banjo" with the feathers of one wing and sang an odd, minor strain which went on interminably. Then she slunk about after Lefnik, watching from behind a tall column which was too straight to hide her profile while Lefnik stuffed his storage-claws and craw with cavier and chocolate ice cream at the buffet.

Then, when Lefnik seized a large, ornate silver nutcracker and slipped it under his robe, Matilda went into action.

"Seize that Crab!" she cried. "He means to assassinate the Stones."

Later, as Howie Pringle escorted a triumphant Matilda home, he said, "Lucky for us that you saw Lefnik conceal that nutcracker under his robe."

"What nutcracker? Without my contact lenses, everything's a blur."

"If you didn't see the nutcracker, how did you know that Lefnik was our man—uh—our Crab and meant to crush the Stones to death?"

"Howie, it was easy. I just remembered what my brilliant, late and wealthy employer, Ambassador Richards, always said, and I knew that the Bird couldn't possibly be the assassin."

"And what did the late Ambassador say which gave you your clue, Matilda?"

"You can't kill two Stones with one Bird."

It could have been worse.

Changeover

by Juleen Brantingham

"With consumer acceptance of credit cards and the Universal Product Code (UPC) and the development of the home videophone/computer console, video shopping was at last practical. This resulted in lowered overhead for businesses and relief for the overburdened postal and traffic systems.

"Unfortunately, theft of credit cards became an almost uncontrollable crime. Even reinstatement of the death penalty for the ringleaders of these MasterCharge criminals provided no relief. While more and more businesses converted entirely to electronic shopping and billing systems, more and more consumers balked at using them. Consumer/supplier relationships were at an all-time low.

"Universal Consumer Code (UCC) was seen as a solution to the theft problem. But this relatively minor change in payment procedures met unexpected resistance."—*Popular Economics* (May 1997)

"Good morning, sir. This is West Side Maternity and Pediatric calling to inform you that two patients, a Ms. Melanie Vickers and Master Sean Robert Vickers, Jr., have been dispatched to your address on the eight o'clock ambu-bus. ETA is 8:07."

Coughing and incomprehensible mumbles, video blanked. "—before I had my coffee—" More mumbles.

"Pardon me, sir. What was that?"

"Bad night," explained a slightly less fuzzy voice. "Now what did you say you were calling about?"

"Your wife and son, sir. They're on their way home. Now about the bill—"

"Jeez. Eight o'clock in the morning. Well, okay. Put it on the screen and let me see the bad news. God—worse than I thought. What's this item—'Megavitamin Therapy (4-SMTW—Ref: AM)'? Vitamins? Good Lord, why couldn't we just buy a bottle of pills? That price is ridiculous!"

"Sir, the vitamin therapy was requested by your wife. It's a little late to argue."

"It always is."

"Now, if you require a print-out of the charges for your records, just press the Request button on your console."

"Damn right I want a print-out—"

"If you have no further questions, please place your identification code on the scanner plate of your console."

Incomprehensible mumble. "—my credit card here somewhere."

"Sir!"

"What?"

"Sir, did I hear you say something about a credit card? I'm sorry, sir, but West Side Maternity and Pediatric has switched over to the new UCC System. You were informed of this when you brought your wife in for delivery. We are no longer equipped to handle credit cards."

"What do you mean you're no longer equipped? I've got the scanner plate right here in front of me. I put my card face down on the plate, your computer reads it, feeds the information into the billing system, and my bank transfers the funds. Just like always."

Righteousness carries well over audio equipment. "Sir, you were *informed* of the change. It's for your own protection. After all, the carrier of Sean Robert Vickers, Sr.'s credit card might not *be* Sean Robert Vickers, Sr. We have no way of knowing."

"Then he wouldn't have any interest in bailing Sean Junior and his mother out of your hospital."

"An explanation of the System has been widely publicized," the voice continued, without pause. "Our computer has been programmed to read a series of magnetic dots impregnated in the consumer's skin. That is the UCC System, a vast improvement over the old-fashioned credit card."

"Yeah? Well, what if I tell you *I* am not equipped for this UC—whatever? Huh? What if I told you I don't have any of those little dots?"

"That would be a lie, sir," the voice said primly. "When the hospital decided to switch over to UCC we offered to apply the identification code to all our clients as a free service. I have it right here on my records that you took advantage of this service."

"Yeah, but nobody told me they were going to put the dots *there*. That's a helluva place to put them."

"Sir, I fail to understand why you are becoming so upset. There was no insult intended, no indignity. Do you realize how much research went into planning the UCC System? They didn't just choose that location at *random*, you know. Accidents can happen. You might lose an arm or leg. But everyone has one of *those*. Now, will you please place your identification code on the scanner plate? I *do* have other clients to call this morning."

Sean Robert Vickers, Sr., gave in to progress ungracefully. Cursing, he leaned over the console and placed his forehead against the scanner plate as he bowed to the inevitable.

Be it ever so humble—

Hometown

by Richard Wilson

Kit stood entranced in front of the old house. "Oh, Thad," she said to her husband, "it's just like the one I was born in. The porch, the dormer windows—everything."

Thad, who had known Kit practically all her life, was aware that her old home was not at all like this one. But he didn't say that to her.

"Sure, Kit," he said. "Very much so. Now let's start

back.'' Then, without thinking, he said something he could have kicked himself for: ''It's getting dark.''

It *was* getting dark, of course, but only in here. And that would make it harder to get her to leave.

''Oh, it *is!*'' she said. ''Isn't it wonderful? The street lights are going on. How softly they glow. And look—there's a light on in *my* house, too.''

''Come on, now,'' Thad said irritably. ''My feet hurt.''

''I'm sorry, darling. We have been tramping all over town, haven't we? We'll just sit in the park awhile and rest. I do love the dusk so.''

They sat down on the wooden bench. He leaned back resignedly. She was perched on the front slat, turning her head this way and that, exclaiming over a tree or a bush, or over the red brick firehouse across the street, or the steeple on the church at the end of town.

Then she saw the chalk marks on the path.

''Oh, look!'' she said delightedly. ''Potsy. One-two-three-four-five. What fun that used to be! . . . I wonder where the children are?''

''Now, Kit,'' her husband said, ''you know there aren't any children.''

She turned to glare at him in a quick change of mood. ''Why do you always have to spoil everything? Isn't it enough to know it without being reminded of it? Can't I have a little fantasy if I want to?''

''It's just that I don't want you to have another—I don't want you to be ill, that's all.''

''Go ahead and say it!'' she cried. ''Another nervous breakdown. You're afraid I'll go crazy is what you mean. You're sorry you ever picked such a neurotic woman, aren't you?''

That tried to soothe her. ''You're not neurotic, Kit. You're just homesick. It happens to everyone here, me included. I just don't think you should let yourself be carried away by all this—''

She jumped to her feet. ''Carried away! I haven't *be-gun* to be carried away.'' She took something out of her bag and tossed it into the first potsy square. ''I'll show you some carrying away.'' She skipped through the boxes. He saw what she had thrown down. An expensive compact he had given her.

Another couple walked along the path toward them. They smiled indulgently at the woman playing a child's game. Thad looked away in embarrassment. He waited till the couple had passed, then got up and grabbed his wife's arm.

"Kit!" he said roughly. "I'm not going to let you act this way." He shook her. "Snap out of it. We're going now."

She shook his hand off. "You go," she said. "Go on back to that cold, sterile world, you big brave pioneer. I'm staying."

"You can't. Be reasonable, Kit."

"There's a hotel down by the church. I saw it. I'll stay there until my time is up. How long is it—six more months? Maybe they have special monthly rates." She started to walk away.

"Kit, it's not real. You know that. The hotel is just a false front, like the movie house and the supermarket and everything else in here."

"Don't say that!" She stopped and turned to him. Her eyes got unnaturally large. "Don't take it away from me again! Not when I've just found it. Don't take it away! Don't!"

She sobbed, then laughed wildly, then sobbed again and went limp. He caught her and lowered her gently to the grass—the artificial grass under the artificial tree, under fake stars in a fake sky.

Someone had seen and an ambulance came clanging, its headlights two reddish gleams. He had to admire the people who ran the place—it was an oldfashioned Earth-style ambulance, authentic right down to the license plate.

Two men jumped out with a stretcher and lifted Kit into it. "Anything serious, Mac?" one of them asked.

"No," Thad said. "Just three and a half years of being a Moon colonist, that's all. Seeing all this was too much for her." He climbed into the back with the stretcher.

As the gates swung open the perpetual light of the Moon caverns banished the artificial dusk. As his wife was transferred to a conventional ambulance, Thad looked back at the sign over the gate:

HOMETOWN, EARTH
Admission $5

And there are 200,000 convictions each day.

The Penalty

by Henry Slesar

On the last day of the trial, the heavenly courtroom was crowded with angelic spectators, seated on the alabaster steps which ringed the arena of justice. It was not morbid curiosity which drew them there; the eyes that looked upon the defendant were liquid with sympathy for his ordeal, if slightly gazed by boredom. There was little unique in the case of Angel John Matthew Kress; his crimes (Scorn, Vanity, and unwarranted Criticism) were common enough, even in Heaven. But, this being the last day, they flocked to witness the drama of the jury's verdict, and to hear the inevitable sentence pronounced by St. David, District Judge of the Eighth Heavenly District.

The cosmos cooperated to heighten the melodramatic mood of the day. The cottony clouds overhead assumed a gray and slightly soiled appearance as the trial's participants awaited the jury's decision. The defendant, seated despondently before the judge's dais, seemed resigned to what must come next, and there was a forlorn, tattered look to his wings.

The bailiff, a broadshouldered Angel with a stern voice, commanded them to silence and announced the arrival of the judge. There was a faint whir of feathers in the courtroom, and St. David entered.

St. David, in his long white robe, was business-like as he took his place behind the marble bench. Whatever sad emotion he felt in the moment was concealed behind an implacable expression. He turned to the jury foreman, and said:

"Have you reached a verdict?"

"We have, your Honor."

"Please announce it to the court."

"We find the defendant guilty as charged."

A sigh, no louder than the breeze, drifted across the arena. The defendant, his fate fixed by a law both ancient and immutable, remained motionless.

"The defendant will rise," St. David said, "and approach the bench."

Slowly, the prisoner lifted himself from the chair, his wings now a hindrance to movement. He went dreamlike towards the judge's dais, and stood with head bowed before him.

"John Matthew Kress," St. David said sonorously, "you have been found guilty of the crimes of Scorn, Vanity, and unwarranted Criticism, crimes ill-befitting an Angel of your rank and service. You have sinned against your fellows without thought to the harm you would create, or the punishment which would surely follow. You have broken sacred commandments we hold dear. You have allowed unsaintly pride to take possession of you, pride which eats away the heart of Love. You have placed yourself above the ancient laws of Heaven, and you must pay for your sin."

St. David paused, and his eyes became grave.

"I have no other course but to pass judgment upon you according to our honorable tradition, harsh as that judgment may seem. Angel John Matthew Kress, I hereby sentence you to Life."

In the Cleveland General Hospital, a baby was born. It was a boy, to be christened John Matthew Kress. And like all newborn infants, it cried and cried, as if it were very angry.

What a pity to waste youth upon the young.

The Pill

by Maggie Nadler

The woman who sat alone on the veranda staring out at the mountains was a beauty. Early morning sunlight glinted on the golden hair that fell loose past her shoulders, and played over the cameo face with its dark eyes and perfect features. Her deep tan was set off against a white summer dress which also brought out the youthful suppleness of her figure. She sat motionless for a long time, gazing far off.

A door opened and a second woman appeared on the porch, a tumbler in her hand. The newcomer was perhaps fifty-five, and dumpy, with lank gray hair and a puffy face that even in her prime could scarcely have been attractive. She approached the seated woman and touched her gently on the shoulder. "It's time for your pill, dear," she said. The other made no response. "Your medicine," she said, more loudly, and when there was still no reply she moved around to face the front of the chair. This time the seated woman raised blank, remote eyes to her. "That's right, darling. Let me help you. Now open your mouth—that's a good girl"—and as the mouth popped obediently open she poured the contents of the glass down the blonde woman's throat. There was a gasping, choking sound as perhaps half the liquid came back up, dribbling out around the even teeth. The dumpy woman forced her own mouth into a smile. "That's just fine. Now I'll go back inside and do a few little things and then we'll go for a nice ride. How will that be?" *I can't take any more,* she screamed inwardly, *I just can't take it. It's a good thing it's all arranged and she's going away today, because I just can't take any more.*

But the blonde hadn't heard her and was already back in her old position, staring unseeingly straight ahead into the distance.

A short time later the dumpy woman emerged from the house once more. In each hand she carried a small suitcase. These she loaded into the trunk of a battered green sedan. Then she returned to the porch for her companion. She helped her to her feet and, moving slowly, guided her carefully down the steps along the walkway and assisted her into the car. She herself took the driver's seat, and only minutes later they were on the main highway. It was a long, silent, tedious drive across barren desert land, the woman at the wheel tense and preoccupied, the other lolling vacantly beside her. At last, after several interminable hours, the rocky landscape gave way to renewed greenery and presently they were driving up a winding tree-lined road which ended abruptly at a pair of great iron gates bearing the legend: GREEN MANSIONS. The gates were open and they drove on through until they came to a sprawling and ancient but apparently well cared-for mansion with a small parking area nearby. They eased into a space near the entrance. The dumpy woman unloaded the suitcases and assisted her companion out of the car and up the two low steps to the slightly open door. Timidly she pushed it farther open and they stepped together, the blonde leaning on her for support, into a large immaculate reception room. The receptionist, a handsome, somewhat hard-faced woman in a smartly tailored suit, looked up and stared. For a moment she seemed startled. Then, "Yes?" she asked sharply.

"I—I'm Margaret Duggins and this is Mrs. Nelson, the patient I called you about last Wednesday. I believe you were expecting us . . ." Her voice trailed off.

"Oh, yes . . . Duggins . . . that's right. You're expected," the receptionist said in a milder tone. "Dottie!" she called toward the open door beyond her desk. A thin, dark-haired girl of about twenty, clad in a nurse's uniform, immediately appeared. She glanced in some surprise at the newcomers.

"Yes, Miss Biggs?"

"We have a new guest. Mrs. Nelson, here." She indicated the blonde, who stood gaping at her new surroundings, saliva trickling from one corner of her mouth.
"A room should be ready for her—you know, No. 19.
Perhaps you'd better take her there now and get her settled."

"Yes, Miss Biggs." The girl took the blonde's arm in
a brisk, business-like manner and led her away. The
woman named Margaret made as if to follow but the receptionist called her back.

"No, Miss Duggins. Not today. We find that it's better
if the relatives and friends stay behind at first. It's less
confusing to the patient, less upsetting. Later, when she's
all settled and comfortable, you can visit her as often as
you like. No, don't worry about her bags—Dottie will
get them later." The dumpy woman dropped back but
continued to peer after the two retreating figures. The corridor was dim; through the gloom, she could make out
vague shapes propped up in chairs staring at what must
have been a television screen down at the far end . . .
She forced her attention back to the receptionist, who
spoke once more. "And now, if you'll just fill out these
papers, there's information we need to have . . ."

About forty-five minutes later, the nurse, Dottie, re-
entered the office. "Well, I finally got her to sleep. Gave
her two sleeping tablets. It wasn't easy, though. Would
you believe it, she started fighting me."

"God, what a pathetic case," muttered Miss Biggs.

"You mean because she dribbles? They all do that,"
said Dottie indifferently. "She's past ninety; what do you
expect?"

"No, not her. I mean the daughter. Did you notice
her?"

A glimmer of understanding came into the nurse's eyes.
"Did I! How could I avoid it? I wonder why people want
to let themselves go like that, anyway. It's awful."

"Why anyone would let themselves become such an
eyesore when the Youth Pill is so cheap is more than I'll
ever see." The receptionist was fifty years old and had
a date with a college junior for that evening.

"I've got an aunt like that," said the nurse reflectively.
"Won't take the Pill, lets herself go, you should just see
her. She's eighty. Says if it can't make the rest of her

young along with her skin she wants no part of it. She's one of those real old-fashioned New England rugged individualist types, so maybe you can excuse her. But I can't understand for the life of me why any Californian would want to act like that. I'm sure going to be taking the Pill by the time *I'm* 25 or 30.''

The older woman sighed philosophically. "Well, you never can tell," she said, shaking her head. "It takes all kinds."

Till the war-drums throb no longer—

The Final Battle

by Harry Harrison

In the evening, after the dinner things have been cleared away, there is nothing we children enjoy more than sitting around the fireplace while Father tells us a story.

You may say that sounds foolish, or old-fashioned, with all the modern forms of entertainment, and if you say that you will forgive me if I smile indulgently?

I am eighteen and, in most other ways, I have put childish things behind me. But Father is an orator and his voice weaves a magic spell that still binds me, and, in all truth, I like it that way. Even though we won the War we lost a great deal in the process and it is a harsh and cruel world out there. I'm going to stay young just as long as I can.

"Tell us about the final battle," that is what the children usually say, and that is the story he usually tells. It is a frightening story, even though we know that it is all over now, but there is nothing like a good shiver up and down your spine before you go to sleep.

Father takes his beer, sips it slowly, then flicks the bits

of foam from his moustache with his finger. That's the signal that he is going to begin.

"War is hell, and don't you forget it," he says, and the two youngest titter because they would have their mouths washed out with soap if *they* said the word.

"War is hell, it always has been, and the only reason I tell you this story is because I do not want you ever to forget that. We've fought the final battle of the last war, and a lot of good men died to win it, and now that it is over I want you always to remember that. If they had any reason for dying it was so that you could live. And never, ever, have to fight a war again.

"Firstly, abandon the idea that there is something ennobling or wonderful about battle. There is not. That is a myth that has been a long time dying and it probably dates from prehistory when war was hand-to-hand single combat, fought at the cave door as a man defended his home from the stranger. Those days are long past, and what was good for the individual can mean death for a civilized community. It meant death for *them*, didn't it?"

Father's big, serious eyes dart around the circle of listening faces, but no one will meet his gaze. For some reason *we* feel guilty, although most of us have been born since the War.

"We've won the War, but it is not really won if we do not learn a lesson from it. The other side might have discovered the Ultimate Weapon first, and if they had we are the ones who would be dead and vanished, and you must never forget that. Just a chance of history saved our culture and destroyed theirs. If this accident of fate can have any meaning for us, it must be that we learn a little humility. We are not gods and we are not perfect—and we must abandon warfare as the way to settle mankind's differences. I was there and I helped to kill them and I know what I am talking about."

After this comes the moment we are expecting and we all hold our breaths, waiting.

"Here it is," Father says, standing and reaching high up on the wall. "This is it, the weapon that rains death from a distance and is the Ultimate Weapon."

Father brandishes the bow over his head and is a dramatic figure in the firelight, his shadow stretching across the cave and up the wall. Even the smallest baby stops scratching for fleas under its fur wrapping and watches, gape-mouthed.

"The man with the club or the stone knife or the spear cannot stand before the bow. We've won our war and we must use this weapon only for peace, to kill the elk and the mammoth. This is our future."

He smiles as he hangs the bow carefully back on its peg.

"The waging of war is too terrible now. The era of perpetual peace has begun."

There's a limit to wandering—

Earthbound

by Lester del Rey

It was hours after the last official ceremony before Clifton could escape the crowd of planetlubbers with their babblings, their eligible daughters, and their stupid self-admiration. They'd paid through the nose to get him here, and they meant to get their money's worth. The exit led only to a little balcony, but it seemed to be deserted. He took a deep breath of the night air and his eyes moved unconsciously toward the stars.

Coming back to Earth had been a mistake, but he'd needed the money. Space Products Unlimited wanted a real deepspace hero to help celebrate its hundredth anniversary, and he'd just finished the Regulation of Rigel, so he'd been picked. Damn them and their silly speeches and awards—and damn Earth! What was one planet when there were a billion up there among the stars?

From the other side of a potted plant there was a soft, quavering sigh. Clifton swung his head, then relaxed as he saw the other man was not looking at him. The eyes behind the dark glasses were directed toward the sky.

"Aldebaran, Sirius, Deneb, Centaurus," the voice whispered. It was a high-pitched voice with an odd accent, but there was the poetry of ancient yearning in it.

He was a small, shrivelled old man. His shoulders were bent. A long beard and dark glasses covered most of his face, but could not entirely conceal the deep wrinkles, even in the moonlight.

Clifton felt a sudden touch of pity and moved closer, without quite knowing why. "Didn't I see you on the platform?"

"Your memory is very good, Captain. I was awarded publicly for fifty years of faithful service making space boots. Well, I was always a good cobbler, and perhaps my boots helped some men out there." The old man's hand swept toward the stars, then fell back to grip the railing tightly. "They gave me a gold watch, though time means nothing to me. And a cheap world cruise ticket, as if there were any spot on this world I could still want to see." He laughed harshly. "Forgive me if I sound bitter. But, you see, I've never been off Earth!"

Clifton stared at him incredulously. "But everyone—"

"Everyone but me," the old man said. "Oh, I tried. I was utterly weary of Earth and I looked at the stars and dreamed. But I failed the early rigid physicals. Then, when things were easier, I tried again. A strange plague grounded the ship. A strike delayed another. Then one exploded on the pad and only a few on board were saved. It was then I realized I was meant to wait here—here on Earth, and nowhere else. So I stayed, making space boots."

Pity and impulse forced unexpected words to Clifton's lips. "I'm taking off for Rigel again in four hours, and there's a spare cabin on the *Maryloo*. You're coming with me."

The old hand that gripped his arm was oddly gentle. "Bless you, Captain. But it would never work. I'm under orders to remain here."

"Nobody can order a man grounded forever. You're coming with me if I have to drag you, Mr.—"

"Ahasuerus." The old man hesitated, as if expecting the name to mean something. Then he sighed and lifted his dark glasses.

Clifton met the other's gaze for less than a second.

Then his own eyes dropped, though the memory of what he had seen was already fading. He vaulted over the balcony railing and began running away from Ahasuerus, toward his ship and the unconfined reaches of space.

Behind him, the Wandering Jew tarried and waited.

The ultimate time-paradox.

Rotating Cylinders and the Possibility of Global Causality Violation

by Larry Niven

"Three hundred years we've been at war," said Quifting, "and I have the means to end it. I can destroy the Hallane Regency." He seemed very pleased with himself, and not at all awed at being in the presence of the emperor of seventy worlds.

The aforementioned emperor said, "That's a neat trick. If you can't pull it off, you can guess what penalties I might impose. None of my generals would dare such a brag."

"Their tools are not mine." Quifting shifted in a valuable antique massage chair. He was small and round and completely hairless: the style of the nonaristocratic professional. He *should* have been overawed, and frightened. "I'm a mathematician. Would you agree that a time machine would be a useful weapon of war?"

"I would," said the emperor. "Or I'd take a faster-than-light starship, if you're offering miracles."

"I'm offering miracles," said Quifting, "but to the enemy."

The emperor wondered if Quifting was mad. Mad or not, he was hardly dangerous. The emperor was halfway around the planet from him, on the night side. His side of the meeting room was only a holographic projection, though Quifting wouldn't know that.

Half a dozen clerks and couriers had allowed this man to reach the emperor's ersatz presence. Why? Possibly Quifting had useful suggestions, but not necessarily. Sometimes they let an entertaining madman through, lest the emperor grow bored.

"It's a very old idea," Quifting said earnestly. "I've traced it back three thousand years, to the era when space-flight itself was only a dream. I can demonstrate that a massive rotating cylinder, infinite in length, can be circled by closed timelike paths. It seems reasonable that a long but finite—"

"Wait. I must have missed something."

"Take a massive cylinder," Quifting said patiently, "and put a rapid spin on it. I can plot a course for a spacecraft that will bring it around the cylinder and back to its starting point in space *and time.*"

"Ah. A functioning time machine, then. Done with relativity, I expect. But must the cylinder be infinitely long?"

"I wouldn't think so. A long but finite cylinder ought to show the same behavior, except near the endpoints."

"And when you say you can demonstrate this . . ."

"To another mathematician. Otherwise I would not have been allowed to meet Your Splendor. In addition, there are historical reasons to think that the cylinder need not be infinite."

Now the emperor was jolted. "Historical? Really?"

"That's surprising, isn't it? But it's easy to design a time machine, given the Terching Effect. You know about the Terching Effect?"

"It's what makes a warship's hull so rigid," confirmed the emperor.

"Yes. The cylinder must be very strong to take the rotation without flying apart. Of course it would be enormously expensive to build. But others have tried it. The Six Worlds Alliance started one during the Free Trade period."

"Really?"

"We have the records. Archeology had them fifty years ago, but they had no idea what the construct was intended to do. Idiots." Quifting's scowl was brief. "Never mind. A thousand years later, during the One Race Wars, the Mao Buddhists started to build such a time machine out in Sol's cometary halo. Again, behind the Coal Sack is a long, massive cylinder, a quasi-Terching-Effect shell enclosing a neutronium core. We think an alien race called the Kchipreesee built it. The ends are flared, possibly to compensate for edge effects, and there are fusion rocket motors in orbit around it, ready for attachment to spin it up to speed."

"Did nobody ever finish one of these, ah, time machines?"

Quifting pounced on the word. "Nobody!" and he leaned forward, grinning savagely at the emperor. No, he was not awed. A mathematician rules his empire absolutely, and it is more predictable, easier to manipulate, than any universe an emperor would dare believe in. "The Six Worlds Alliance fell apart before their project was barely started. The Mao Buddhist attempt—well, you know what happened to Sol system during the One Race Wars. As for the Kchipreesee, I'm told that many generations of space travel killed them off through biorhythm upset."

"That's ridiculous."

"It may be, but they are certainly extinct, and they certainly left their artifact half-finished."

"I don't understand," the emperor admitted. He was tall, muscular, built like a middleweight boxer. Health was the mark of aristocracy in this age. "You seem to be saying that building a time machine is simple but expensive, that it would handle any number of ships—It would, wouldn't it?"

"Oh, yes."

"—and send them back in time to exterminate one's enemies' ancestors. Others have tried it. But in practice, the project is always interrupted or abandoned."

"Exactly."

"Why?"

"Do you believe in cause and effect?"

"Of course. I . . . suppose that means I don't believe in time travel, doesn't it?"

"A working time machine would destroy the cause-and-effect relationship of the universe. It seems the universe resists such meddling. No time machine had ever been put into working condition. If the Hallane Regency tries it something will stop them. The Coal Sack is in Hallane space. They need only attach motors to the Kchipreesee device and spin it up.''

''Bringing bad luck down upon their foolish heads. *Hubris*. The pride that challenges the gods. I like it. Yes. Let me see . . .'' The emperor generally left war to his generals, but he took a high interest in espionage. He tapped at a pocket computer and said, ''Get me Director Chilbreez.''

To Quifting he said, ''The director doesn't always arrest enemy spies. Sometimes he just watches 'em. I'll have him pick one and give him a lucky break. Let him stumble on a vital secret, as it were.''

''You'd have to back it up—''

''Ah, but we're already trying to recapture Coal Sack space. We'll step up the attacks a little. We should be able to convince the Hallanes that we're trying to take away their time machine. Even if you're completely wrong—which I suspect is true—we'll have them wasting some of their industrial capacity. Maybe start some factional disputes, too. Pro- and anti-time-machine. Hah!'' The emperor's smile suddenly left him. ''Suppose they actually build a time machine?''

''They won't.''

''But a time machine is possible? The mathematics works?''

''But that's the point, Your Splendor. The universe itself resists such things.'' Quifting smiled confidently. ''Don't you believe in cause and effect?''

''Yes.''

Violet-white light blazed through the windows behind the mathematician, making of him a sharp-edged black shadow. Quifting ran forward and smashed into the holograph wall. His eyes were shut tight, his clothes were afire. ''What is it?'' he screamed. ''What's happening?''

''I imagine the sun has gone nova,'' said the emperor.

The wall went black.

A dulcet voice spoke. ''Director Chilbreez on the line.''

''Never mind.'' There was no point now in telling the director how to get an enemy to build a time machine. The universe protected its cause-and-effect basis with humorless ferocity. Director Chilbreez was doomed; and perhaps Quifting had ended the war after all. The emperor went to the window. A churning aurora blazed bright as day, and grew brighter still.

They came tha-a-at close!

The Voice in the Garden

by Harlan Ellison

After the bomb, the last man on Earth wandered through the rubble of Cleveland, Ohio. It had never been a particularly jaunty town, nor even remotely appealing to aesthetes. But now, like Detroit and Rangoon and Minsk and Yokohama, it had been reduced to a petulantly shattered Tinkertoy of lath and brickwork, twisted steel girders and melted glass.

As he picked his way around the dust heap that had been the Soldiers and Sailors Monument in what had been Public Square, his eyes red-rimmed from crying at the loss of humanity, he saw something he had not seen in Beirut or Venice or London. He saw the movement of another human being.

Celestial choruses sang in his head as he broke into a run across the pitted and blasted remains of Euclid Avenue. It was a woman!

She saw him, and in the very posture of her body, he knew she was filled with the same glory he felt. She knew! She began running toward him, her arms outstretched. They seemed to swim toward each other in a ballet of slow motion. He stumbled once, but got to his feet quickly and went on. They detoured around the crumpled tin of tortured metal that had once been automobiles, and met in front of the shattered carcass that was, in a time seemingly eons before, The May Co.

"I'm the last man!" he blurted. He could not keep the words inside, they fought to fill the air. "I'm the last, the very last. They're all dead, everyone but us. I'm the last man, and you're the last woman, and we'll have to mate and start the race again, and this time we'll do it right. No war, no hate, no bigotry, nothing but goodness . . . we'll do it, you'll see, it'll be fine, a bright new shining world from all this death and terror."

Her face was lit with an ethereal beauty, even beneath the soot and deprivation. "Yes, yes," she said. "It'll be just like that. I love you, because we're all there is left to love, each other."

He touched her hand. "I love you. What is your name?"

She flushed slightly. "Eve," she said. "What's yours?"

"Bernard," he said.

We might all have been better off.

If Eve Had Failed to Conceive

by Edward Wellen